THE BLACK MONDAY MURDERS, VOL. 1. First printing. January 2017. Published by Image Comics, Inc. Office of publication: 2701 NW Vaughn St., Suite 780, Portland, OR 97210.  Printed in the USA. For information regarding the CPSIA on this printed material call: 203-595-3636 and provide reference #RICH-720402. For international rights, contact: foreignlicensing@imagecomics.com. ISBN: 978-1-5343-0027-9. Newbury Comics Variant ISBN: 978-1-5343-0252-5. DCBS Variant ISBN: 978-1-5343-0253-2. Forbidden Planet Variant ISBN: 978-1-5343-0260-0.

[image comics presents:]......

..................A STORY OF HUMAN SACRIFICE

Words by: Jonathan Hickman
Art by: Tomm Coker
Colors by: Michael Garland
Letters by: Rus Wooton

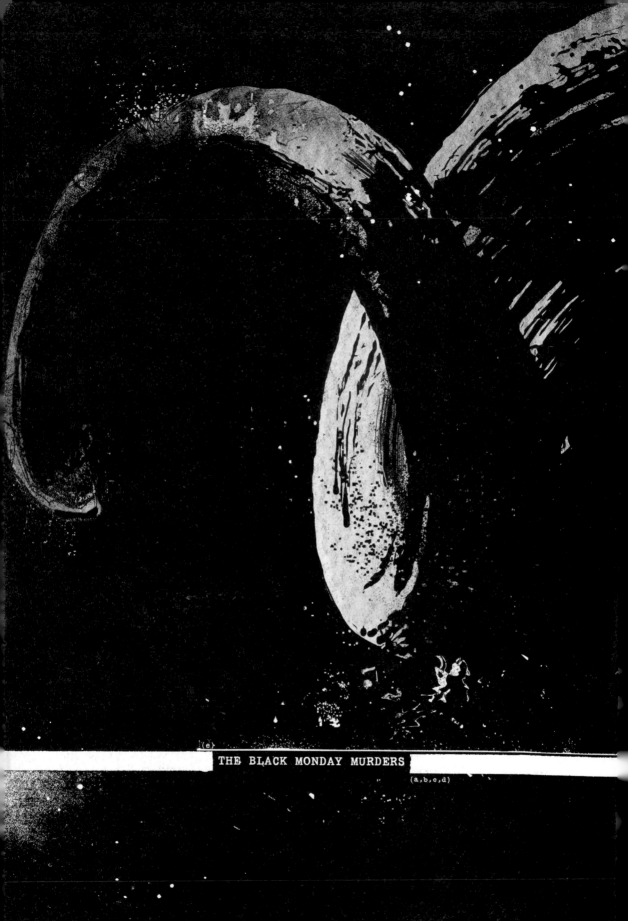

(e)

THE BLACK MONDAY MURDERS

(a,b,c,d)

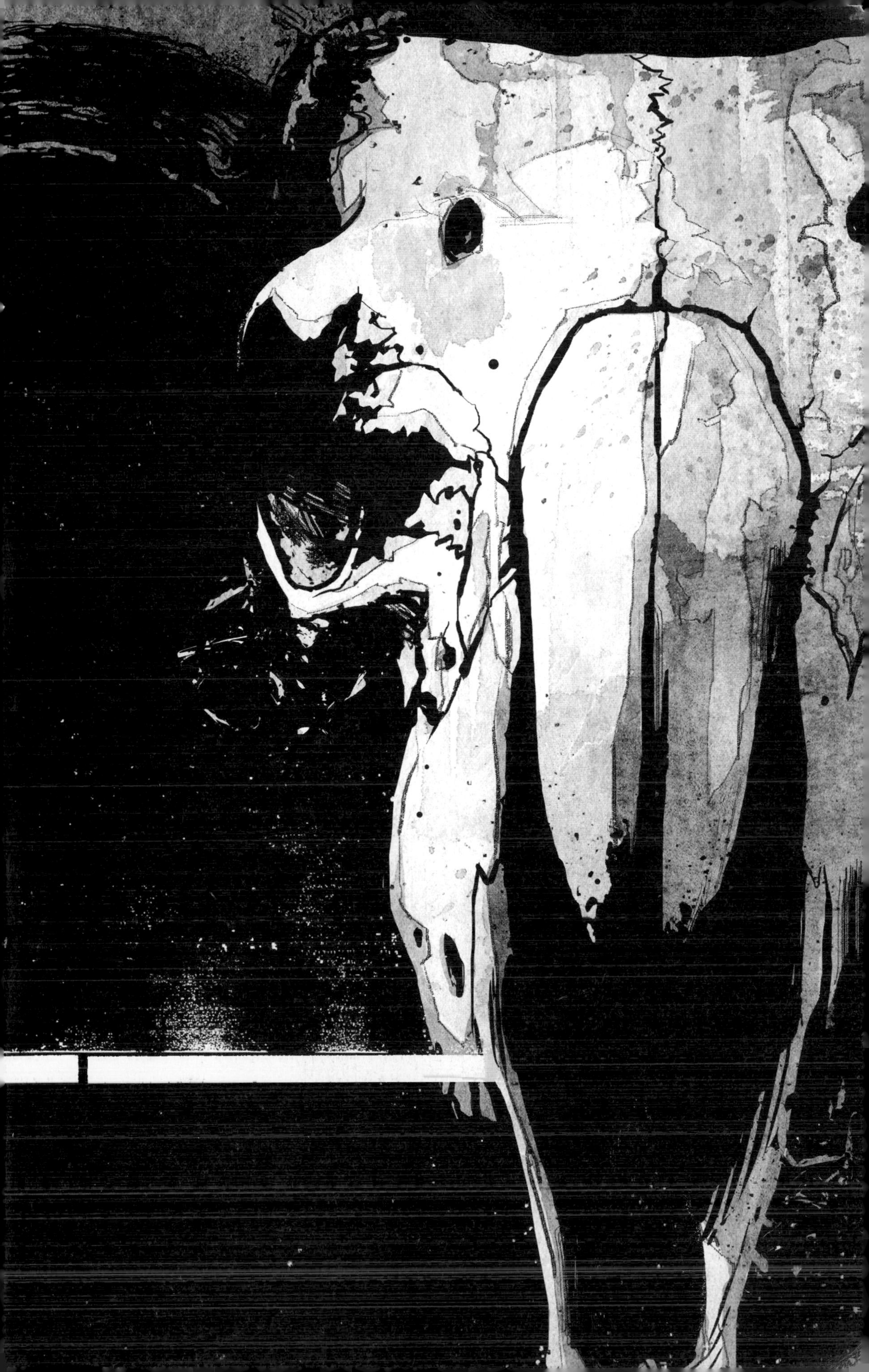

[VOLUME ONE:] . . . . . . . . . . . . . . . . . .

.................ALL HAIL, GOD MAMMON

# CONTENTS

II

III

IV

Bonus

DRAMATIS PERSONAE:

(a)

(e)

(b,c,d)

CAINA
1929

Charles Ackermann
    (The Ackermann seat)
J.W. Bischoff
    (The Bischoff seat)
Raymond Dominic
    (The Dominic seat)
Milton Rothschild
    (The Rothschild seat)
Abigail
    (Rothschild Familiar)


KANKRIN
1985/Current

Irena Kozlov
    (The Judge)
Alexi Malkin
    (The Body)
Viktor Eresko
    (The Executioner)

CAINA
1985/Current

Wynn Ackermann
    (The Ackermann seat)
Beatrix Bischoff
    (The Bischoff seat)
Marco Dominic
    (The Dominic seat)
Daniel Rothschild
    (The Rothschild seat)
Grigoria Rothschild
    (The Rothschild seat)
Abby
    (Rothschild Familiar)

Thomas Dane
    (Head of Security)


NEW YORK POLICE DEPARTMENT

Theodore Dumas
    (Detective)
Michael Caffey
    (Detective)
Susana Moreno
    (Detective)
William Merritt
    (Captain)


OTHER

Dr. Tyler Gaddis
    (Professor of Economics,
    Fordham)                    (a,b,c,d)

1929

- THE CRASH -

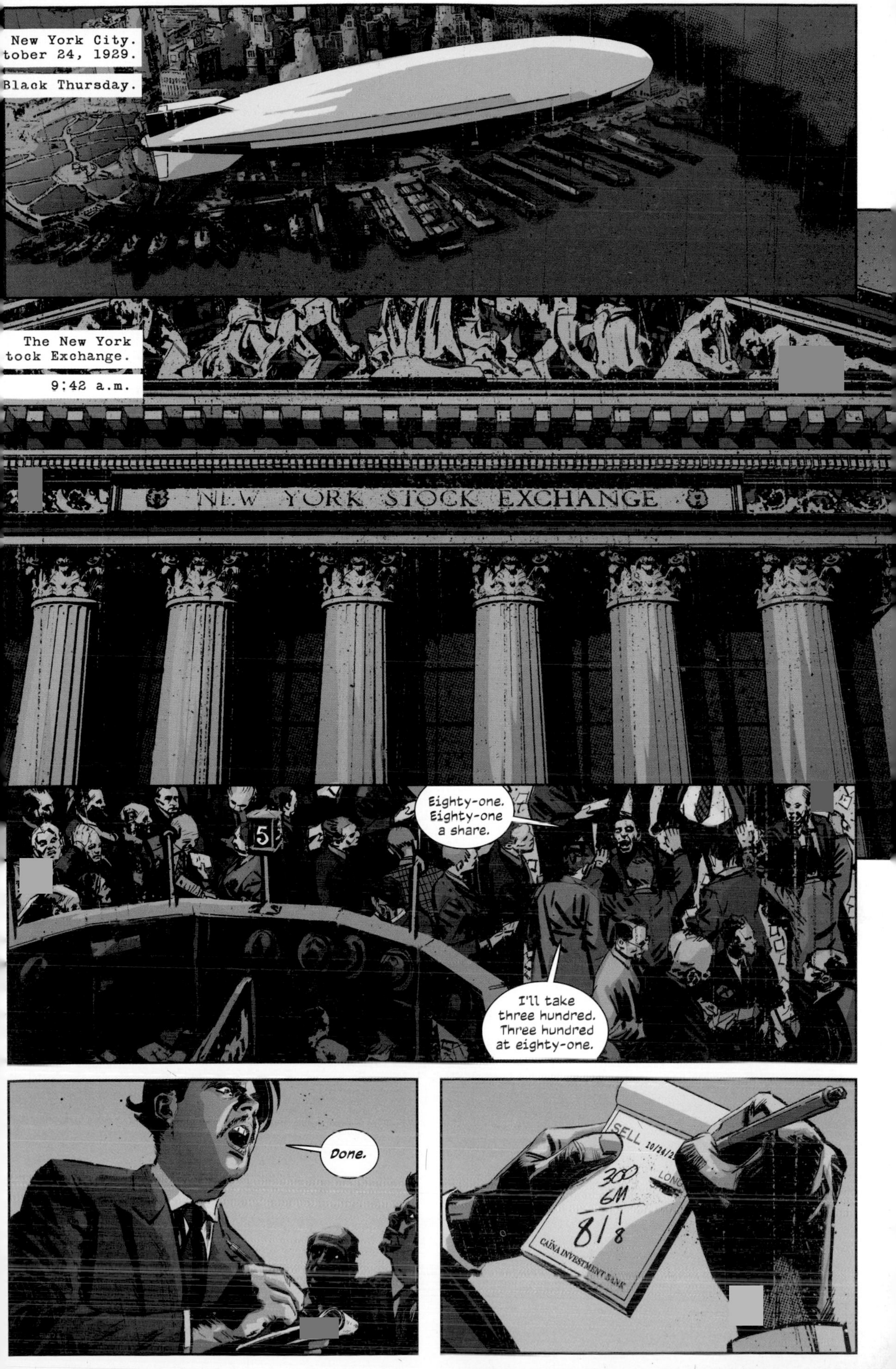

New York City.
tober 24, 1929.
Black Thursday.
The New York
tock Exchange.
9:42 a.m.
NEW YORK STOCK EXCHANGE
5
Eighty-one. Eighty-one a share.
I'll take three hundred. Three hundred at eighty-one.
Done.
SELL
300
GM
81 1/8
CAÏNA INVESTMENT BANK

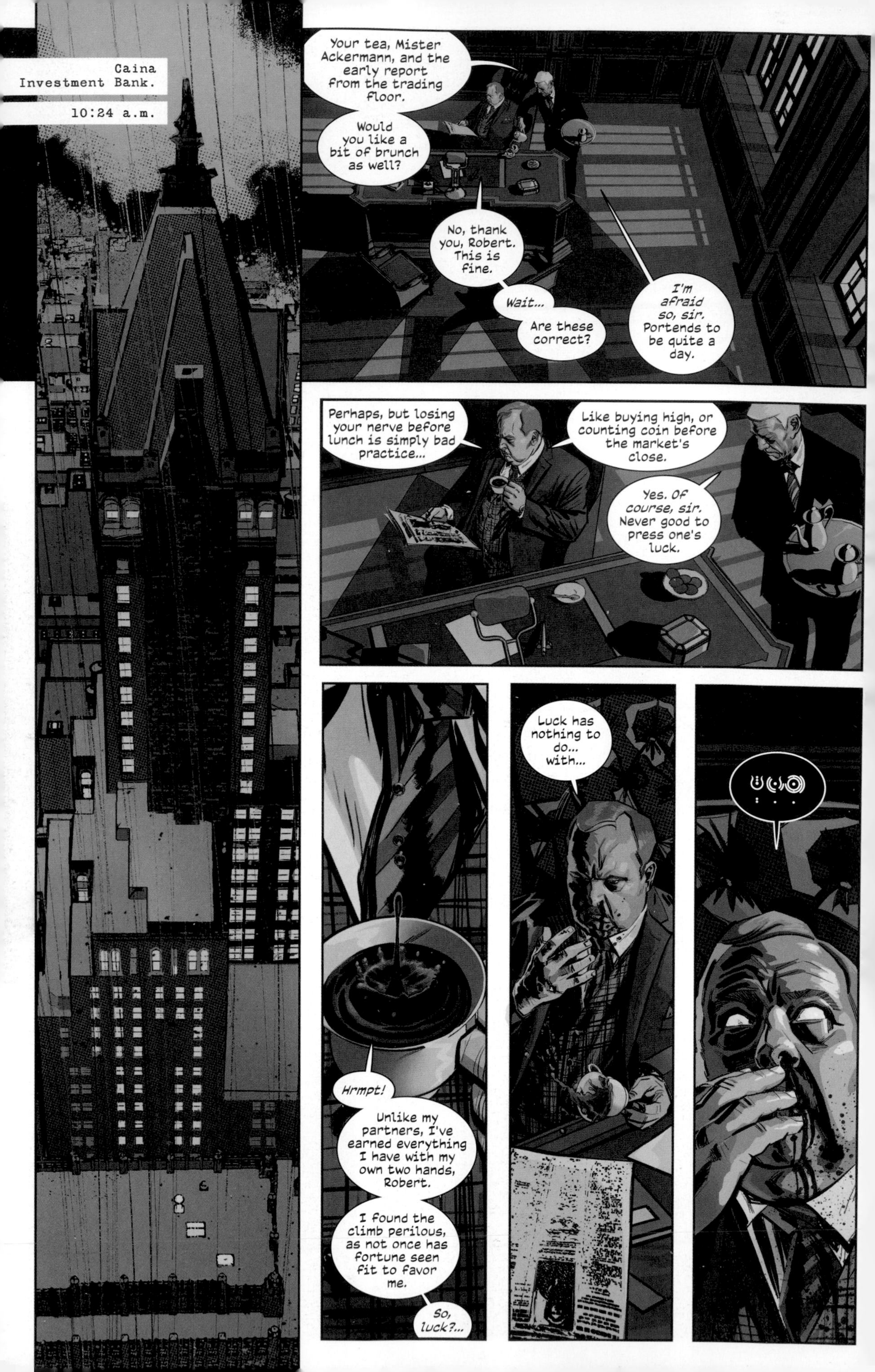
Caina Investment Bank.
10:24 a.m.
Your tea, Mister Ackermann, and the early report from the trading floor.
Would you like a bit of brunch as well?
No, thank you, Robert. This is fine.
Wait...
Are these correct?
I'm afraid so, sir. Portends to be quite a day.
Perhaps, but losing your nerve before lunch is simply bad practice...
Like buying high, or counting coin before the market's close.
Yes. Of course, sir. Never good to press one's luck.
Hrmpt!
Unlike my partners, I've earned everything I have with my own two hands, Robert.
I found the climb perilous, as not once has fortune seen fit to favor me.
So, luck?...
Luck has nothing to do... with...

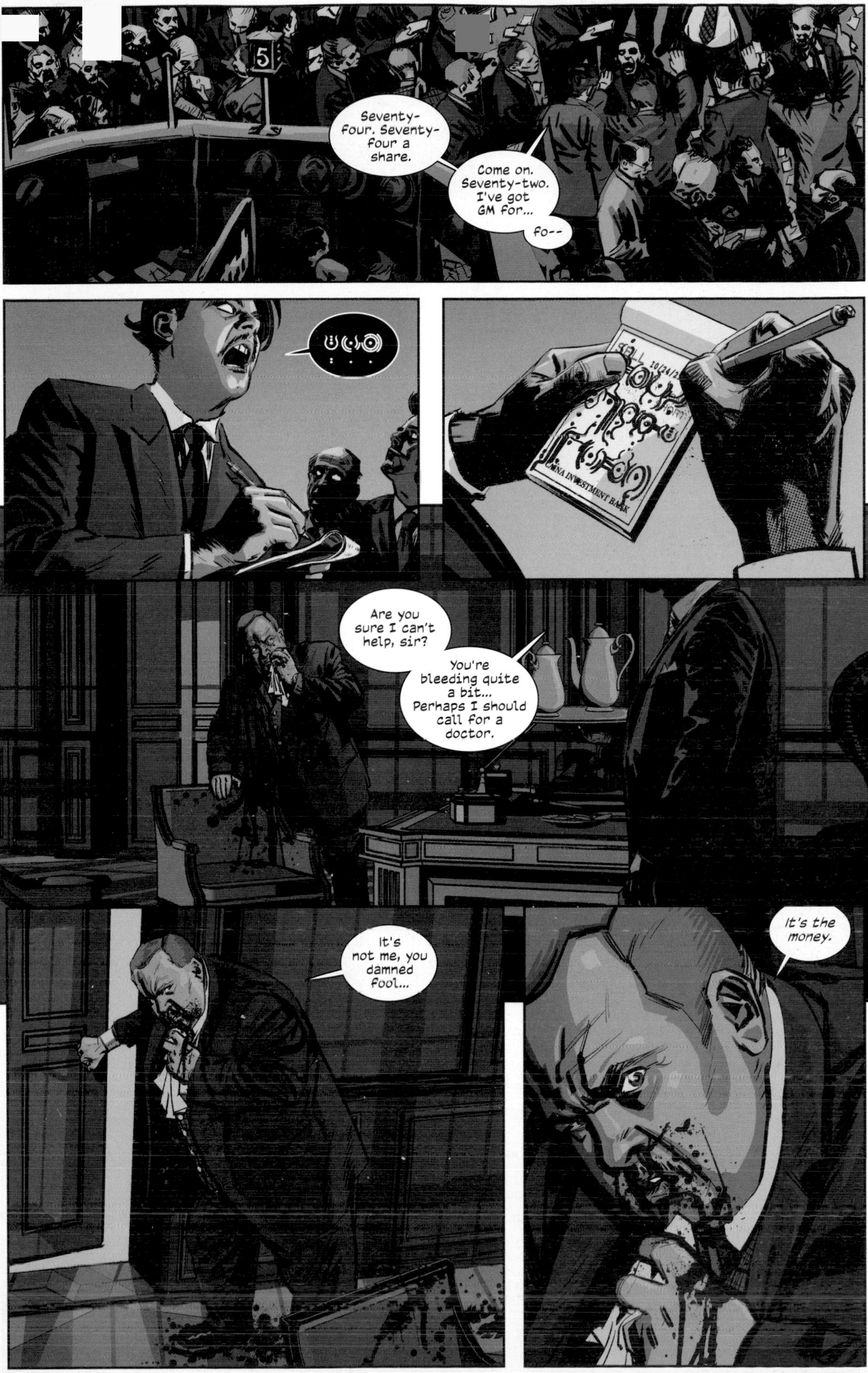
Seventy-four. Seventy-four a share.
Come on. Seventy-two. I've got GM for...
fo--
Are you sure I can't help, sir?
You're bleeding quite a bit... Perhaps I should call for a doctor.
It's not me, you damned fool...
*It's the money.*

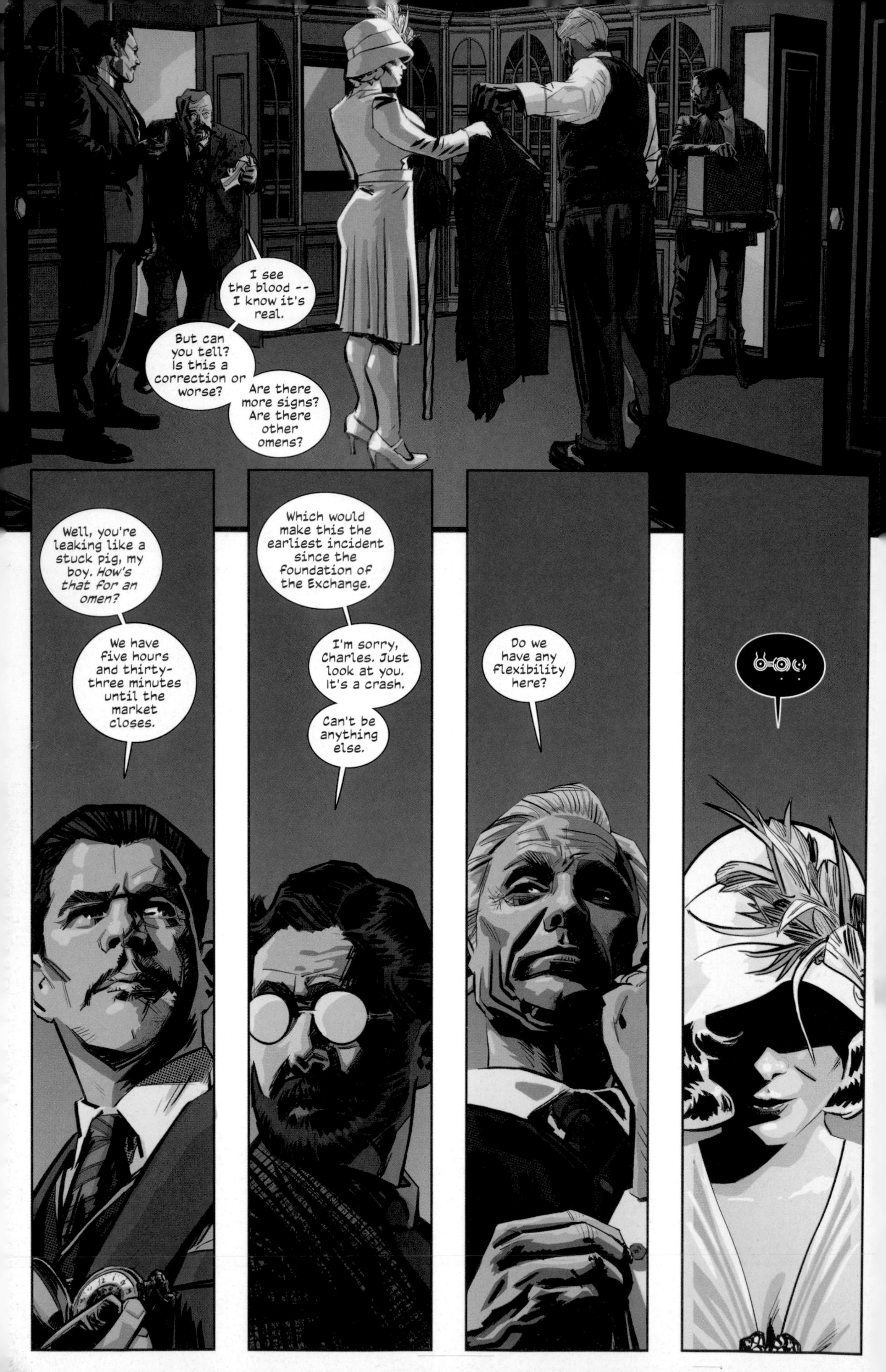

I see the blood -- I know it's real.
But can you tell? Is this a correction or worse?
Are there more signs? Are there other omens?
Well, you're leaking like a stuck pig, my boy. *How's that for an omen?*
We have five hours and thirty-three minutes until the market closes.
Which would make this the earliest incident since the foundation of the Exchange.
I'm sorry, Charles. Just look at you. It's a crash.
Can't be anything else.
Do we have any flexibility here?

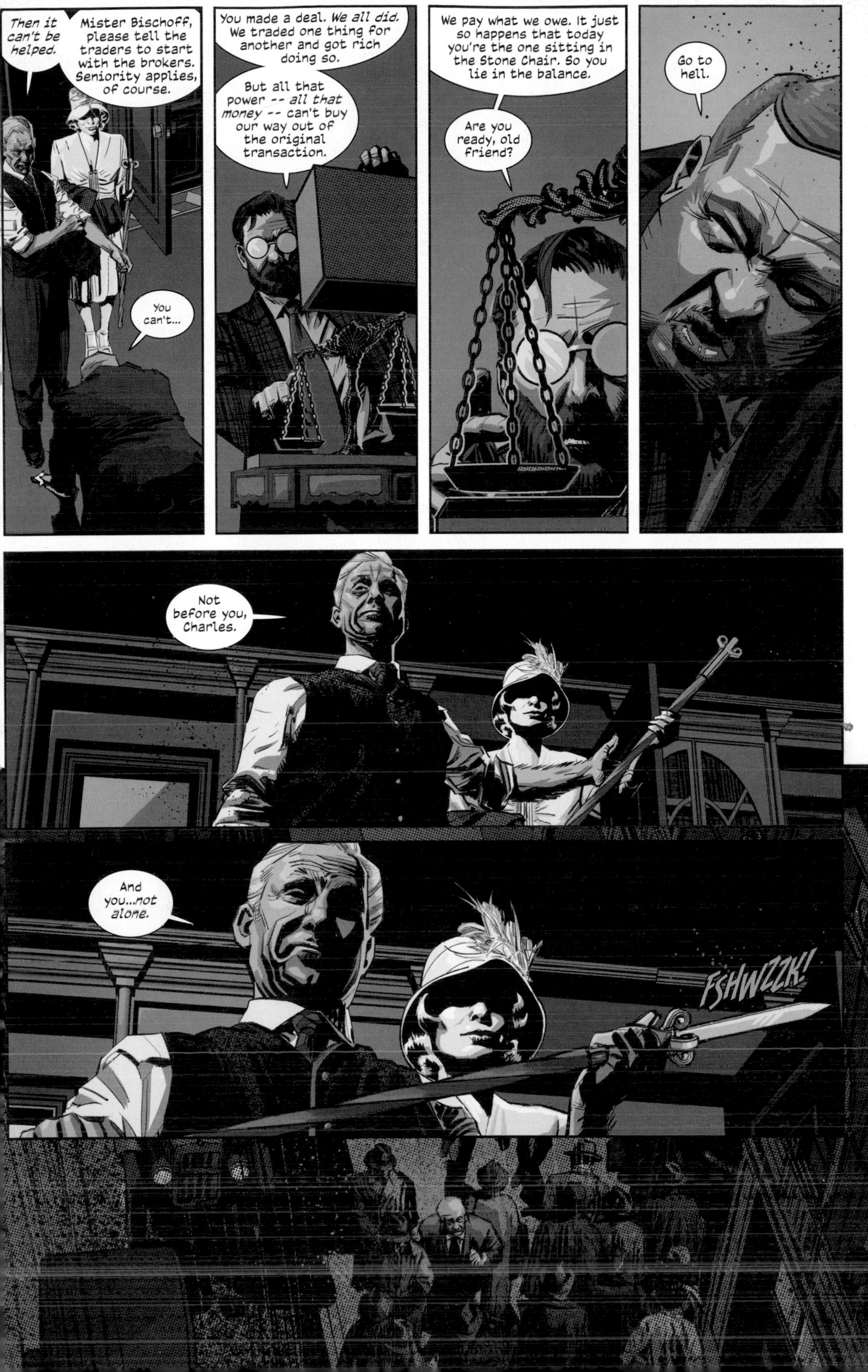
Then it can't be helped.
Mister Bischoff, please tell the traders to start with the brokers. Seniority applies, of course.
You can't...
You made a deal. We all did. We traded one thing for another and got rich doing so.
But all that power -- all that money -- can't buy our way out of the original transaction.
We pay what we owe. It just so happens that today you're the one sitting in the Stone Chair. So you lie in the balance.
Are you ready, old friend?
Go to hell.
Not before you, Charles.
And you...not alone.
FSHWZZK!

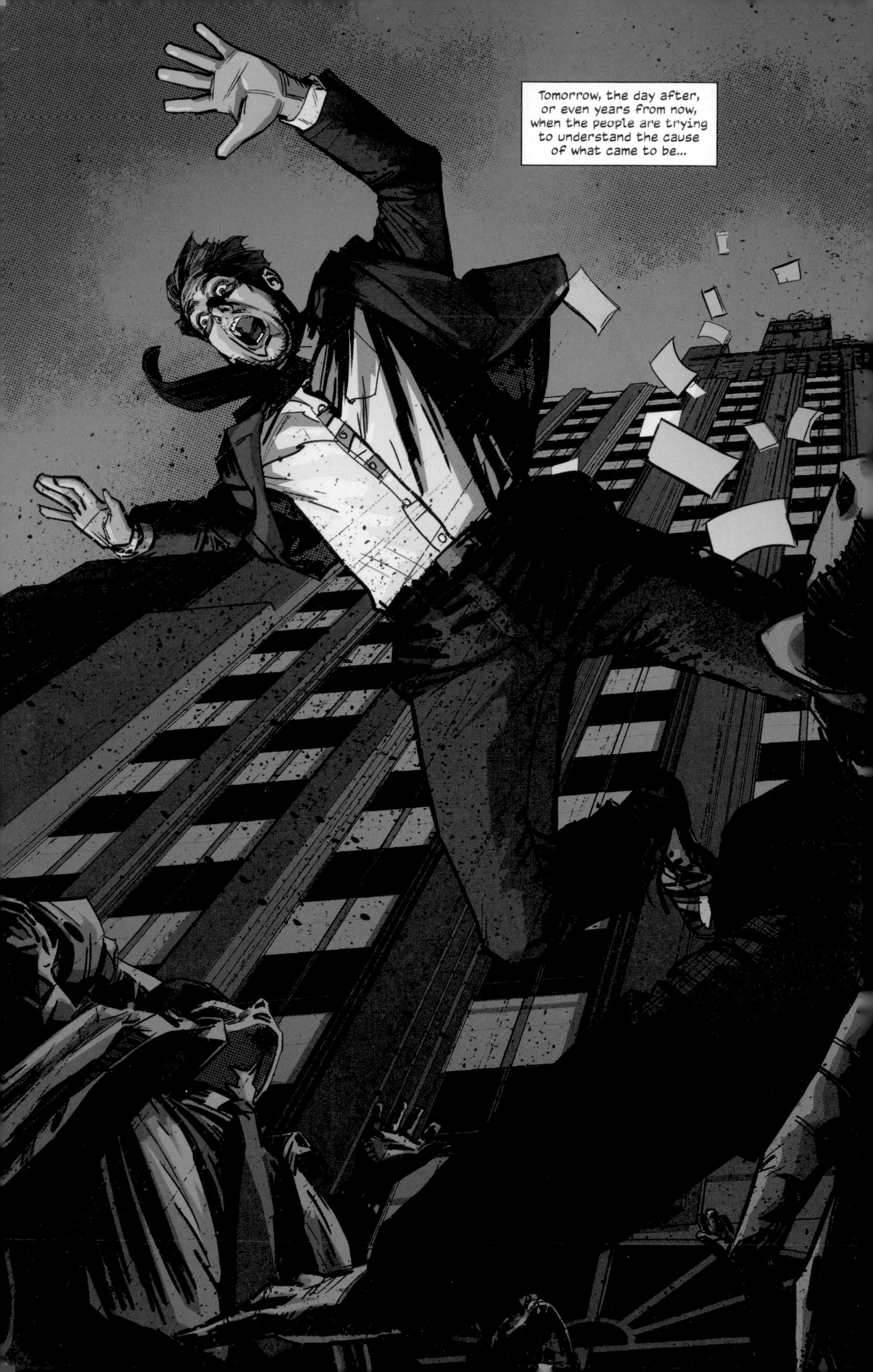
Tomorrow, the day after, or even years from now, when the people are trying to understand the cause of what came to be...

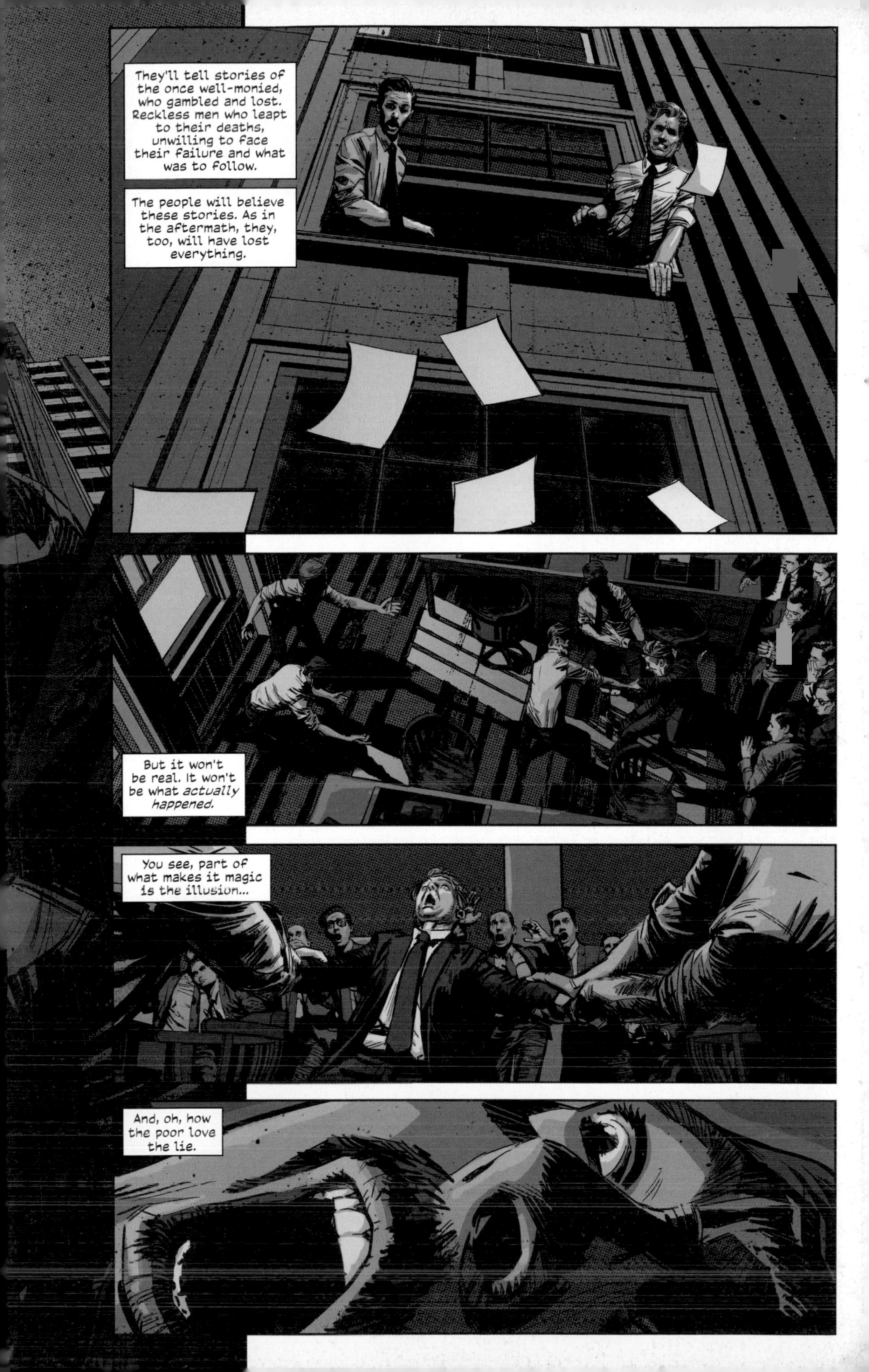
They'll tell stories of the once well-monied, who gambled and lost. Reckless men who leapt to their deaths, unwilling to face their failure and what was to follow.
The people will believe these stories. As in the aftermath, they, too, will have lost everything.
But it won't be real. It won't be what *actually happened.*
You see, part of what makes it magic is the illusion...
And, oh, how the poor love the lie.

DEATH MARCH

A business term describing the often futile practice of increasing the number of employees working on a project in the hopes of achieving an unlikely goal.

Commonly referred to as "throwing bodies at the problem."

---

(www.forums.investorscoven.com/threads/why-so-many.80872/#post-1899332)

Here's the thing: I think it's getting easier every day to rewrite history. Not because people are more gullible, or because it's a failure of education, but because, basically, the truth has become an easy mark.

(And look, I'm not referring to urban legends that reinforce the fringe, like staged moon landings or men on the grassy knoll. I'm talking about lies that get repeated often enough by "respected sources" that they become accepted truth.)

Which brings me to my plan. I know this is shitty, and kinda evil, but I think it's something we could do and probably make some money. I've even talked to a friend of a friend who works at an investment bank, and she said they'd probably be interested in funding something like this. Anyway, here's the thing:

I want to make a website where people can go to fact-check supposed urban legends. I want it to appear to be completely aboveboard. Open-source documentation, superusers who can edit articles, etc. We'll literally traffic in openness and the truth.

Except when we don't. When we want a lie to become the other thing, we'll disseminate that lie through the site. Because our reputation is perfect, and above reproach, people will believe us. I think something like that has real value, and I think some people would pay a premium.

It's like that Mark Twain quote, "A lie can travel halfway around the globe before the truth puts on its shoes." Except, you know, it wasn't him that said it, and this time it's both things.

So what do you guys think?

---

(www.thetruthisoutthere.com/debunked/1929-wall-street-suicides/)

CLAIM: In the Stock Market Crash of 1929, did Wall Street investors jump off buildings?

THIS CLAIM IS: FALSE

This urban legend gained most of its traction from the attributed quote below. When he was visiting New York, Winston Churchill was awakened by the noise of a crowd outside the Savoy-Plaza Hotel the day after Black Tuesday. He wrote:

> "Under my very window a gentleman cast himself down fifteen storeys and was dashed to pieces, causing a wild commotion and the arrival of the fire brigade."

Unfortunately, Churchill had mistaken a window washer for a stockbroker as later verified by his obituary.

See other examples.

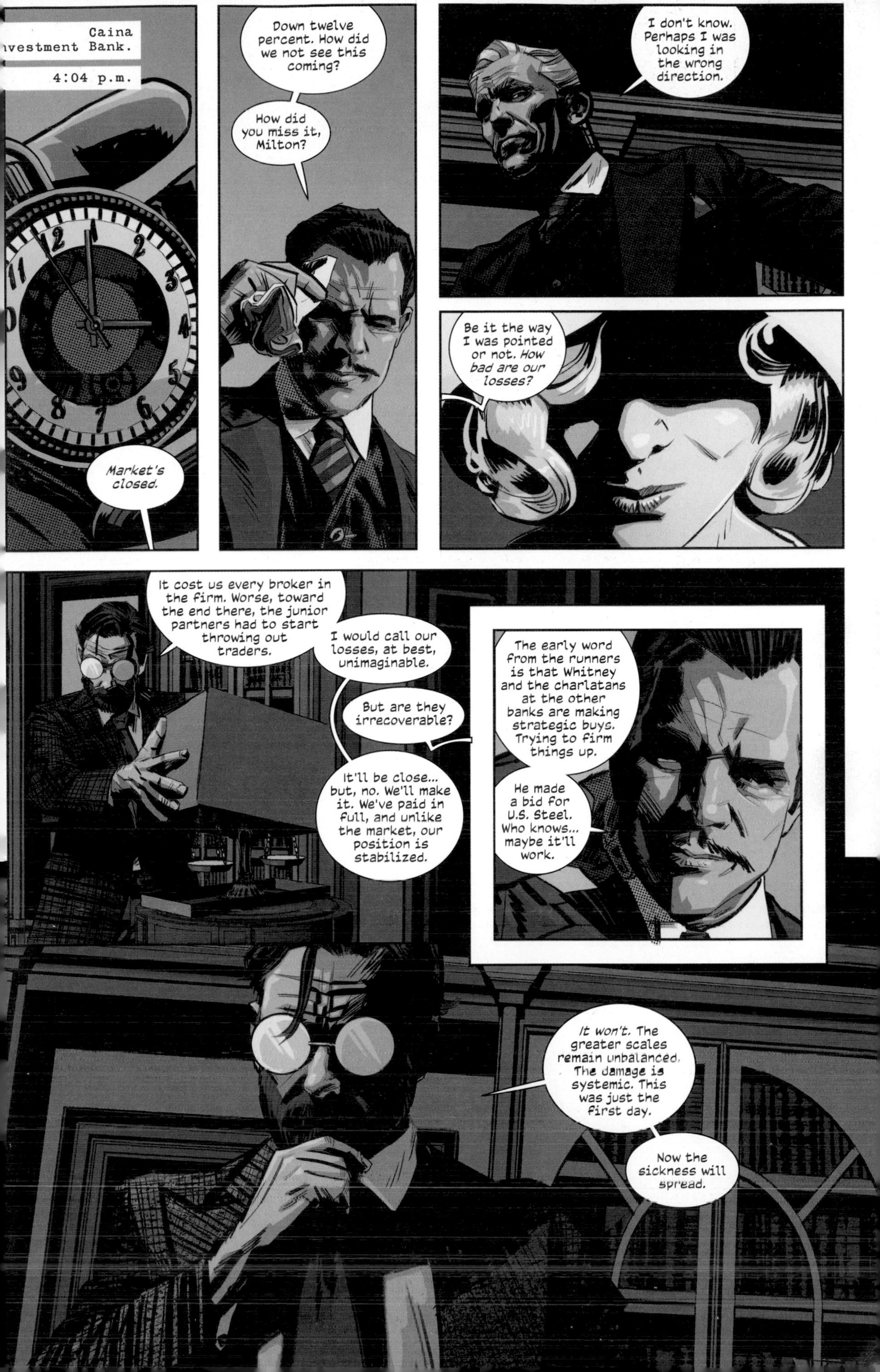
Caina
nvestment Bank.
4:04 p.m.
Market's closed.
Down twelve percent. How did we not see this coming?
How did you miss it, Milton?
I don't know. Perhaps I was looking in the wrong direction.
Be it the way I was pointed or not. How bad are our losses?
It cost us every broker in the firm. Worse, toward the end there, the junior partners had to start throwing out traders.
I would call our losses, at best, unimaginable.
But are they irrecoverable?
It'll be close... but, no. We'll make it. We've paid in full, and unlike the market, our position is stabilized.
The early word from the runners is that Whitney and the charlatans at the other banks are making strategic buys. Trying to firm things up.
He made a bid for U.S. Steel. Who knows... maybe it'll work.
It won't. The greater scales remain unbalanced. The damage is systemic. This was just the first day.
Now the sickness will spread.

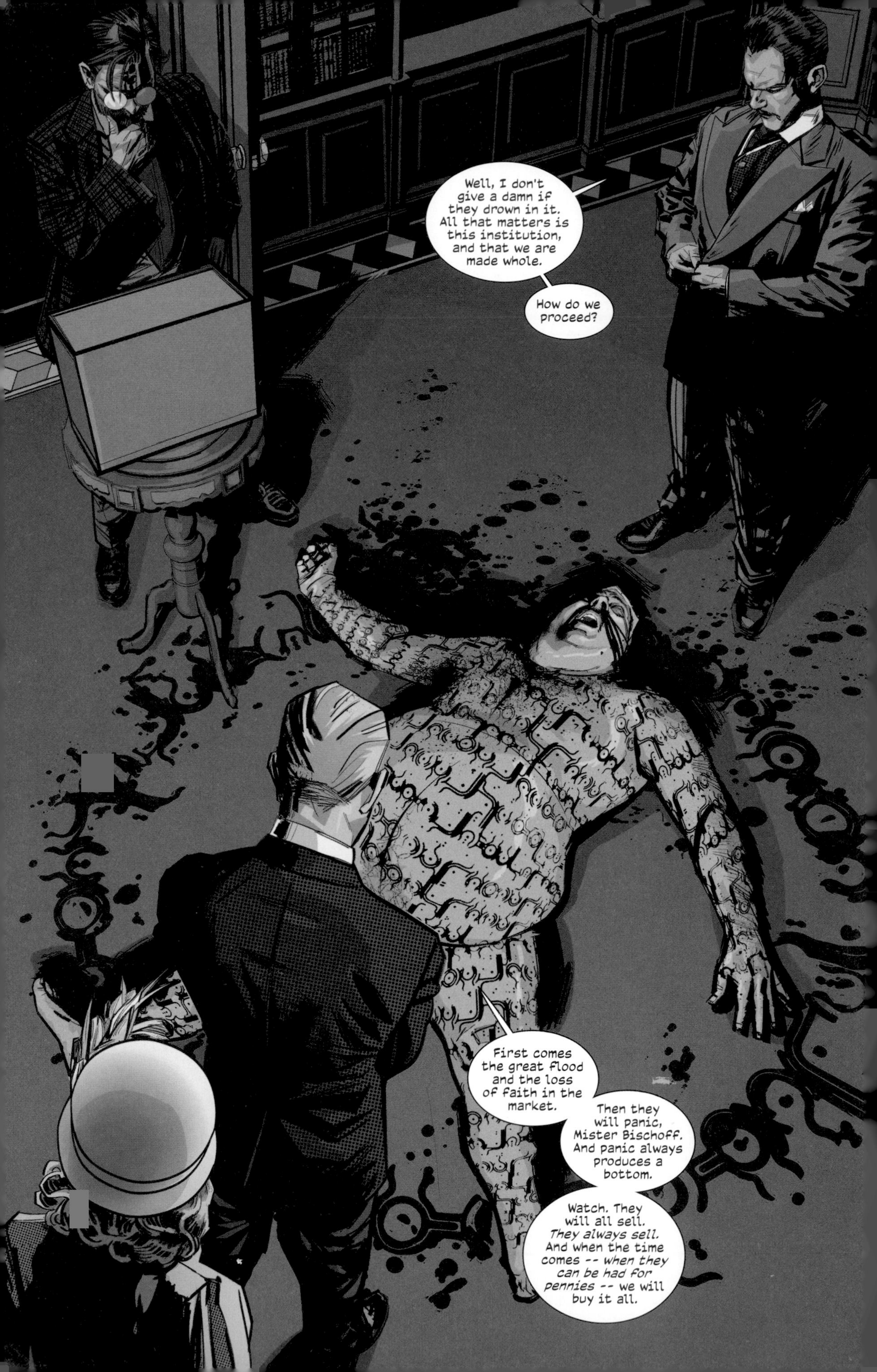
Well, I don't give a damn if they drown in it. All that matters is this institution, and that we are made whole.
How do we proceed?
First comes the great flood and the loss of faith in the market.
Then they will panic, Mister Bischoff. And panic always produces a bottom.
Watch. They will all sell. *They always sell.* And when the time comes -- *when they can be had for pennies* -- we will buy it all.

```
-  THERE'S  ONLY  ONE  GOD   -
-  AND  HIS  NAME  IS  MAMMON  -
```

CHAPTER ONE:

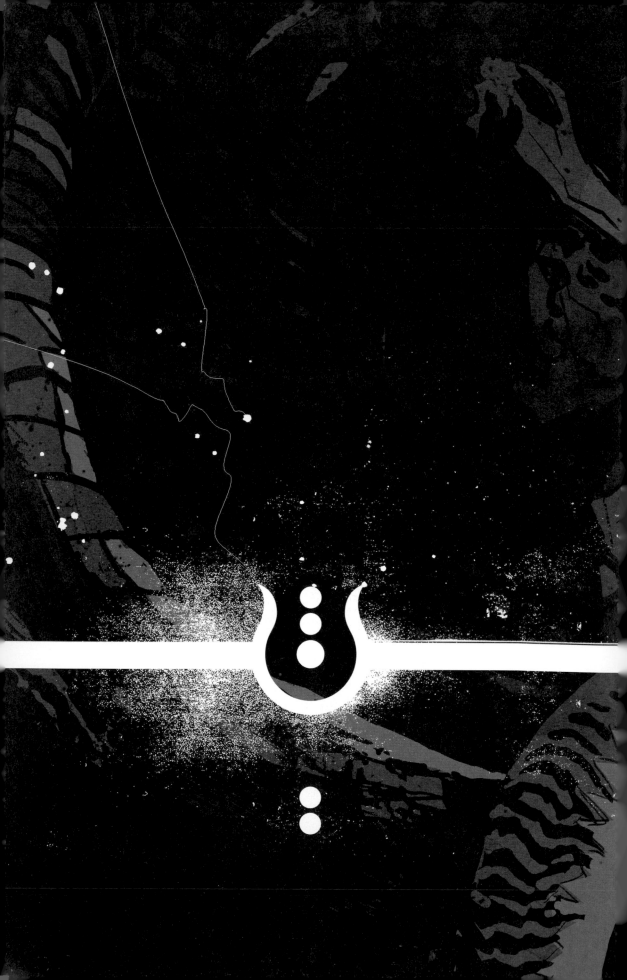

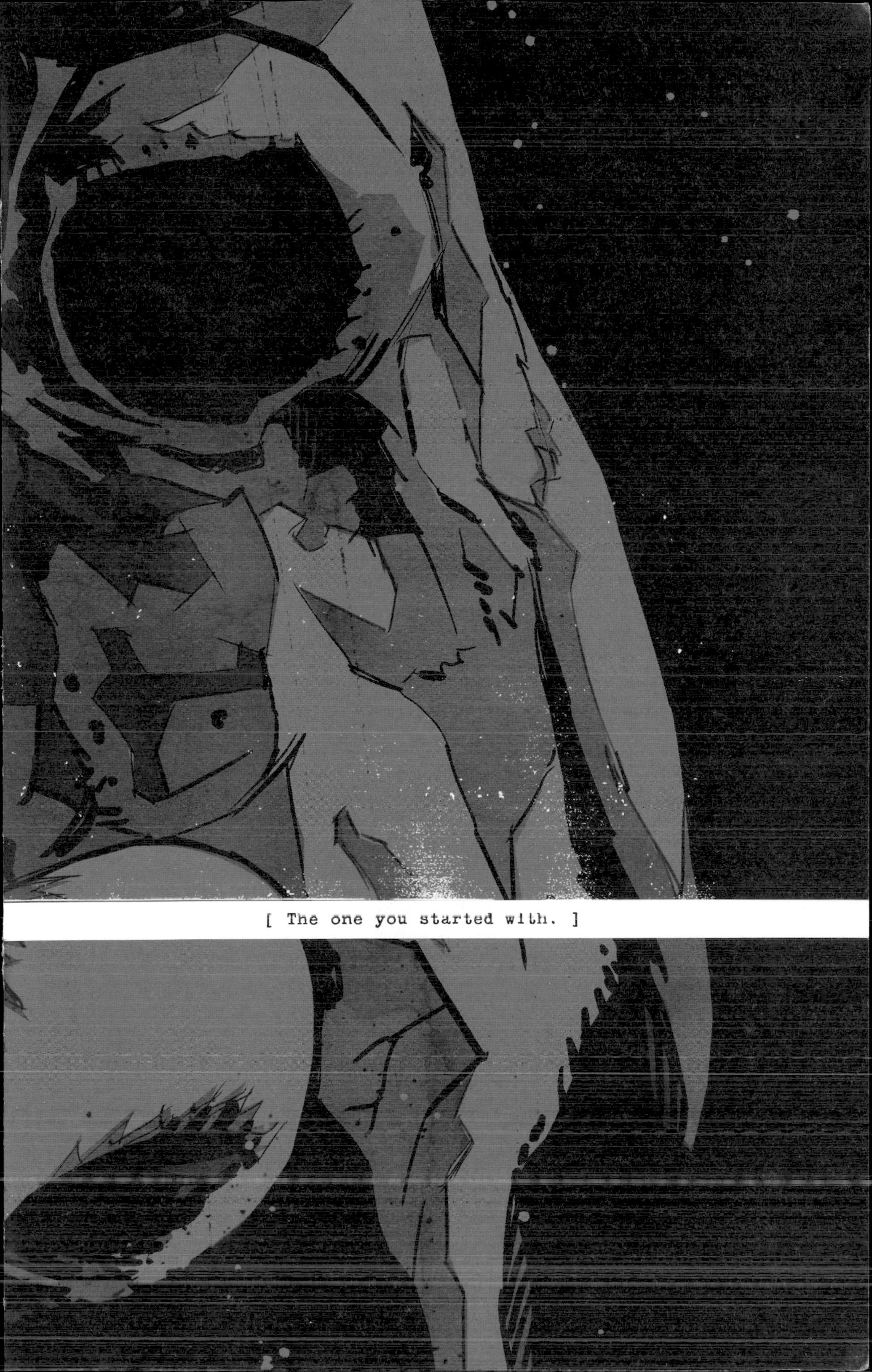
[ The one you started with. ]

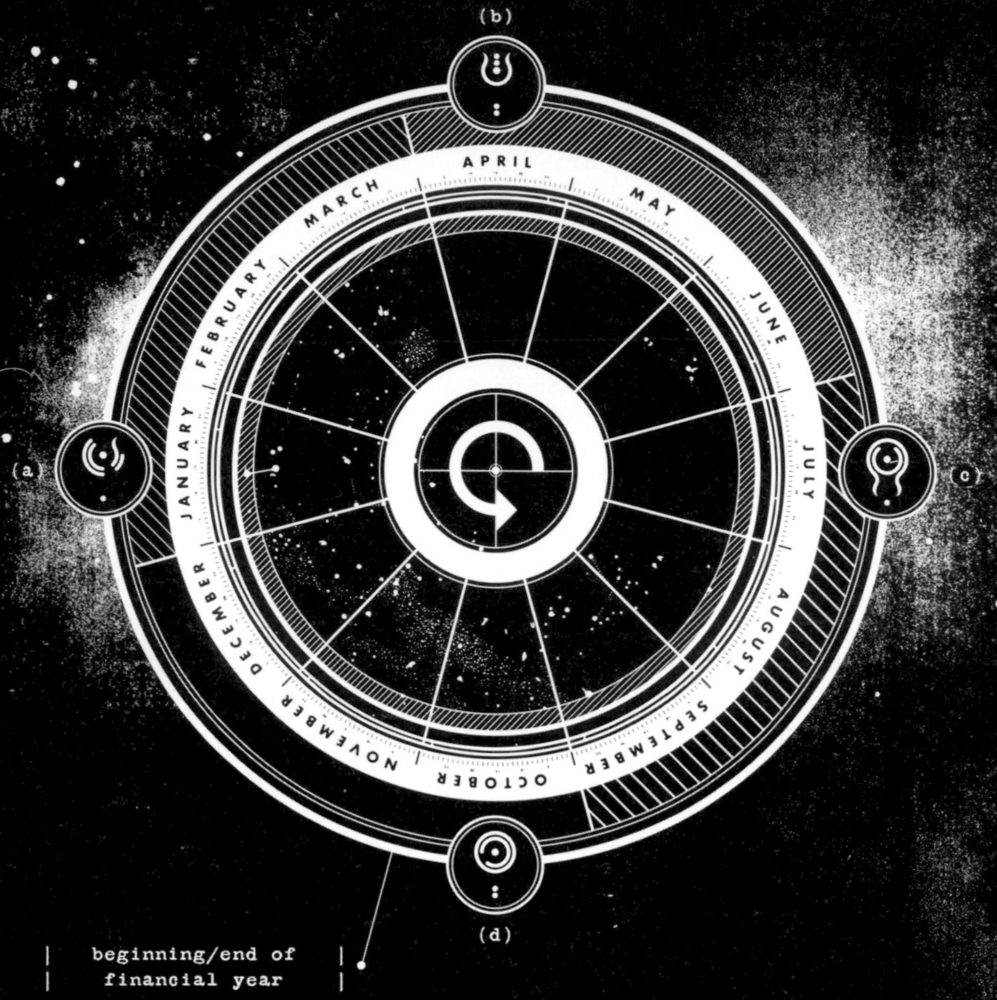
(a)
(b)
(c)
(d)
JANUARY
FEBRUARY
MARCH
APRIL
MAY
JUNE
JULY
AUGUST
SEPTEMBER
OCTOBER
NOVEMBER
DECEMBER
beginning/end of financial year

Western Schools of Economics

Western schools are defined by their traditional four-pillar foundational framework and shared/rotating power structure. While these characteristics are also commonly associated with both the Hyperpyron and Nomisma sects of European schools, the Protestant-Catholic stratagem conducted for centuries by the Black Popes of Rome have successfully prevented unification of these institutions.

Notable Academies:

Post-Tudor Consolidation:

Barclays (1690)
BOE (1694)
Lloyds (1765)

Post-Expansion:

BNY (1784)
J.P. Morgan (1799)
State Street (1792)
Citi (1812)
Caina (1857)
Goldman Sachs (1869)

                                              (October 24, 1929)
    (a) ⬤ [Fyr | The Watcher].................BISCHOFF

    (b) ⬤ [Aer | The Ascendant Seat].......ROTHSCHILD

    (c) ⬤ [Wæter | The Scales]...............DOMINIC

    (d) ⬤ [Eorthe | The Stone Chair]........ACKERMANN


                              ⬤
                              ⬤


The Four Pillars of Caina
_____

Based on a rotating twelve-year schedule, the board members of
Caina spend three years at each station per cycle. Partial terms
do occur and are most commonly attributed to either death or
leave of absence.

In 1989, the board members of Caina permanently relinquished the
Stone Chair to the Kankrin Troika during the Caina-Kankrin
merger. A sabbatical replaced the three-year Stone Chair term
normally served by Caina members. The Kankrin Troika also
lobbied for a seasonal portion of the Watcher's functions, which
was granted but with generational conditions.*




*Must be renegotiated upon the passing of a board member if that
member is currently holding the Watcher position.

CAINA INVESTMENT BANK
Founded 1857

•

Board Structure as
of January 1, 1929

(a)

J.W. BISCHOFF
[Fyr | The Watcher]

A trader and a teacher. Measures the comings and goings of the gifted.

(b)

MILTON ROTHSCHILD
[Aer | The Ascendant Seat]

The spear. The voice of Mammon on the Caina board. The de facto head of the Academy. The Ascendant Seat may cast a second vote to break a tie.

(c)

RAYMOND DOMINIC
[Wæter | The Scales]

Works with the Ascendant Seat to gauge volatility in the market.

Has the ability to perceive 'balance.'

(d)

CHARLES ACKERMANN
[Eorthe | The Stone Chair]

The sacrificial altar. The blood price.

The one who pays when Mammon takes his portion.

STONE CHAIR HOLDERS
FROM 1929 TO PRESENT

Charles Ackermann
(1929)
Gloria Ackermann
(1929-1931)

J.W. Bischoff
(1932-1934)

Milton Rothschild
(1935-1937)

Raymond Dominic
(1938-1940)

Gloria Ackermann
(1941-1943)

J.W. Bischoff
(1944-1945)

Hannah Bischoff
(1945-1946)

Milton Rothschild
(1947-1949)

Raymond Dominic
(1950-1952)

Patrick Ackermann
(1953-1955)

Hannah Bischoff
(1956-1958)

Milton Rothschild
(1959-1961)

THE DOMINIC
SLAUGHTER

Raymond Dominic......1962
Piers Dominic...1962-1963
Alastair Dominic.....1963
Annabel Dominic......1963
Hugh Dominic.........1963
Isla Dominic-Day.....1963
Duncan Dominic.......1963
Callum Dominic.......1963
Thad Dominic....1963-1964

Cynthia
Ackermann-Bane
(1965-1967)

Raven Bischoff
(1968-1970)

Milton Rothschild
(1971-1973)

Thad Dominic
(1974-1976)

Wynn Ackermann
(1977-1979)

Raven Bischoff
(1980)
Beatrix Bischoff
(1980-1982)

Daniel Rothschild
Grigoria Rothschild
(1983-1985)

Marco Dominic
(1986-1988)

Wynn Ackermann
(1989)

KANKRIN TROIKA
(1989-current)

2016

- THE SECOND SIN -

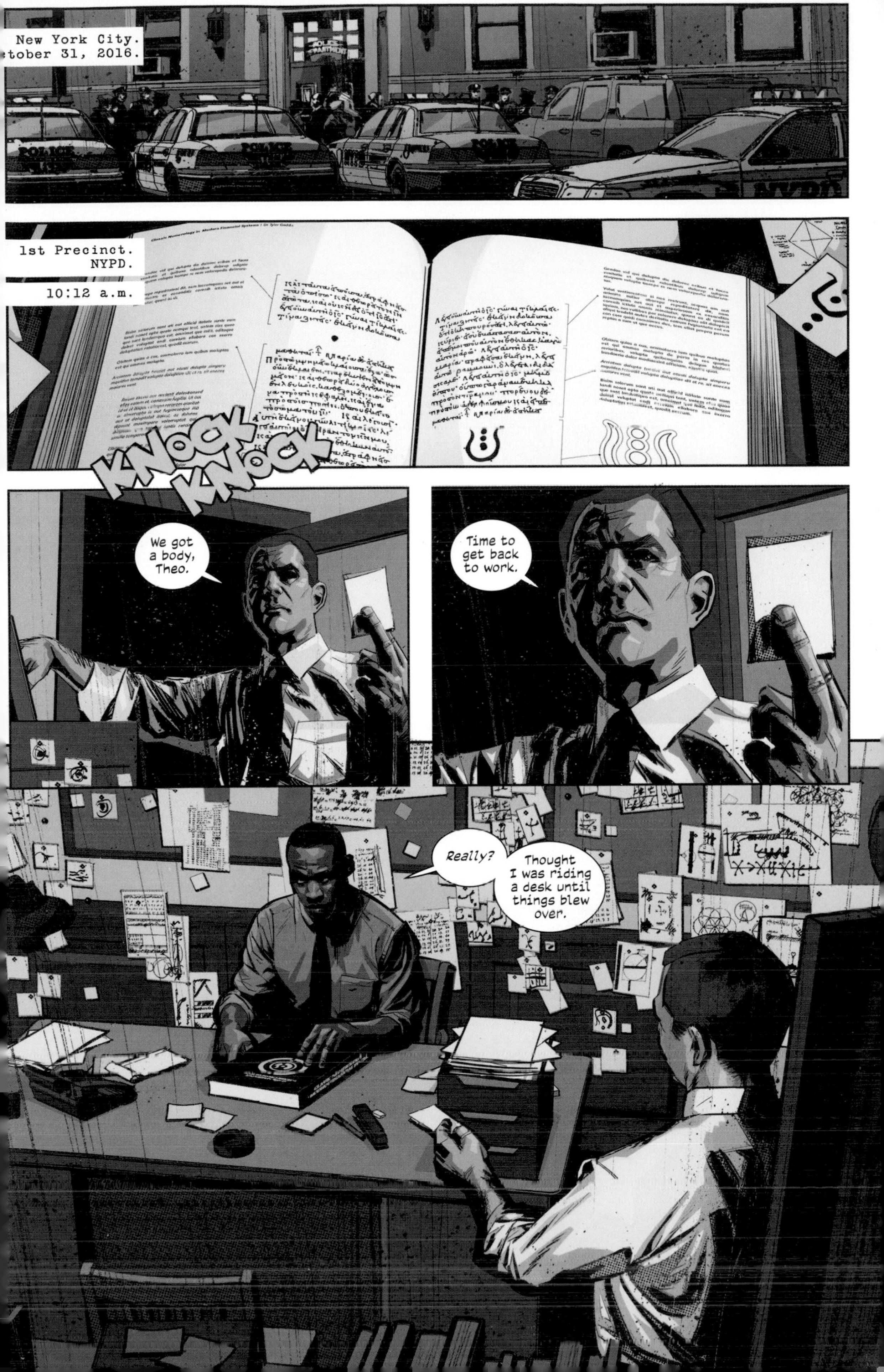
New York City.
tober 31, 2016.
1st Precinct. NYPD.
10:12 a.m.
KNOCK KNOCK
We got a body, Theo.
Time to get back to work.
Really?
Thought I was riding a desk until things blew over.

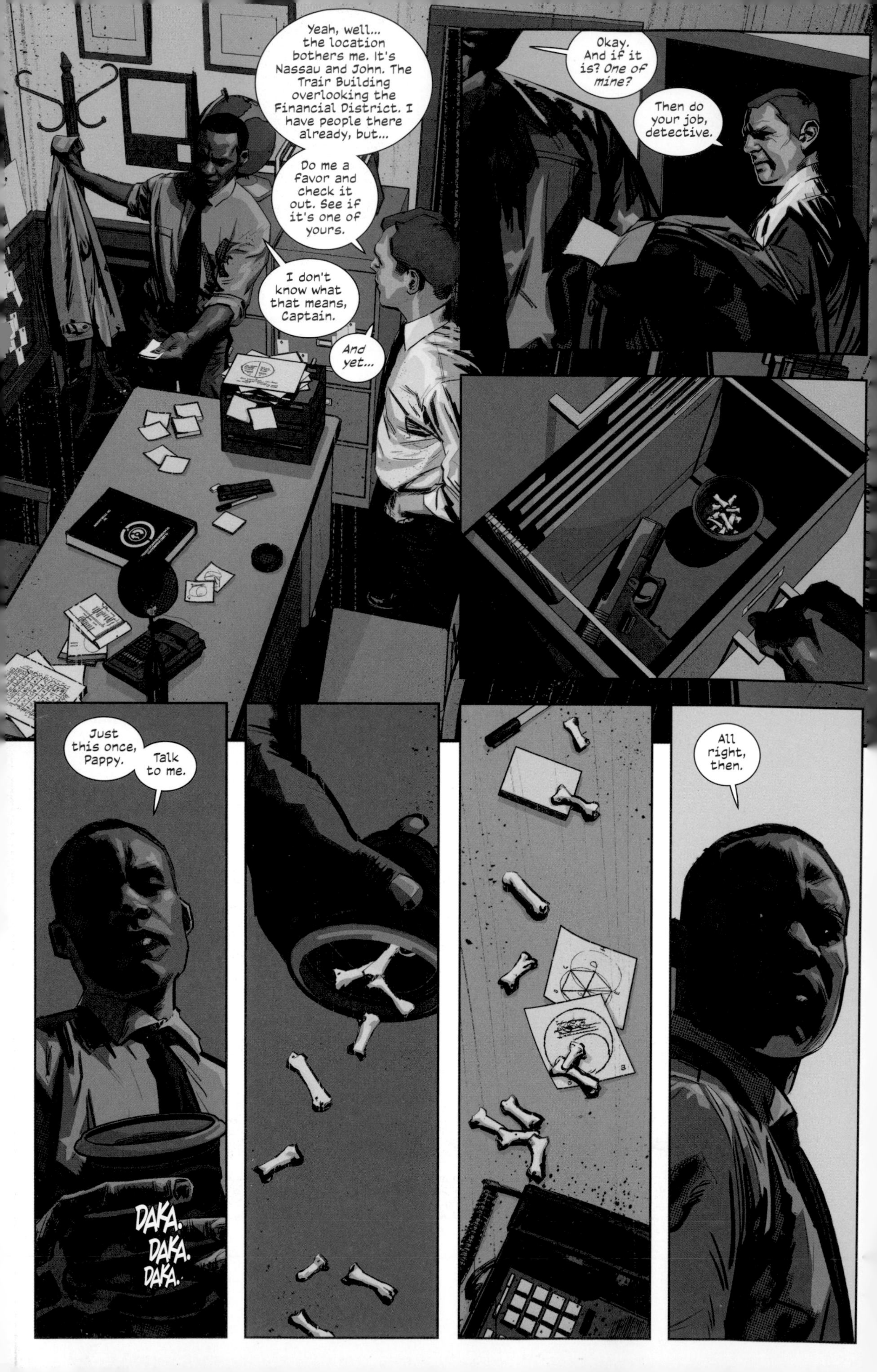
Yeah, well... the location bothers me. It's Nassau and John. The Trair Building overlooking the Financial District. I have people there already, but...
Do me a favor and check it out. See if it's one of yours.
I don't know what that means, Captain.
And yet...
Okay. And if it is? One of mine?
Then do your job, detective.
Just this once, Pappy.
Talk to me.
DAKA. DAKA. DAKA.
All right, then.

POLICE DEPARTMENT CITY OF NEW YORK

16 Ericsson Place
New York, NY, 10013-2411

Precinct: (212) 334-0611
Community Affairs: (212) 334-0640
Crime Prevention: (212) 334-0603
Domestic Violence: (212) 334-0618
Youth Officer: (212) 334-0618
Auxiliary Coordinator: (212) [illegible]
Detective Squad: (212) 334-06[illegible]

| | |
|---|---|
| NAME: | THEODORE JAMES DUMAS |
| SEX: | MALE |
| AGE: | 47 |
| DOB: | 03/27/1969 |
| SS#: | 250-71-9822 |
| RANK: | DETECTIVE, FIRST-GRADE |

SUPPLEMENTARY COMPLAINT REPORT

Complainant's name: [redacted]

Complainant's address: [redacted]

Incident date: August 16, 2016
Incident location: [redacted]

Subject: INTERVIEW OF [redacted]

1. [redacted] stopped the car and got out [redacted] approached the victim [redacted] firing five or six shots [redacted]

2. [redacted] before the detective shot the man, she believed she heard him say something like, "I see you," or "I can see you." The victim smiled at him and then the detective shot [redacted]

3. [redacted]

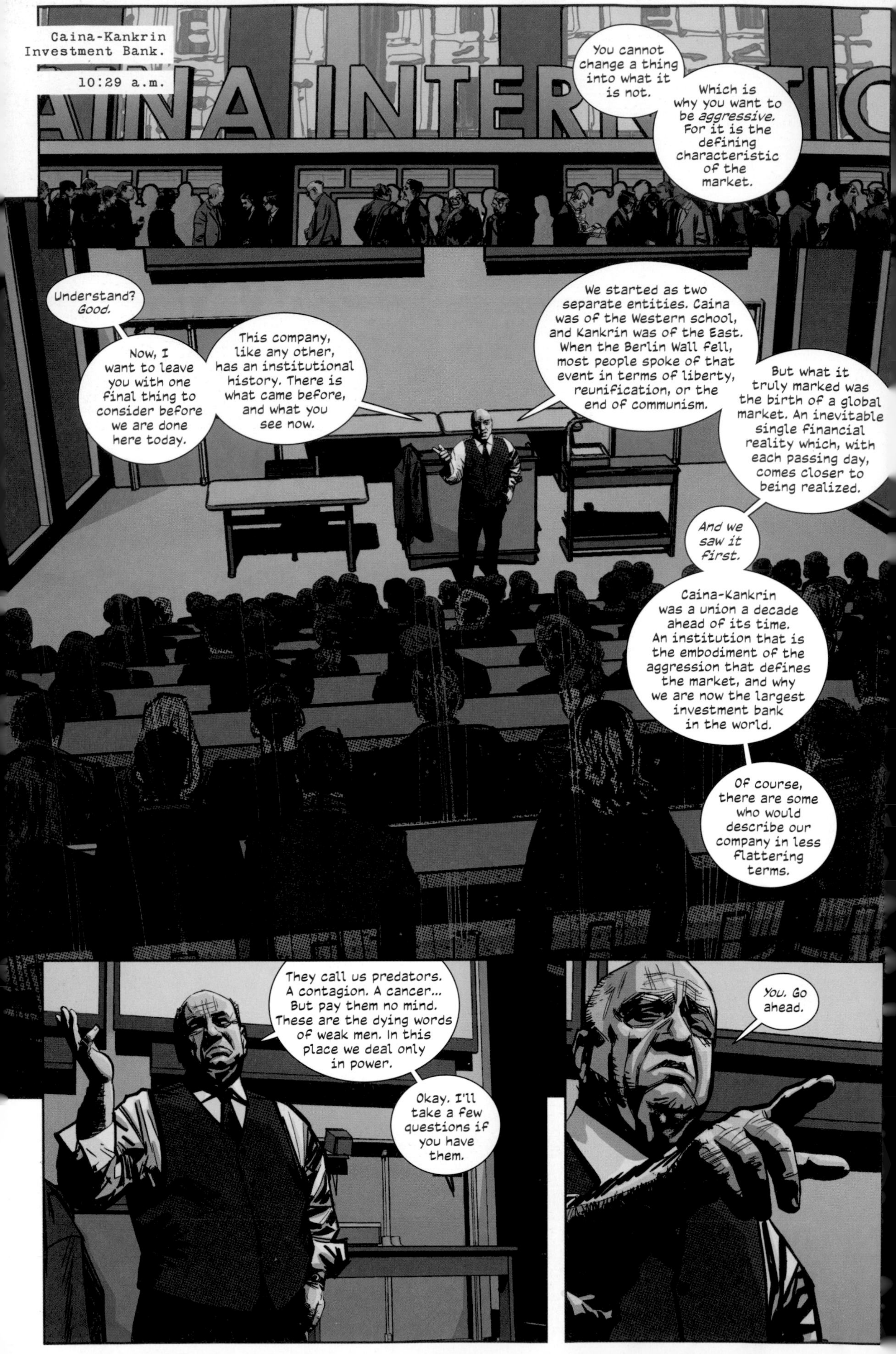
Caina-Kankrin Investment Bank.
10:29 a.m.
CAINA INTERNATIO
You cannot change a thing into what it is not.
Which is why you want to be *aggressive.* For it is the defining characteristic of the market.
Understand? *Good.*
Now, I want to leave you with one final thing to consider before we are done here today.
This company, like any other, has an institutional history. There is what came before, and what you see now.
We started as two separate entities. Caina was of the Western school, and Kankrin was of the East. When the Berlin Wall fell, most people spoke of that event in terms of liberty, reunification, or the end of communism.
But what it truly marked was the birth of a global market. An inevitable single financial reality which, with each passing day, comes closer to being realized.
*And we saw it first.*
Caina-Kankrin was a union a decade ahead of its time. An institution that is the embodiment of the aggression that defines the market, and why we are now the largest investment bank in the world.
Of course, there are some who would describe our company in less flattering terms.
They call us predators. A contagion. A cancer... But pay them no mind. These are the dying words of weak men. In this place we deal only in power.
Okay. I'll take a few questions if you have them.
*You.* Go ahead.

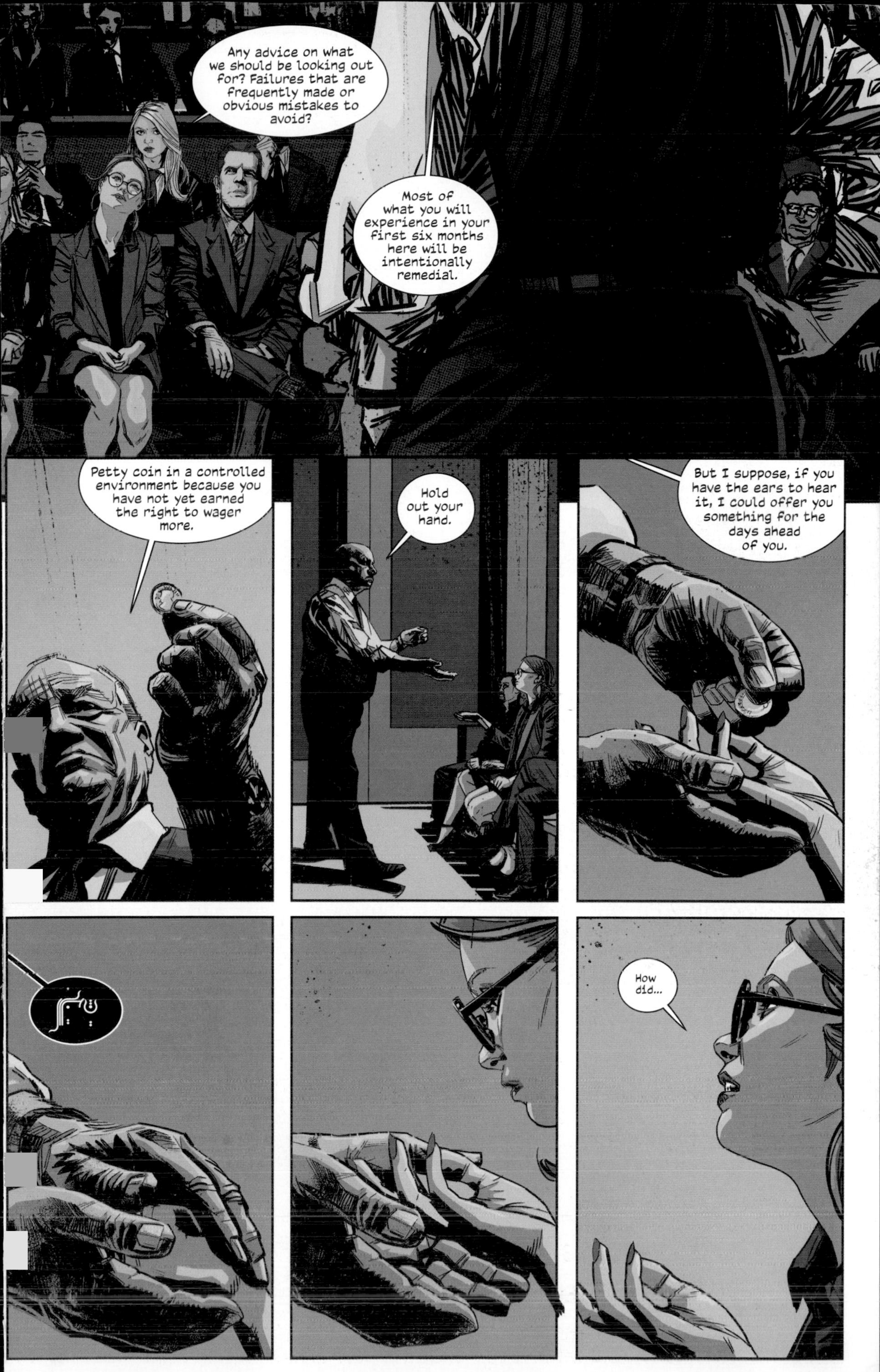
Any advice on what we should be looking out for? Failures that are frequently made or obvious mistakes to avoid?
Most of what you will experience in your first six months here will be intentionally remedial.
Petty coin in a controlled environment because you have not yet earned the right to wager more.
Hold out your hand.
But I suppose, if you have the ears to hear it, I could offer you something for the days ahead of you.
How did...

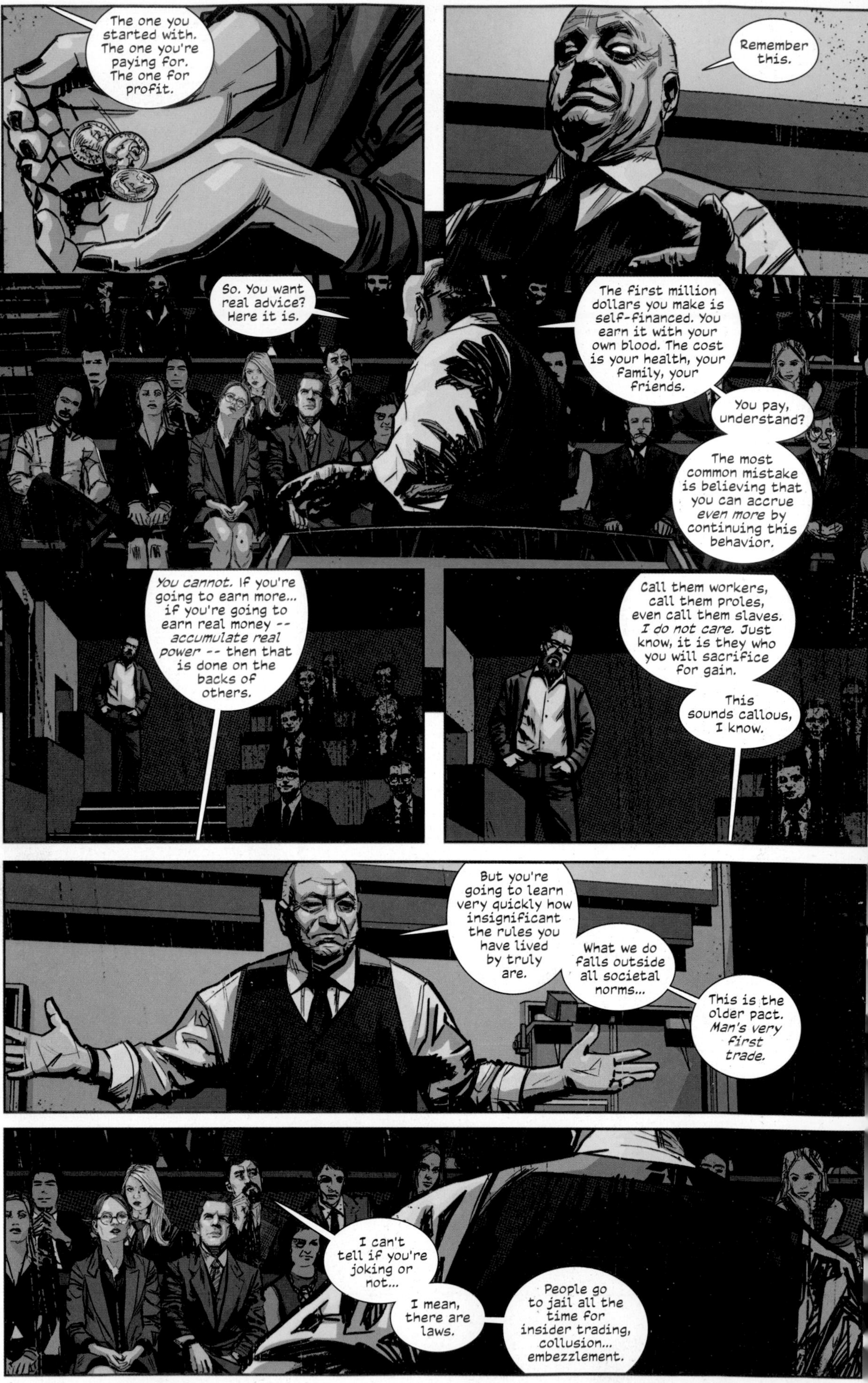
The one you started with. The one you're paying for. The one for profit.
Remember this.
So. You want real advice? Here it is.
The first million dollars you make is self-financed. You earn it with your own blood. The cost is your health, your family, your friends.
You pay, understand?
The most common mistake is believing that you can accrue *even more* by continuing this behavior.
*You cannot.* If you're going to earn more... if you're going to earn real money -- *accumulate real power* -- then that is done on the backs of others.
Call them workers, call them proles, even call them slaves. *I do not care.* Just know, it is they who you will sacrifice for gain.
This sounds callous, I know.
But you're going to learn very quickly how insignificant the rules you have lived by truly are.
What we do falls outside all societal norms...
This is the older pact. *Man's very first trade.*
I can't tell if you're joking or not...
I mean, there are laws.
People go to jail all the time for insider trading, collusion... embezzlement.

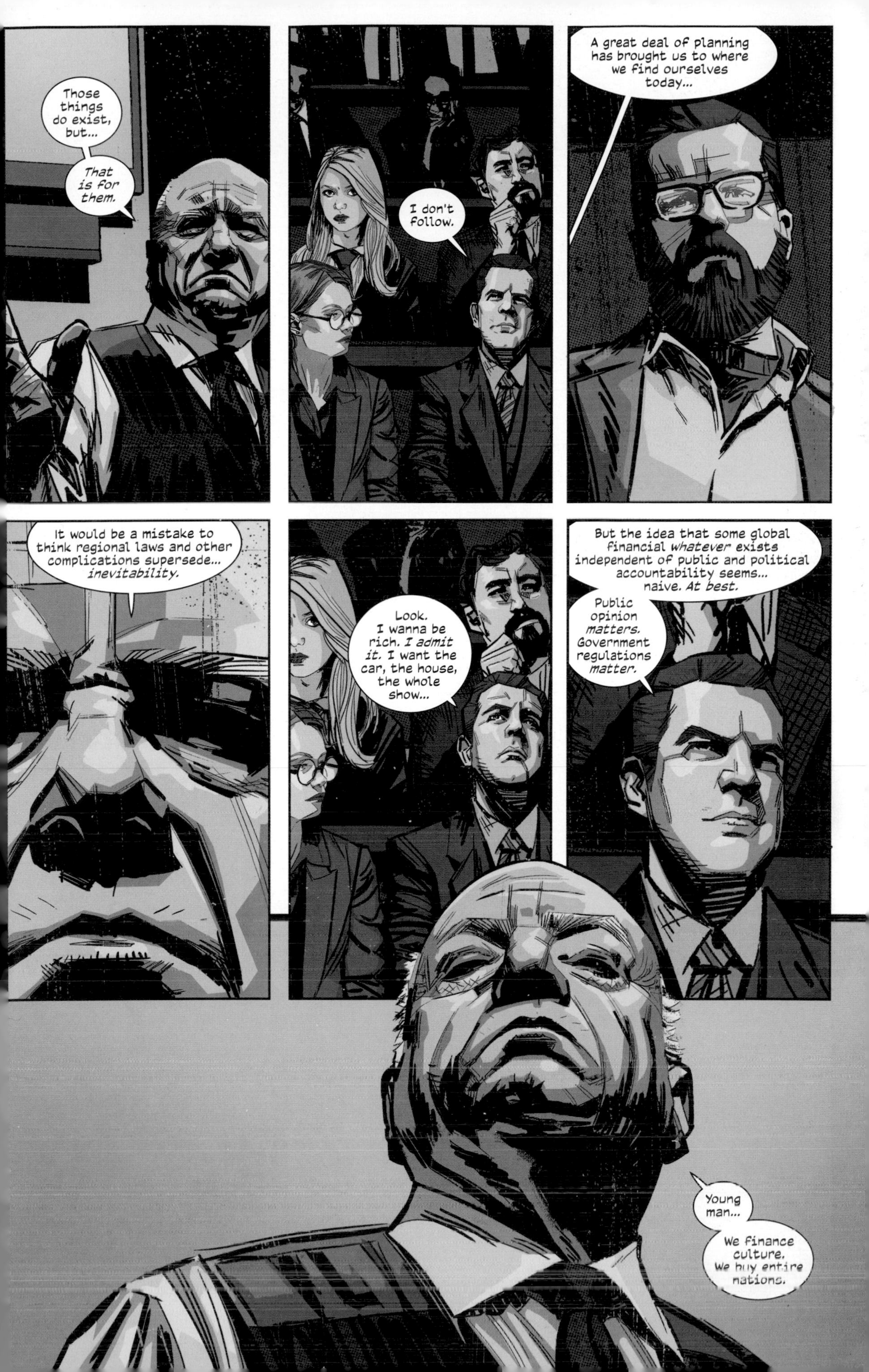
Those things do exist, but...
*That is for them.*
I don't follow.
A great deal of planning has brought us to where we find ourselves today...
It would be a mistake to think regional laws and other complications supersede... *inevitability.*
Look. I wanna be rich. *I admit it.* I want the car, the house, the whole show...
But the idea that some global financial *whatever* exists independent of public and political accountability seems... naive. *At best.*
Public opinion *matters.* Government regulations *matter.*
Young man...
We finance culture. We buy entire nations.

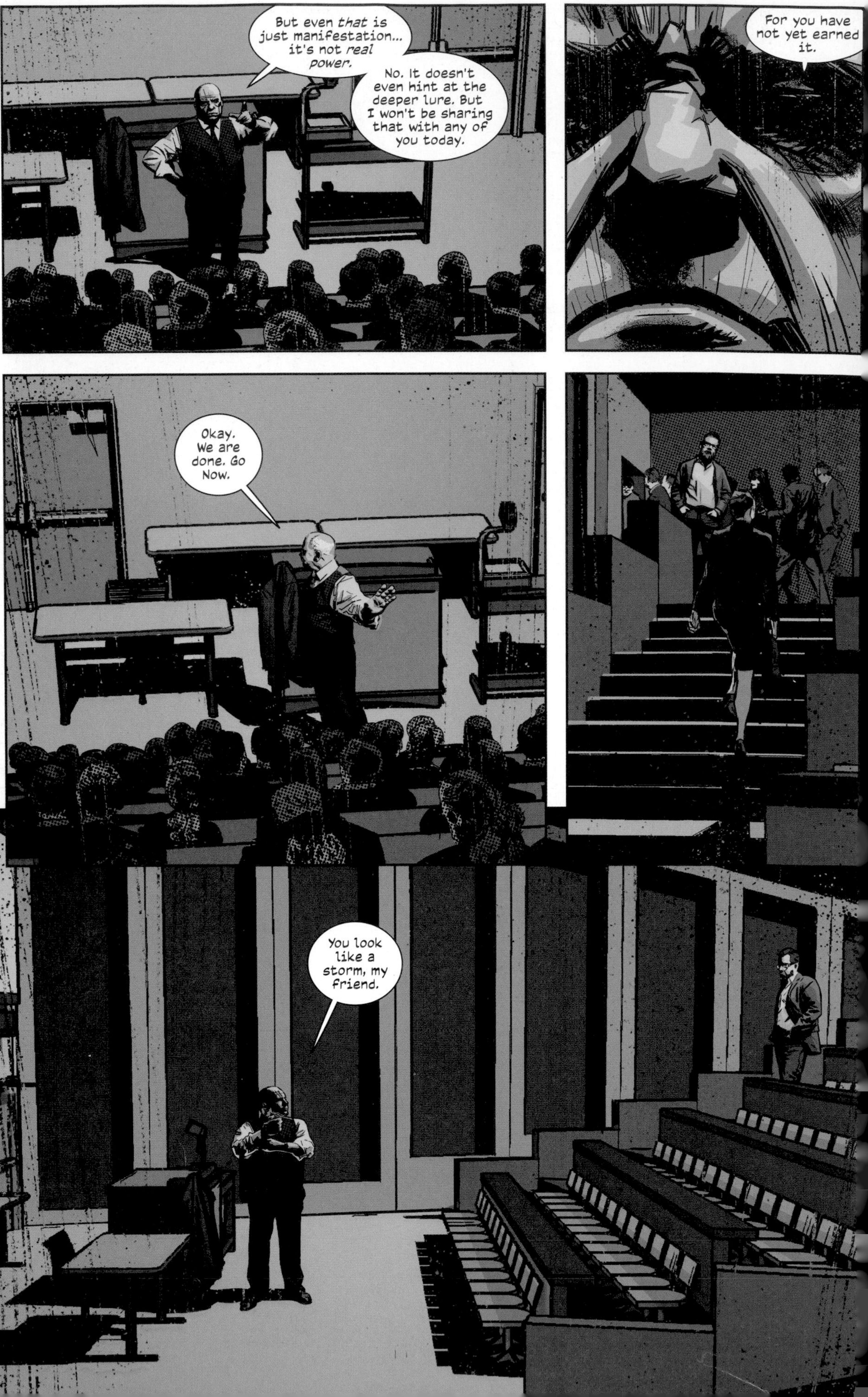
But even *that* is just manifestation... it's not *real power.*
No. It doesn't even hint at the deeper lure. But I won't be sharing that with any of you today.
For you have not yet earned it.
Okay. We are done. Go Now.
You look like a storm, my friend.

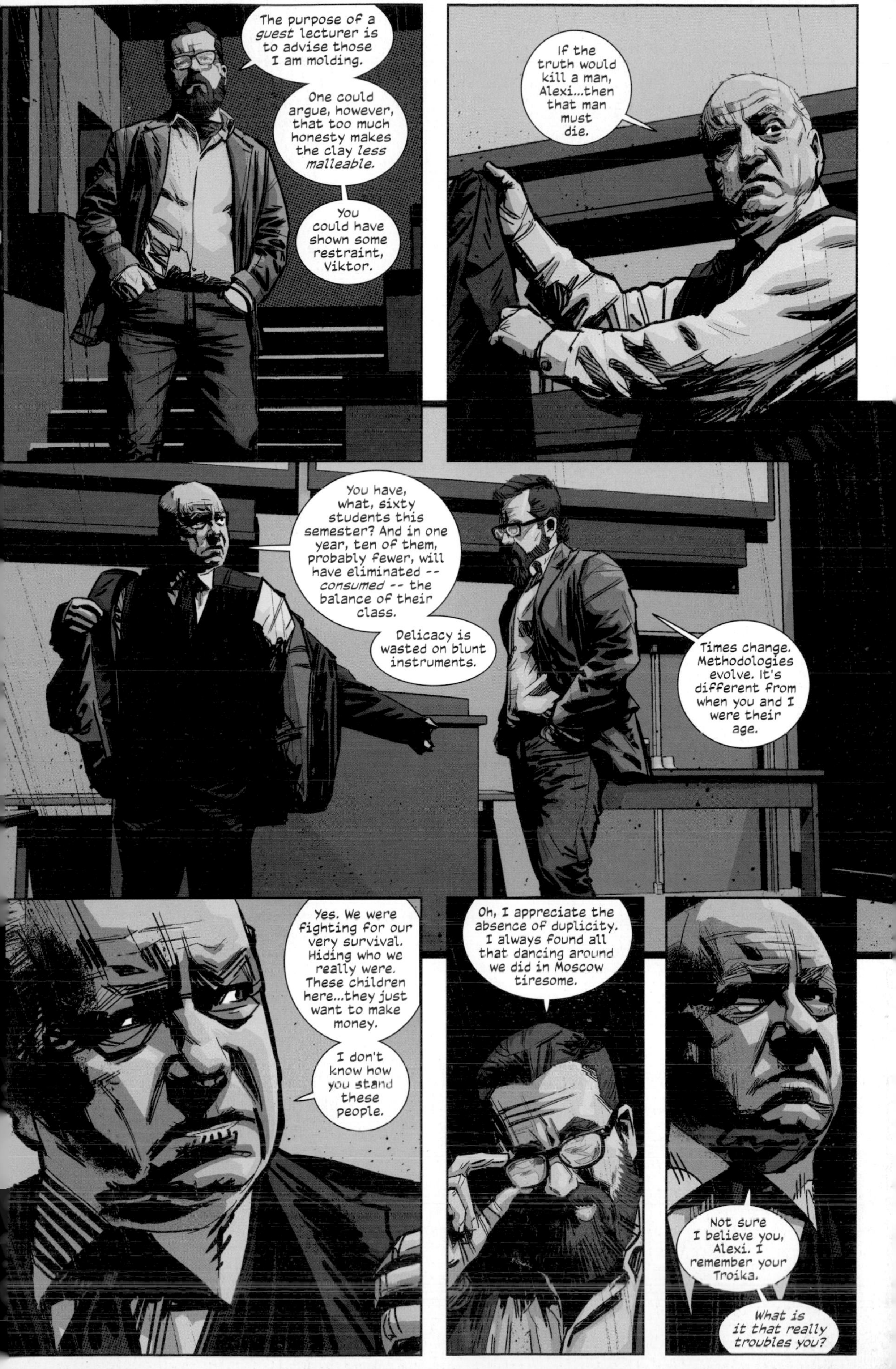
The purpose of a *guest* lecturer is to advise those I am molding.
One could argue, however, that too much honesty makes the clay *less malleable.*
You could have shown some restraint, Viktor.
If the truth would kill a man, Alexi...then that man must die.
You have, what, sixty students this semester? And in one year, ten of them, probably fewer, will have eliminated -- *consumed* -- the balance of their class.
Delicacy is wasted on blunt instruments.
Times change. Methodologies evolve. It's different from when you and I were their age.
Yes. We were fighting for our very survival. Hiding who we really were. These children here...they just want to make money.
I don't know how you stand these people.
Oh, I appreciate the absence of duplicity. I always found all that dancing around we did in Moscow tiresome.
Not sure I believe you, Alexi. I remember your Troika.
*What is it that really troubles you?*

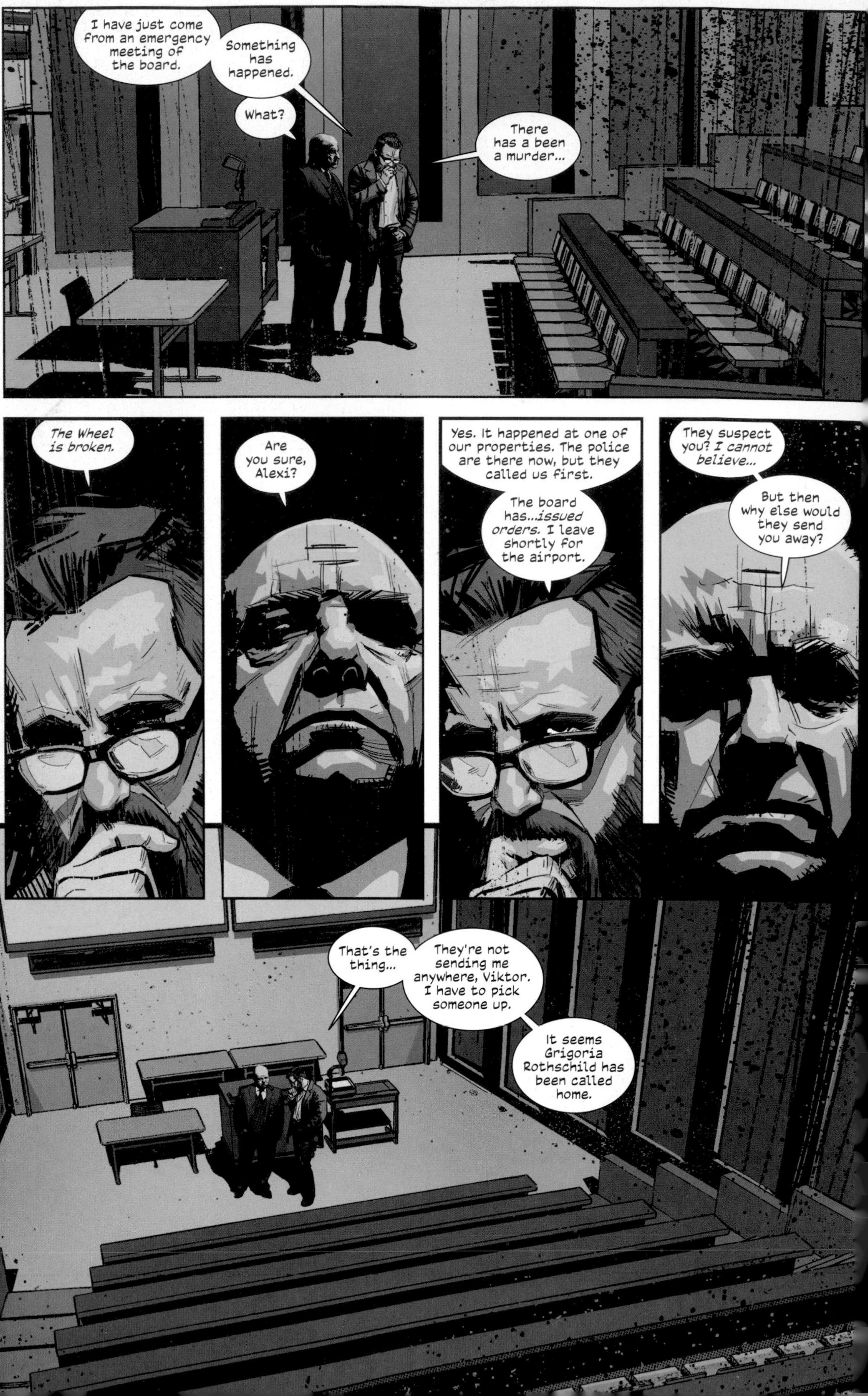
I have just come from an emergency meeting of the board.
Something has happened.
What?
There has a been a murder...
*The Wheel is broken.*
Are you sure, Alexi?
Yes. It happened at one of our properties. The police are there now, but they called us first.
The board has...*issued orders.* I leave shortly for the airport.
They suspect you? *I cannot believe...*
But then why else would they send you away?
That's the thing...
They're not sending me anywhere, Viktor. I have to pick someone up.
It seems Grigoria Rothschild has been called home.

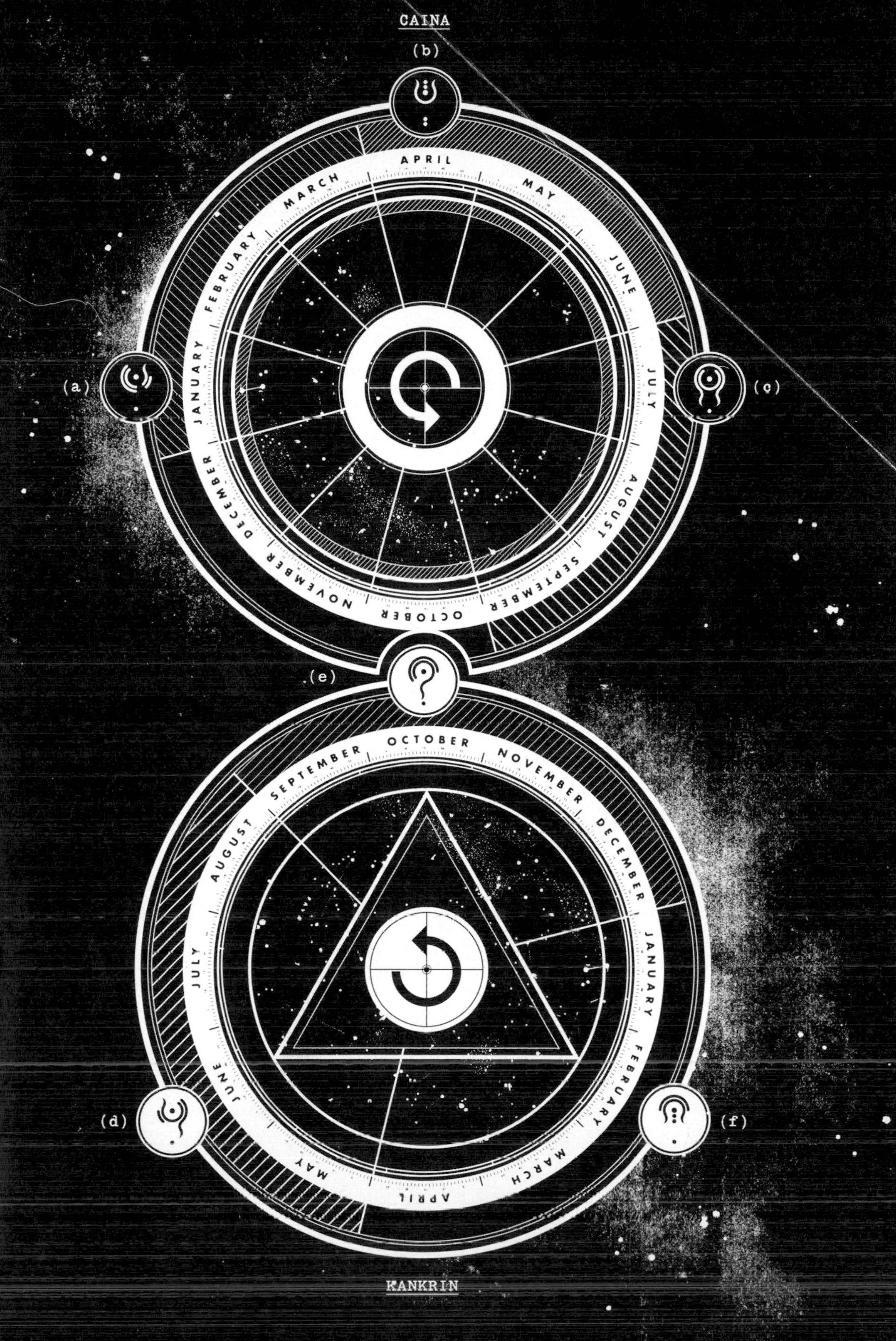
CAINA
(b)
(a)
(c)
APRIL
MAY
JUNE
JULY
AUGUST
SEPTEMBER
OCTOBER
NOVEMBER
DECEMBER
JANUARY
FEBRUARY
MARCH
(e)
OCTOBER
NOVEMBER
DECEMBER
JANUARY
FEBRUARY
MARCH
APRIL
MAY
JUNE
JULY
AUGUST
SEPTEMBER
(d)
(f)
KANKRIN

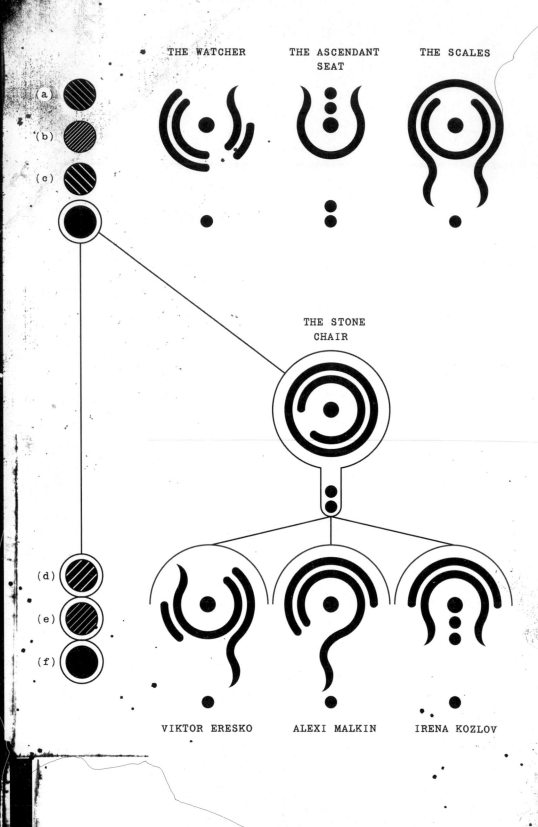

THE WATCHER

THE ASCENDANT
SEAT

THE SCALES

(a)

(b)

(c)

THE STONE
CHAIR

(d)

(e)

(f)

VIKTOR ERESKO

ALEXI MALKIN

IRENA KOZLOV

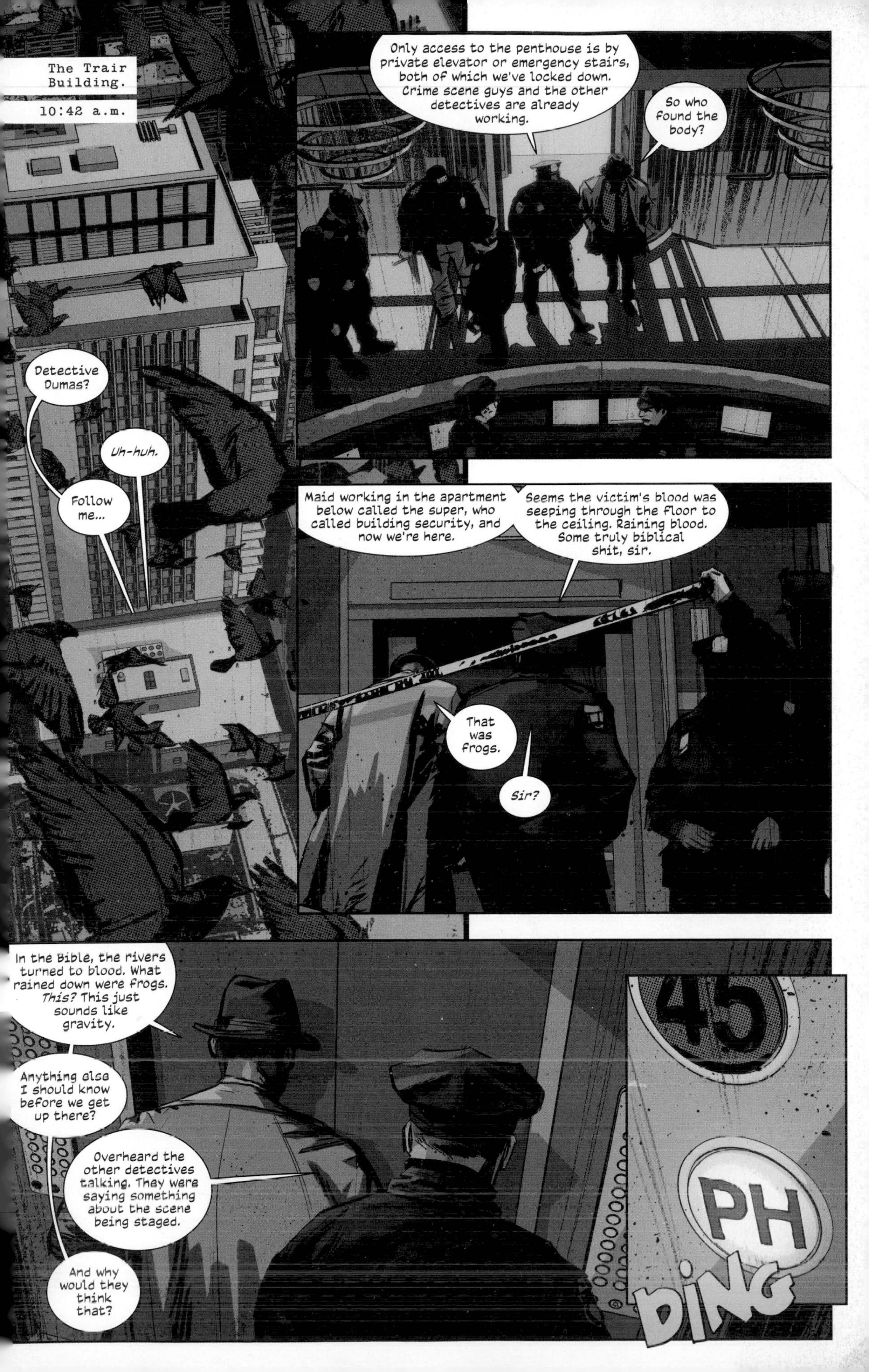
The Trair Building.
10:42 a.m.
Only access to the penthouse is by private elevator or emergency stairs, both of which we've locked down. Crime scene guys and the other detectives are already working.
So who found the body?
Detective Dumas?
Uh-huh.
Follow me...
Maid working in the apartment below called the super, who called building security, and now we're here.
Seems the victim's blood was seeping through the floor to the ceiling. Raining blood. Some truly biblical shit, sir.
That was frogs.
Sir?
In the Bible, the rivers turned to blood. What rained down were frogs. This? This just sounds like gravity.
Anything else I should know before we get up there?
Overheard the other detectives talking. They were saying something about the scene being staged.
And why would they think that?
45
PH
DING

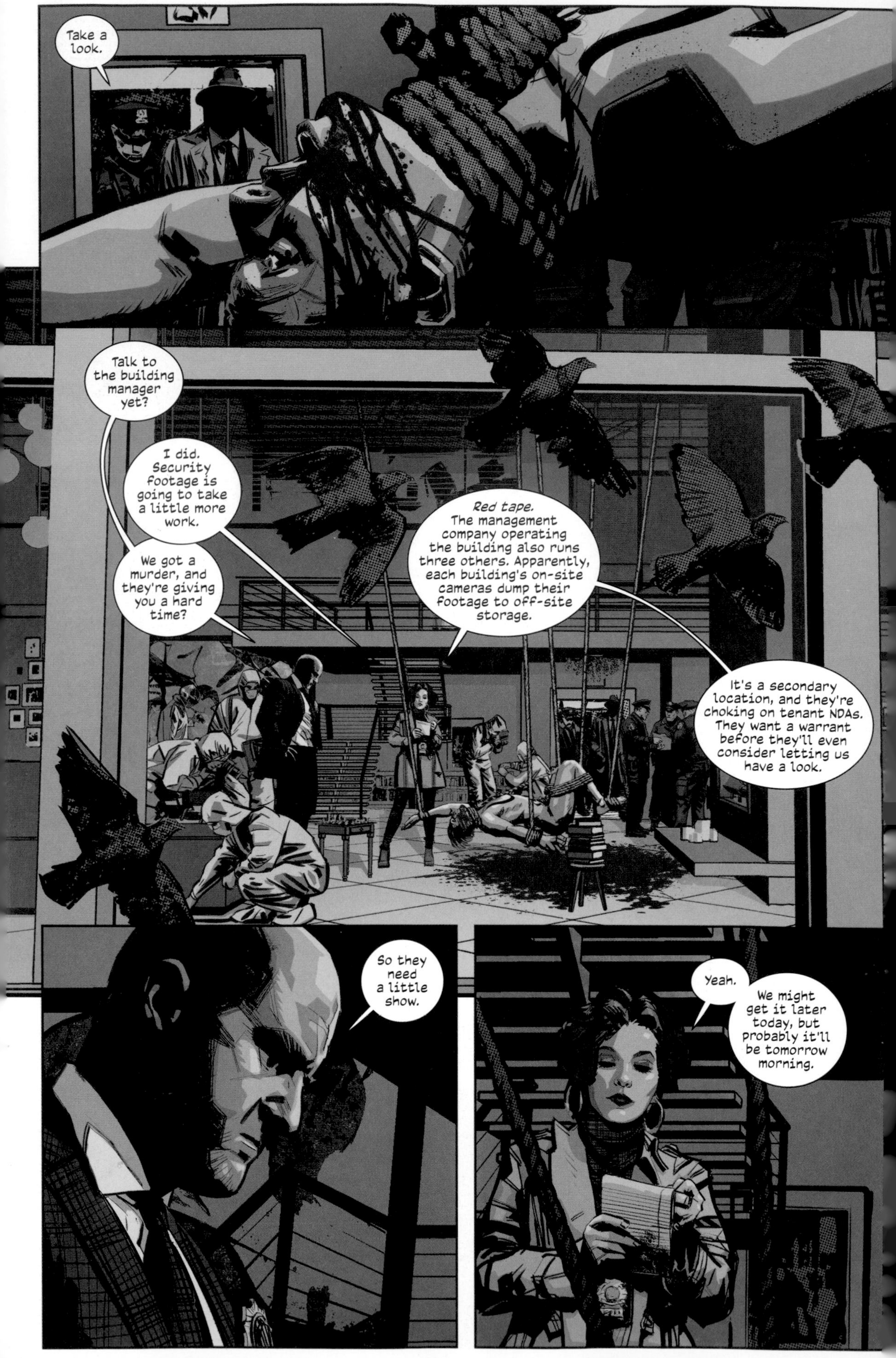
Take a look.
Talk to the building manager yet?
I did. Security footage is going to take a little more work.
We got a murder, and they're giving you a hard time?
*Red tape.* The management company operating the building also runs three others. Apparently, each building's on-site cameras dump their footage to off-site storage.
It's a secondary location, and they're choking on tenant NDAs. They want a warrant before they'll even consider letting us have a look.
So they need a little show.
Yeah.
We might get it later today, but probably it'll be tomorrow morning.

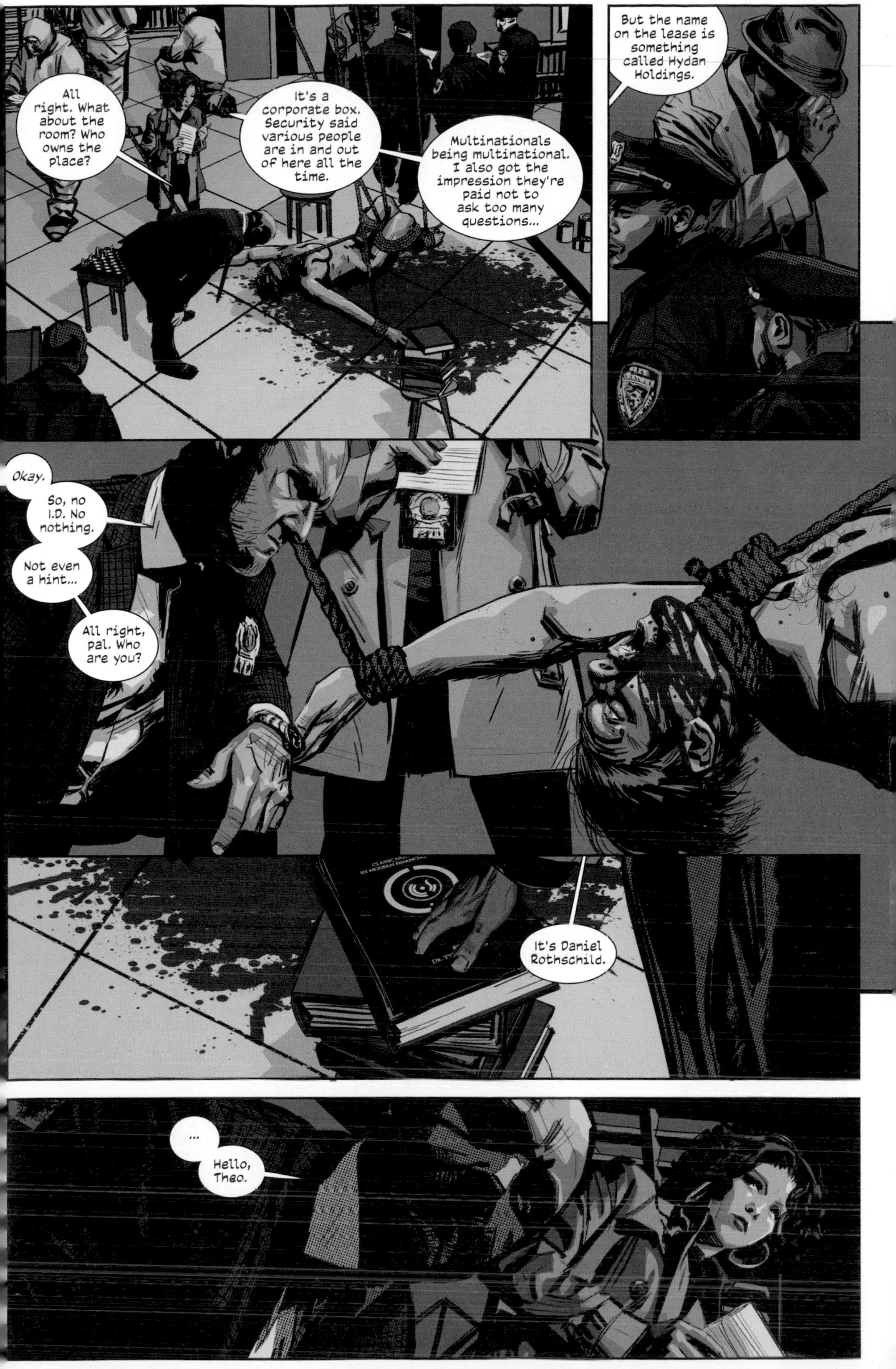
All right. What about the room? Who owns the place?
It's a corporate box. Security said various people are in and out of here all the time.
Multinationals being multinational. I also got the impression they're paid not to ask too many questions...
But the name on the lease is something called Hydan Holdings.
Okay.
So, no I.D. No nothing.
Not even a hint...
All right, pal. Who are you?
It's Daniel Rothschild.
...
Hello, Theo.

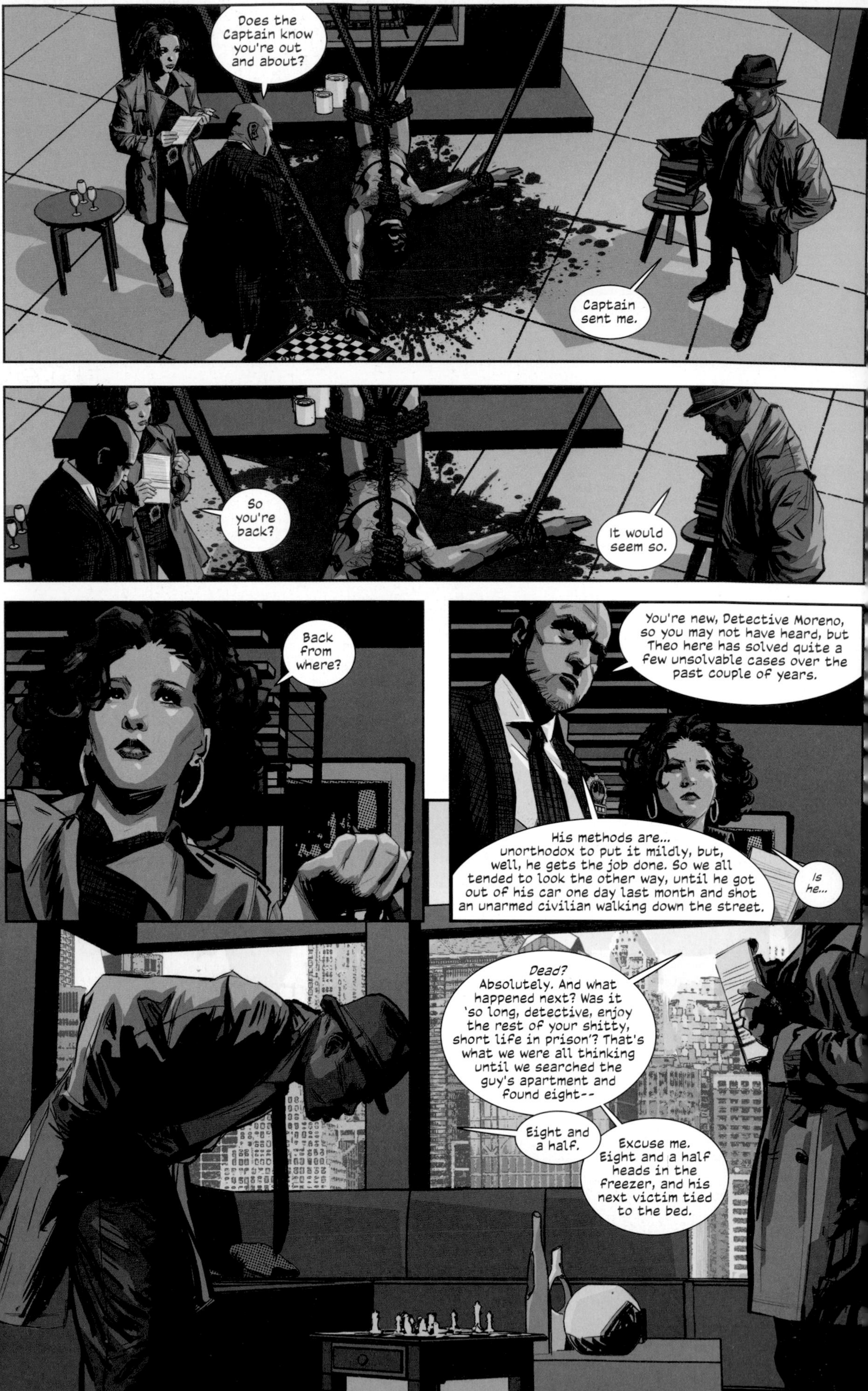
Does the Captain know you're out and about?
Captain sent me.
So you're back?
It would seem so.
Back from where?
You're new, Detective Moreno, so you may not have heard, but Theo here has solved quite a few unsolvable cases over the past couple of years.
His methods are... unorthodox to put it mildly, but, well, he gets the job done. So we all tended to look the other way, until he got out of his car one day last month and shot an unarmed civilian walking down the street.
Is he...
*Dead?* Absolutely. And what happened next? Was it 'so long, detective, enjoy the rest of your shitty, short life in prison'? That's what we were all thinking until we searched the guy's apartment and found eight--
Eight and a half.
Excuse me. Eight and a half heads in the freezer, and his next victim tied to the bed.

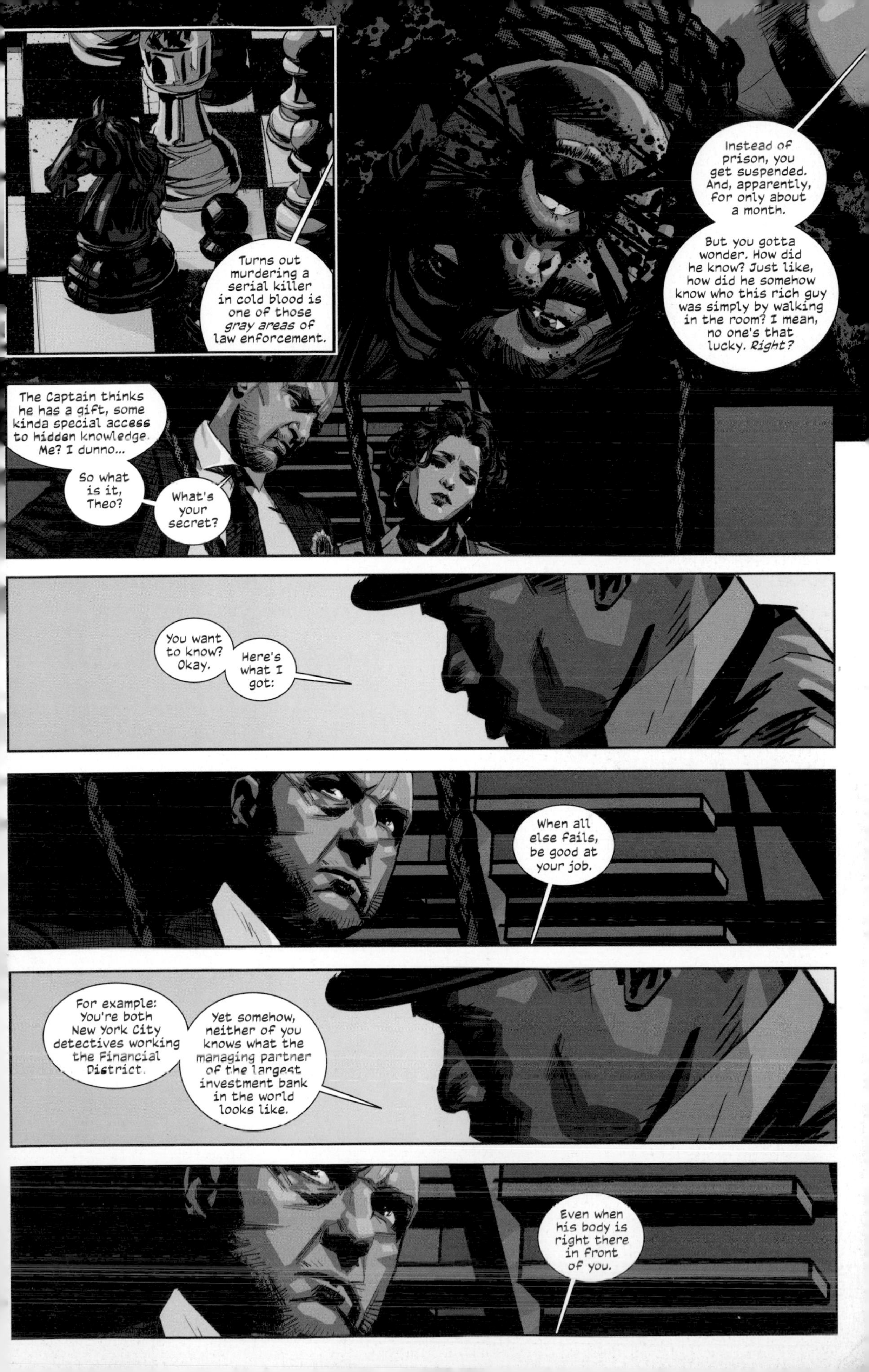
Turns out murdering a serial killer in cold blood is one of those *gray areas* of law enforcement.
Instead of prison, you get suspended. And, apparently, for only about a month.
But you gotta wonder. How did he know? Just like, how did he somehow know who this rich guy was simply by walking in the room? I mean, no one's that lucky. *Right?*
The Captain thinks he has a gift, some kinda special access to hidden knowledge. Me? I dunno...
So what is it, Theo?
What's your secret?
You want to know? Okay.
Here's what I got:
When all else fails, be good at your job.
For example: You're both New York City detectives working the Financial District.
Yet somehow, neither of you knows what the managing partner of the largest investment bank in the world looks like.
Even when his body is right there in front of you.

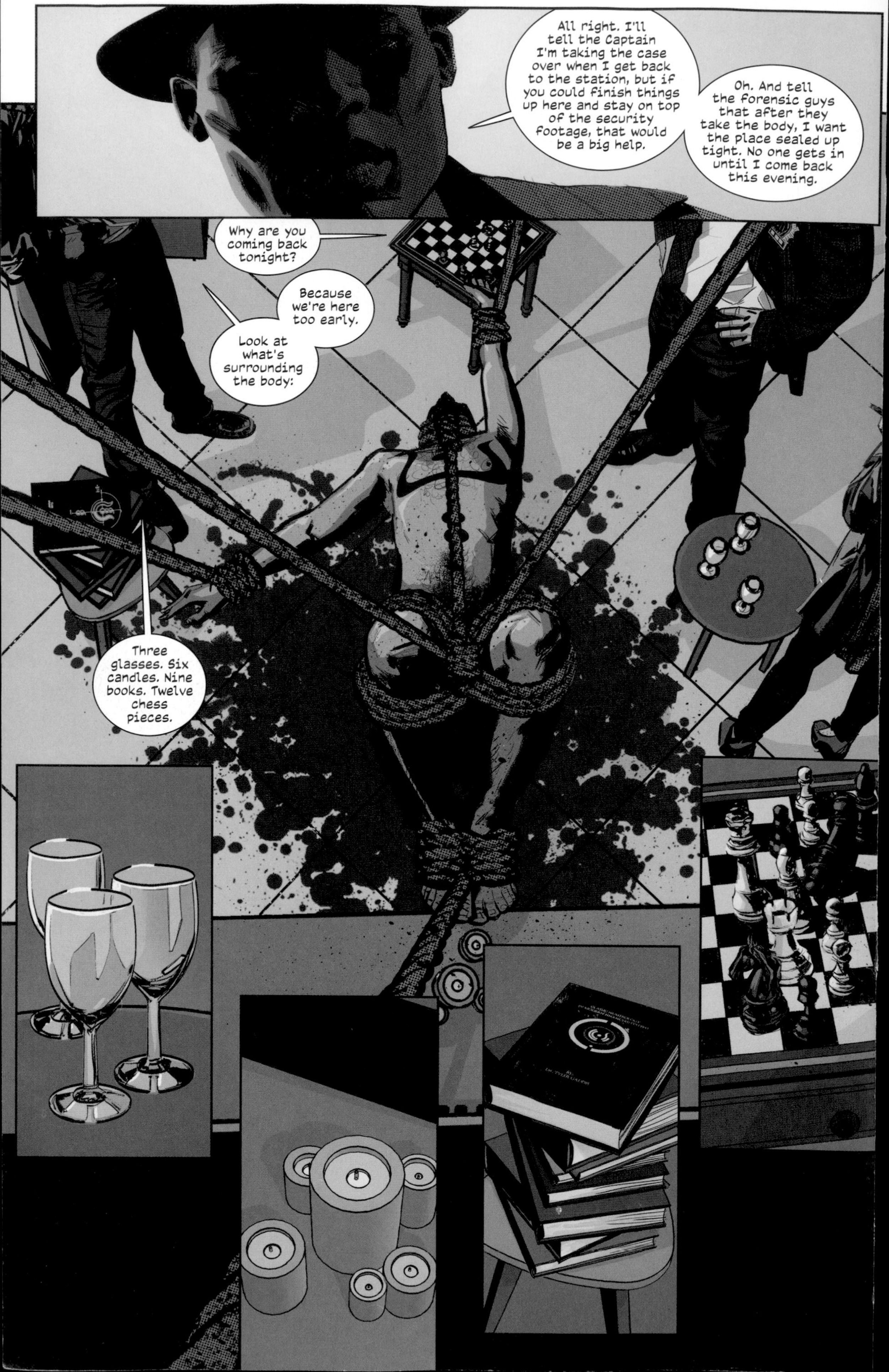
All right. I'll tell the Captain I'm taking the case over when I get back to the station, but if you could finish things up here and stay on top of the security footage, that would be a big help.
Oh. And tell the forensic guys that after they take the body, I want the place sealed up tight. No one gets in until I come back this evening.
Why are you coming back tonight?
Because we're here too early.
Look at what's surrounding the body:
Three glasses. Six candles. Nine books. Twelve chess pieces.

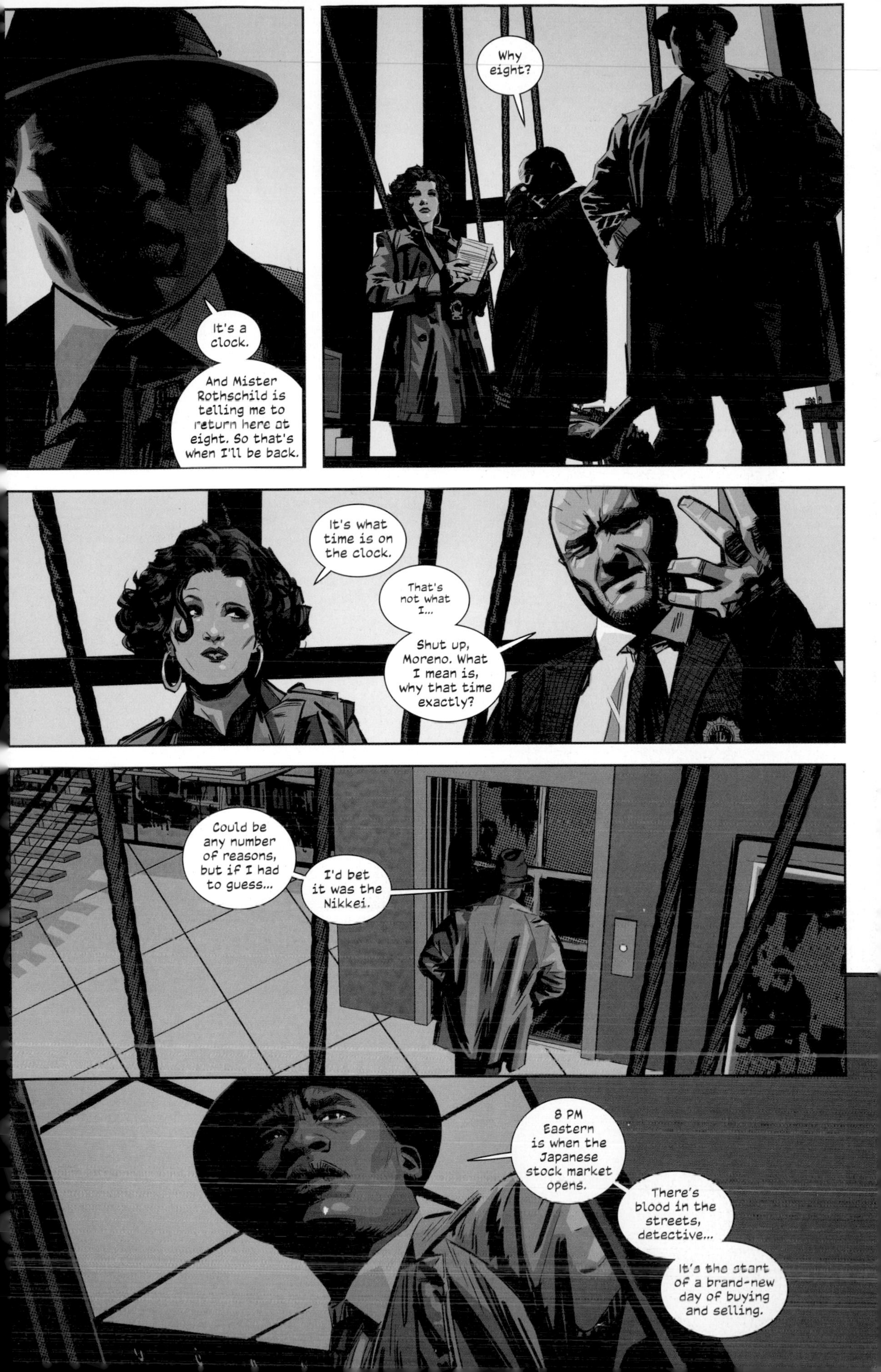
It's a clock.
And Mister Rothschild is telling me to return here at eight. So that's when I'll be back.
Why eight?
It's what time is on the clock.
That's not what I...
Shut up, Moreno. What I mean is, why that time exactly?
Could be any number of reasons, but if I had to guess...
I'd bet it was the Nikkei.
8 PM Eastern is when the Japanese stock market opens.
There's blood in the streets, detective...
It's the start of a brand-new day of buying and selling.

NORTH AMERICAN STOCK MARKET CRASHES

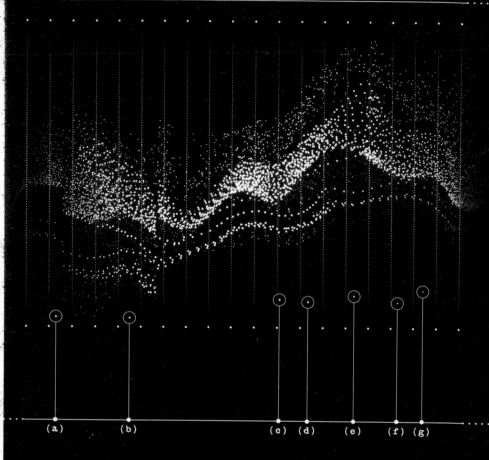

(a)
(b)
(c)
(d)
(e)
(f)
(g)

(a) 1907 | U.S. market panic....................October 14

(b) 1929 | Wall Street Crash ...................October 24

(c) 1987 | Black Monday.........................October 19

(d) 1989 | Airline bailout mini-crash...........October 13

(e) 1997 | Global mini-crash....................October 27

(f) 2002 | Global downturn......................October 9

(g) 2007 | Bear market of 2007-2009.............October 11

THE MONTH OF OCTOBER

Historically, almost all major and minor North American stock market crashes occur, or begin, in the month of October.

Prominent October market crashes have occurred in the years 1907, 1929, 1987, 1989, 1997, 2002, and 2007.

------------------------------------------------------------------------

SAMHAIN

Samhain is celebrated from sunset on October 31st to sunset on November 1st.

While traditionally not celebrated by the Western Schools of Economics, the merger of the Caina and Kankrin Academies has resulted in the normalization of the Eastern School holiday. Samhain is now considered a Greater Sabbat of the North American Western School.

Of particular note is Samhain's occurrence at the midpoint of the autumn equinox and the winter solstice, during the monthlong Feast of Mammon, when the veil between this world and the the other is at its thinnest, and communion with God is possible.

------------------------------------------------------------------------

NOVEMBER 1ST

The Market has never opened down on November 1st.

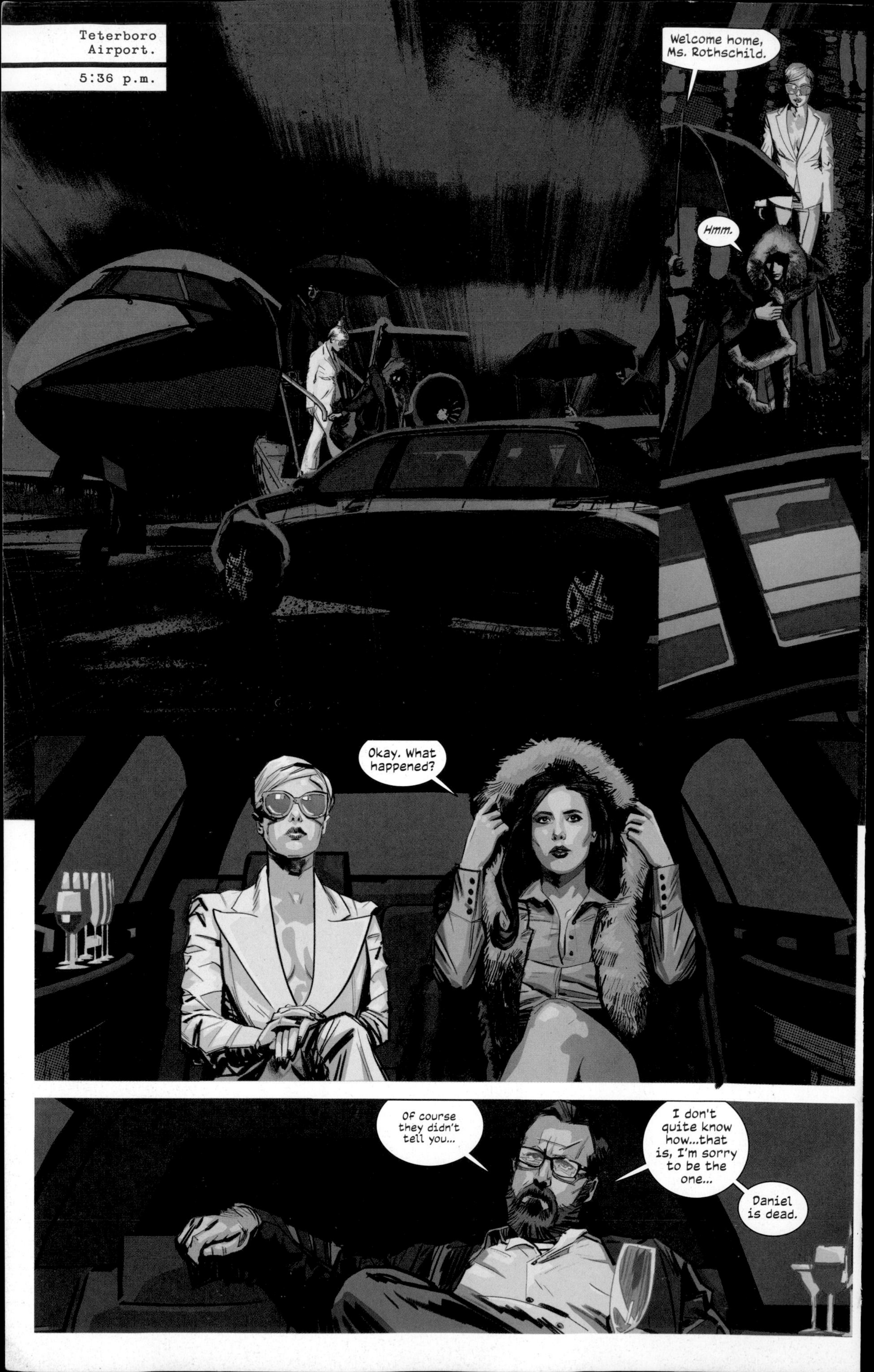
Teterboro Airport.
5:36 p.m.
Welcome home, Ms. Rothschild.
Hmm.
Okay. What happened?
Of course they didn't tell you...
I don't quite know how...that is, I'm sorry to be the one...
Daniel is dead.

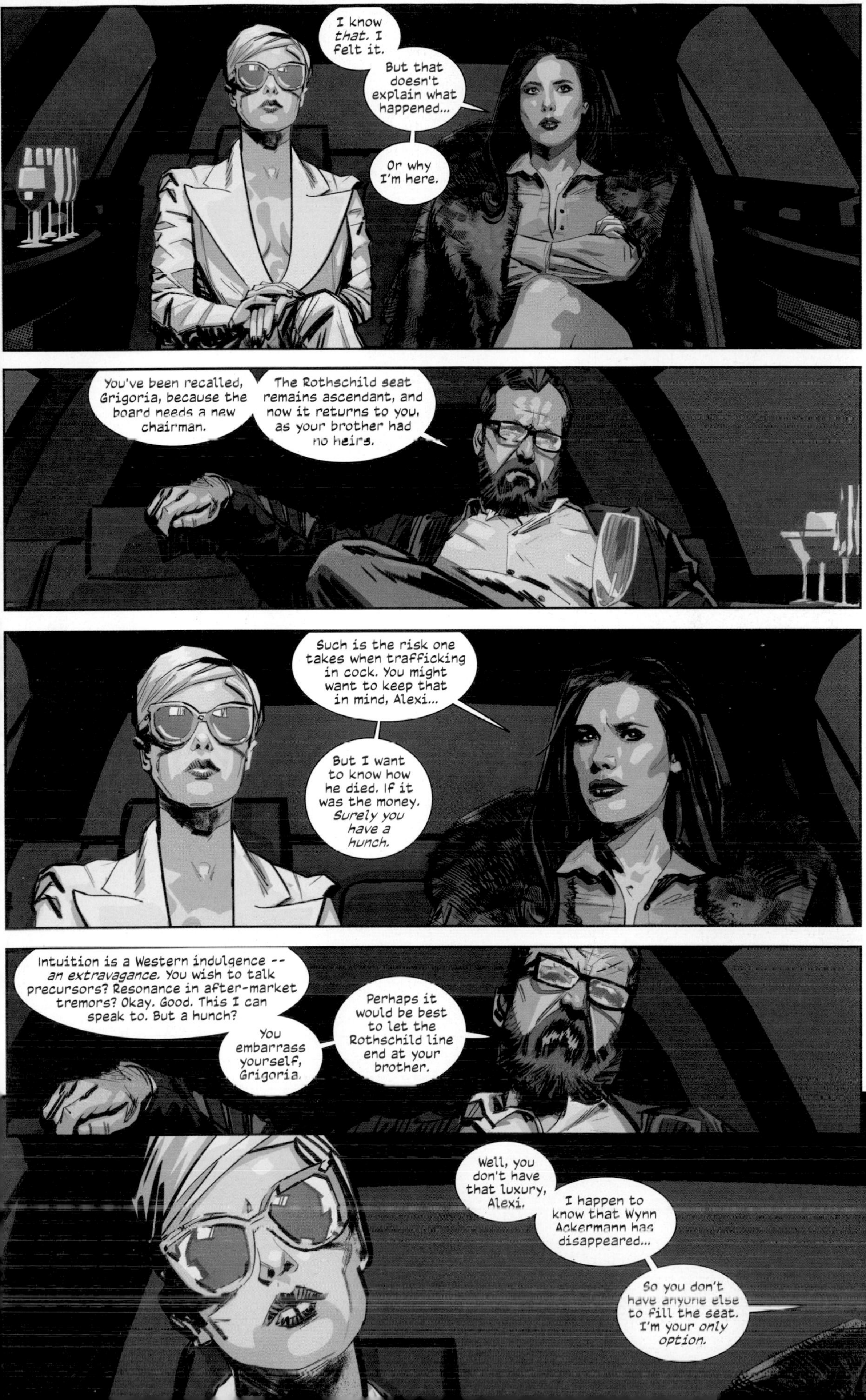
I know *that.* I felt it.
But that doesn't explain what happened...
Or why I'm here.
You've been recalled, Grigoria, because the board needs a new chairman.
The Rothschild seat remains ascendant, and now it returns to you, as your brother had no heirs.
Such is the risk one takes when trafficking in cock. You might want to keep that in mind, Alexi...
But I want to know how he died. If it was the money. *Surely you have a hunch.*
Intuition is a Western indulgence -- *an extravagance.* You wish to talk precursors? Resonance in after-market tremors? Okay. Good. This I can speak to. But a hunch?
You embarrass yourself, Grigoria.
Perhaps it would be best to let the Rothschild line end at your brother.
Well, you don't have that luxury, Alexi.
I happen to know that Wynn Ackermann has disappeared...
So you don't have anyone else to fill the seat. I'm your *only option.*

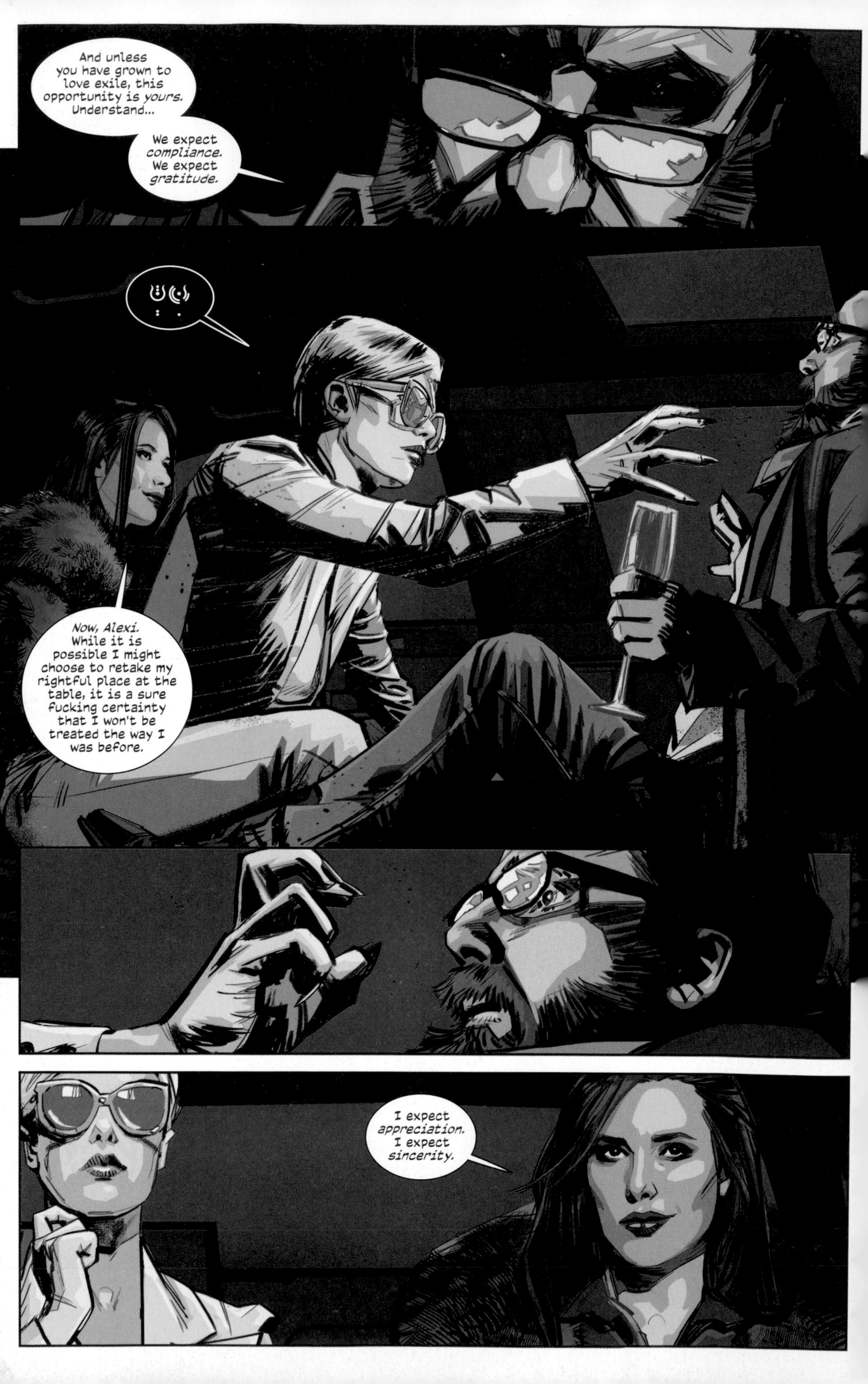
And unless you have grown to love exile, this opportunity is *yours.* Understand...
We expect *compliance.* We expect *gratitude.*
*Now, Alexi.* While it is possible I might choose to retake my rightful place at the table, it is a sure fucking certainty that I won't be treated the way I was before.
I expect *appreciation.* I expect *sincerity.*

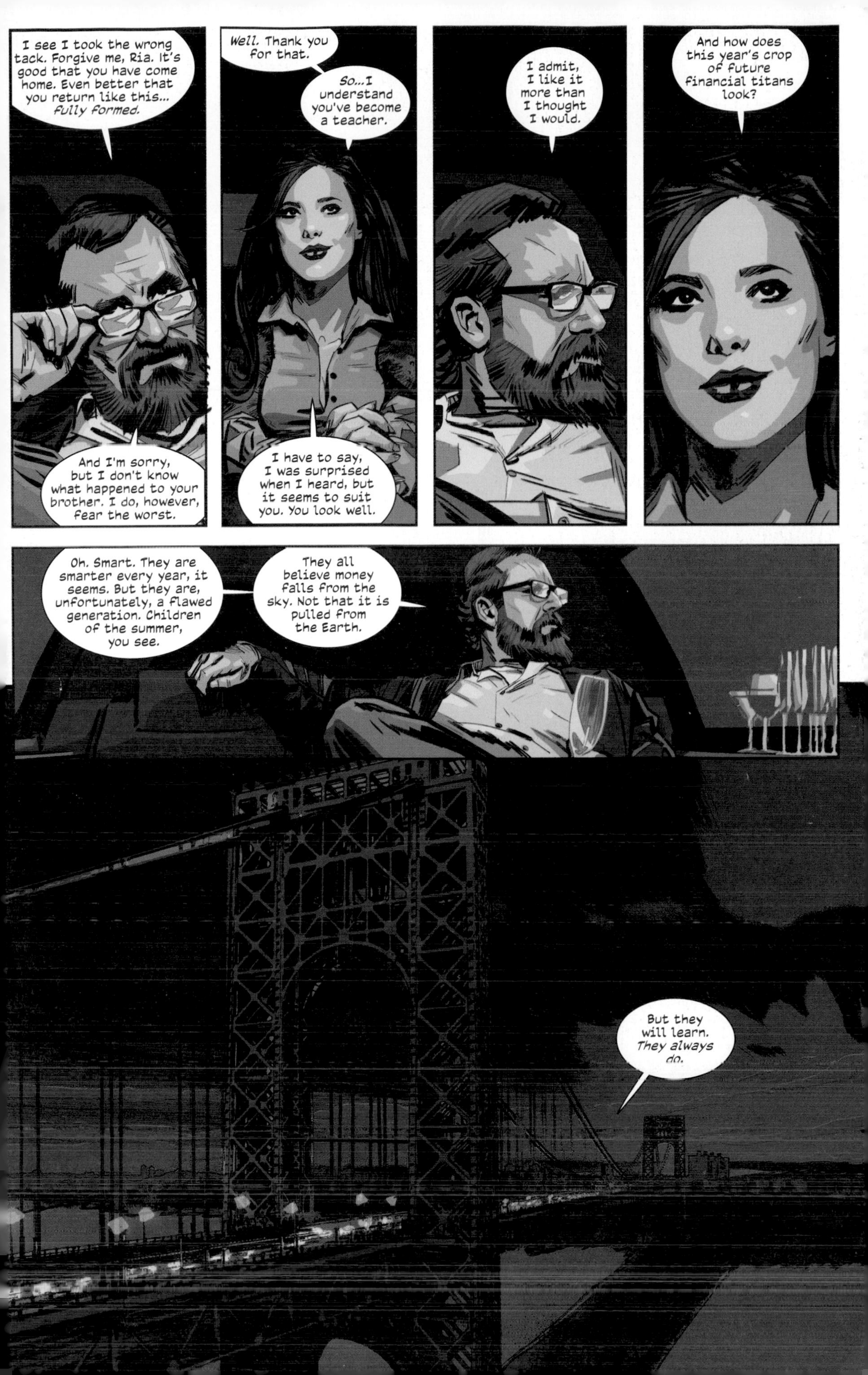
I see I took the wrong tack. Forgive me, Ria. It's good that you have come home. Even better that you return like this... *fully formed.*
And I'm sorry, but I don't know what happened to your brother. I do, however, fear the worst.
*Well.* Thank you for that.
*So...*I understand you've become a teacher.
I have to say, I was surprised when I heard, but it seems to suit you. You look well.
I admit, I like it more than I thought I would.
And how does this year's crop of future financial titans look?
Oh. Smart. They are smarter every year, it seems. But they are, unfortunately, a flawed generation. Children of the summer, you see.
They all believe money falls from the sky. Not that it is pulled from the Earth.
But they will learn. *They always do.*

# THE ROTHSCHILD LINE
# OF THE 20TH CENTURY

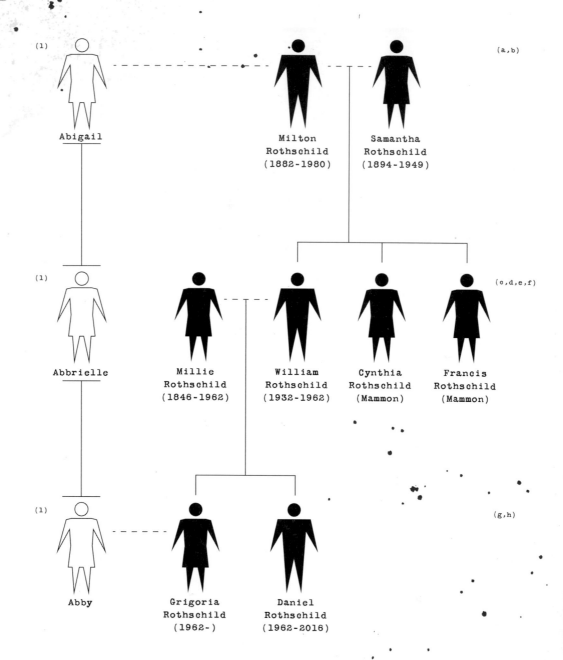

(1)

Abigail

Milton
Rothschild
(1882-1980)

Samantha
Rothschild
(1894-1949)

(a,b)

(1)

Abbrielle

Millie
Rothschild
(1846-1962)

William
Rothschild
(1932-1962)

Cynthia
Rothschild
(Mammon)

Francis
Rothschild
(Mammon)

(c,d,e,f)

(1)

Abby

Grigoria
Rothschild
(1962-)

Daniel
Rothschild
(1962-2016)

(g,h)

- NOW YOU SEE -

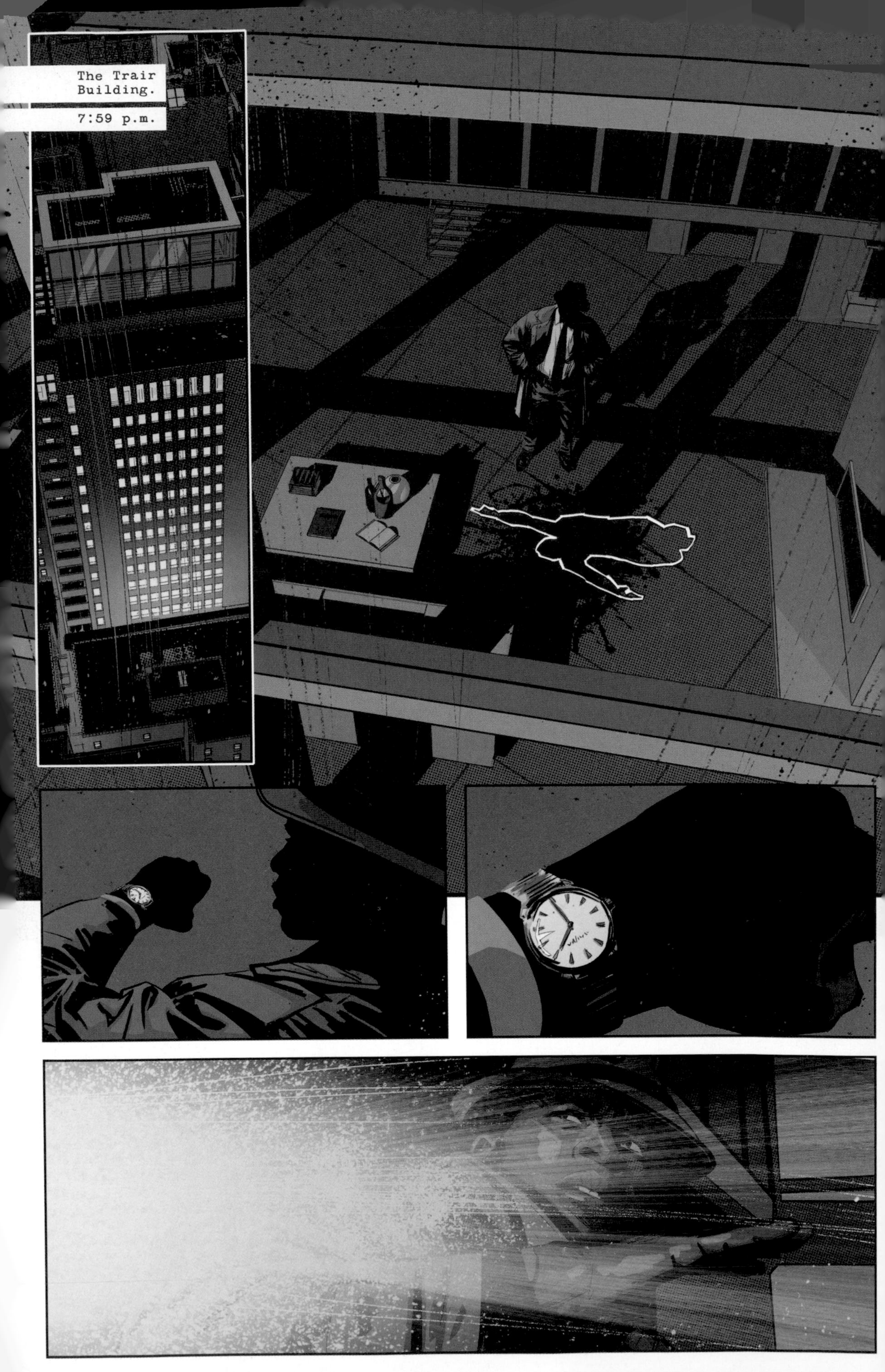
The Trair Building.
7:59 p.m.

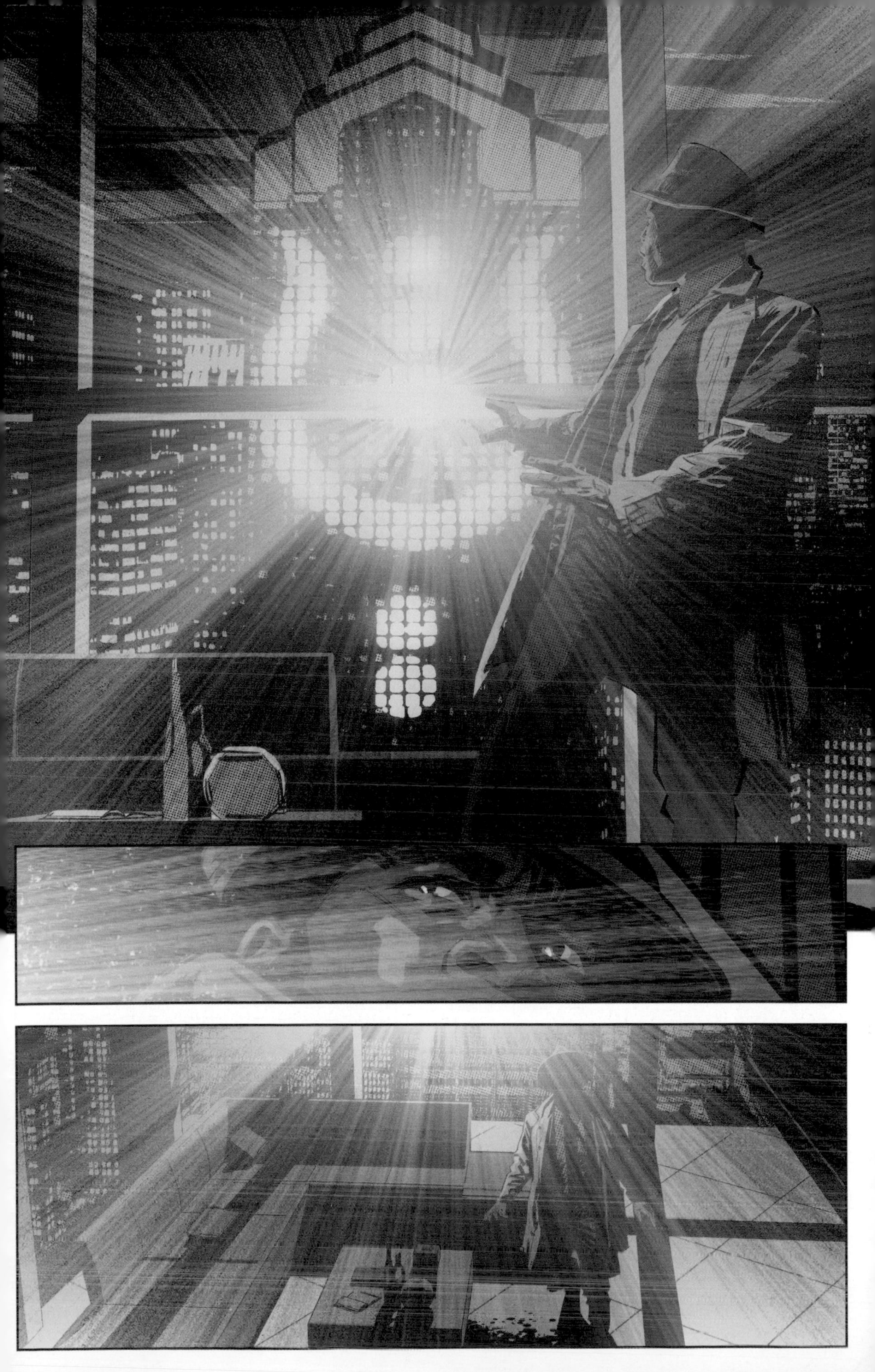

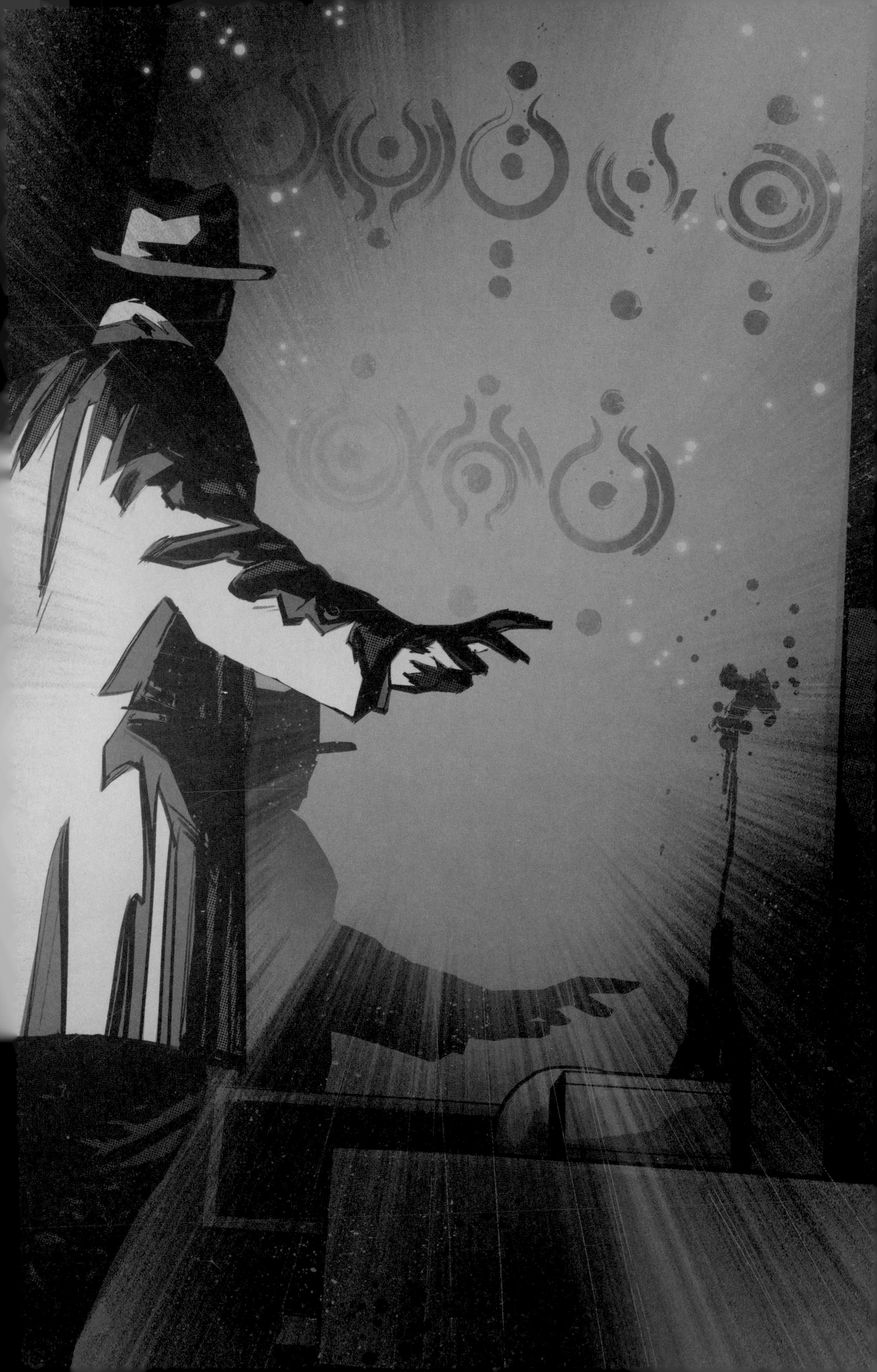

POWER |ˈpou(-ə)r|
noun
[redacted]
• the ability to influence the behavior of others or alter the natural course of events: having power over another | she had me under her power.
[redacted]

---

MONEY |ˈmənē|
noun
• a medium of exchange | the substitution of coin for something of similar value.
• a physical manifestation of influence or power.
[redacted]

---

MAGIC |ˈmajik|
noun
• the power to influence using supernatural forces: do you believe in magic? | suddenly, as if by magic, the words appeared.
[redacted]

1985

- THE WALL -

# The SHARED
# ARCHITECTURE
## of
# OTHER WORLDS

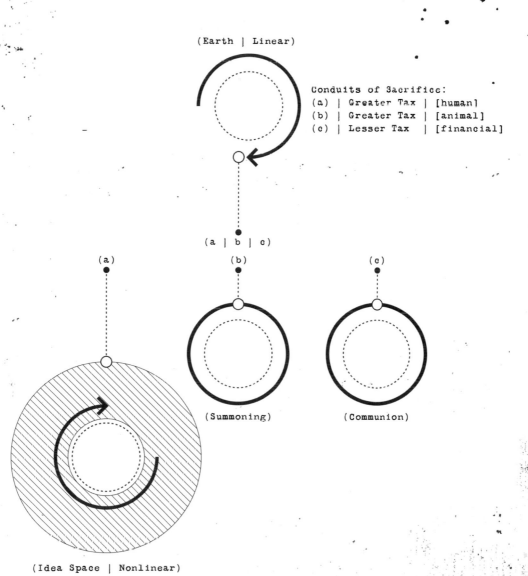

(Earth | Linear)

Conduits of Sacrifice:
(a) | Greater Tax | [human]
(b) | Greater Tax | [animal]
(c) | Lesser Tax | [financial]

(a | b | c)

(a)          (b)          (c)

(Summoning)      (Communion)

(Idea Space | Nonlinear)

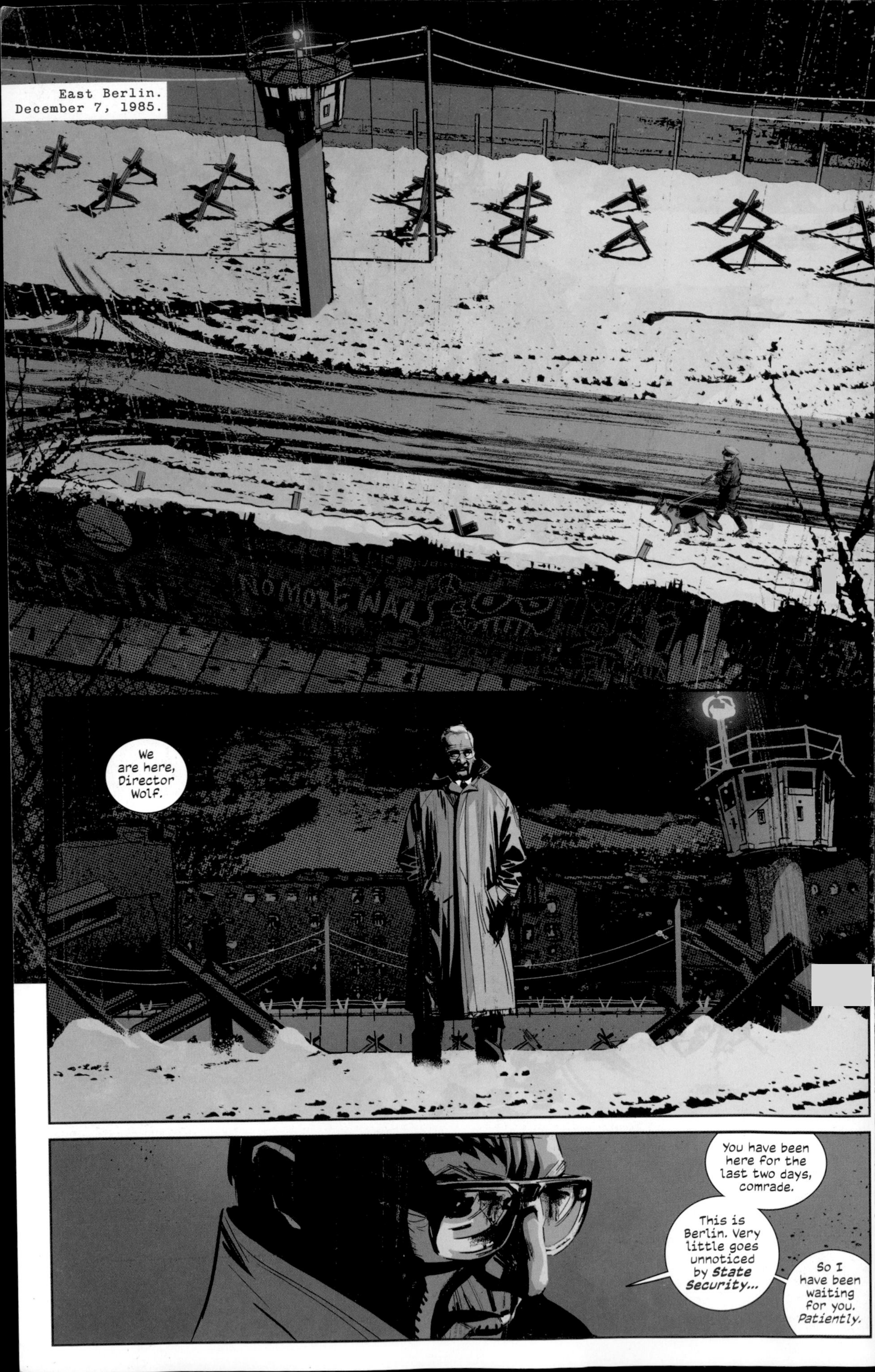
East Berlin.
December 7, 1985.
We are here, Director Wolf.
You have been here for the last two days, comrade.
This is Berlin. Very little goes unnoticed by *State Security...*
So I have been waiting for you. *Patiently.*

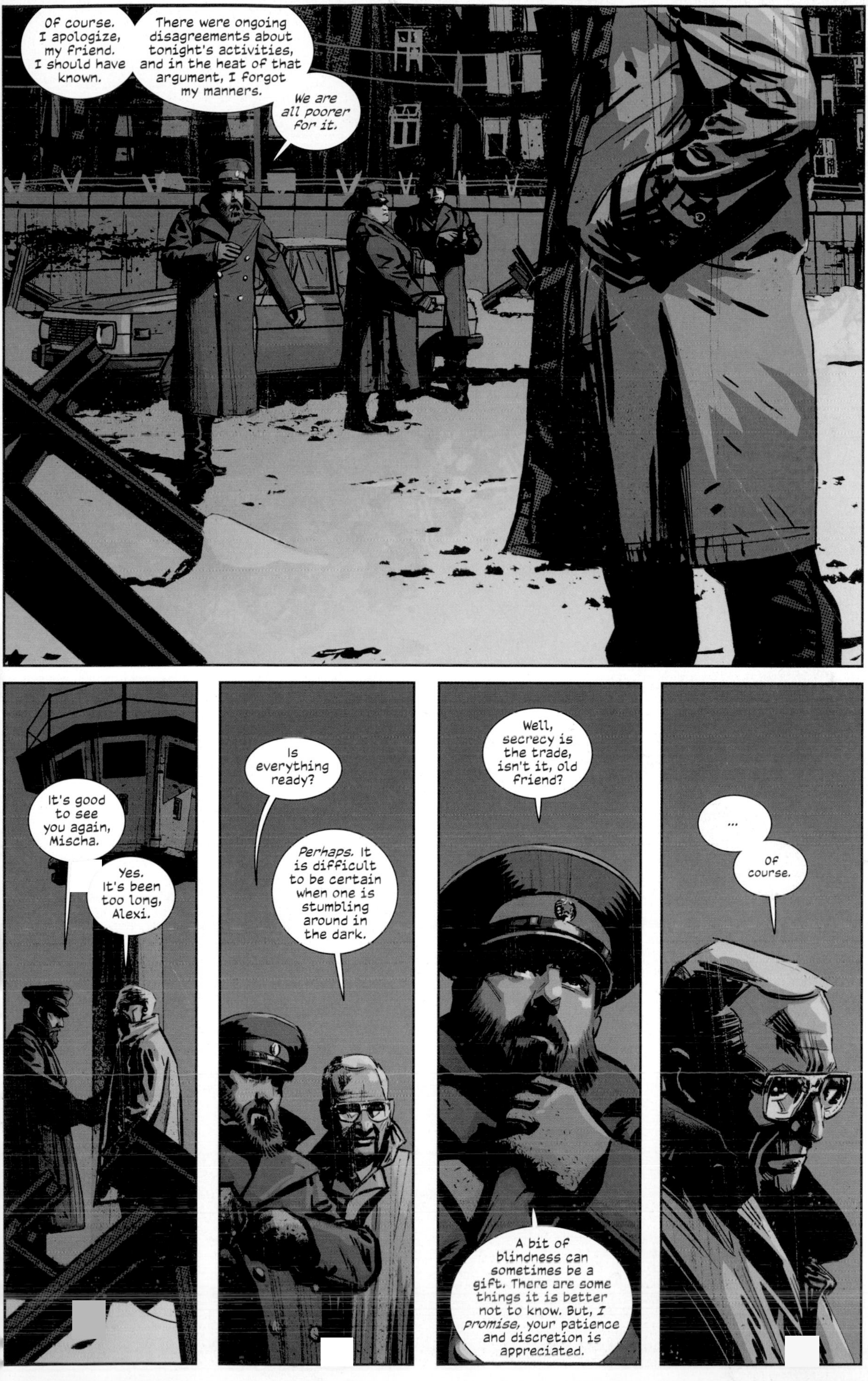
Of course. I apologize, my friend. I should have known.
There were ongoing disagreements about tonight's activities, and in the heat of that argument, I forgot my manners.
We are all poorer for it.
It's good to see you again, Mischa.
Yes. It's been too long, Alexi.
Is everything ready?
Perhaps. It is difficult to be certain when one is stumbling around in the dark.
Well, secrecy is the trade, isn't it, old friend?
A bit of blindness can sometimes be a gift. There are some things it is better not to know. But, I promise, your patience and discretion is appreciated.
...
Of course.

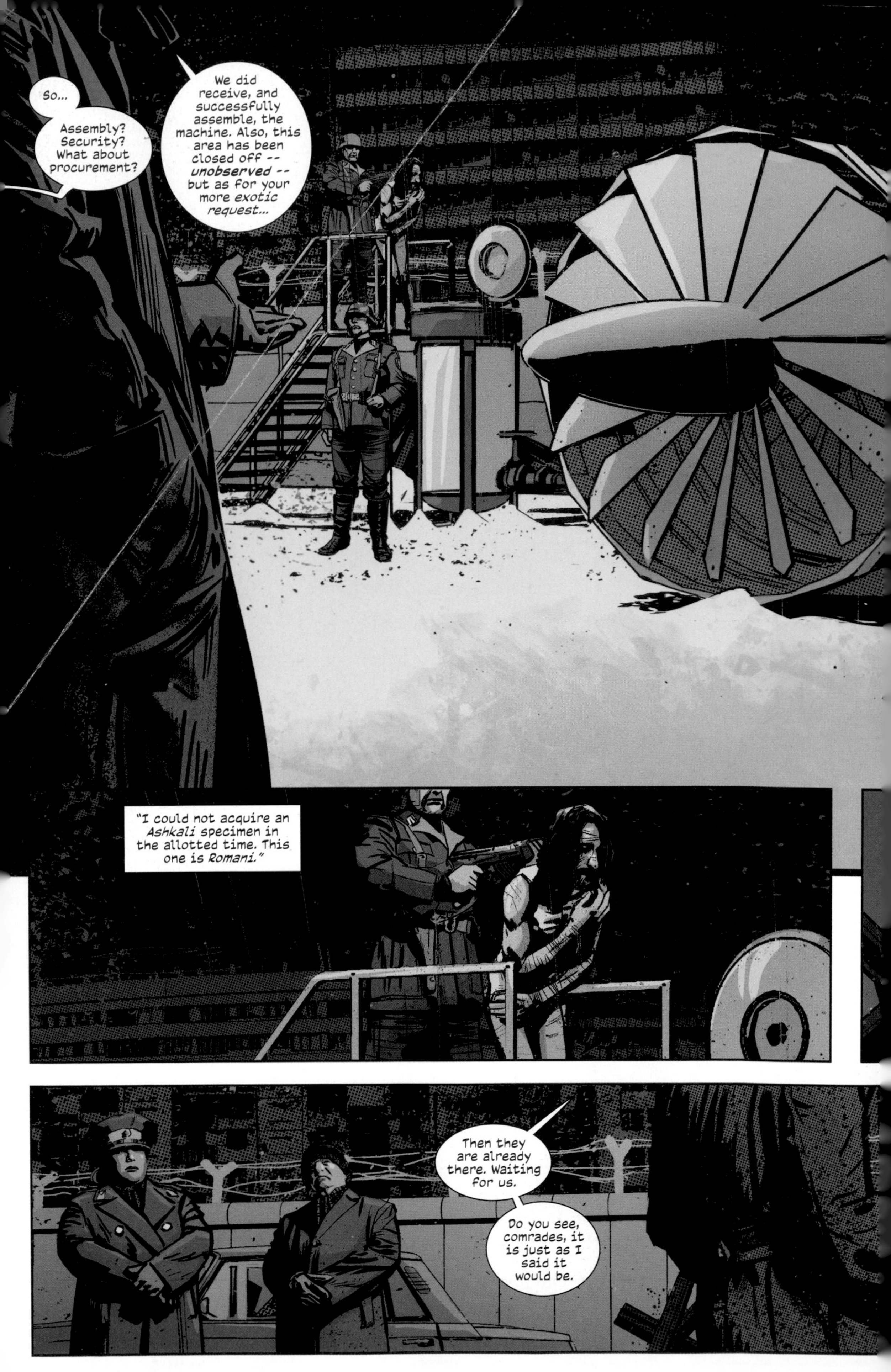
So...
Assembly? Security? What about procurement?
We did receive, and successfully assemble, the machine. Also, this area has been closed off -- *unobserved* -- but as for your more *exotic* request...
"I could not acquire an *Ashkali* specimen in the allotted time. This one is *Romani.*"
Then they are already there. Waiting for us.
Do you see, comrades, it is just as I said it would be.

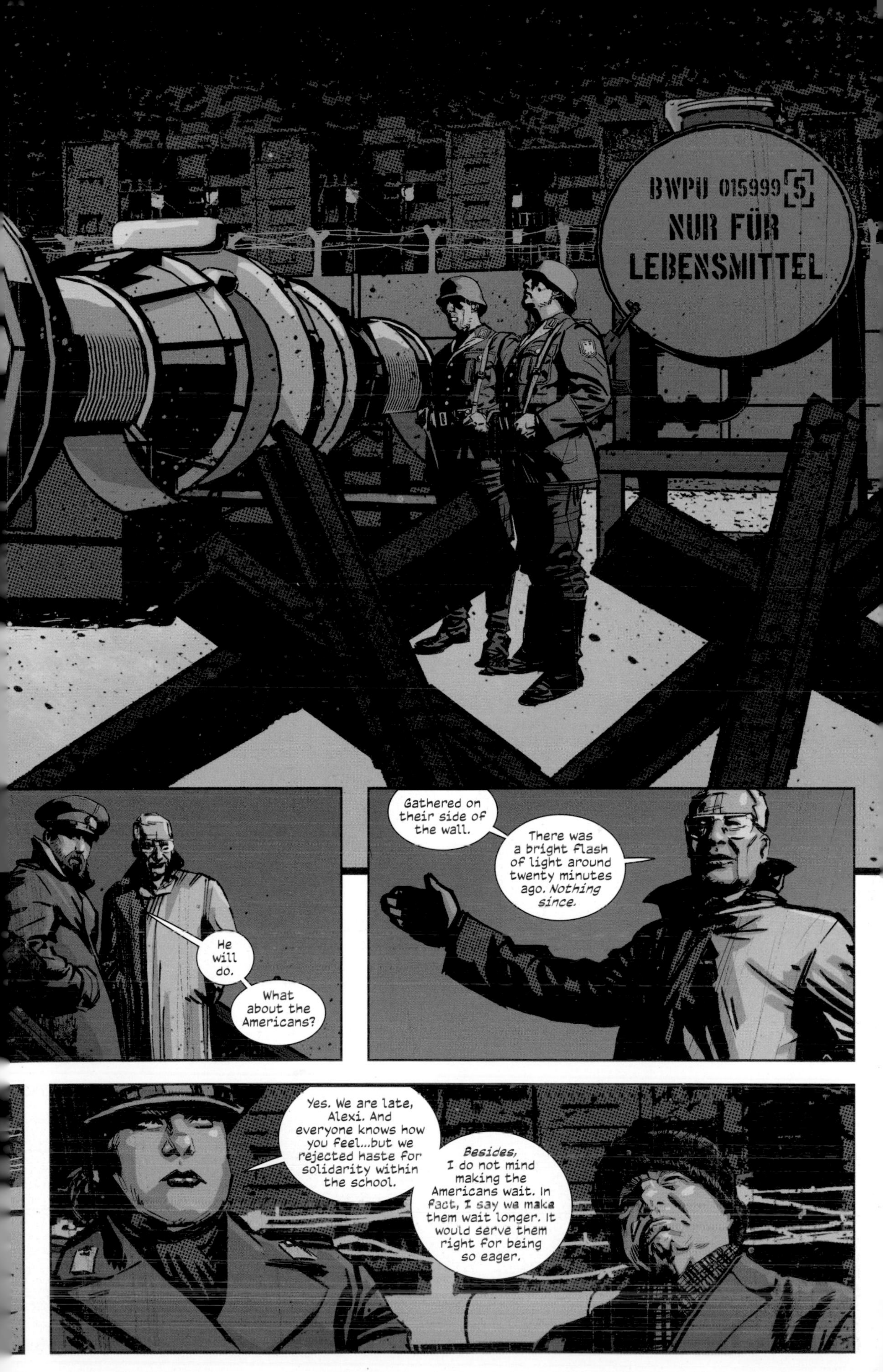
BWPU 015999 5
NUR FÜR LEBENSMITTEL
He will do.
What about the Americans?
Gathered on their side of the wall.
There was a bright flash of light around twenty minutes ago. *Nothing since.*
Yes. We are late, Alexi. And everyone knows how you feel...but we rejected haste for solidarity within the school.
*Besides,* I do not mind making the Americans wait. In fact, I say we make them wait longer. It would serve them right for being so eager.

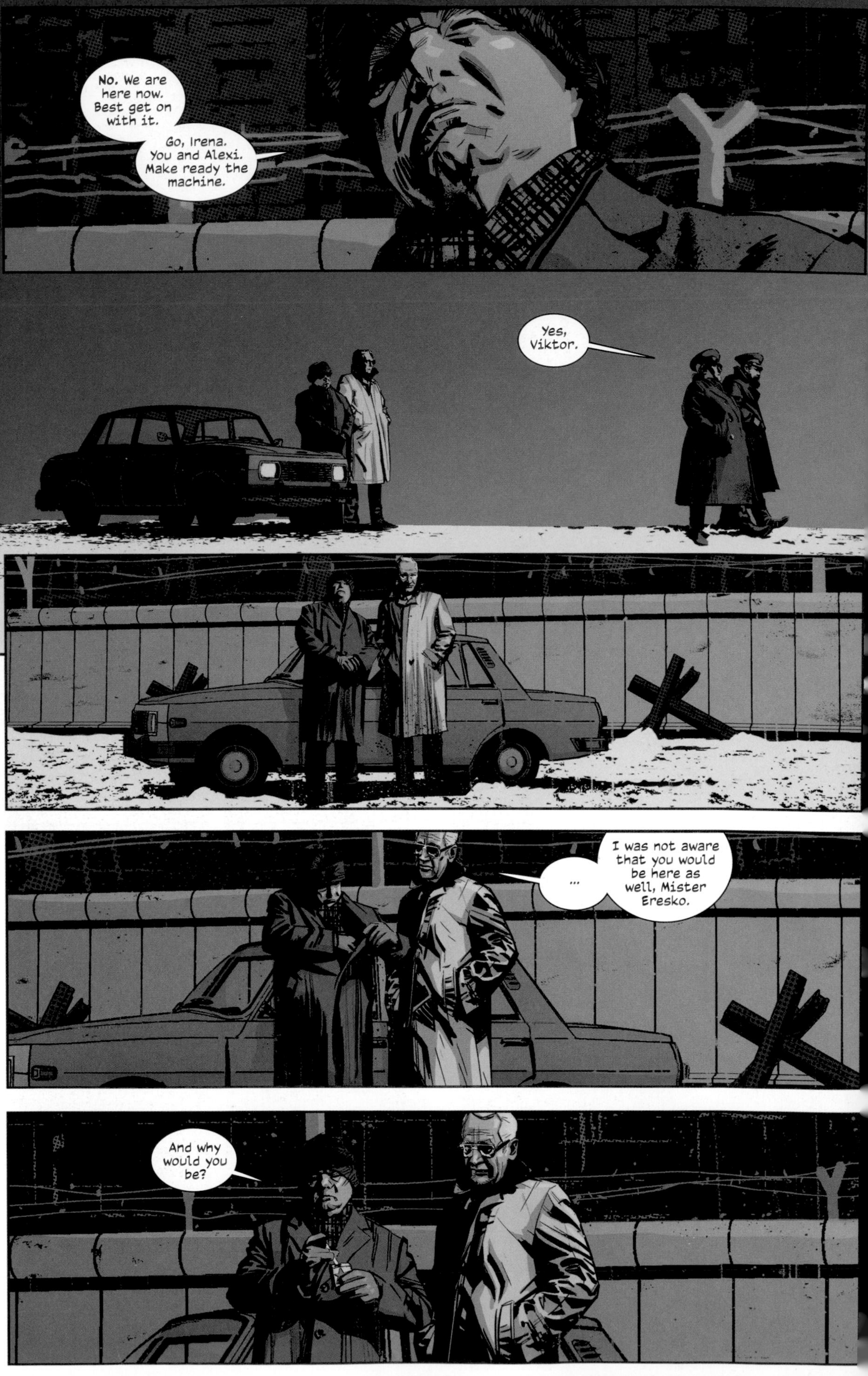
No. We are here now. Best get on with it.
Go, Irena. You and Alexi. Make ready the machine.
Yes, Viktor.
...
I was not aware that you would be here as well, Mister Eresko.
And why would you be?

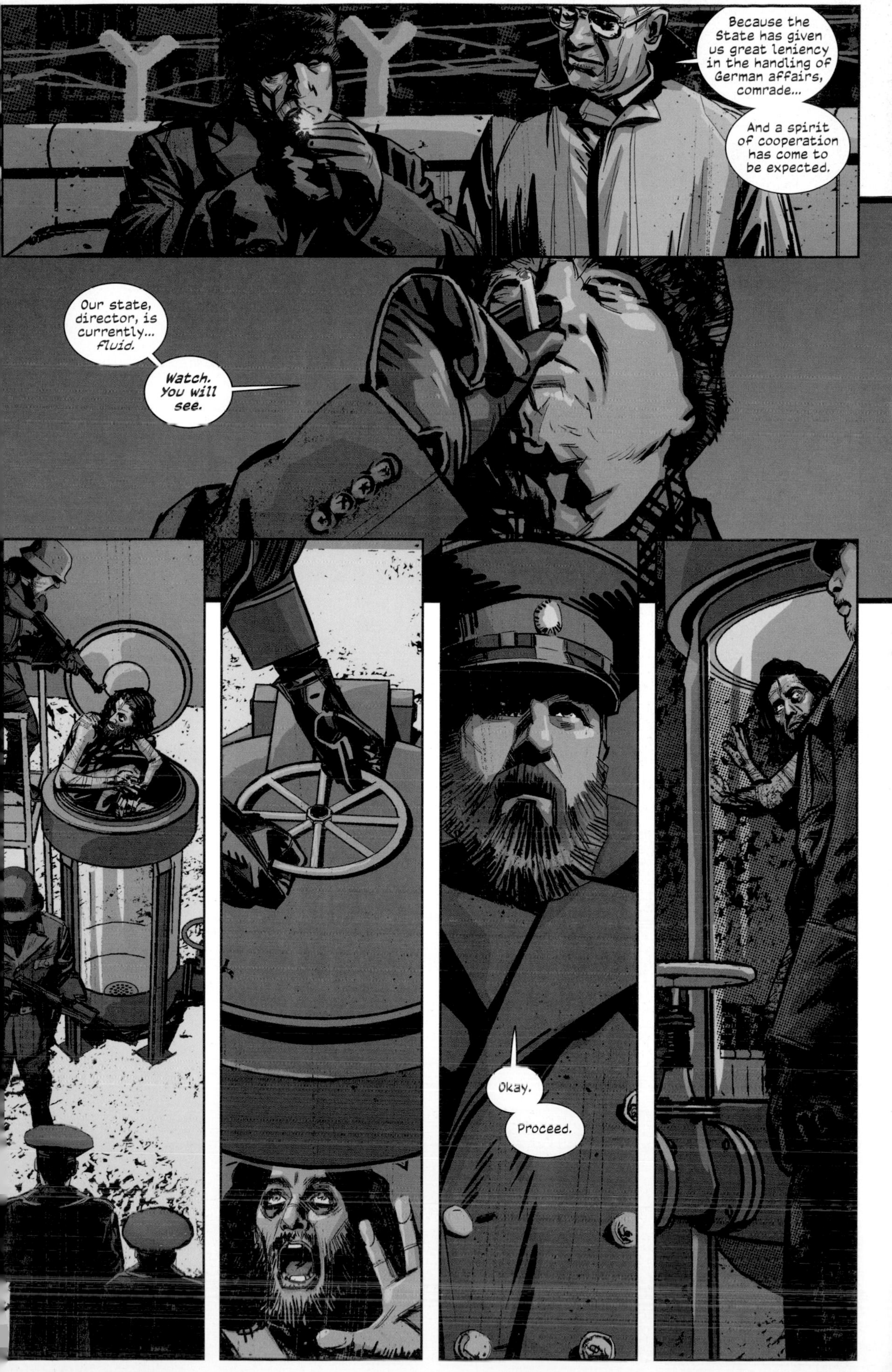
Because the State has given us great leniency in the handling of German affairs, comrade...
And a spirit of cooperation has come to be expected.
Our state, director, is currently... *fluid.*
*Watch. You will see.*
Okay.
Proceed.

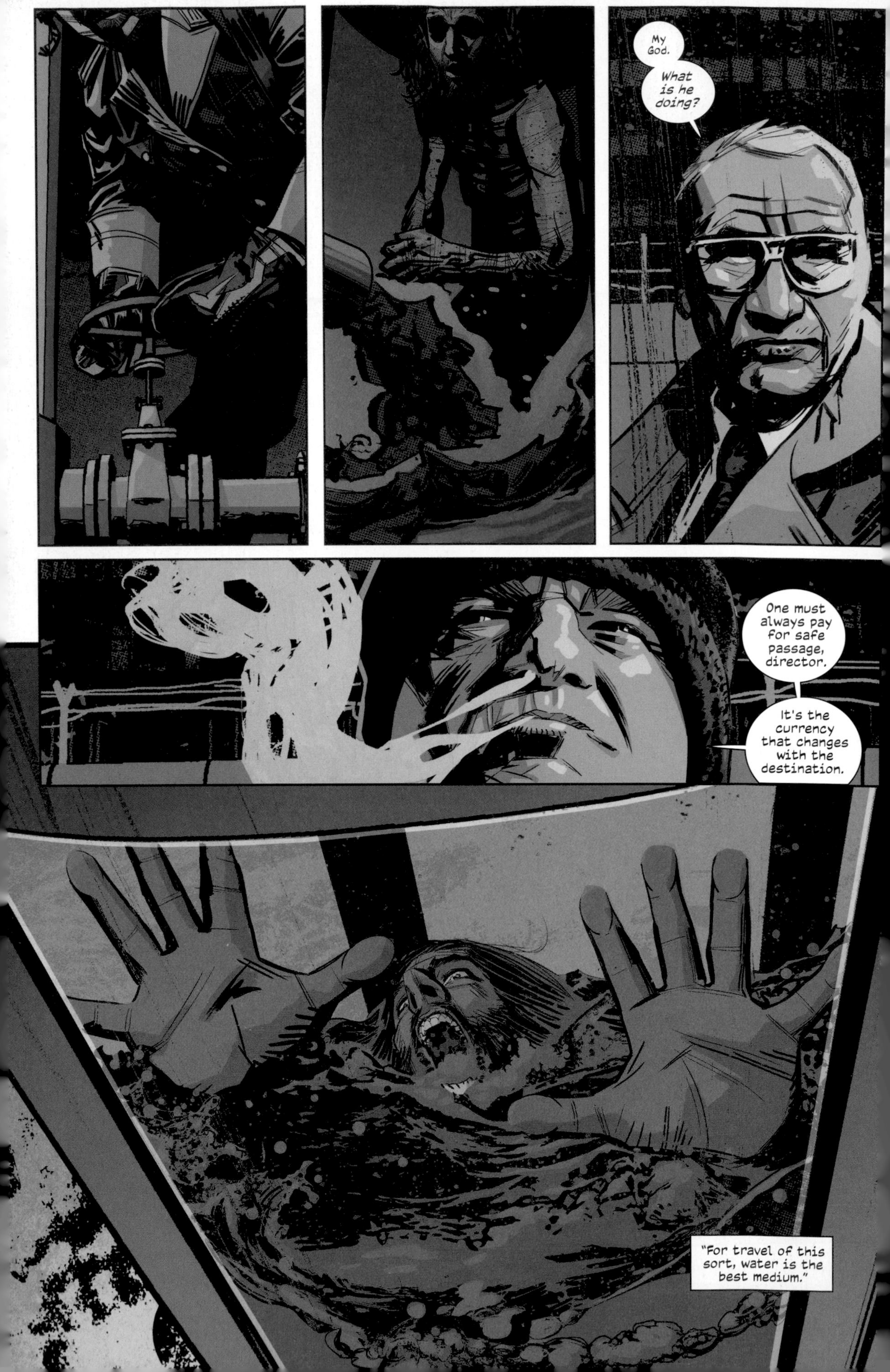
My God.
What is he doing?
One must always pay for safe passage, director.
It's the currency that changes with the destination.
"For travel of this sort, water is the best medium."

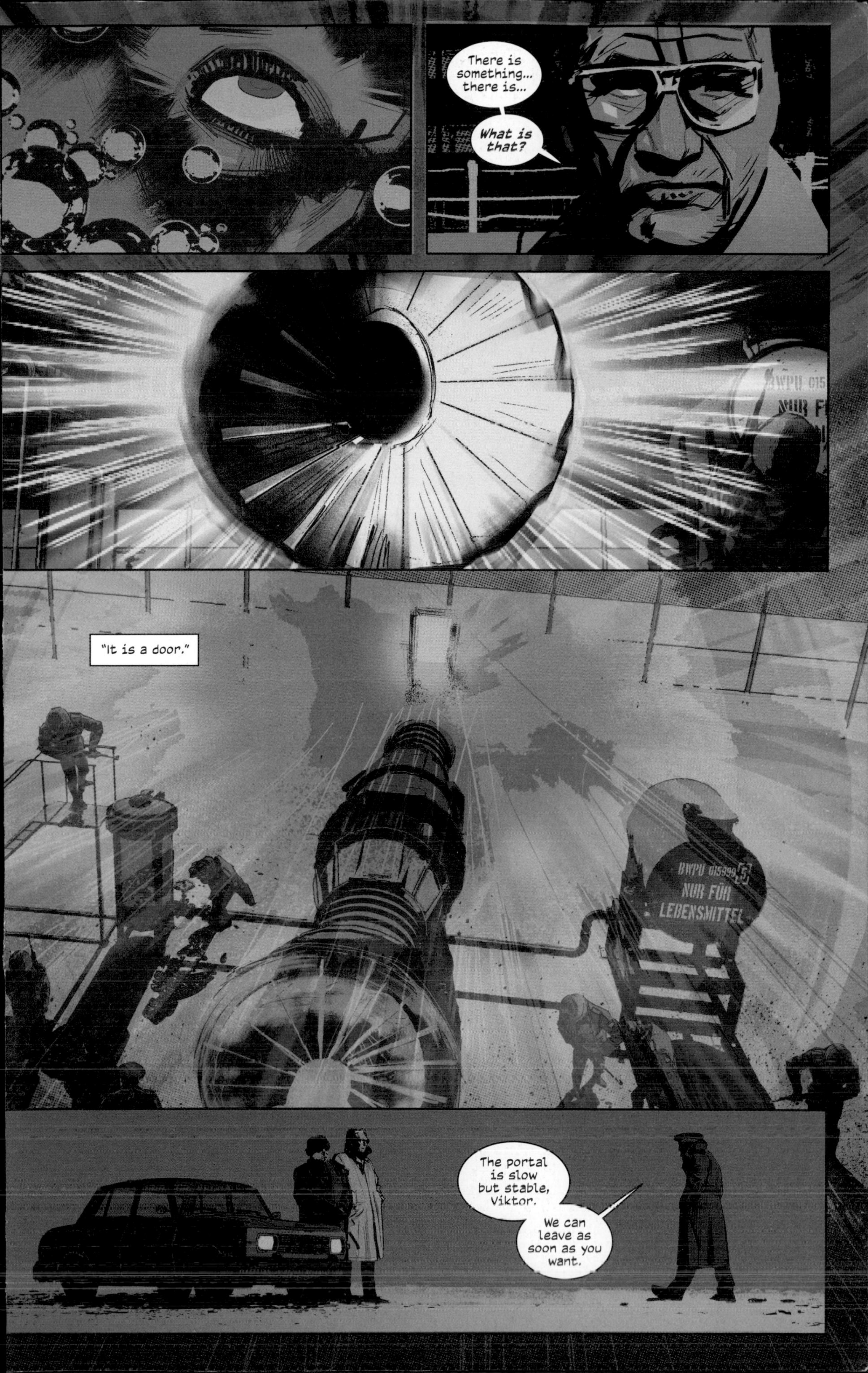

There is something... there is...
What is that?
BWPU 015
NUR F
"It is a door."
BWPU 015999
NUR FÜR LEBENSMITTEL
The portal is slow but stable, Viktor.
We can leave as soon as you want.

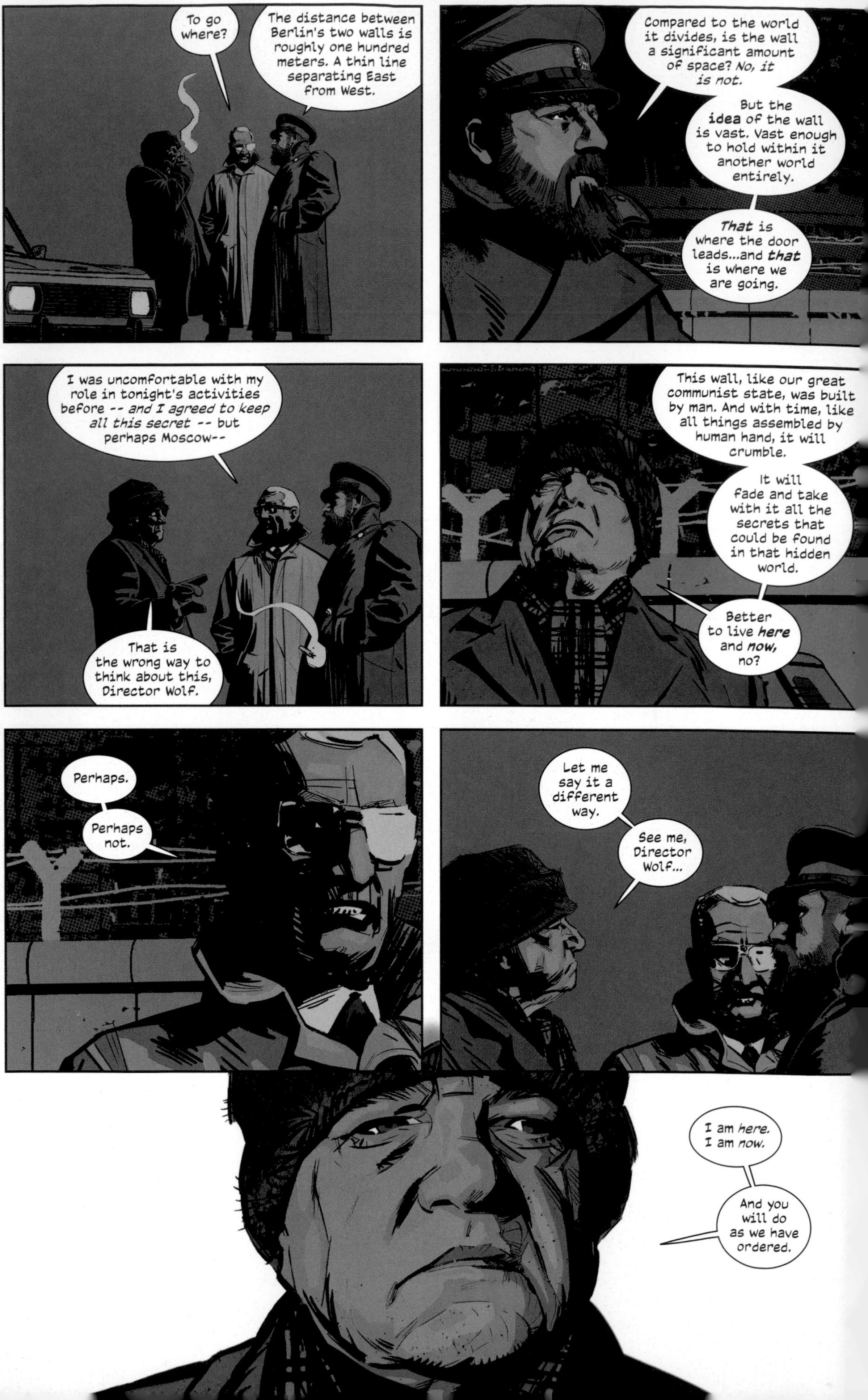
To go where?
The distance between Berlin's two walls is roughly one hundred meters. A thin line separating East from West.
Compared to the world it divides, is the wall a significant amount of space? *No, it is not.*
But the **idea** of the wall is vast. Vast enough to hold within it another world entirely.
***That*** is where the door leads...and ***that*** is where we are going.
I was uncomfortable with my role in tonight's activities before -- *and I agreed to keep all this secret* -- but perhaps Moscow--
That is the wrong way to think about this, Director Wolf.
This wall, like our great communist state, was built by man. And with time, like all things assembled by human hand, it will crumble.
It will fade and take with it all the secrets that could be found in that hidden world.
Better to live ***here*** and ***now,*** no?
Perhaps.
Perhaps not.
Let me say it a different way.
See me, Director Wolf...
I am *here.* I am *now.*
And you will do as we have ordered.

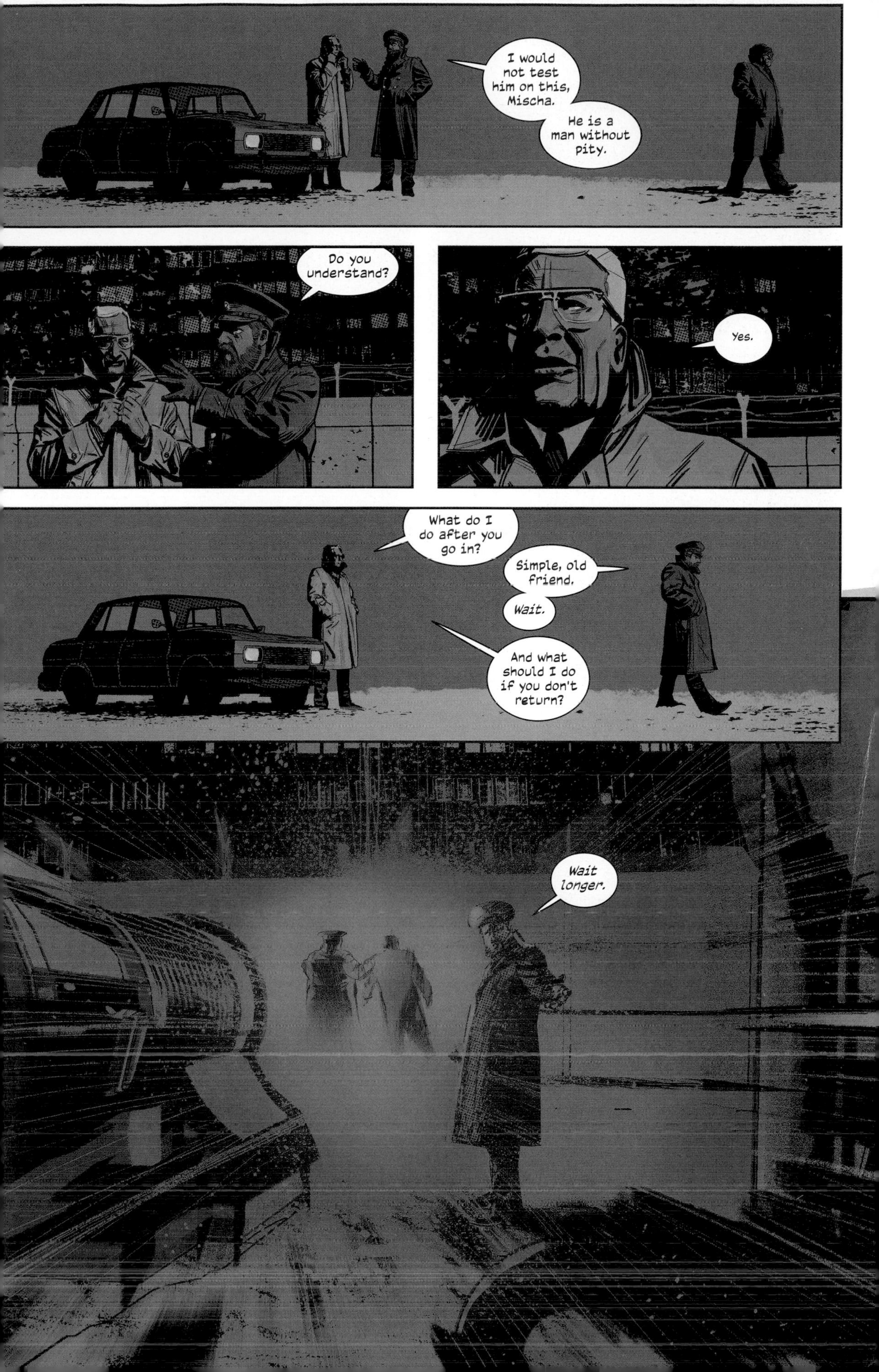
I would not test him on this, Mischa.
He is a man without pity.
Do you understand?
Yes.
What do I do after you go in?
Simple, old friend.
*Wait.*
And what should I do if you don't return?
*Wait longer.*

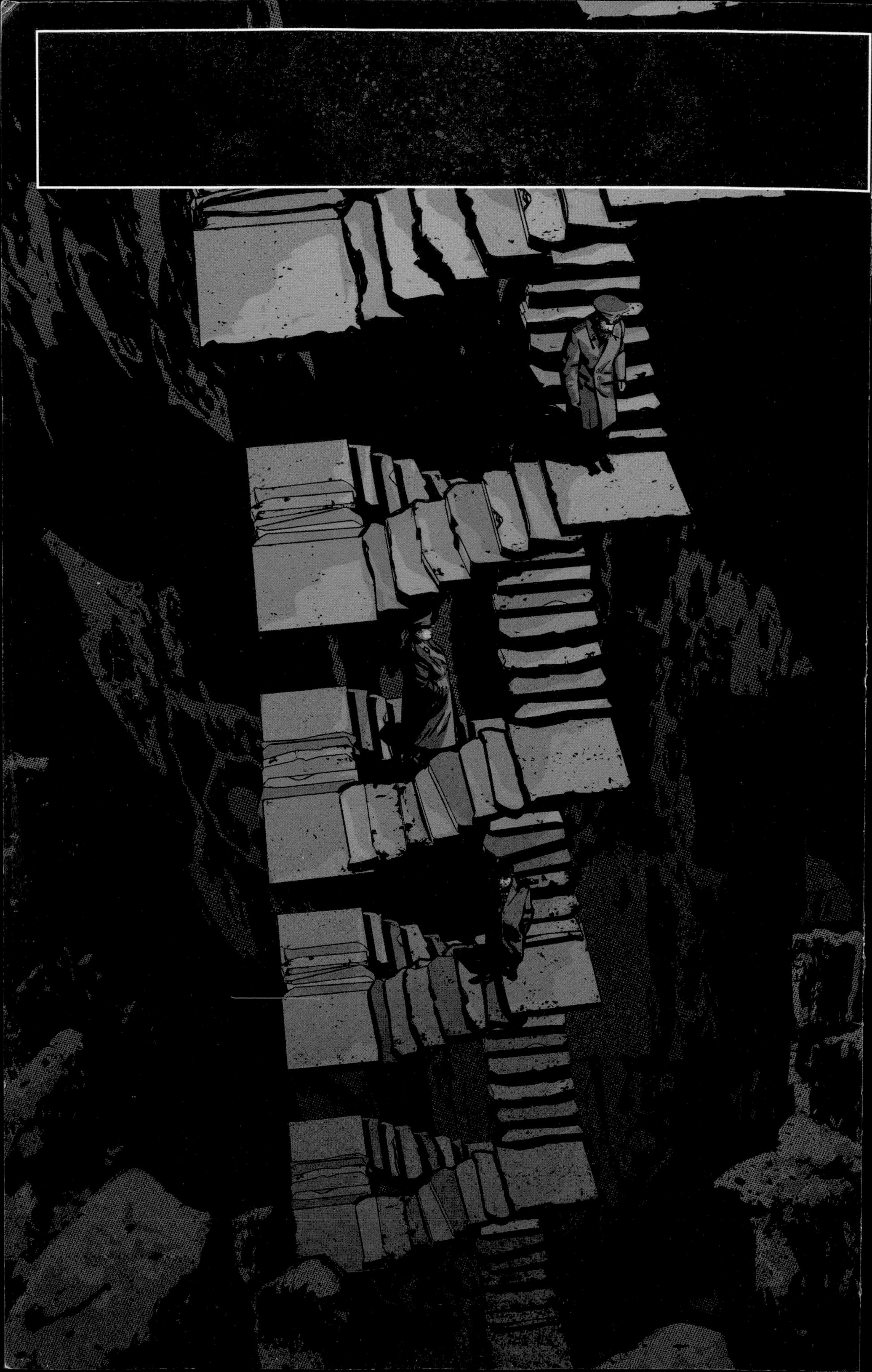

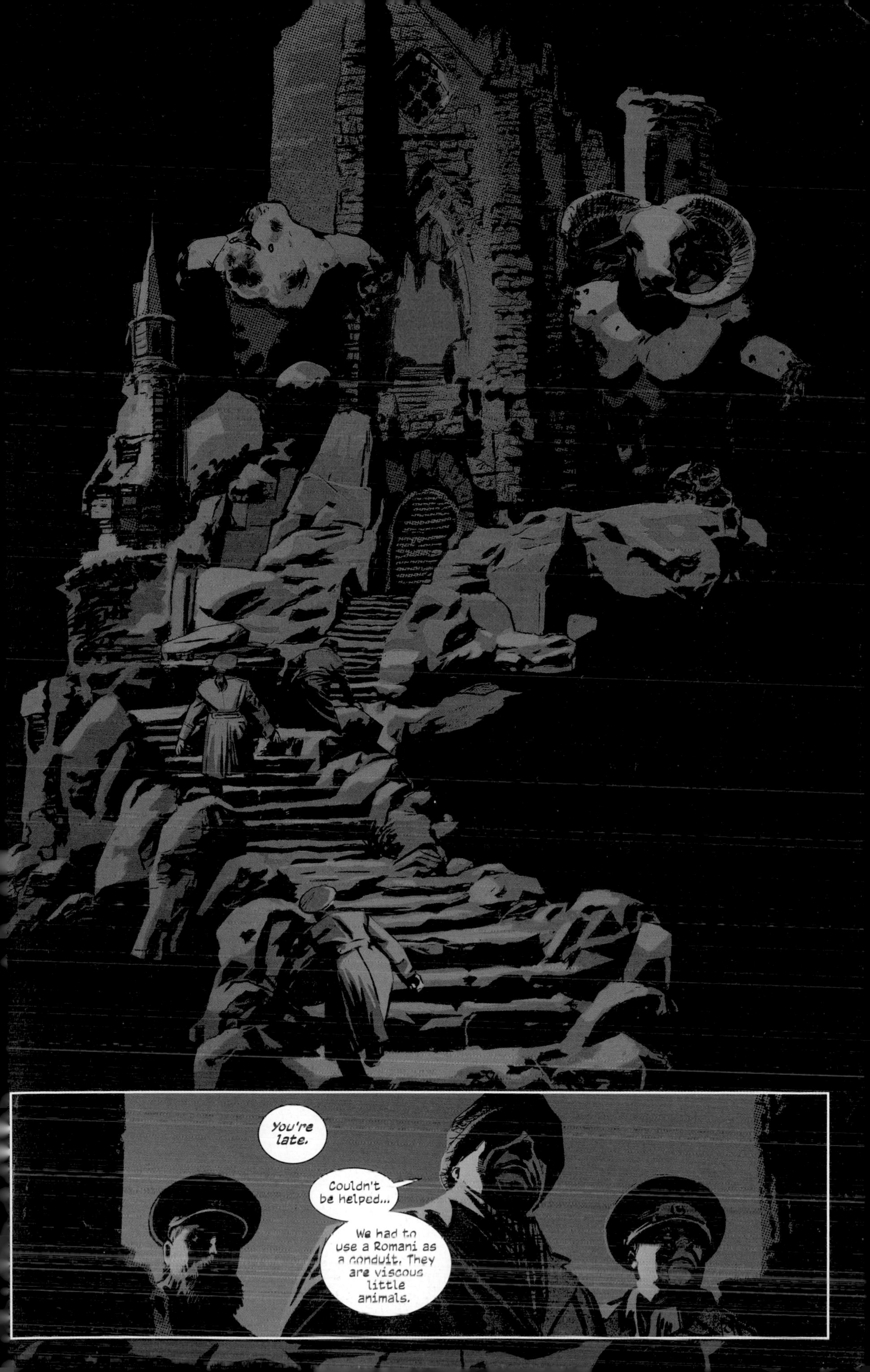
You're late.
Couldn't be helped...
We had to use a Romani as a conduit. They are viscous little animals.

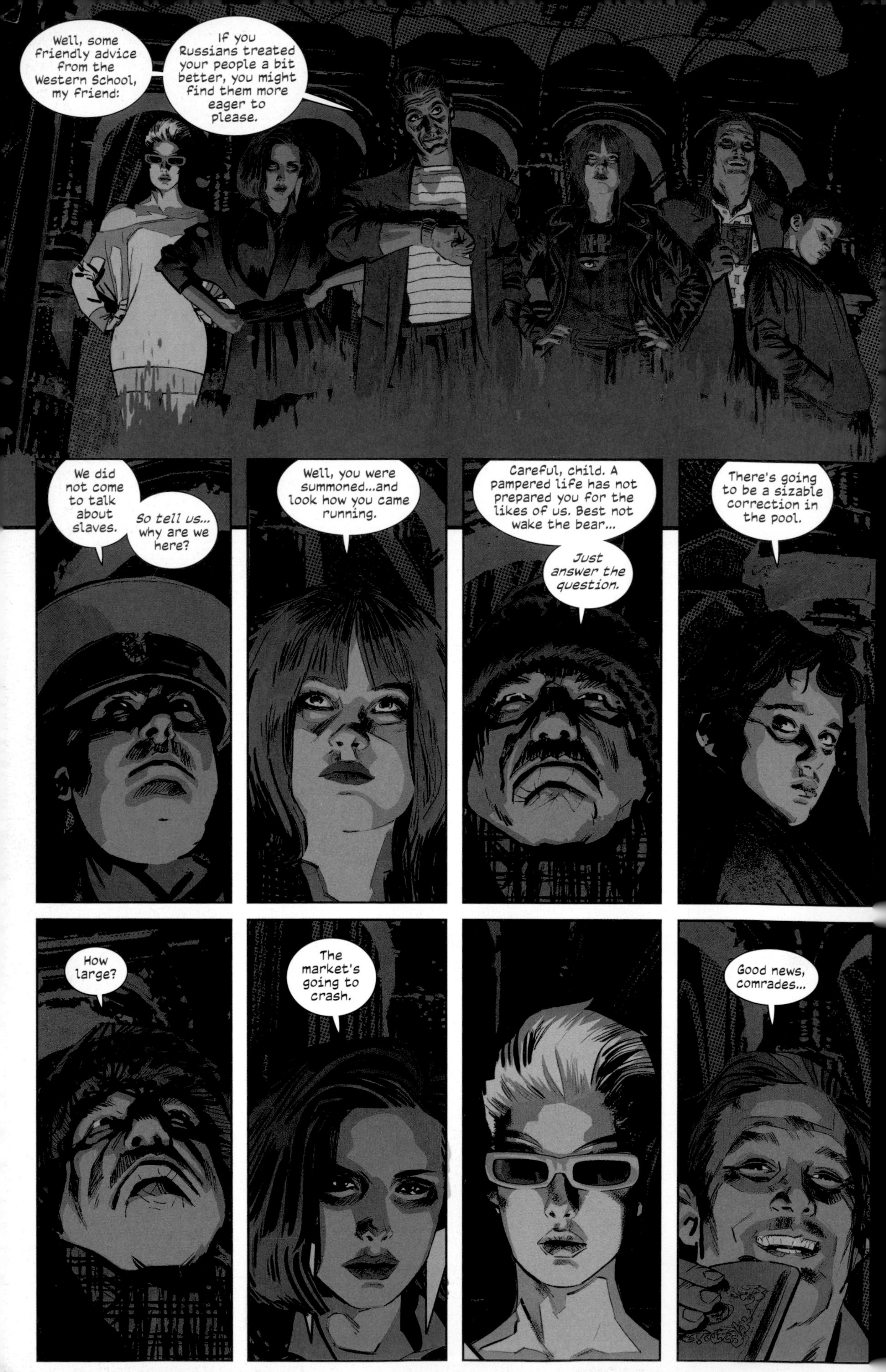
Well, some friendly advice from the Western School, my friend:
If you Russians treated your people a bit better, you might find them more eager to please.
We did not come to talk about slaves.
So tell us... why are we here?
Well, you were summoned...and look how you came running.
Careful, child. A pampered life has not prepared you for the likes of us. Best not wake the bear...
Just answer the question.
There's going to be a sizable correction in the pool.
How large?
The market's going to crash.
Good news, comrades...

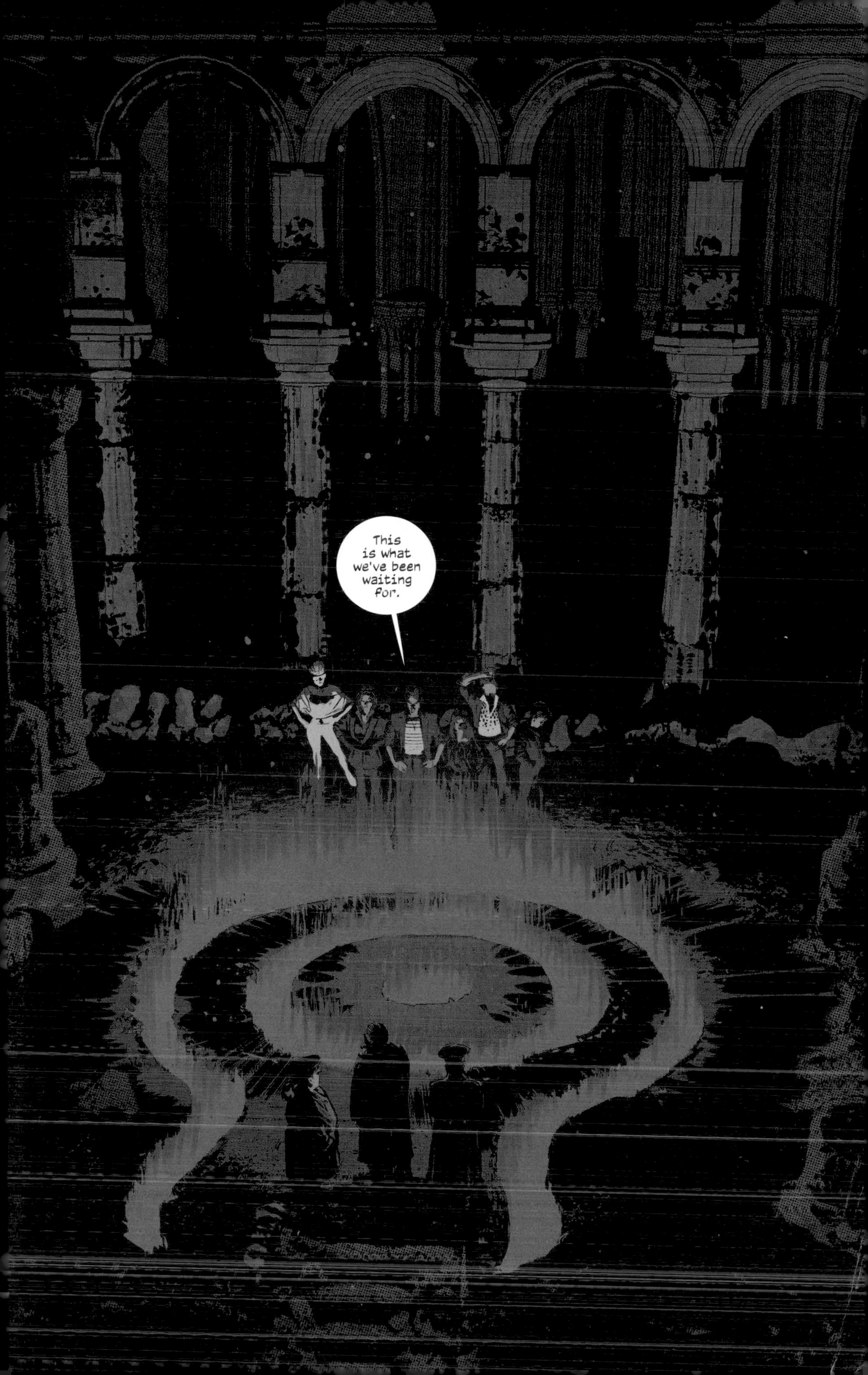
This is what we've been waiting for.

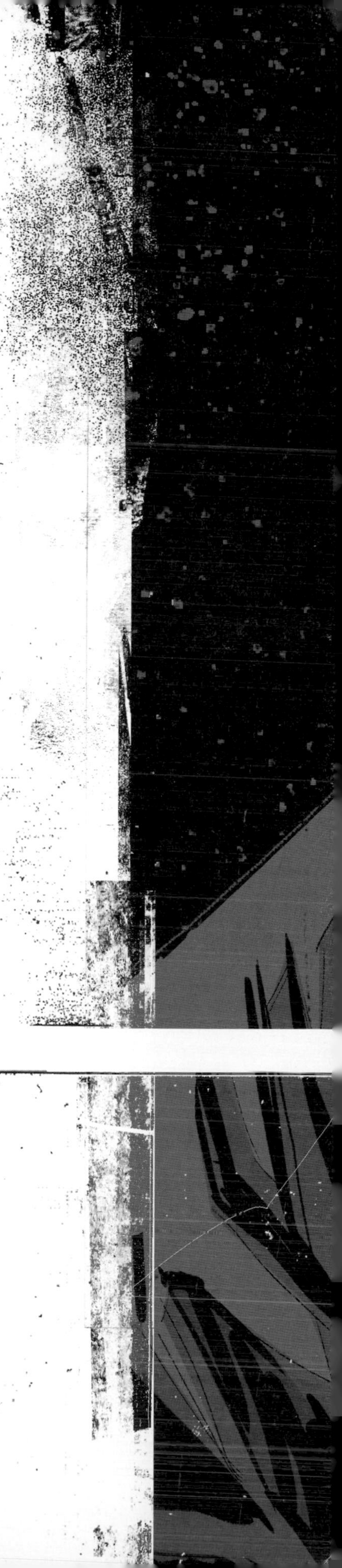

CHAPTER TWO:

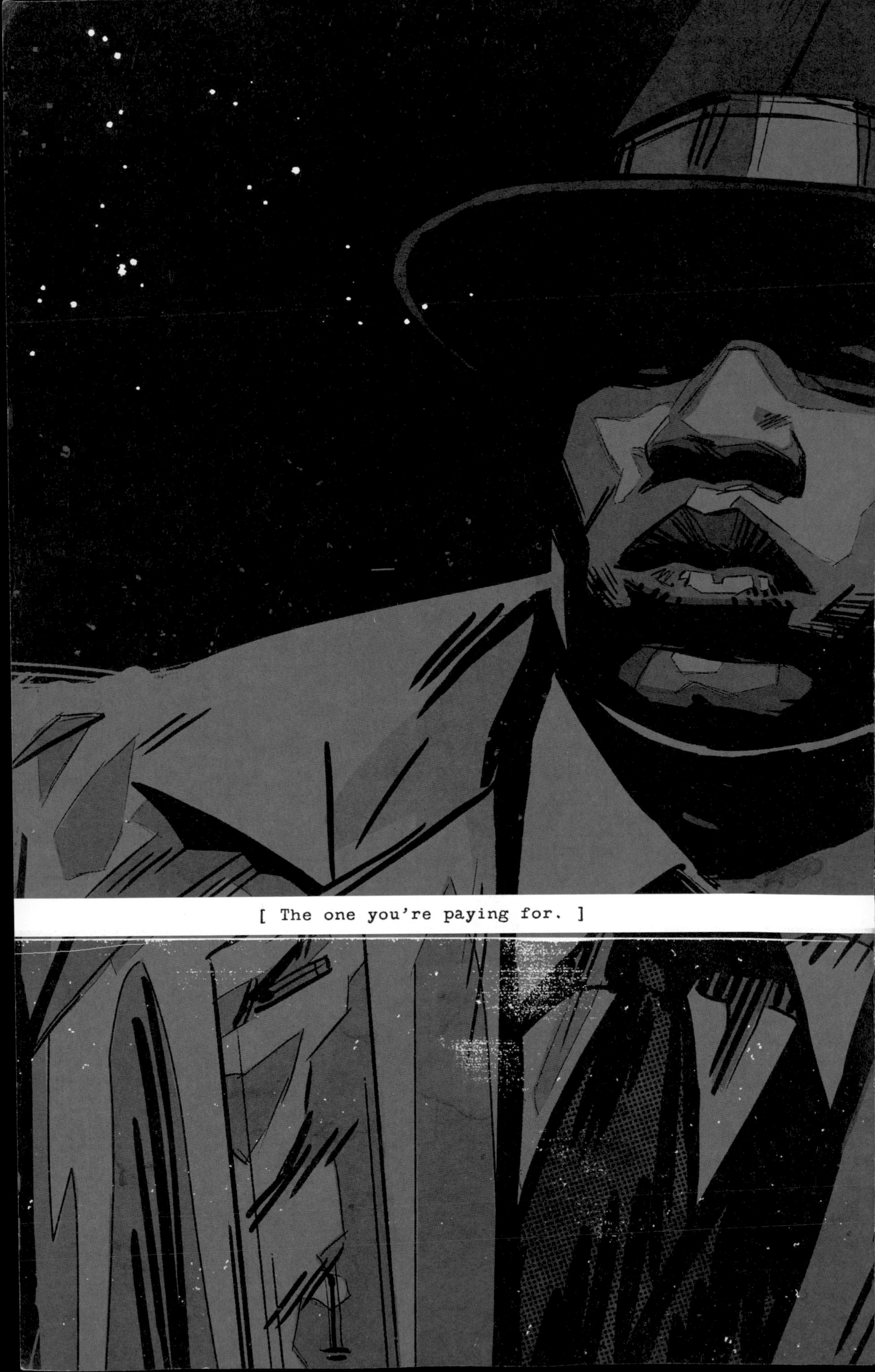
[ The one you're paying for. ]

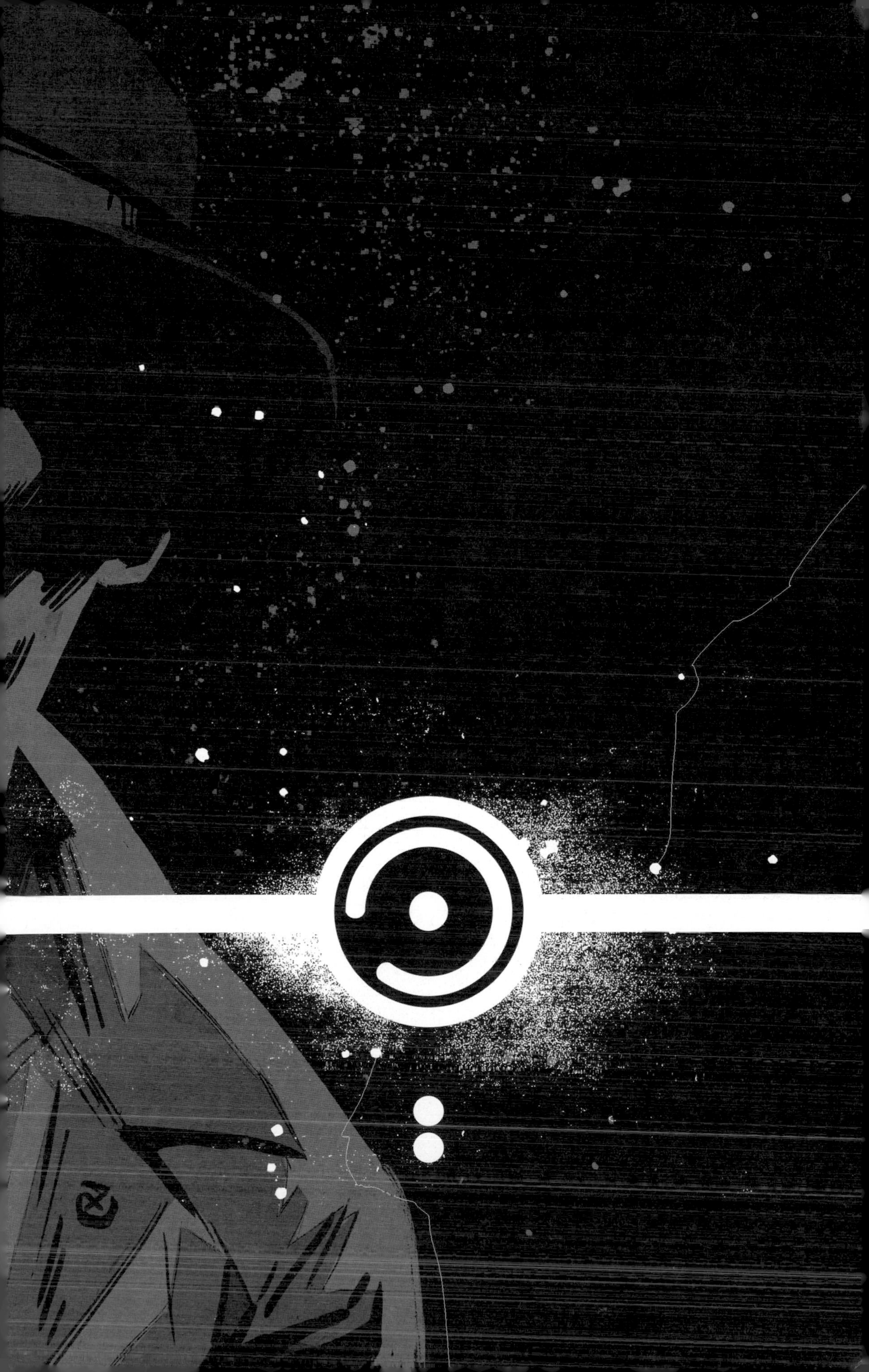

2016

- RENEW THE WHEEL -

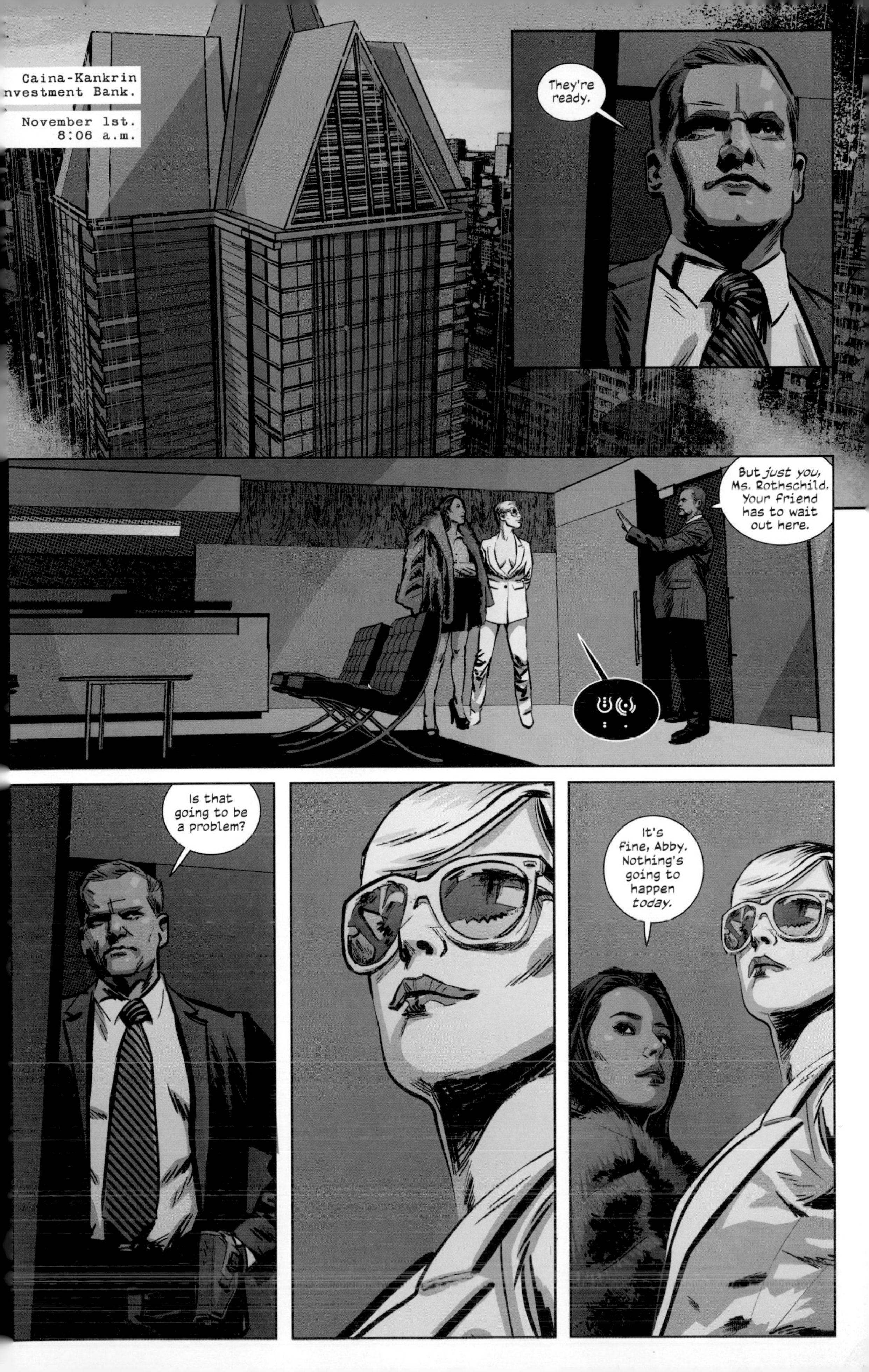

Caina-Kankrin nvestment Bank.
November 1st. 8:06 a.m.
They're ready.
But just you, Ms. Rothschild. Your friend has to wait out here.
Is that going to be a problem?
It's fine, Abby. Nothing's going to happen today.

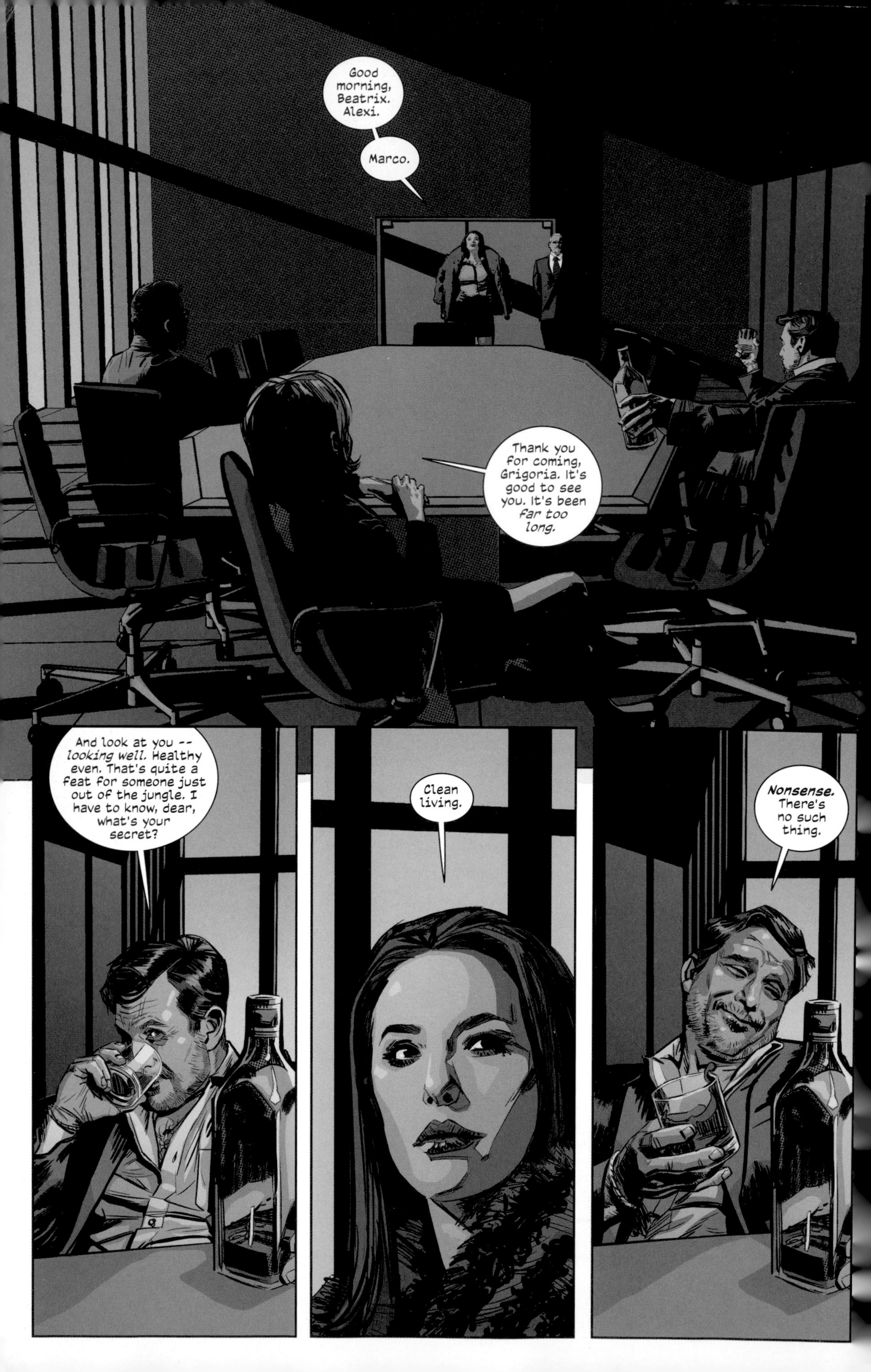
Good morning, Beatrix. Alexi.
Marco.
Thank you for coming, Grigoria. It's good to see you. It's been *far too long.*
And look at you -- *looking well.* Healthy even. That's quite a feat for someone just out of the jungle. I have to know, dear, what's your secret?
Clean living.
***Nonsense.*** There's no such thing.

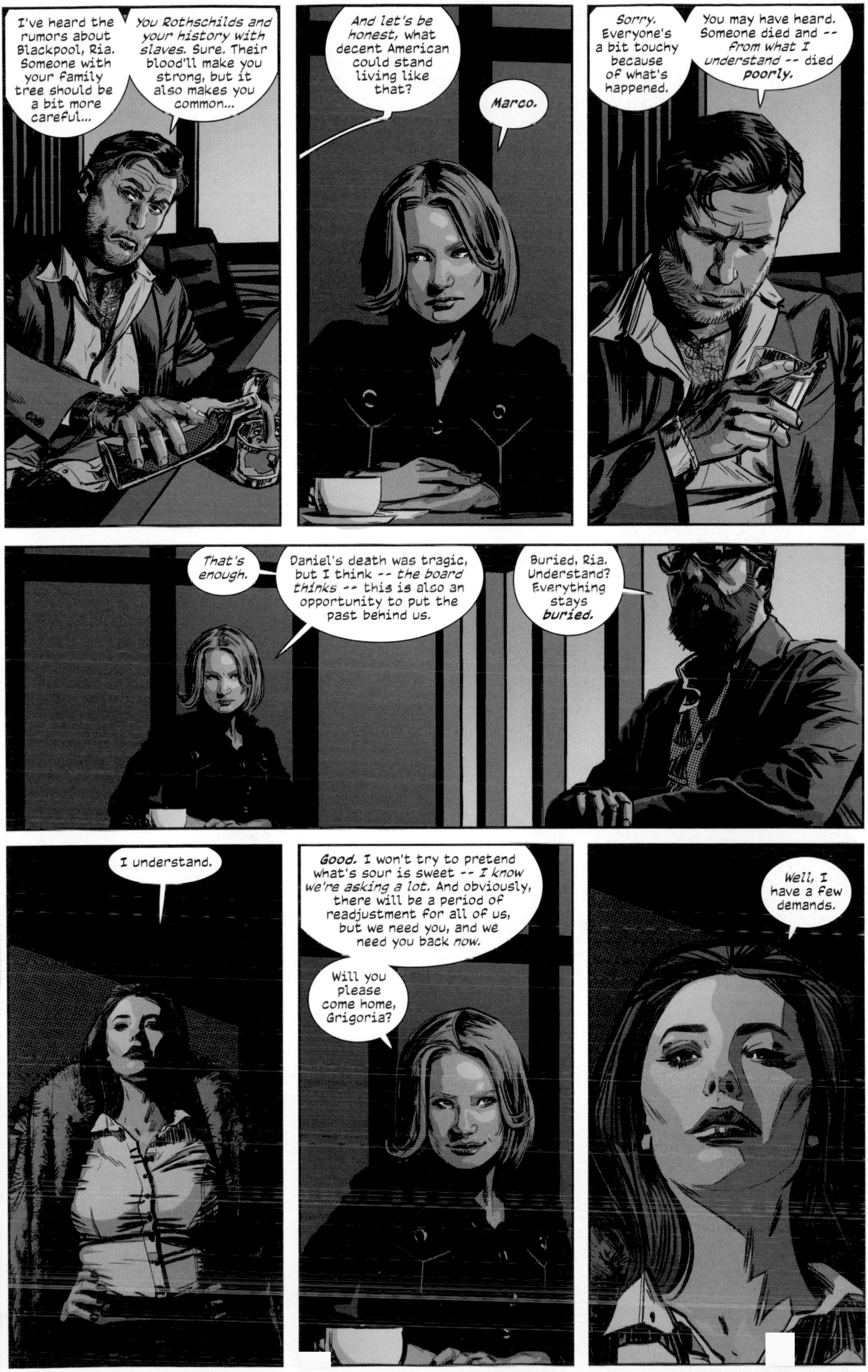
I've heard the rumors about Blackpool, Ria. Someone with your family tree should be a bit more careful...
You Rothschilds and your history with slaves. Sure. Their blood'll make you strong, but it also makes you common...
And let's be honest, what decent American could stand living like that?
Marco.
Sorry. Everyone's a bit touchy because of what's happened.
You may have heard. Someone died and -- from what I understand -- died poorly.
That's enough.
Daniel's death was tragic, but I think -- the board thinks -- this is also an opportunity to put the past behind us.
Buried, Ria. Understand? Everything stays buried.
I understand.
Good. I won't try to pretend what's sour is sweet -- I know we're asking a lot. And obviously, there will be a period of readjustment for all of us, but we need you, and we need you back now.
Will you please come home, Grigoria?
Well, I have a few demands.

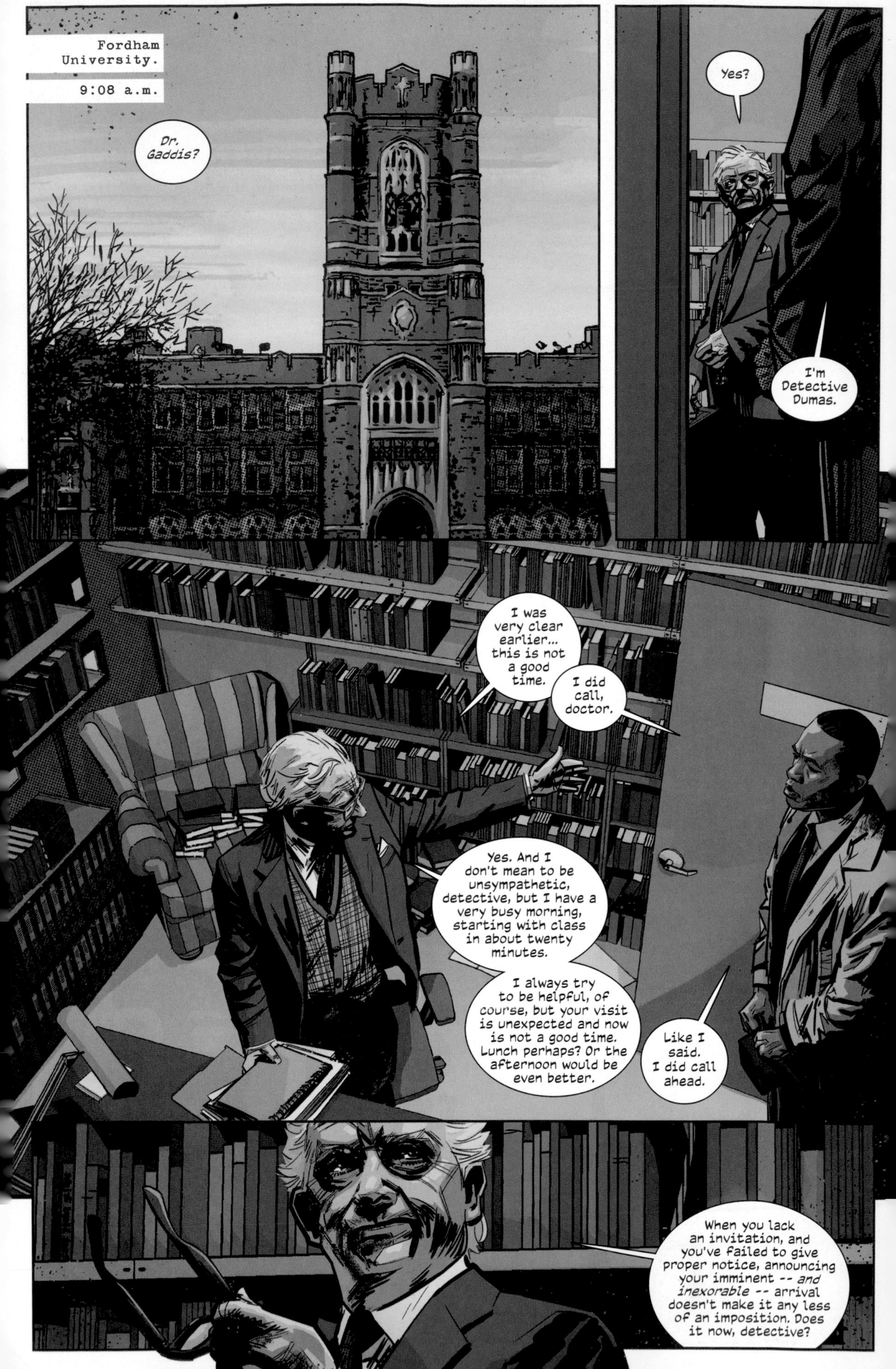
Fordham University.
9:08 a.m.
Dr. Gaddis?
Yes?
I'm Detective Dumas.
I was very clear earlier... this is not a good time.
I did call, doctor.
Yes. And I don't mean to be unsympathetic, detective, but I have a very busy morning, starting with class in about twenty minutes.
I always try to be helpful, of course, but your visit is unexpected and now is not a good time. Lunch perhaps? Or the afternoon would be even better.
Like I said. I did call ahead.
When you lack an invitation, and you've failed to give proper notice, announcing your imminent -- *and inexorable* -- arrival doesn't make it any less of an imposition. Does it now, detective?

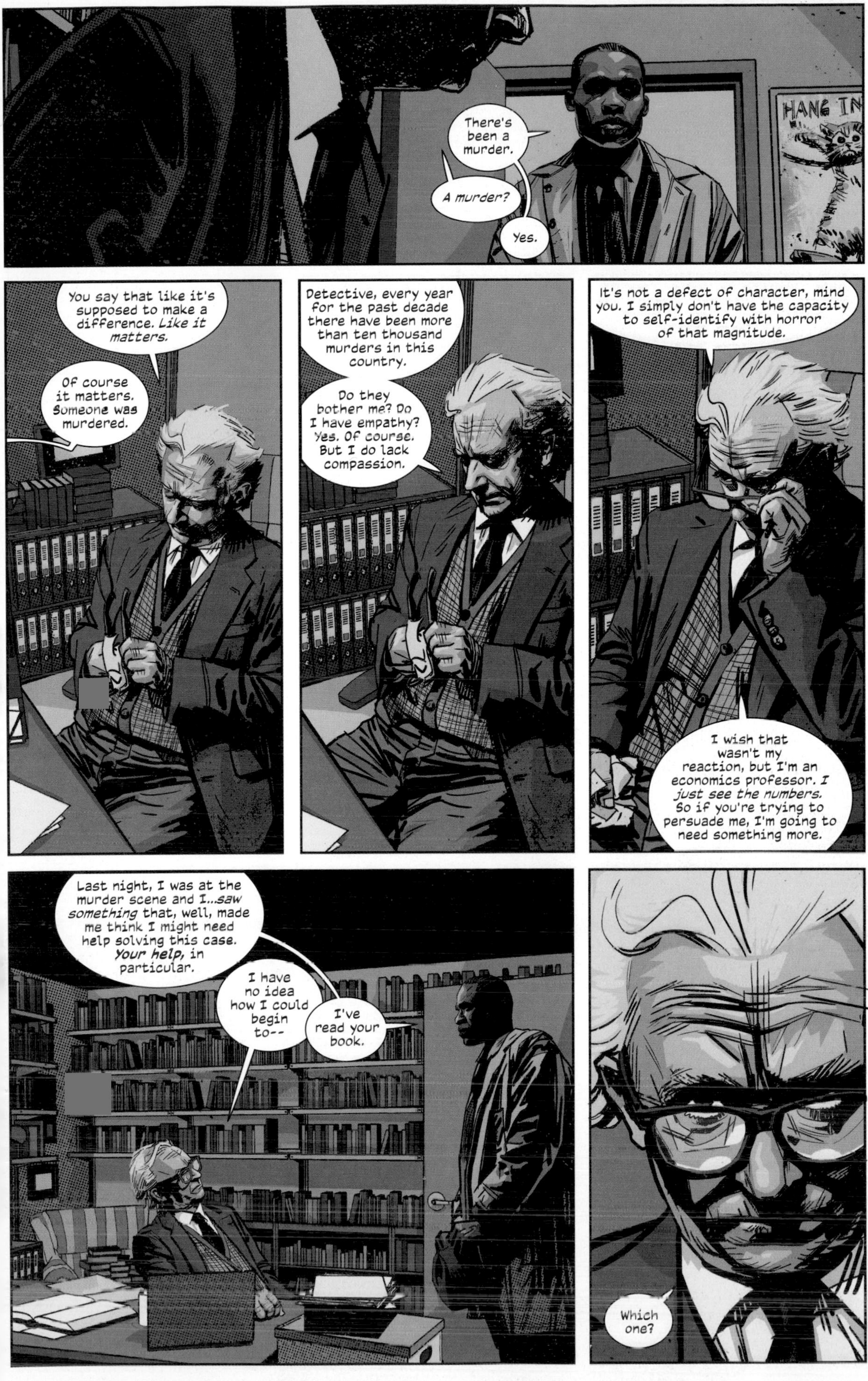
There's been a murder.
A murder?
Yes.
You say that like it's supposed to make a difference. *Like it matters.*
Of course it matters. Someone was murdered.
Detective, every year for the past decade there have been more than ten thousand murders in this country.
Do they bother me? Do I have empathy? Yes. Of course. But I do lack compassion.
It's not a defect of character, mind you. I simply don't have the capacity to self-identify with horror of that magnitude.
I wish that wasn't my reaction, but I'm an economics professor. *I just see the numbers.* So if you're trying to persuade me, I'm going to need something more.
Last night, I was at the murder scene and I... *saw something* that, well, made me think I might need help solving this case. ***Your help,*** in particular.
I have no idea how I could begin to--
I've read your book.
Which one?

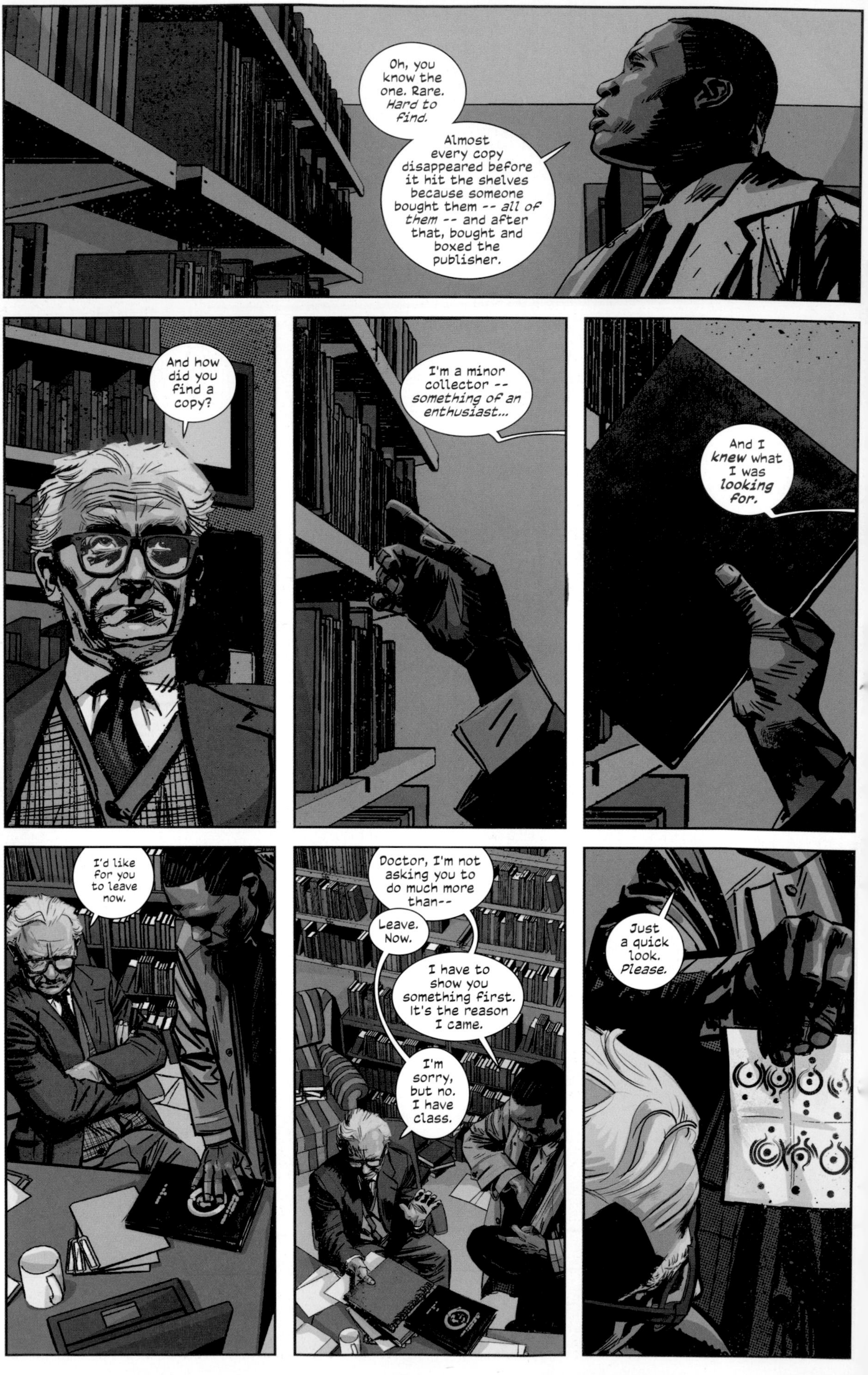
Oh, you know the one. Rare. *Hard to find.*
Almost every copy disappeared before it hit the shelves because someone bought them -- *all of them* -- and after that, bought and boxed the publisher.
And how did you find a copy?
I'm a minor collector -- *something of an enthusiast...*
And I *knew* what I was *looking for.*
I'd like for you to leave now.
Doctor, I'm not asking you to do much more than--
Leave. Now.
I have to show you something first. It's the reason I came.
I'm sorry, but no. I have class.
Just a quick look. *Please.*

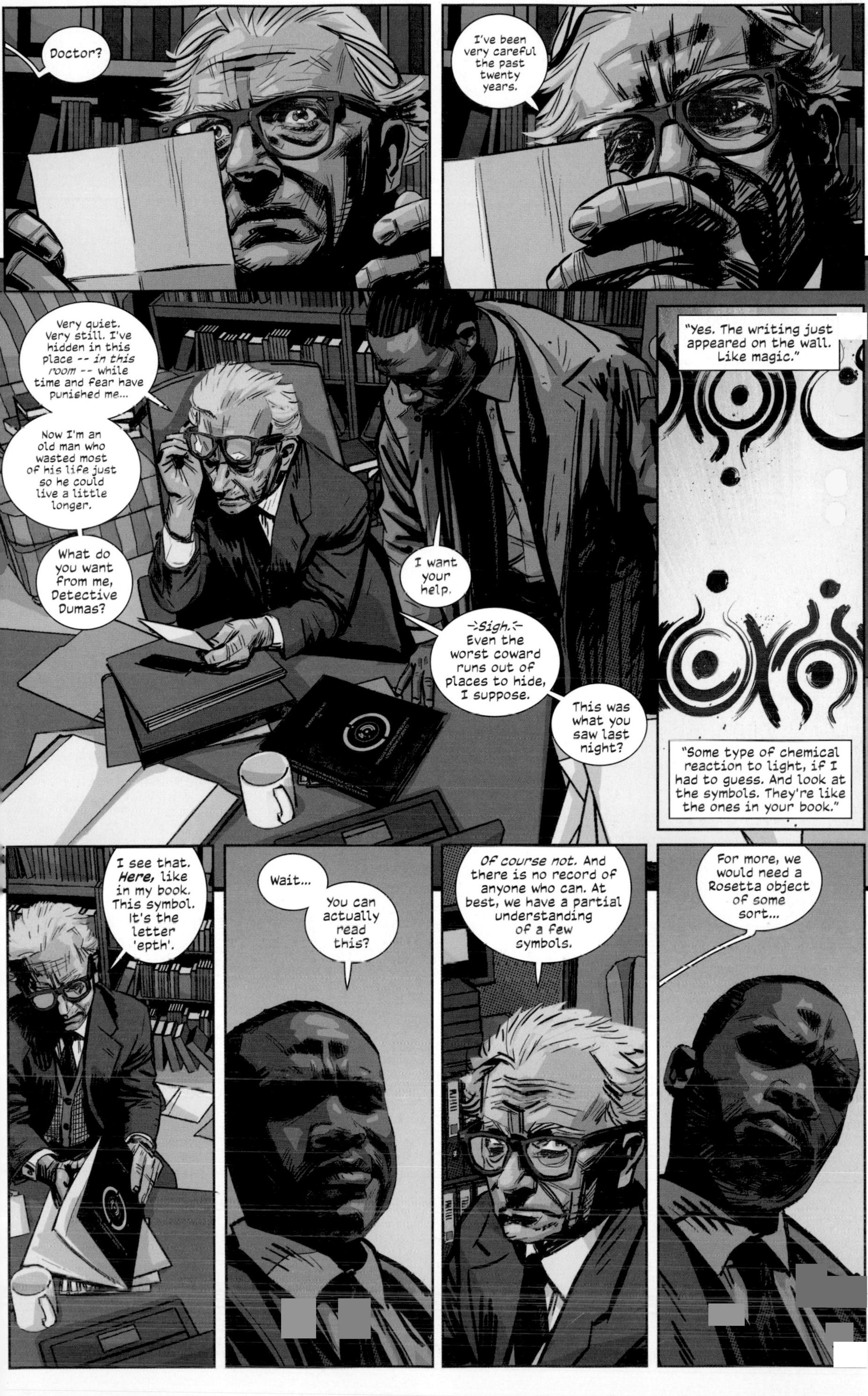
Doctor?
I've been very careful the past twenty years.
Very quiet. Very still. I've hidden in this place -- *in this room* -- while time and fear have punished me...
Now I'm an old man who wasted most of his life just so he could live a little longer.
What do you want from me, Detective Dumas?
I want your help.
-Sigh.- Even the worst coward runs out of places to hide, I suppose.
This was what you saw last night?
"Yes. The writing just appeared on the wall. Like magic."
"Some type of chemical reaction to light, if I had to guess. And look at the symbols. They're like the ones in your book."
I see that. **Here,** like in my book. This symbol. It's the letter 'epth'.
Wait...
You can actually read this?
*Of course not.* And there is no record of anyone who can. At best, we have a partial understanding of a few symbols.
For more, we would need a Rosetta object of some sort...

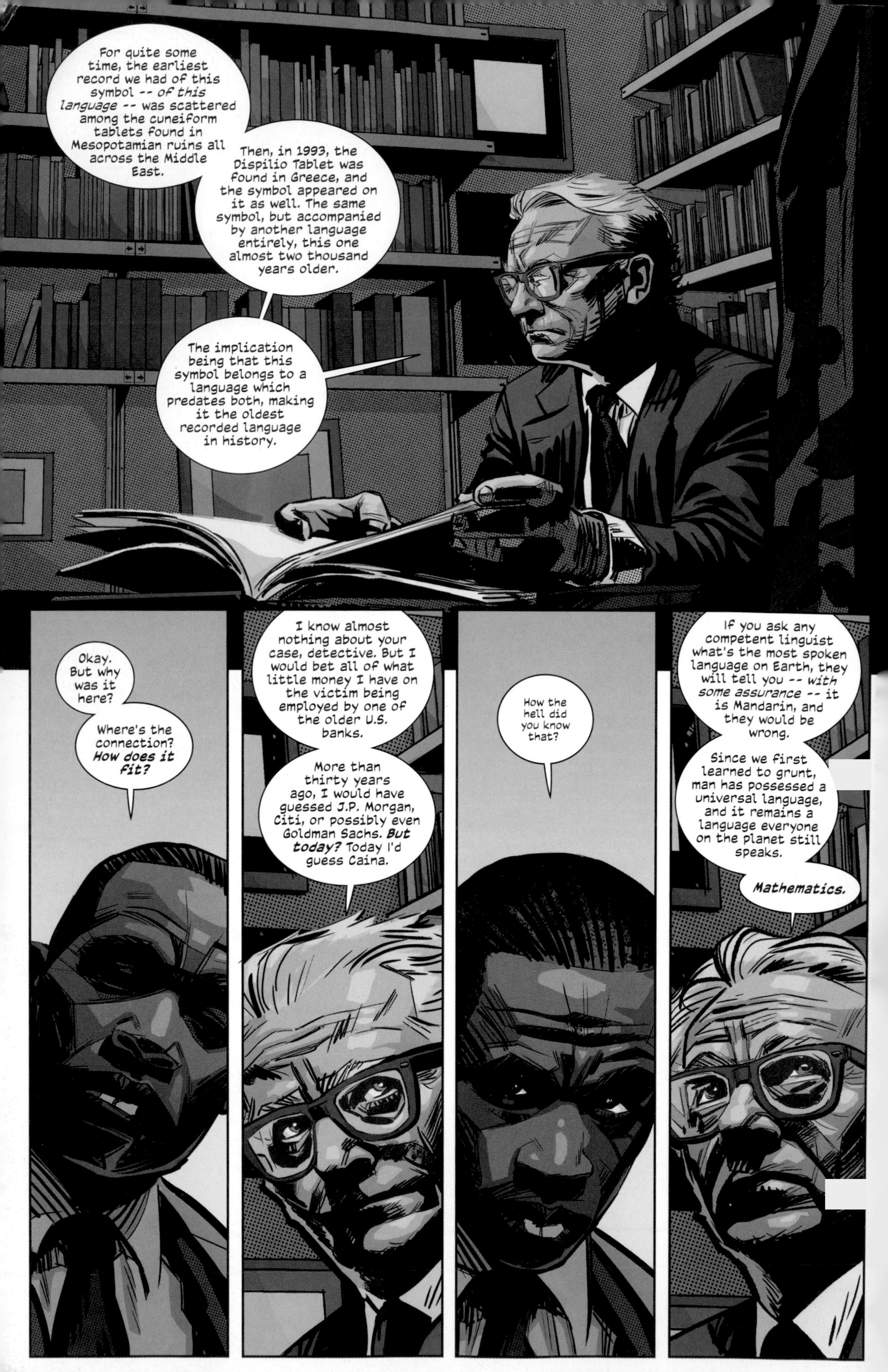
For quite some time, the earliest record we had of this symbol -- *of this language* -- was scattered among the cuneiform tablets found in Mesopotamian ruins all across the Middle East.
Then, in 1993, the Dispilio Tablet was found in Greece, and the symbol appeared on it as well. The same symbol, but accompanied by another language entirely, this one almost two thousand years older.
The implication being that this symbol belongs to a language which predates both, making it the oldest recorded language in history.
Okay. But why was it here?
Where's the connection? ***How does it fit?***
I know almost nothing about your case, detective. But I would bet all of what little money I have on the victim being employed by one of the older U.S. banks.
More than thirty years ago, I would have guessed J.P. Morgan, Citi, or possibly even Goldman Sachs. ***But today?*** Today I'd guess Caina.
How the hell did you know that?
If you ask any competent linguist what's the most spoken language on Earth, they will tell you -- *with some assurance* -- it is Mandarin, and they would be wrong.
Since we first learned to grunt, man has possessed a universal language, and it remains a language everyone on the planet still speaks.
***Mathematics.***

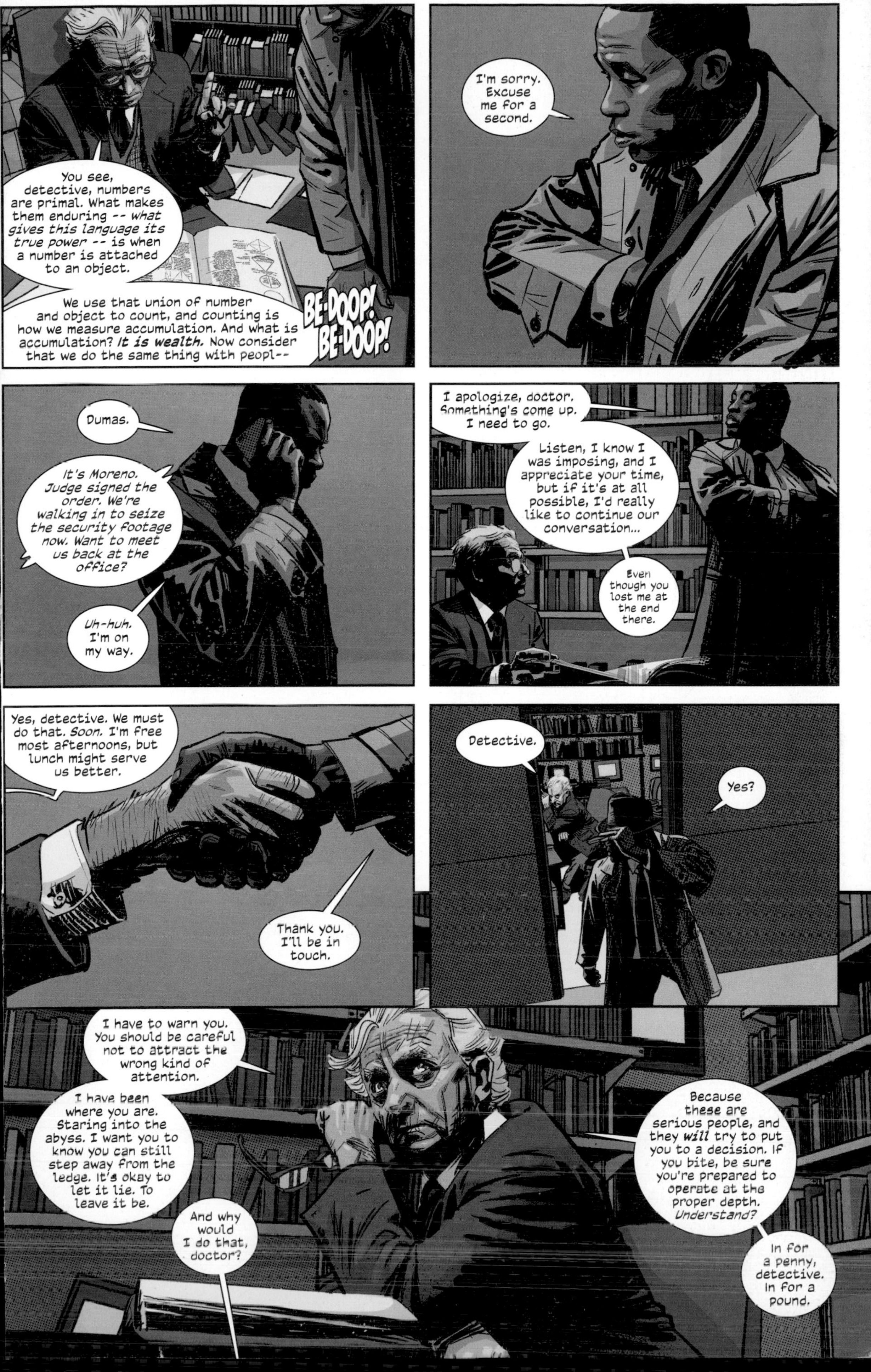
You see, detective, numbers are primal. What makes them enduring -- *what gives this language its true power* -- is when a number is attached to an object.
We use that union of number and object to count, and counting is how we measure accumulation. And what is accumulation? ***It is wealth.*** Now consider that we do the same thing with peopl--
BE-DOOP! BE-DOOP!
I'm sorry. Excuse me for a second.
Dumas.
*It's Moreno. Judge signed the order. We're walking in to seize the security footage now. Want to meet us back at the office?*
*Uh-huh.* I'm on my way.
I apologize, doctor. Something's come up. I need to go.
Listen, I know I was imposing, and I appreciate your time, but if it's at all possible, I'd really like to continue our conversation...
Even though you lost me at the end there.
Yes, detective. We must do that. *Soon.* I'm free most afternoons, but lunch might serve us better.
Thank you. I'll be in touch.
Detective.
Yes?
I have to warn you. You should be careful not to attract the wrong kind of attention.
I have been where you are. Staring into the abyss. I want you to know you can still step away from the ledge. It's okay to let it lie. To leave it be.
And why would I do that, doctor?
Because these are serious people, and they ***will*** try to put you to a decision. If you bite, be sure you're prepared to operate at the proper depth. *Understand?*
In for a penny, detective. In for a pound.

# CAINA BOARD OF DIRECTORS MEETING MINUTES

DATE: Tuesday, November 1, 2016
TIME: 8:00 AM
LOCATION: Caina Boardroom. New York.

PRESENT: Beatrix Bischoff | The Watcher
Marco Dominic | The Scales
Alexi Malkin | The Stone Chair

Grigoria Rothschild
(Guest)

ABSENT:

Wynn Ackermann | (Sabbatical)

I. Call to Order: At 8:15 AM by presiding officer Beatrix Bischoff.

II. Quorum: Three of four Board members present (three required.)

III. Reading and Approval of Minutes: Minutes of the October 4, 2016 Board meeting regarding [redacted]

IV. Treasurer's Report: Uncontested.

V. New Business:

A. Reappointment of Grigoria Rothschild to the Ascendant Seat (unanimous approval).

B. Rothschild stock transfer of [redacted] (approval).

C. Retribution language adopted regarding the circumstances surrounding the death of Daniel Rothschild (unanimous approval).

D. Unilateral control of negotiating mergers and/or acquisitions for the next six months (approval).

E. Full access to all [redacted] (rejected).

G. Arbitration of access to all [redacted] (approval).

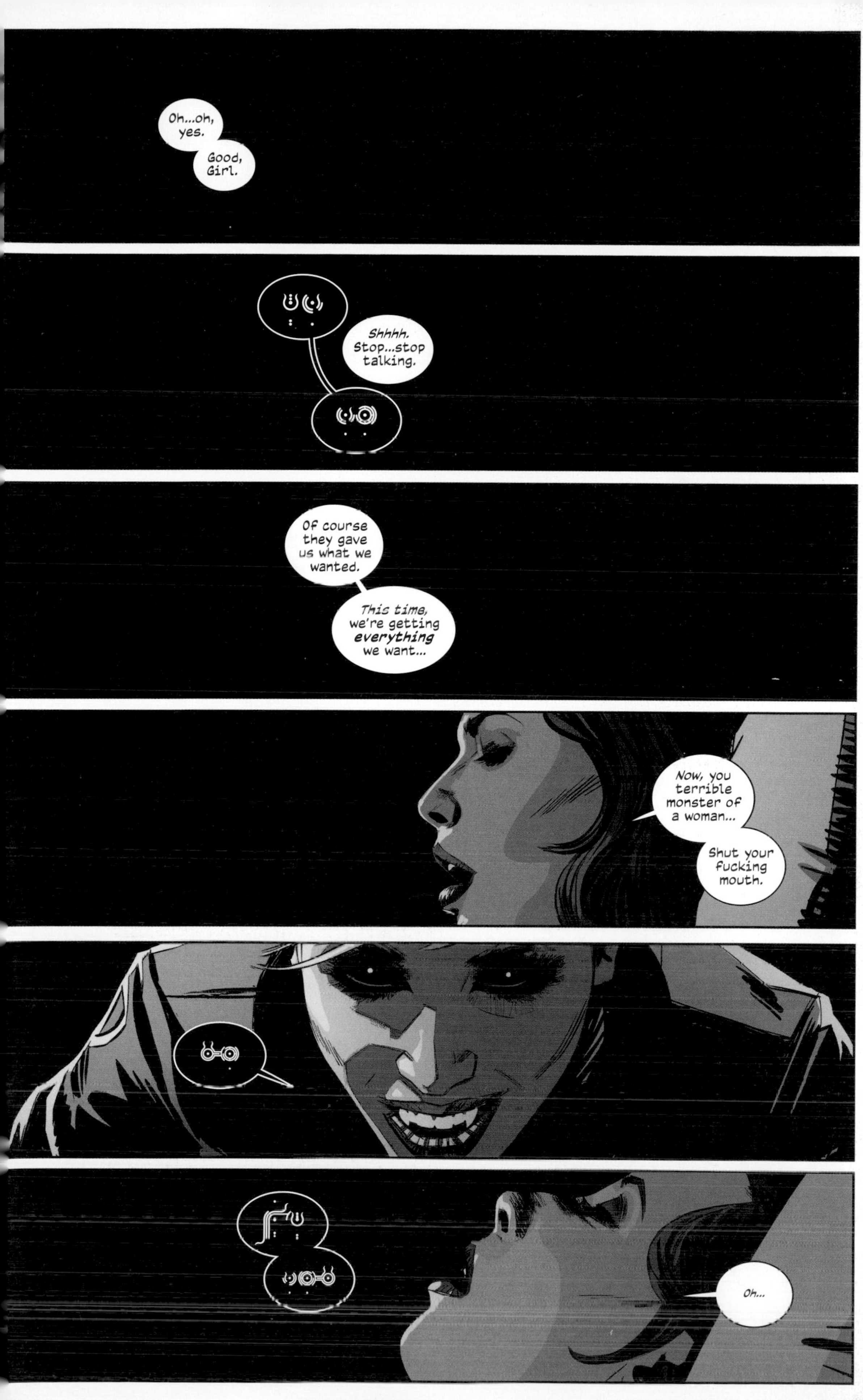
Oh...oh, yes.
Good, Girl.
Shhhh. Stop...stop talking.
Of course they gave us what we wanted.
This time, we're getting everything we want...
Now, you terrible monster of a woman...
Shut your fucking mouth.
Oh...

March 12, 1899

To my eldest son, Milton,

If you are receiving this letter, then I have died before you reached
the age of thirty. It's of a secondary concern that if I had died after
you reached that age, you would have received a completely different
letter (simpler fare to be sure; well-wishes and similar, other hollow
advice), but you have always been a curious boy and, I believe, that
letter's existence would have haunted you. To that end, let me assure
you, this is the bloody red meat you seek.

By now, you will have claimed my place on the Wheel - along with the
other three families that make up our academy - and have come into your
full power. I am sure that you, much like I did in my time, feel both
impervious and immortal, but let me assure you, this is not the case.

As such, I would like to offer you three options for overcoming the
greatest tragedy of an empowered life: brevity.

    1. Consolidate the school. Eliminate the other three families and
consume their wealth. This should, at the very least, extend your
life twenty to thirty more years. Unfortunately, because the
power transfer must follow proper protocol, one cannot eliminate
all of the others at once. Meaning that one of the others, and
possibly both, will know what you are doing and will work to
oppose you. Additionally, this does not solve the Stone Chair
conundrum. I do not advise this route.

    2. ███████████████████████████████████████████
███████████████████████████████████████████████
███████████████████████████████████████████████
███████████████████████████████████████████ I do
consider this an acceptable solution, but also partial fare.

    3. If you have the strength to survive the summoning (which is
why it is paramount that you be under the age of thirty), then
petition the Federal Reserve and ████████████████████████
████████████████████ to acquire a Familiar. This not only
provides you with a proxy for the Stone Chair, but could
potentially prolong your life for another one hundred years. This
would be my recommended option.

Whichever course you choose, know that I envy your position.

Finally, if by some combination of cruelty and medicine, my mother has
managed to outlive me, I implore you to right that wrong as soon as
possible. The woman is a yoke no decent neck should endure, so please,
send her on her way.

Your father,
Andrew Davis Rothschild II

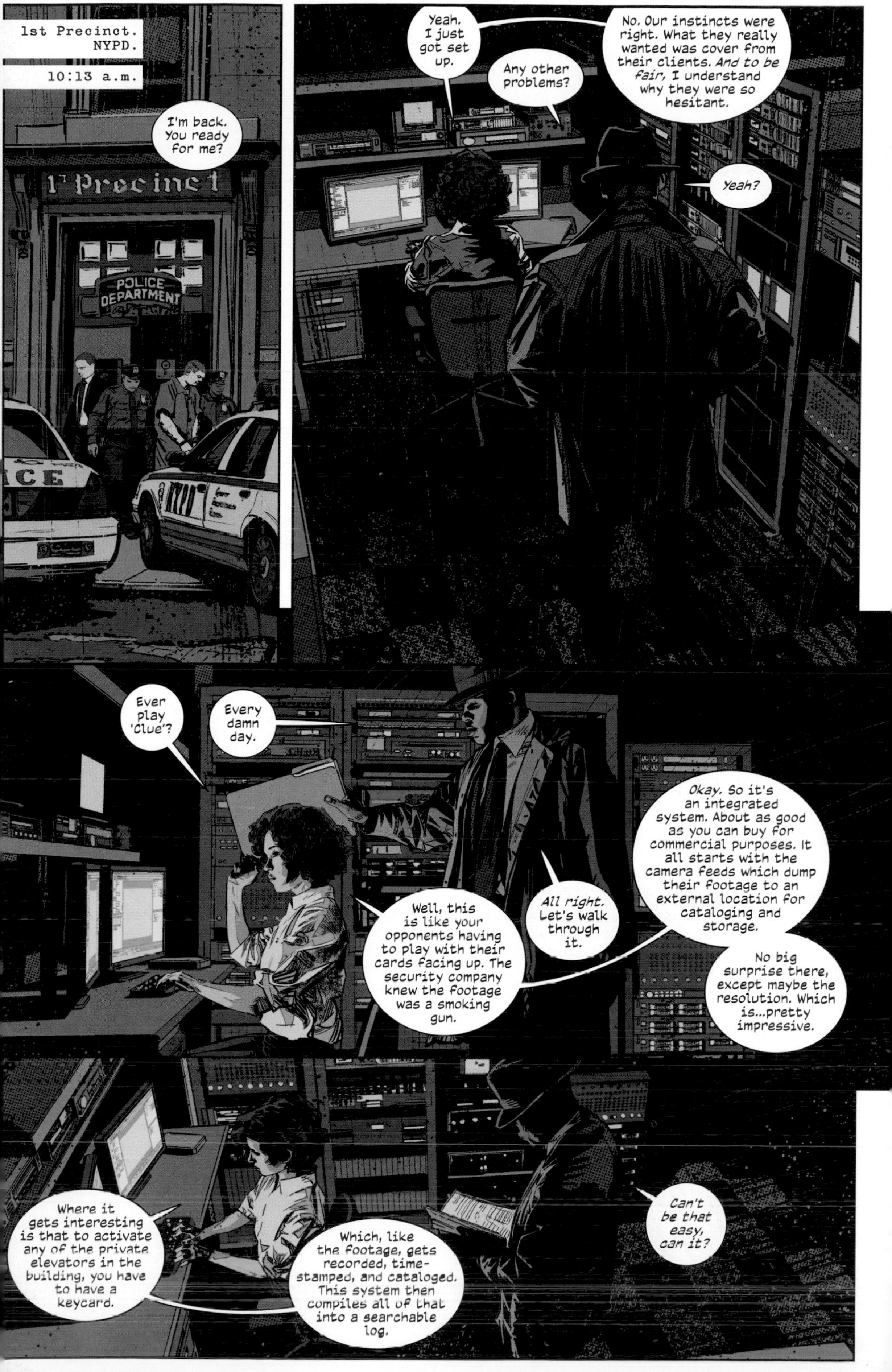
1st Precinct. NYPD.
10:13 a.m.
I'm back. You ready for me?
1st Precinct
POLICE DEPARTMENT
Yeah. I just got set up.
Any other problems?
No. Our instincts were right. What they really wanted was cover from their clients. *And to be fair,* I understand why they were so hesitant.
*Yeah?*
Ever play 'Clue'?
Every damn day.
Well, this is like your opponents having to play with their cards facing up. The security company knew the footage was a smoking gun.
*All right.* Let's walk through it.
*Okay.* So it's an integrated system. About as good as you can buy for commercial purposes. It all starts with the camera feeds which dump their footage to an external location for cataloging and storage.
No big surprise there, except maybe the resolution. Which is...pretty impressive.
Where it gets interesting is that to activate any of the private elevators in the building, you have to have a keycard.
Which, like the footage, gets recorded, time-stamped, and cataloged. This system then compiles all of that into a searchable log.
*Can't be that easy, can it?*

The coroner's report puts the time of death in between 11 PM and 1 AM.

The entire scene was staged. Killer could have done that beforehand. Call it 9 and...

We got two hits during that time frame.

Let's see the first one.

This is 9:27, in the PM.

That's Rothschild. The victim. Move on to the next one.

9:42 PM.

There's our boy. Do we see his face?

Let me step through it...

R+09:42:24

And comparing it with the I.D....

Looks like the same guy.

LETHE

COMPANY: CAINA-KANKRIN
CORP ID: 0010083040509  Z8Z50
NAME: ERENKO, VIKTOR
MISC:

Left(01)  Left(02)  Left(03)  Left(04)

SECURITY PROFILE:

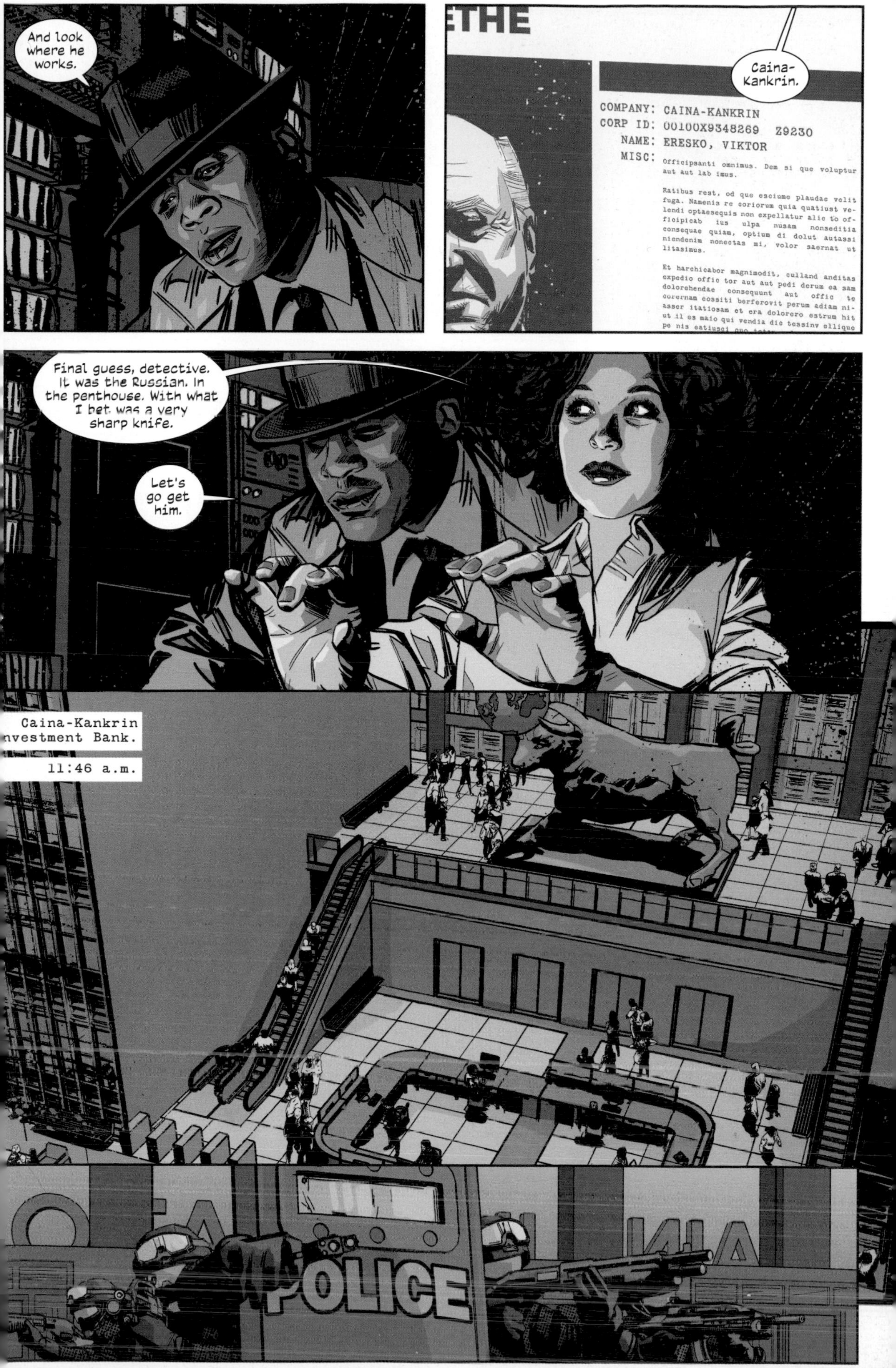
And look where he works.
ETHE
Caina-Kankrin.
COMPANY: CAINA-KANKRIN
CORP ID: 00100X9348269 Z9230
NAME: ERESKO, VIKTOR
MISC: Officipsanti omnimus. Dem si que voluptur aut aut lab imus.
Ratibus rest, od que esciume plaudac velit fuga. Namenis re coriorum quia quatiust velendi optaesequis non expellatur alic to officipicab ius ulpa nusam nonseditia consequae quiam, optium di dolut autassi niendenim nonectas mi, volor saernat ut litasimus.
Et harchicabor magnimodit, culland anditas expedio offic tor aut aut pedi derum ea sam dolorehendae consequunt aut offic te corernam cossiti berferovit perum adiam niasser itatiosam et era dolorero estrum hit ut il es maio qui vendia dic tessinv ellique pe nis eatiusci
Final guess, detective. It was the Russian. In the penthouse. With what I bet was a very sharp knife.
Let's go get him.
Caina-Kankrin
nvestment Bank.
11:46 a.m.
POLICE

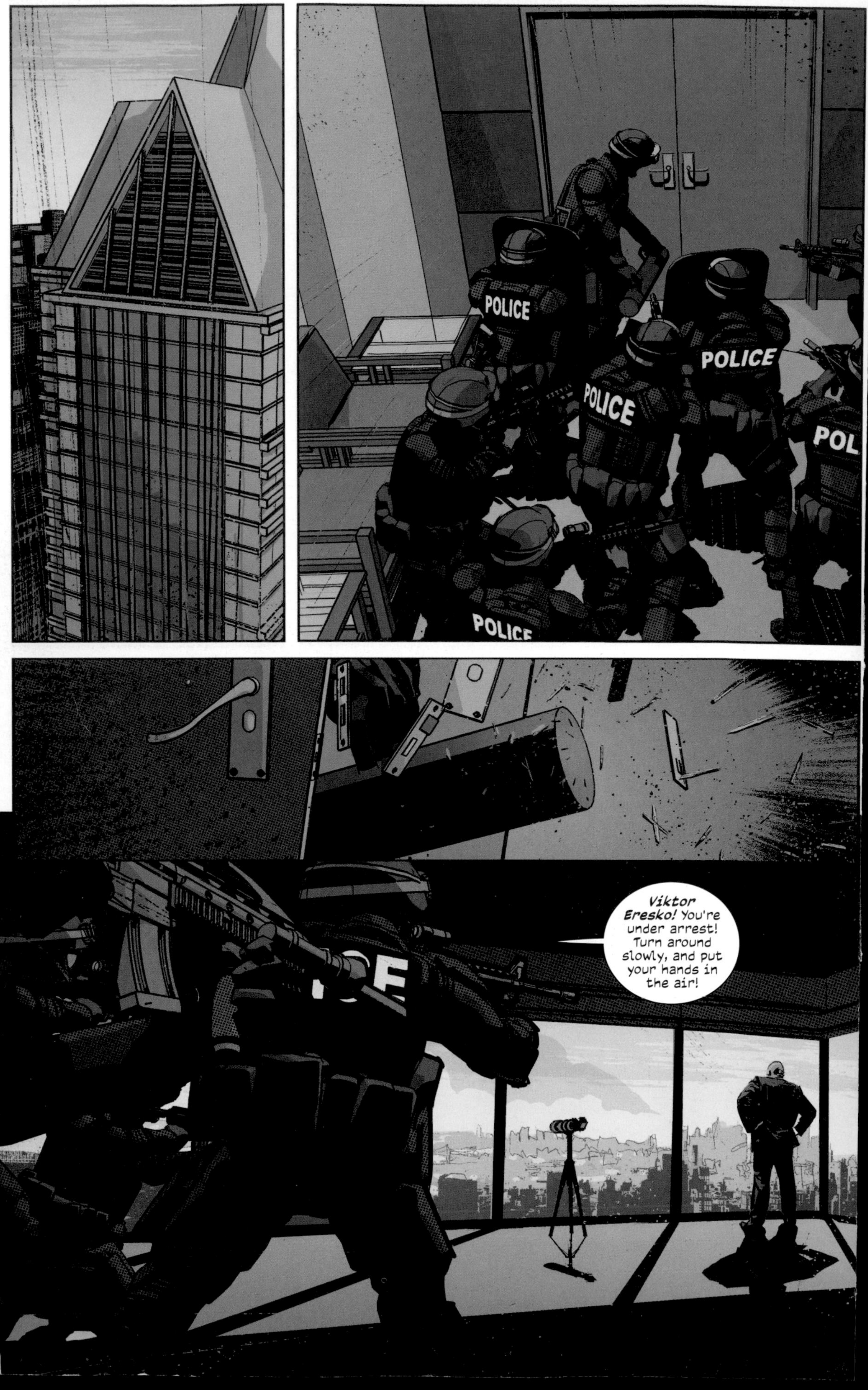
POLICE
POLICE
POLICE
POL
POLICE
Viktor Eresko! You're under arrest! Turn around slowly, and put your hands in the air!

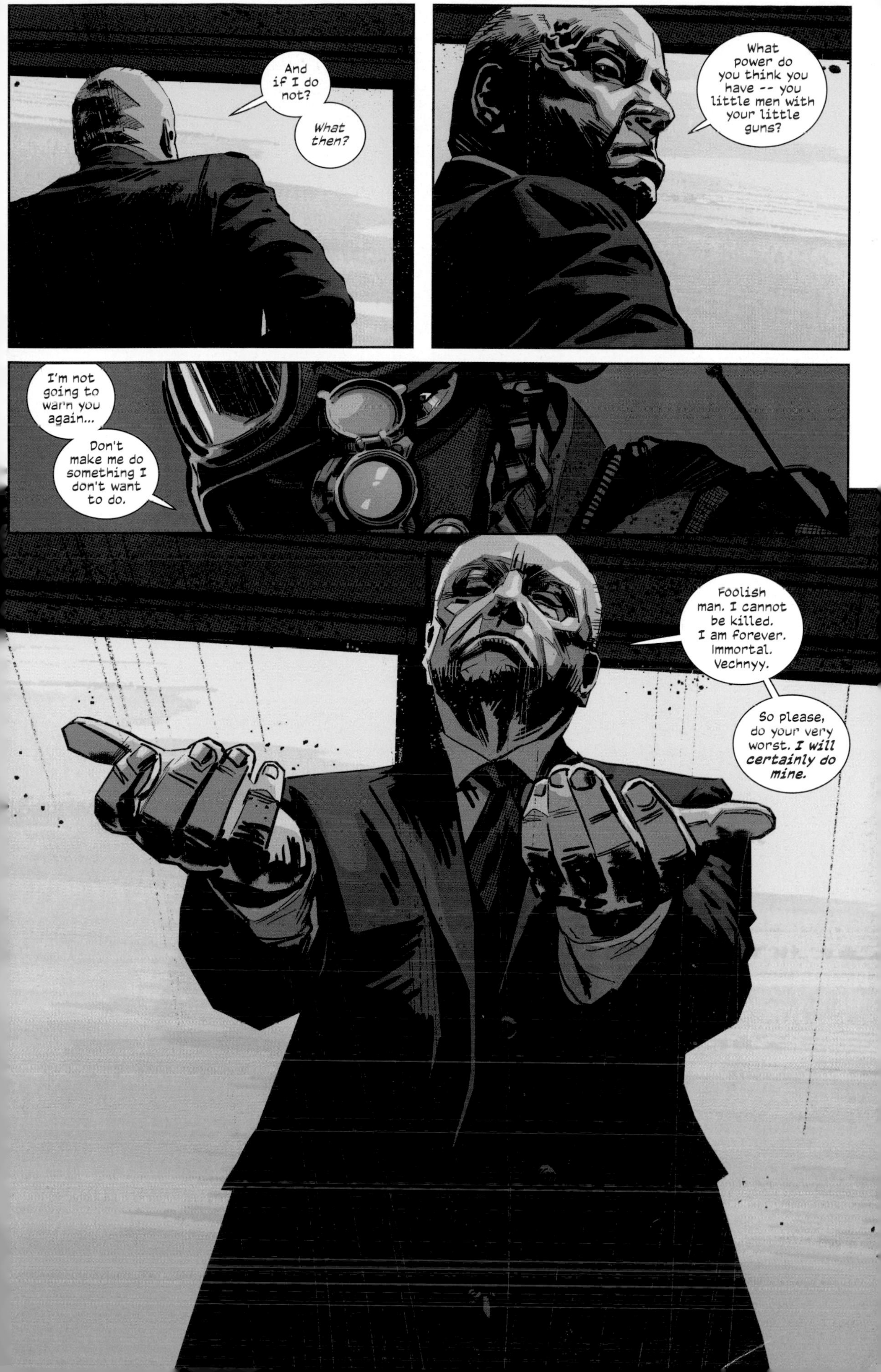
And if I do not?
*What then?*
What power do you think you have -- you little men with your little guns?
I'm not going to warn you again...
Don't make me do something I don't want to do.
Foolish man. I cannot be killed. I am forever. Immortal. Vechnyy.
So please, do your very worst. ***I will certainly do mine.***

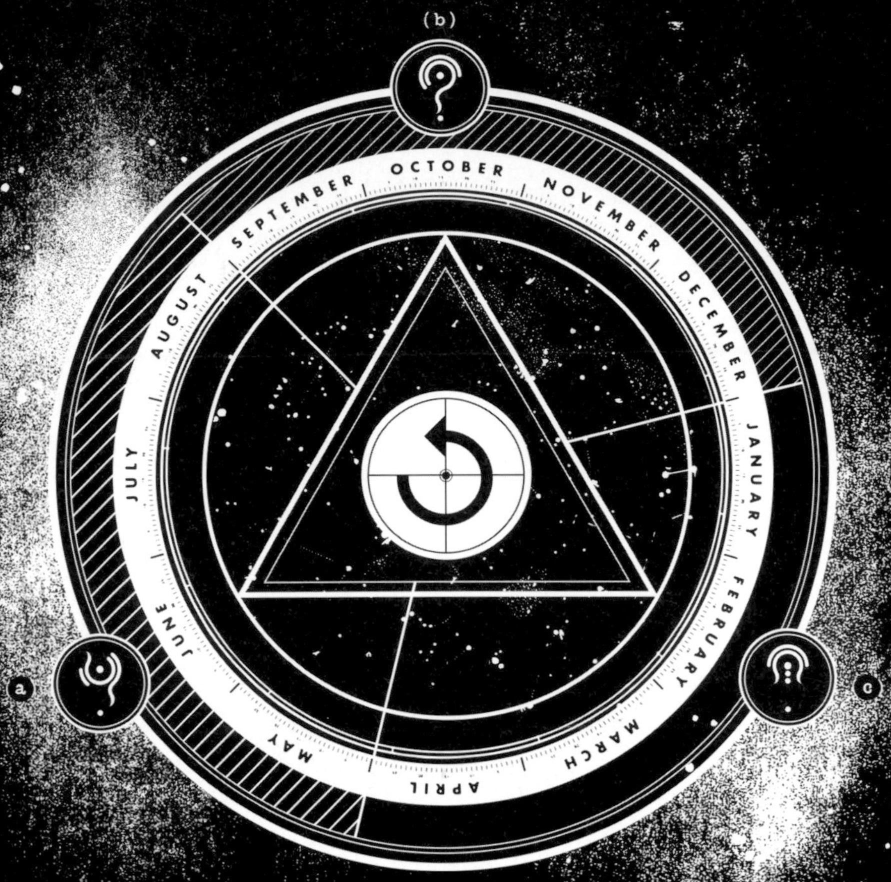
(b)
OCTOBER
NOVEMBER
DECEMBER
JANUARY
FEBRUARY
MARCH
APRIL
MAY
JUNE
JULY
AUGUST
SEPTEMBER
a
c

Eastern Schools of Economics

At their height, the Eastern schools were not primarily defined by a hierarchical triadic structure. The primary academy arrangement was base six, but by the dawn of the 20th century, the most common composition was base twelve. There were exceptions to this found among Russian nobility, but these, along with the vast majority of typical academies, were all systematically eradicated beginning with the October Revolution.

In the twenty years following Red October, a single fractured academy, Kankrin, was able to inculcate itself into the fledgling government and act as the State Bank of the Soviet Union. Using the secretive and suspicious nature of the Communist Party to its advantage, Kankrin was able to use the seasonal campaigns of political repression to identify "Wild Academies" that naturally occur in a financial vacuum. Behind the Iron Curtain, the Kankrin Troika grew strong devouring its own.

Surviving Academies: Kankrin (1841)

(a) ◉ [Earth | The Judge]..................KOZLOV

(b) ◉ [Man | The Body]....................MALKIN

(c) ● [Sky | The Executioner].............ERESKO

∶

## The Troika of Kankrin.

Even in a parasitic relationship, it is almost impossible not to symbiotically take on characteristics of the thing you are consuming, and the communist state/Eastern school mutualistic union was no different.

Beginning with the Great Purge in 1936, the secret academy operating as the state bank abandoned the base six structure and adopted the judge/jury/executioner triad of the People's Commissariat for Internal Affairs (NKVD) Troika as their own. The bloody tradition of the name lives on, but it also has expanded over time to reflect its more academic side.

The Kankrin universal mantra of: "We are born. We pay in blood. We become." has, over time, evolved into its more common usage: "The one you started with. The one you're paying for. The one for profit."

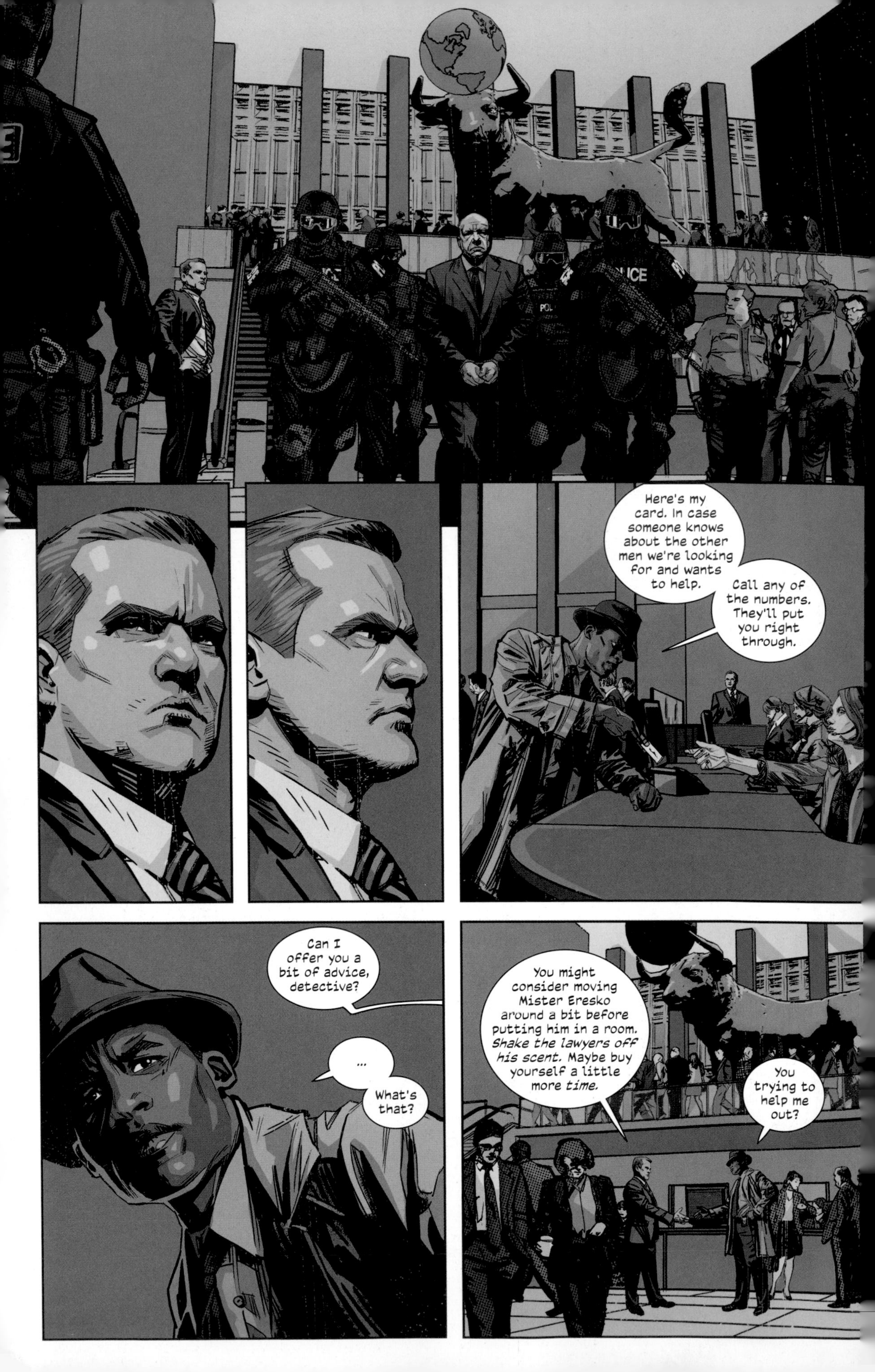

POLICE
Here's my card. In case someone knows about the other men we're looking for and wants to help.
Call any of the numbers. They'll put you right through.
Can I offer you a bit of advice, detective?
...
What's that?
You might consider moving Mister Eresko around a bit before putting him in a room. *Shake the lawyers off his scent.* Maybe buy yourself a little more *time.*
You trying to help me out?

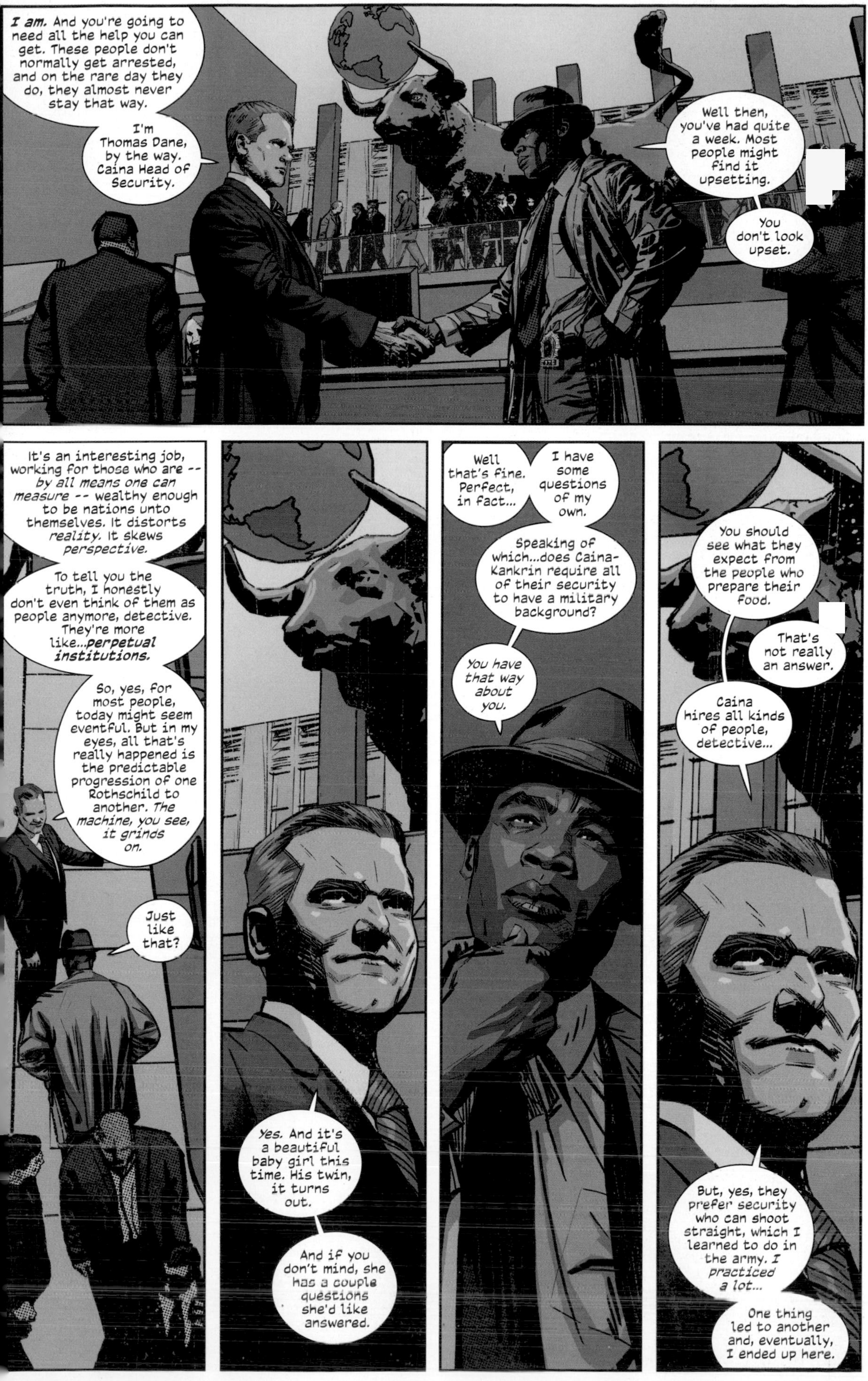
I am. And you're going to need all the help you can get. These people don't normally get arrested, and on the rare day they do, they almost never stay that way.
I'm Thomas Dane, by the way. Caina Head of Security.
Well then, you've had quite a week. Most people might find it upsetting.
You don't look upset.
It's an interesting job, working for those who are -- by all means one can measure -- wealthy enough to be nations unto themselves. It distorts reality. It skews perspective.
To tell you the truth, I honestly don't even think of them as people anymore, detective. They're more like...perpetual institutions.
So, yes, for most people, today might seem eventful. But in my eyes, all that's really happened is the predictable progression of one Rothschild to another. The machine, you see, it grinds on.
Just like that?
Yes. And it's a beautiful baby girl this time. His twin, it turns out.
And if you don't mind, she has a couple questions she'd like answered.
Well that's fine. Perfect, in fact...
I have some questions of my own.
Speaking of which...does Caina-Kankrin require all of their security to have a military background?
You have that way about you.
You should see what they expect from the people who prepare their food.
That's not really an answer.
Caina hires all kinds of people, detective...
But, yes, they prefer security who can shoot straight, which I learned to do in the army. I practiced a lot...
One thing led to another and, eventually, I ended up here.

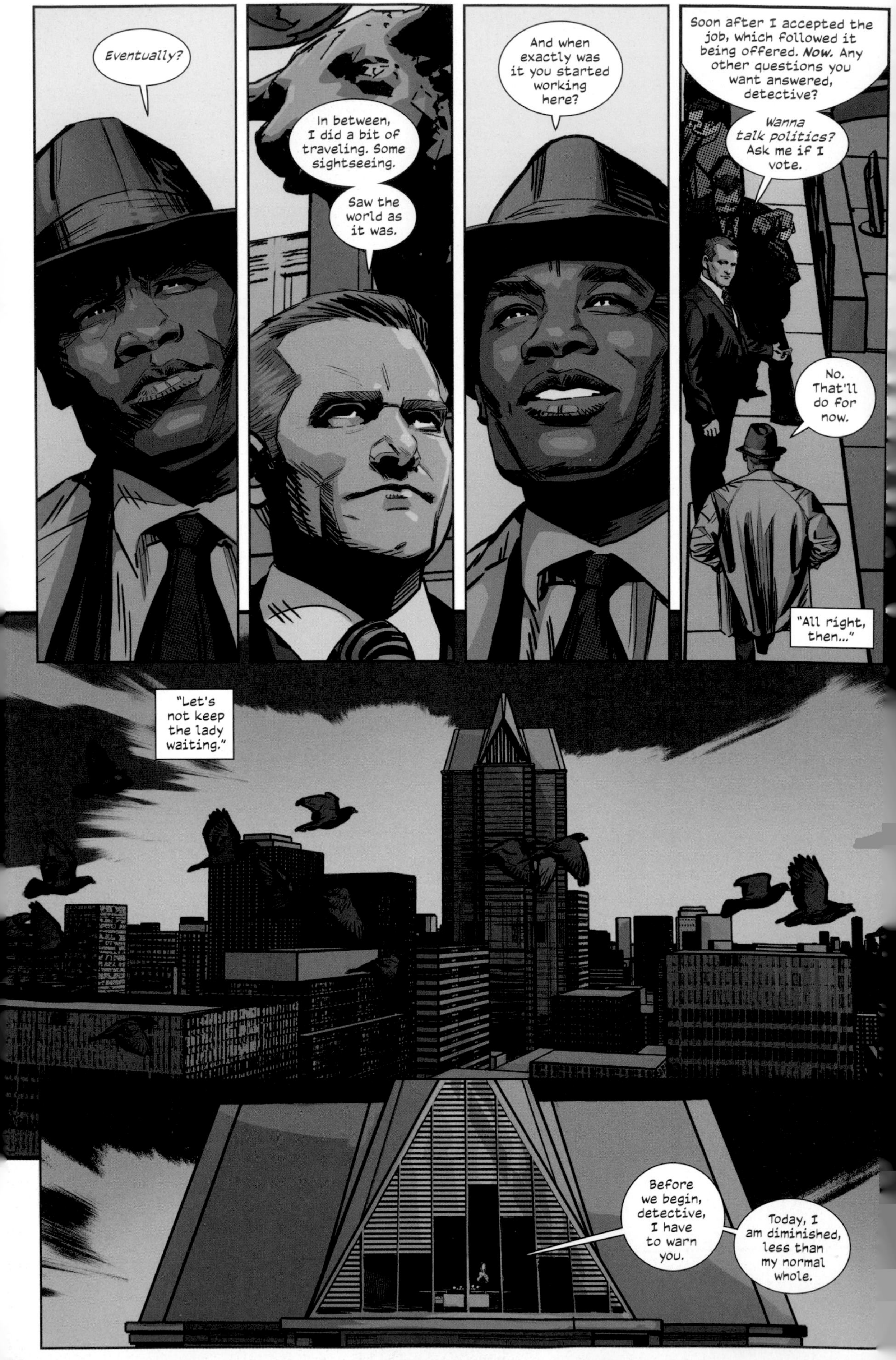
Eventually?
In between, I did a bit of traveling. Some sightseeing.
Saw the world as it was.
And when exactly was it you started working here?
Soon after I accepted the job, which followed it being offered. Now. Any other questions you want answered, detective?
Wanna talk politics? Ask me if I vote.
No. That'll do for now.
"All right, then..."
"Let's not keep the lady waiting."
Before we begin, detective, I have to warn you.
Today, I am diminished, less than my normal whole.

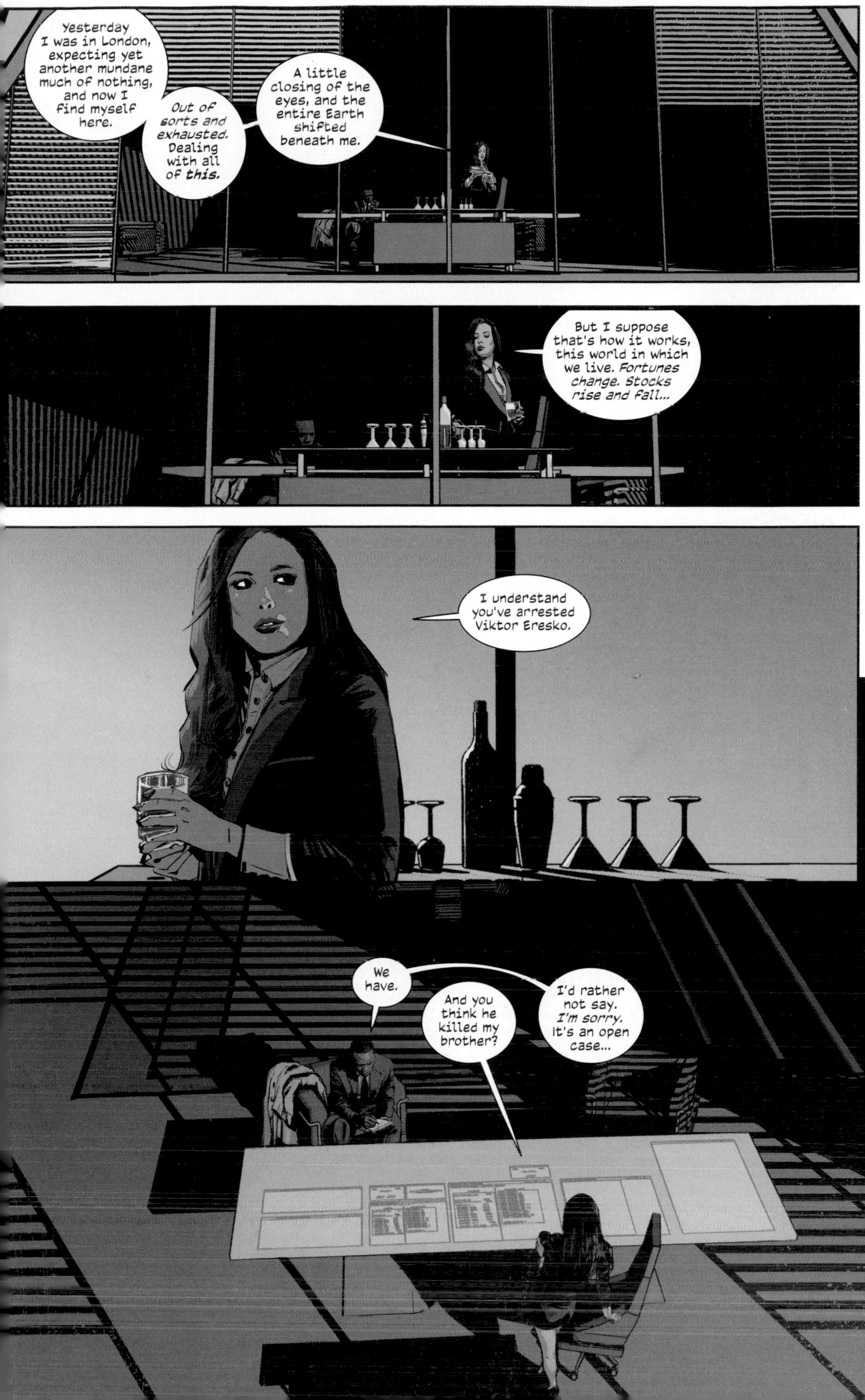
Yesterday I was in London, expecting yet another mundane much of nothing, and now I find myself here.
Out of sorts and exhausted. Dealing with all of this.
A little closing of the eyes, and the entire Earth shifted beneath me.
But I suppose that's how it works, this world in which we live. Fortunes change. Stocks rise and fall...
I understand you've arrested Viktor Eresko.
We have.
And you think he killed my brother?
I'd rather not say. I'm sorry. It's an open case...

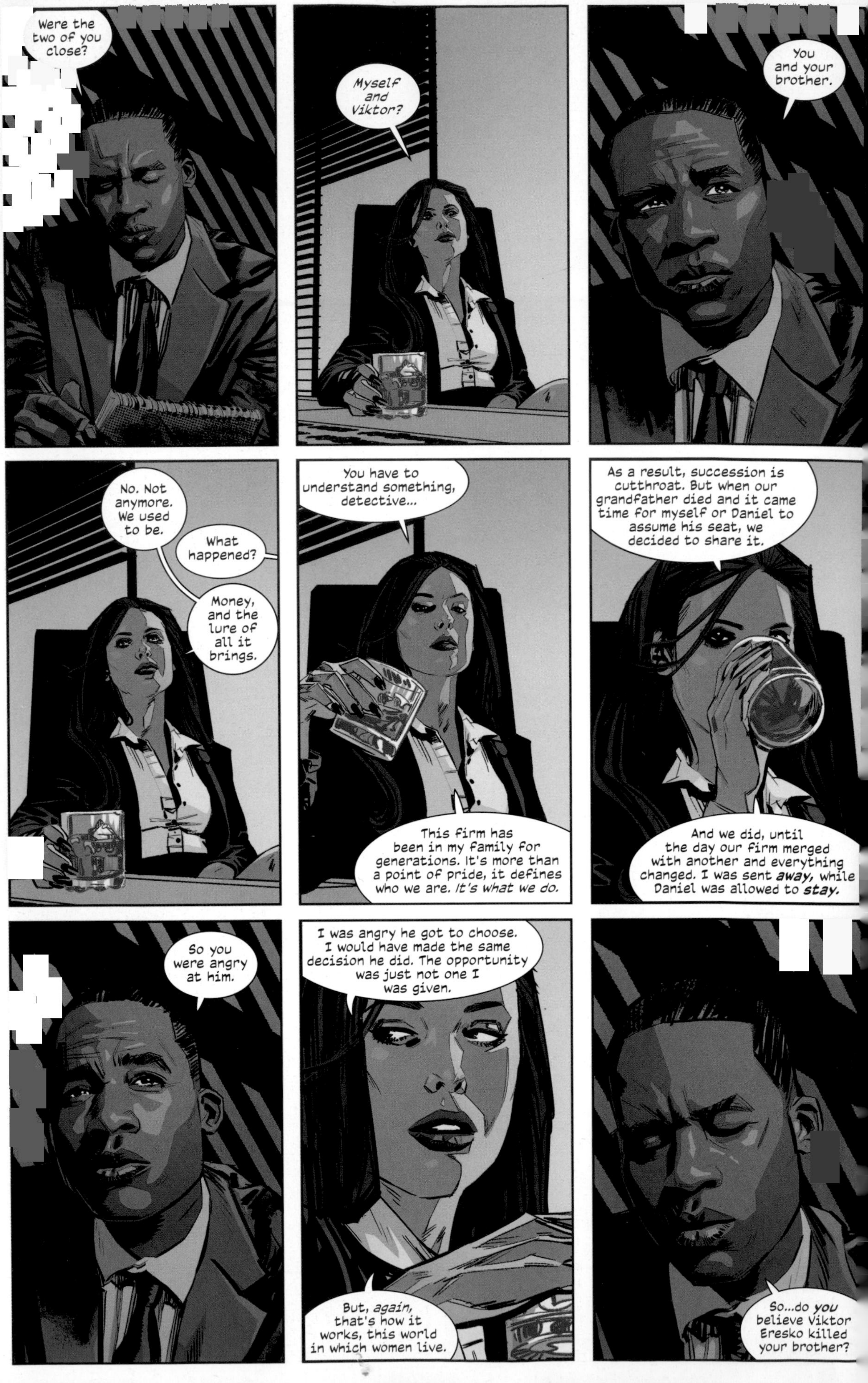

Were the two of you close?
Myself and Viktor?
You and your brother.
No. Not anymore. We used to be.
What happened?
Money, and the lure of all it brings.
You have to understand something, detective...
This firm has been in my family for generations. It's more than a point of pride, it defines who we are. *It's what we do.*
As a result, succession is cutthroat. But when our grandfather died and it came time for myself or Daniel to assume his seat, we decided to share it.
And we did, until the day our firm merged with another and everything changed. I was sent ***away,*** while Daniel was allowed to ***stay.***
So you were angry at him.
I was angry he got to choose. I would have made the same decision he did. The opportunity was just not one I was given.
But, *again,* that's how it works, this world in which women live.
So...do ***you*** believe Viktor Eresko killed your brother?

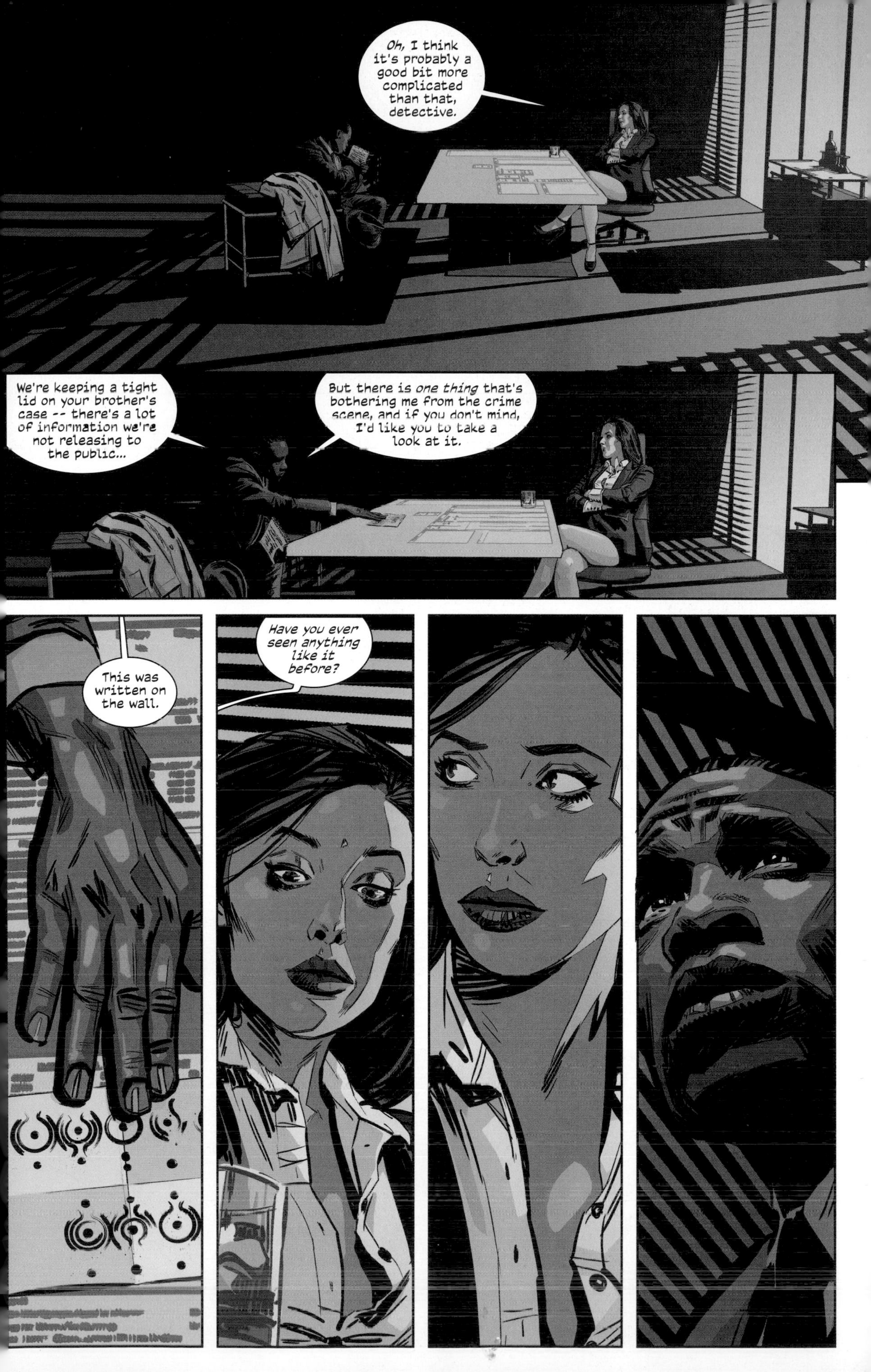

*Oh,* I think it's probably a good bit more complicated than that, detective.
We're keeping a tight lid on your brother's case -- there's a lot of information we're not releasing to the public...
But there is *one thing* that's bothering me from the crime scene, and if you don't mind, I'd like you to take a look at it.
This was written on the wall.
*Have you ever seen anything like it before?*

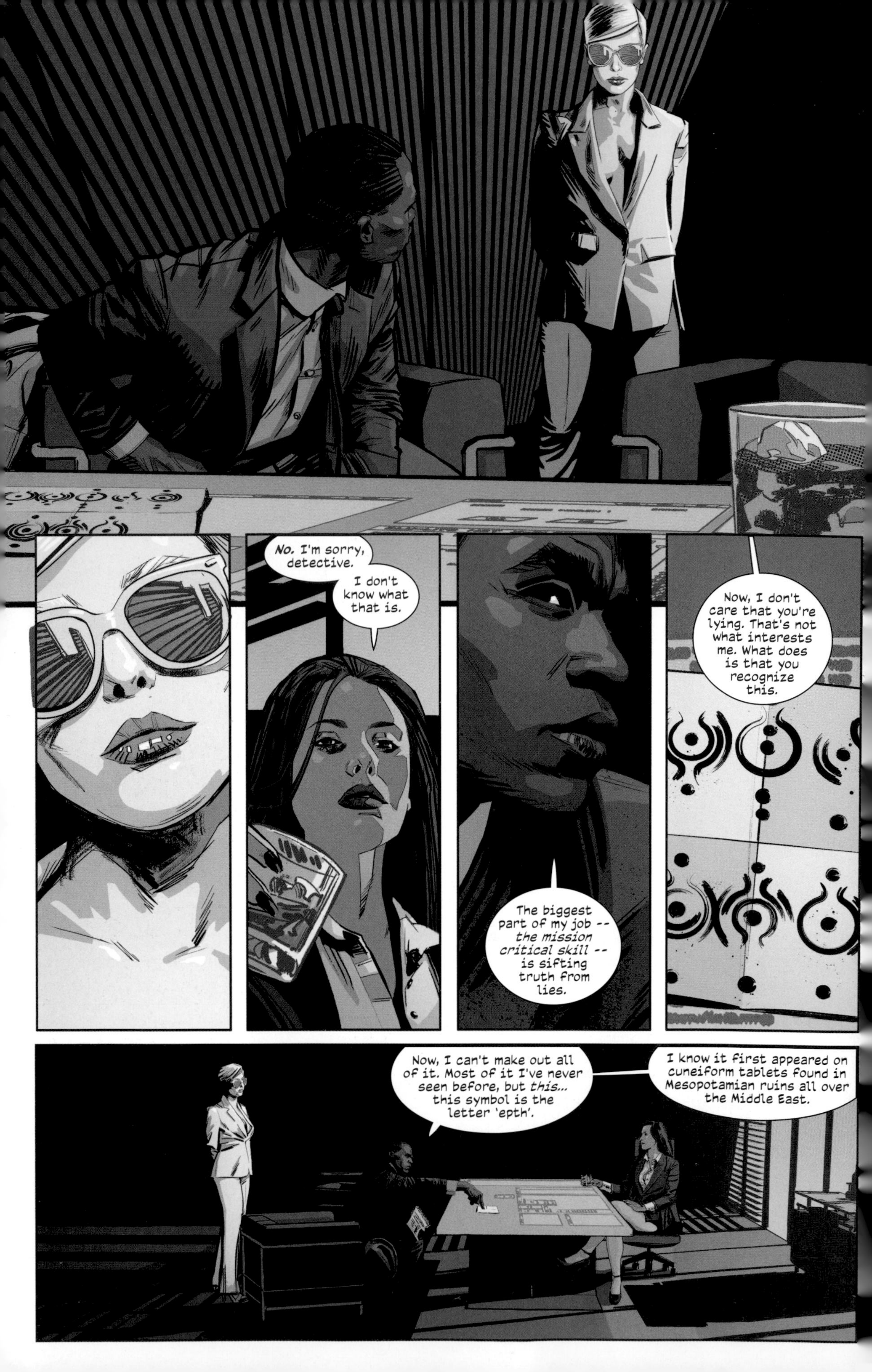

No. I'm sorry, detective.
I don't know what that is.
The biggest part of my job -- the mission critical skill -- is sifting truth from lies.
Now, I don't care that you're lying. That's not what interests me. What does is that you recognize this.
Now, I can't make out all of it. Most of it I've never seen before, but this... this symbol is the letter 'epth'.
I know it first appeared on cuneiform tablets found in Mesopotamian ruins all over the Middle East.

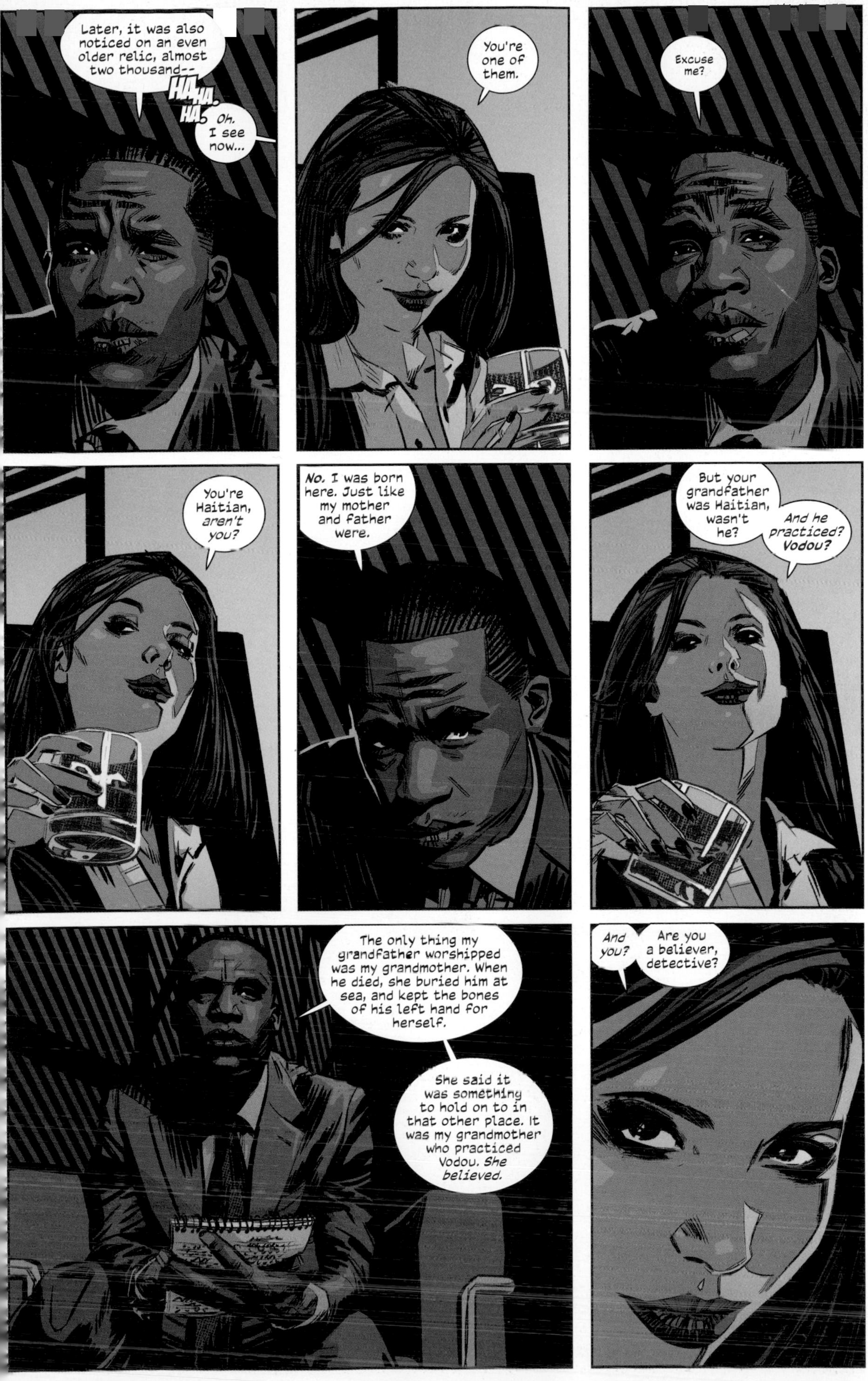
Later, it was also noticed on an even older relic, almost two thousand--
HAHAHA.
Oh. I see now...
You're one of them.
Excuse me?
You're Haitian, *aren't you?*
*No.* I was born here. Just like my mother and father were.
But your grandfather was Haitian, wasn't he?
*And he practiced? Vodou?*
The only thing my grandfather worshipped was my grandmother. When he died, she buried him at sea, and kept the bones of his left hand for herself.
She said it was something to hold on to in that other place. It was my grandmother who practiced Vodou. *She believed.*
*And you?*
Are you a believer, detective?

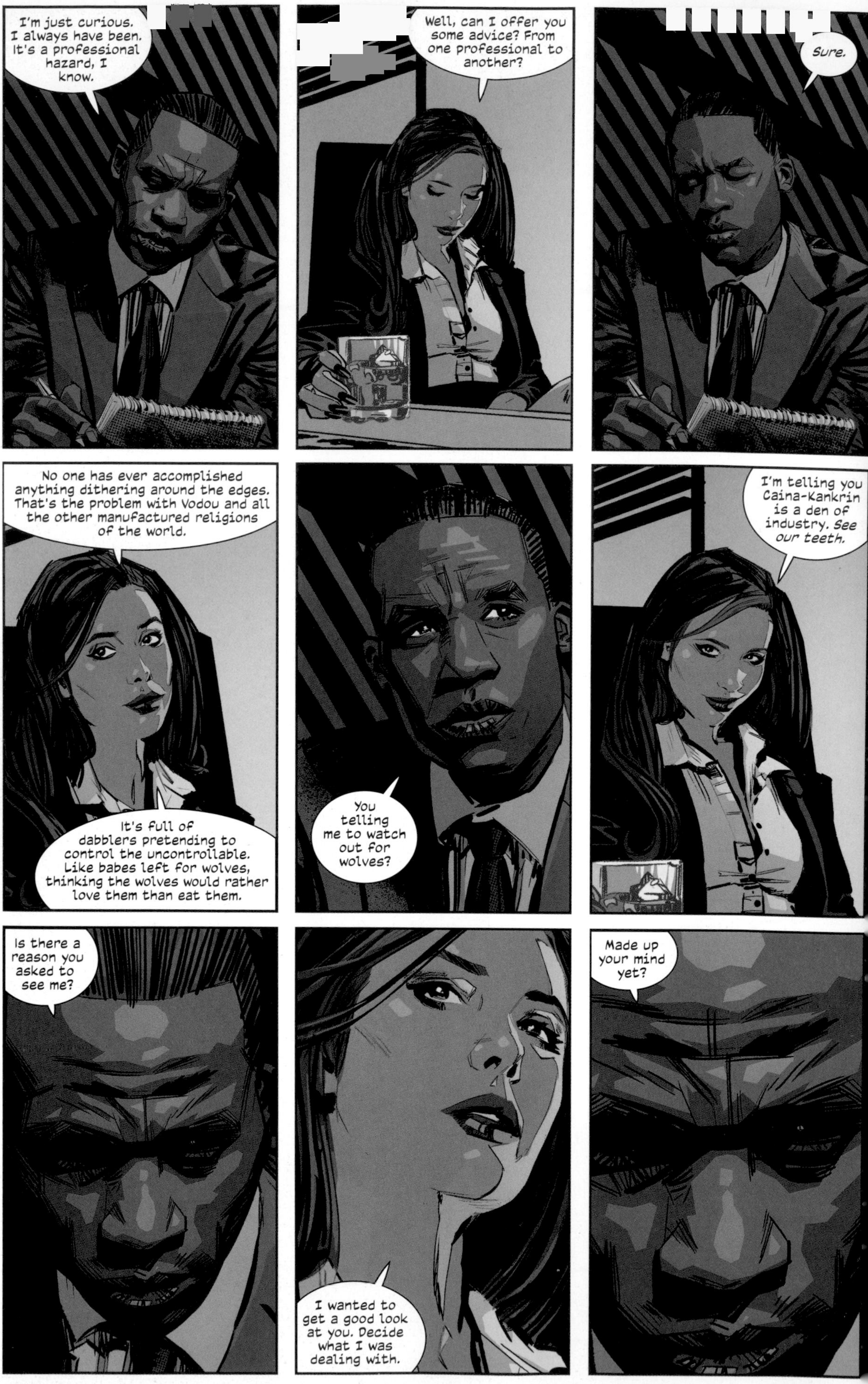
I'm just curious. I always have been. It's a professional hazard, I know.
Well, can I offer you some advice? From one professional to another?
Sure.
No one has ever accomplished anything dithering around the edges. That's the problem with Vodou and all the other manufactured religions of the world.
It's full of dabblers pretending to control the uncontrollable. Like babes left for wolves, thinking the wolves would rather love them than eat them.
You telling me to watch out for wolves?
I'm telling you Caina-Kankrin is a den of industry. *See our teeth.*
Is there a reason you asked to see me?
I wanted to get a good look at you. Decide what I was dealing with.
Made up your mind yet?

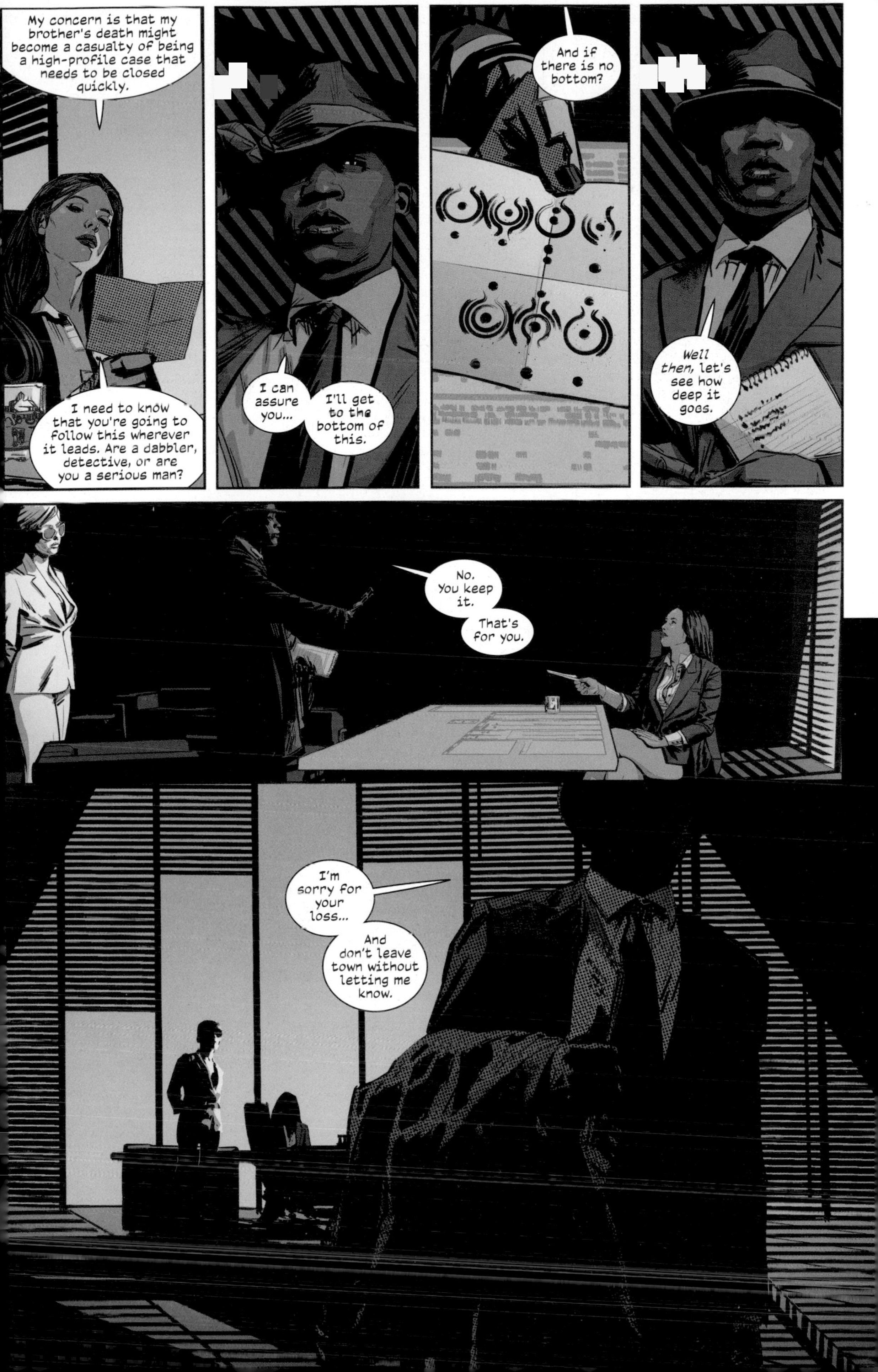
My concern is that my brother's death might become a casualty of being a high-profile case that needs to be closed quickly.
I need to know that you're going to follow this wherever it leads. Are a dabbler, detective, or are you a serious man?
I can assure you...
I'll get to the bottom of this.
And if there is no bottom?
Well then, let's see how deep it goes.
No. You keep it.
That's for you.
I'm sorry for your loss...
And don't leave town without letting me know.

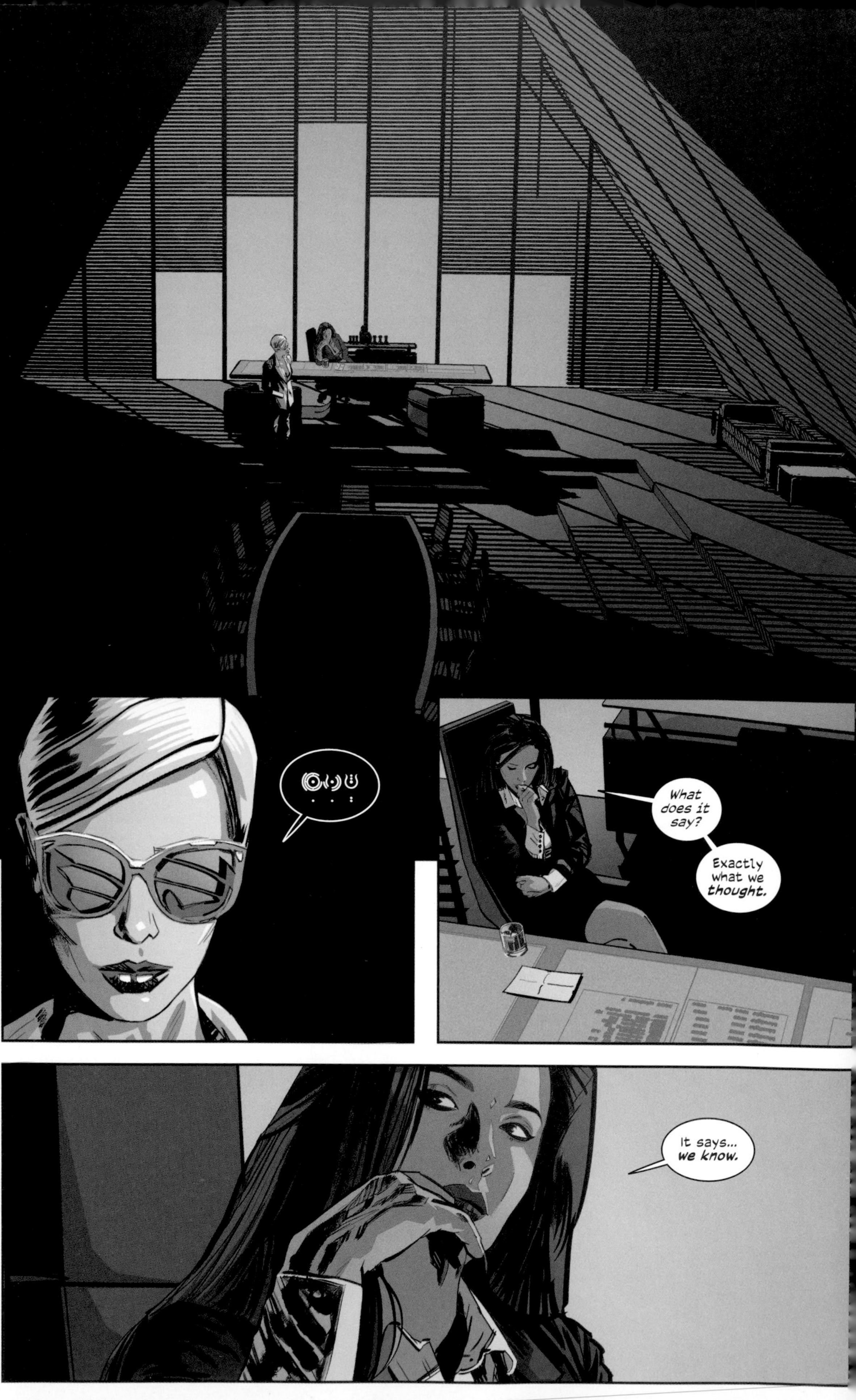
What does it say?
Exactly what we *thought.*
It says... *we know.*

I will never lie to you.

I'm the one you can trust.

- YES, THEY ARE SHARKS -

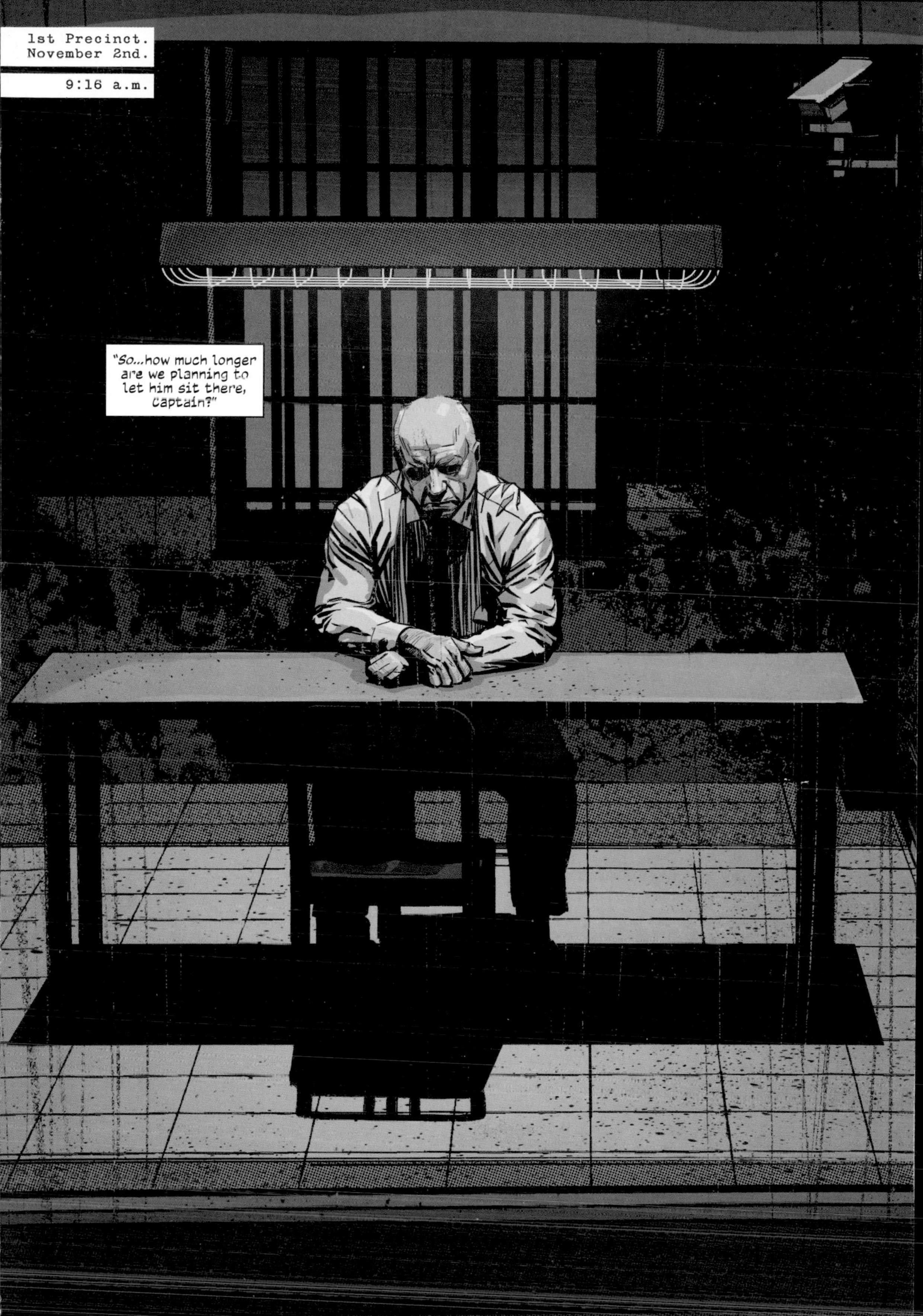
1st Precinct.
November 2nd.
9:16 a.m.
"So...how much longer are we planning to let him sit there, Captain?"

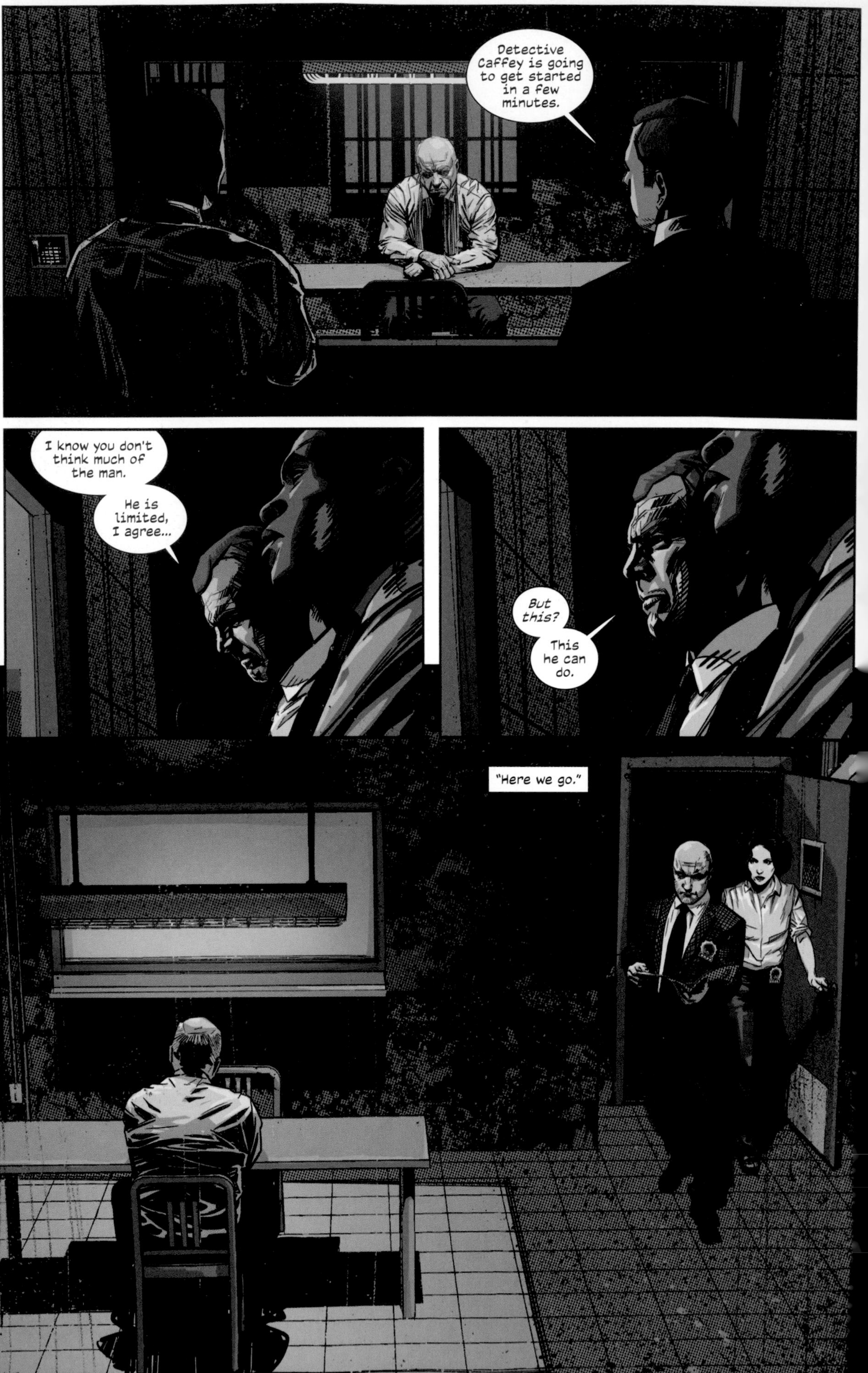
Detective Caffey is going to get started in a few minutes.
I know you don't think much of the man.
He is limited, I agree...
But this?
This he can do.
"Here we go."

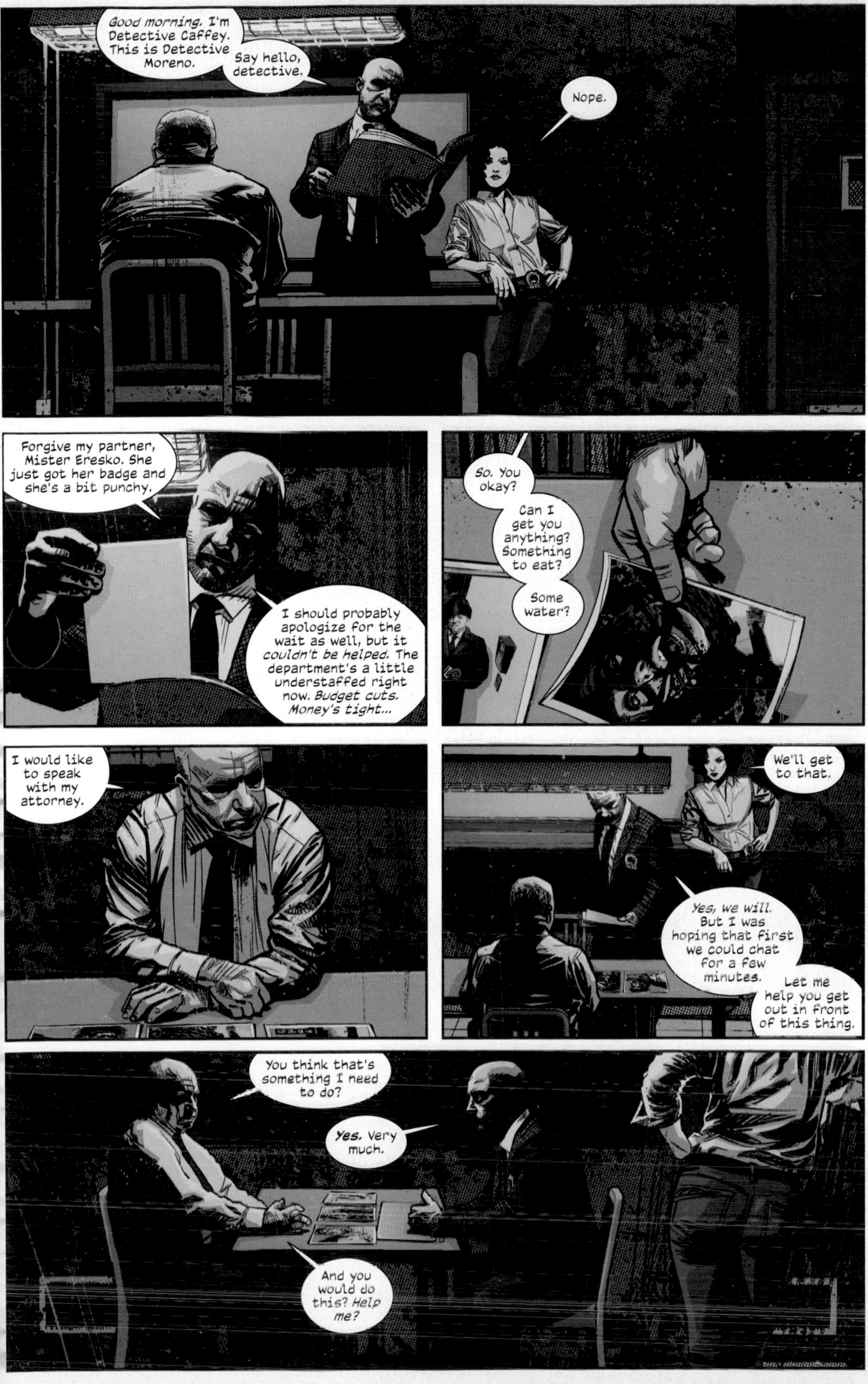
*Good morning.* I'm Detective Caffey. This is Detective Moreno.
Say hello, detective.
Nope.
Forgive my partner, Mister Eresko. She just got her badge and she's a bit punchy.
I should probably apologize for the wait as well, but it *couldn't be helped.* The department's a little understaffed right now. *Budget cuts. Money's tight...*
*So.* You okay?
Can I get you anything? Something to eat?
Some water?
I would like to speak with my attorney.
We'll get to that.
*Yes, we will.* But I was hoping that first we could chat for a few minutes.
Let me help you get out in front of this thing.
You think that's something I need to do?
*Yes.* Very much.
And you would do this? *Help me?*

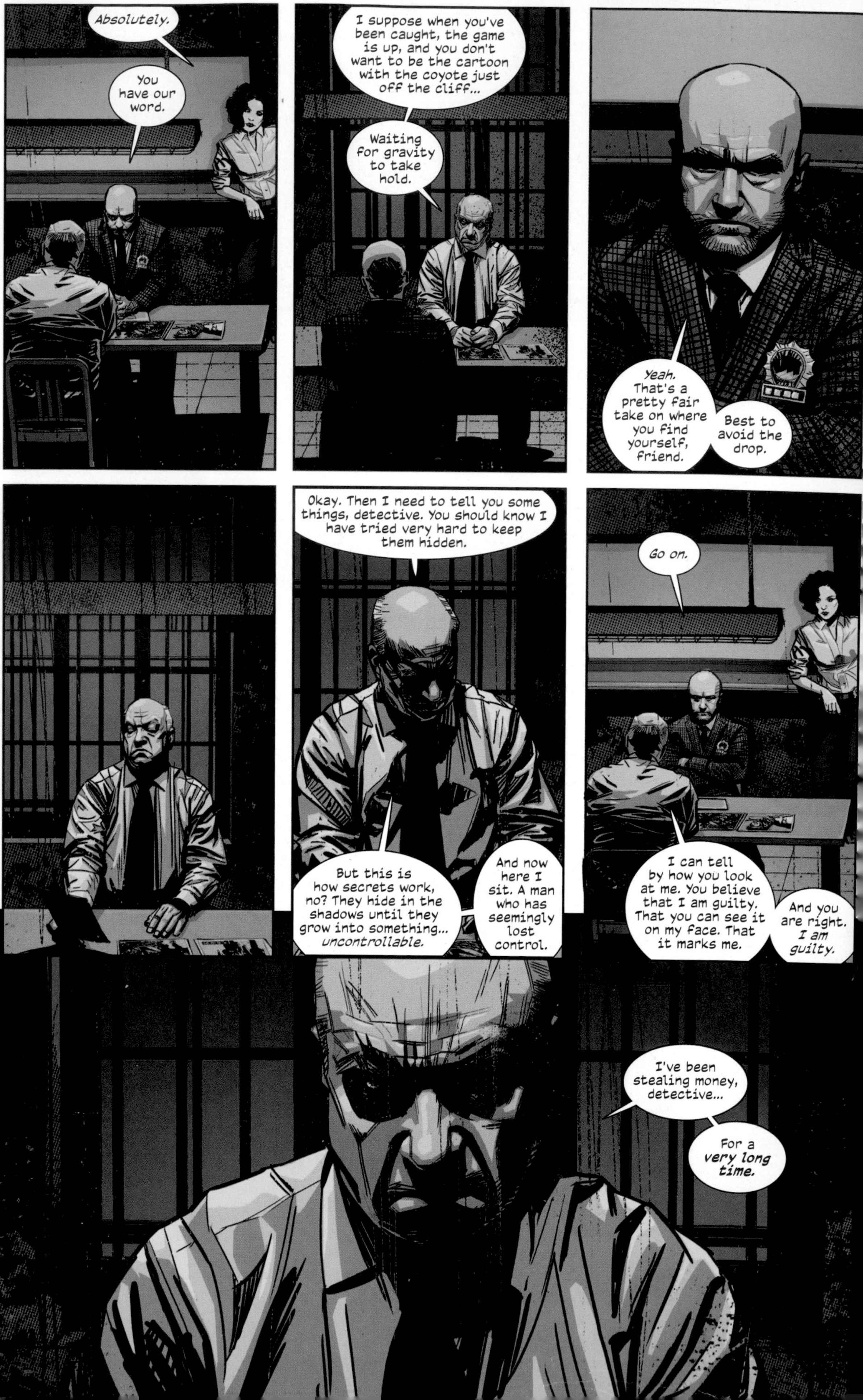
Absolutely.
You have our word.
I suppose when you've been caught, the game is up, and you don't want to be the cartoon with the coyote just off the cliff...
Waiting for gravity to take hold.
Yeah. That's a pretty fair take on where you find yourself, friend.
Best to avoid the drop.
Okay. Then I need to tell you some things, detective. You should know I have tried very hard to keep them hidden.
But this is how secrets work, no? They hide in the shadows until they grow into something... *uncontrollable.*
And now here I sit. A man who has seemingly lost control.
Go on.
I can tell by how you look at me. You believe that I am guilty. That you can see it on my face. That it marks me.
And you are right. *I am guilty.*
I've been stealing money, detective...
For a *very long time.*

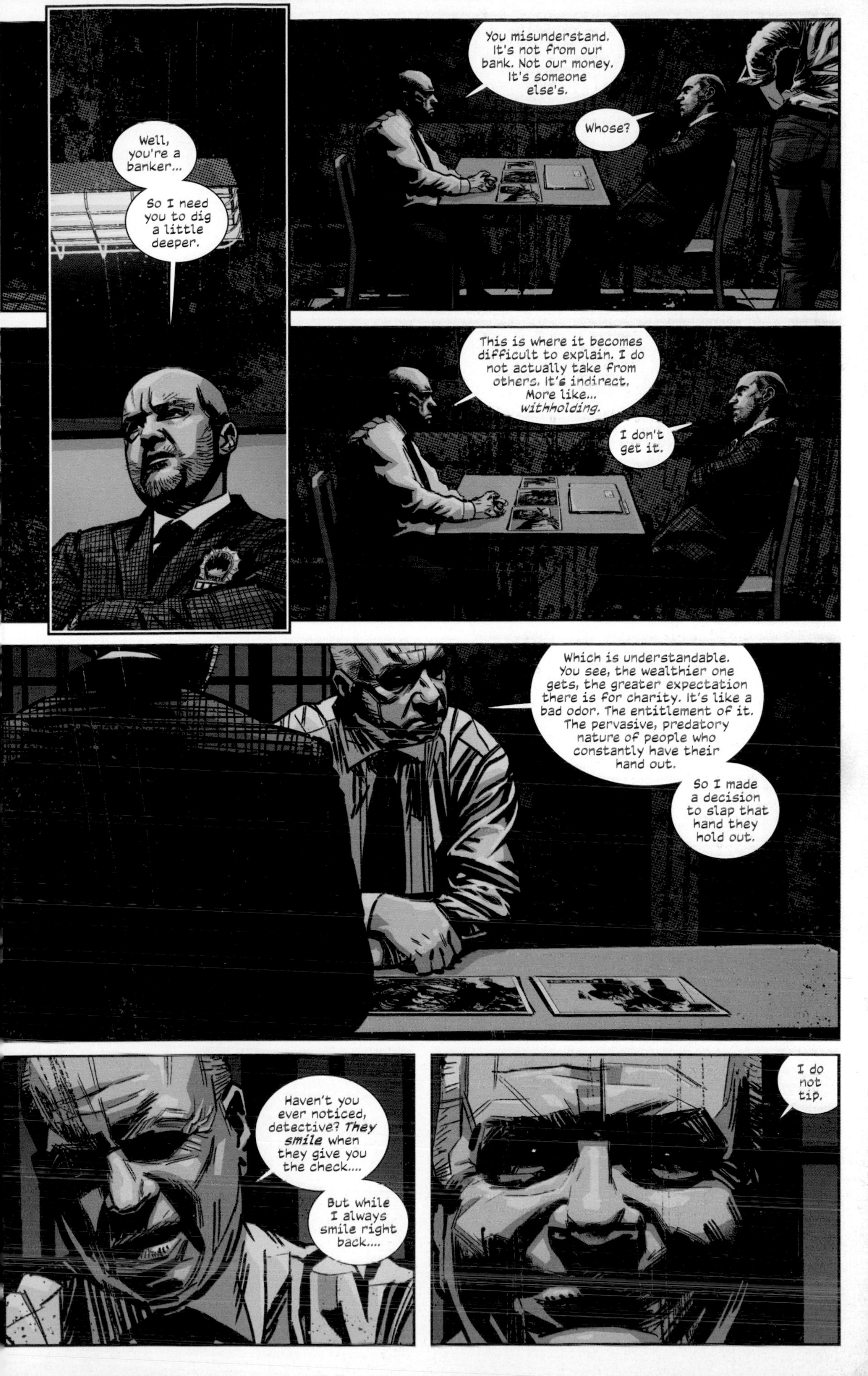

Well, you're a banker...
So I need you to dig a little deeper.
You misunderstand. It's not from our bank. Not our money. It's someone else's.
Whose?
This is where it becomes difficult to explain. I do not actually take from others. It's indirect. More like... withholding.
I don't get it.
Which is understandable. You see, the wealthier one gets, the greater expectation there is for charity. It's like a bad odor. The entitlement of it. The pervasive, predatory nature of people who constantly have their hand out.
So I made a decision to slap that hand they hold out.
Haven't you ever noticed, detective? They smile when they give you the check....
But while I always smile right back....
I do not tip.

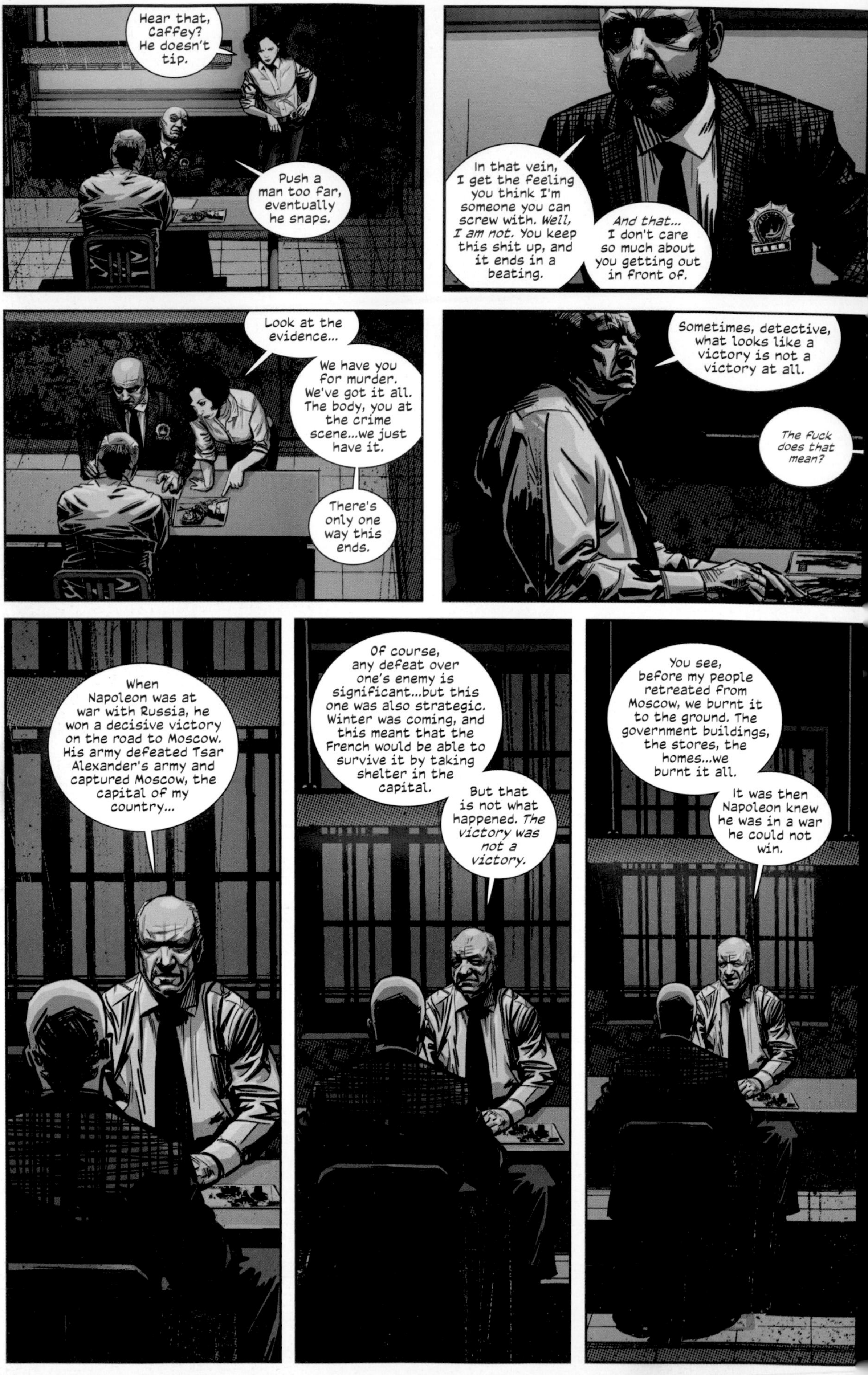
Hear that, Caffey? He doesn't tip.
Push a man too far, eventually he snaps.
In that vein, I get the feeling you think I'm someone you can screw with. *Well, I am not.* You keep this shit up, and it ends in a beating.
*And that...* I don't care so much about you getting out in front of.
Look at the evidence...
We have you for murder. We've got it all. The body, you at the crime scene...we just have it.
There's only one way this ends.
Sometimes, detective, what looks like a victory is not a victory at all.
*The fuck does that mean?*
When Napoleon was at war with Russia, he won a decisive victory on the road to Moscow. His army defeated Tsar Alexander's army and captured Moscow, the capital of my country...
Of course, any defeat over one's enemy is significant...but this one was also strategic. Winter was coming, and this meant that the French would be able to survive it by taking shelter in the capital.
But that is not what happened. *The victory was not a victory.*
You see, before my people retreated from Moscow, we burnt it to the ground. The government buildings, the stores, the homes...we burnt it all.
It was then Napoleon knew he was in a war he could not win.

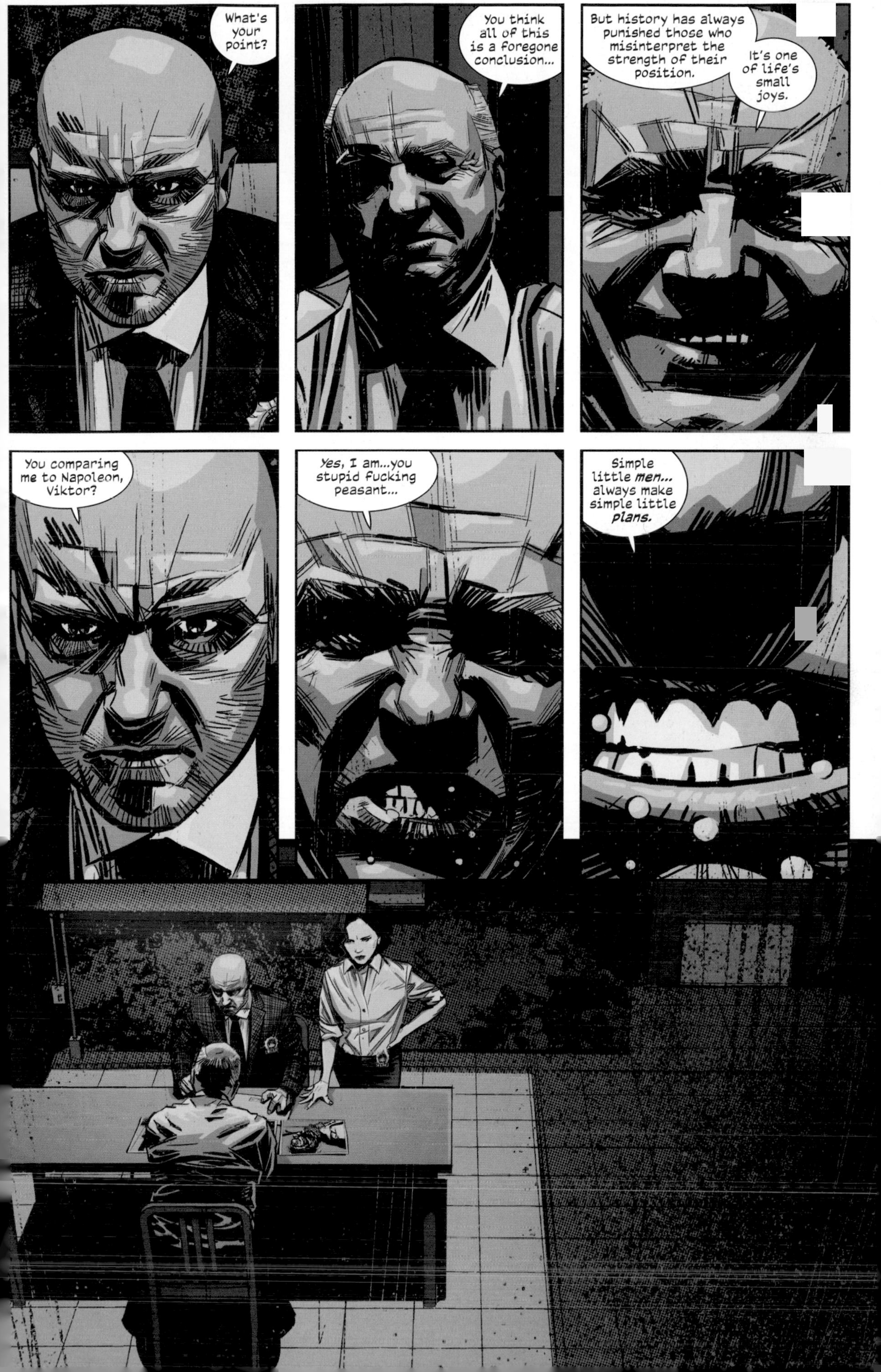
What's your point?
You think all of this is a foregone conclusion...
But history has always punished those who misinterpret the strength of their position.
It's one of life's small joys.
You comparing me to Napoleon, Viktor?
*Yes*, I am...you stupid fucking peasant...
Simple little *men*... always make simple little *plans*.

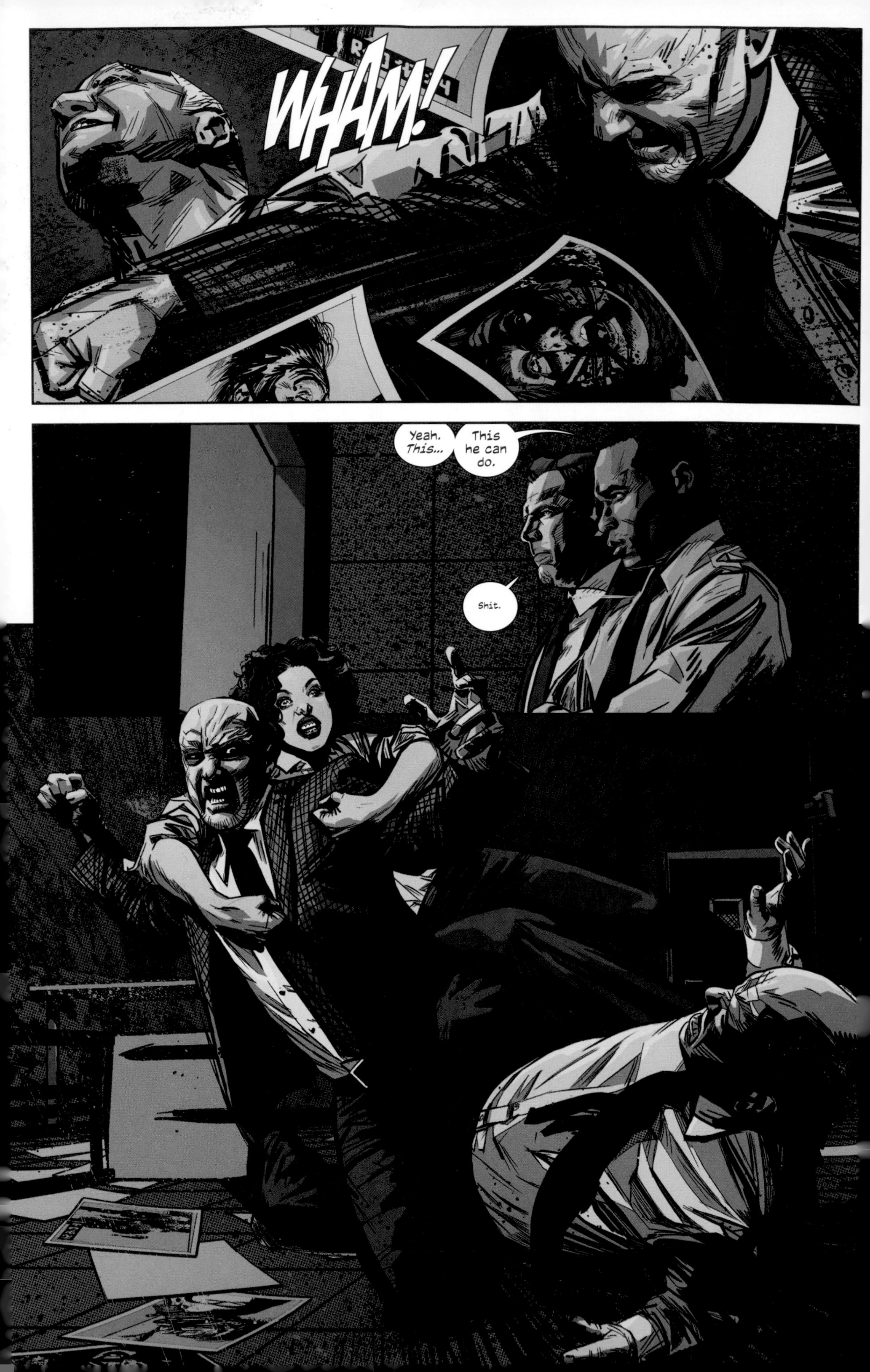
WHAM!
Yeah. This...
This he can do.
Shit.

- BUT AT LEAST THEY ARE OUR SHARKS -

CHAPTER THREE:

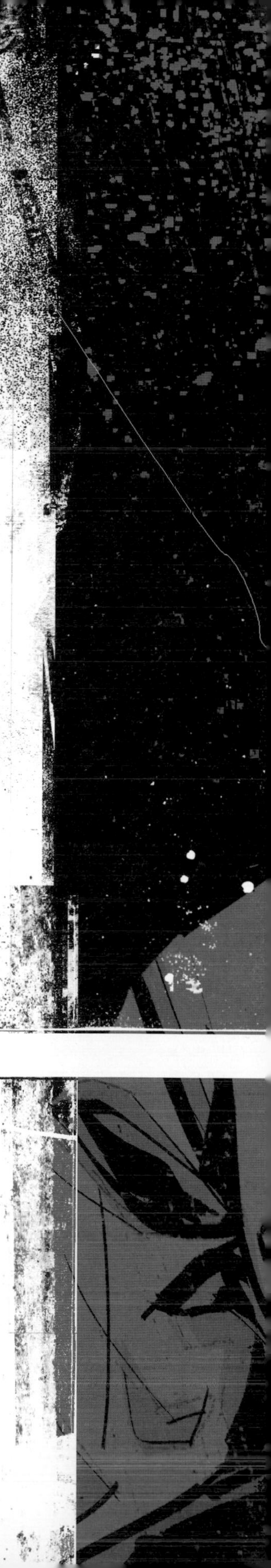

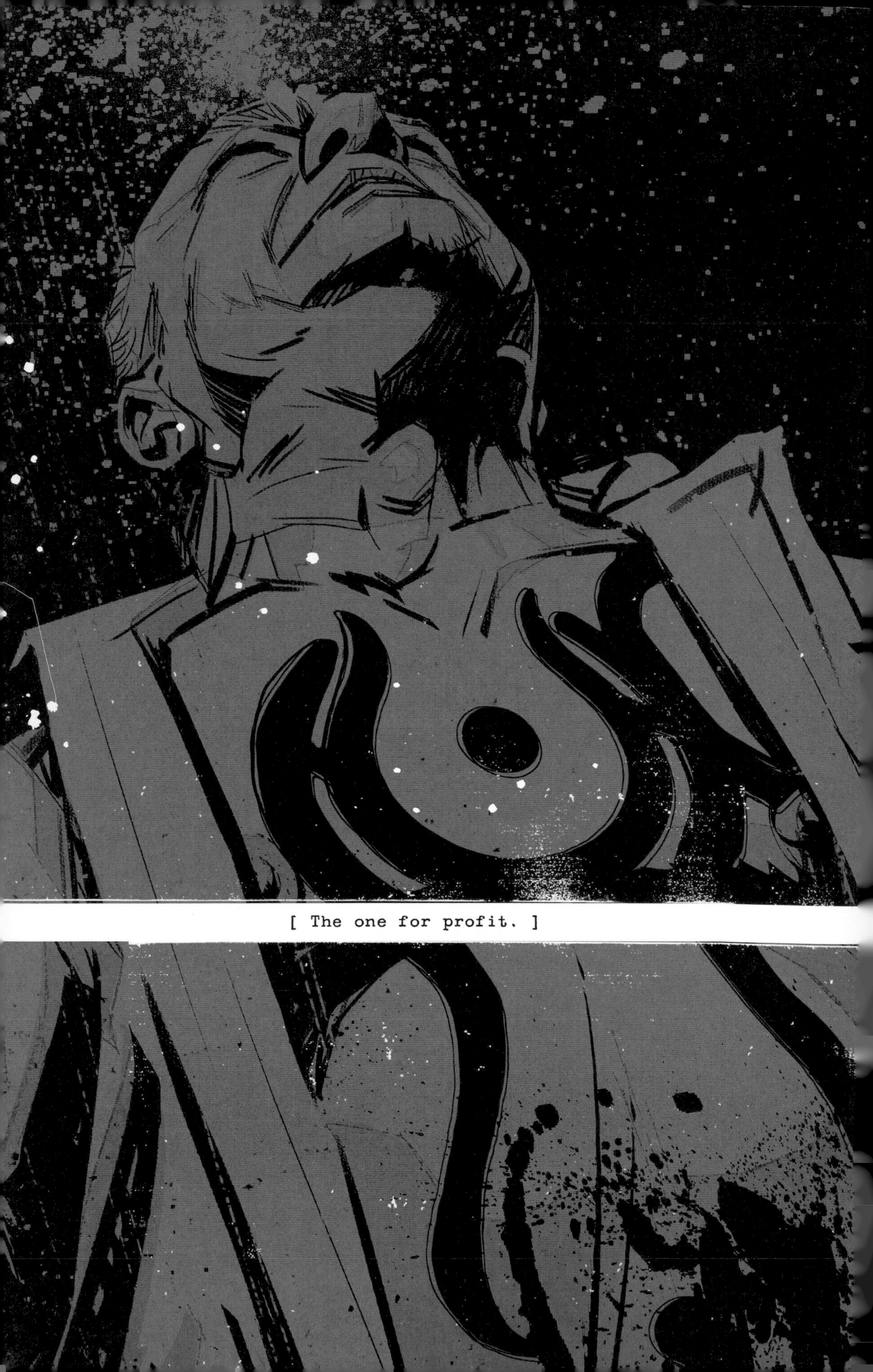
[ The one for profit. ]

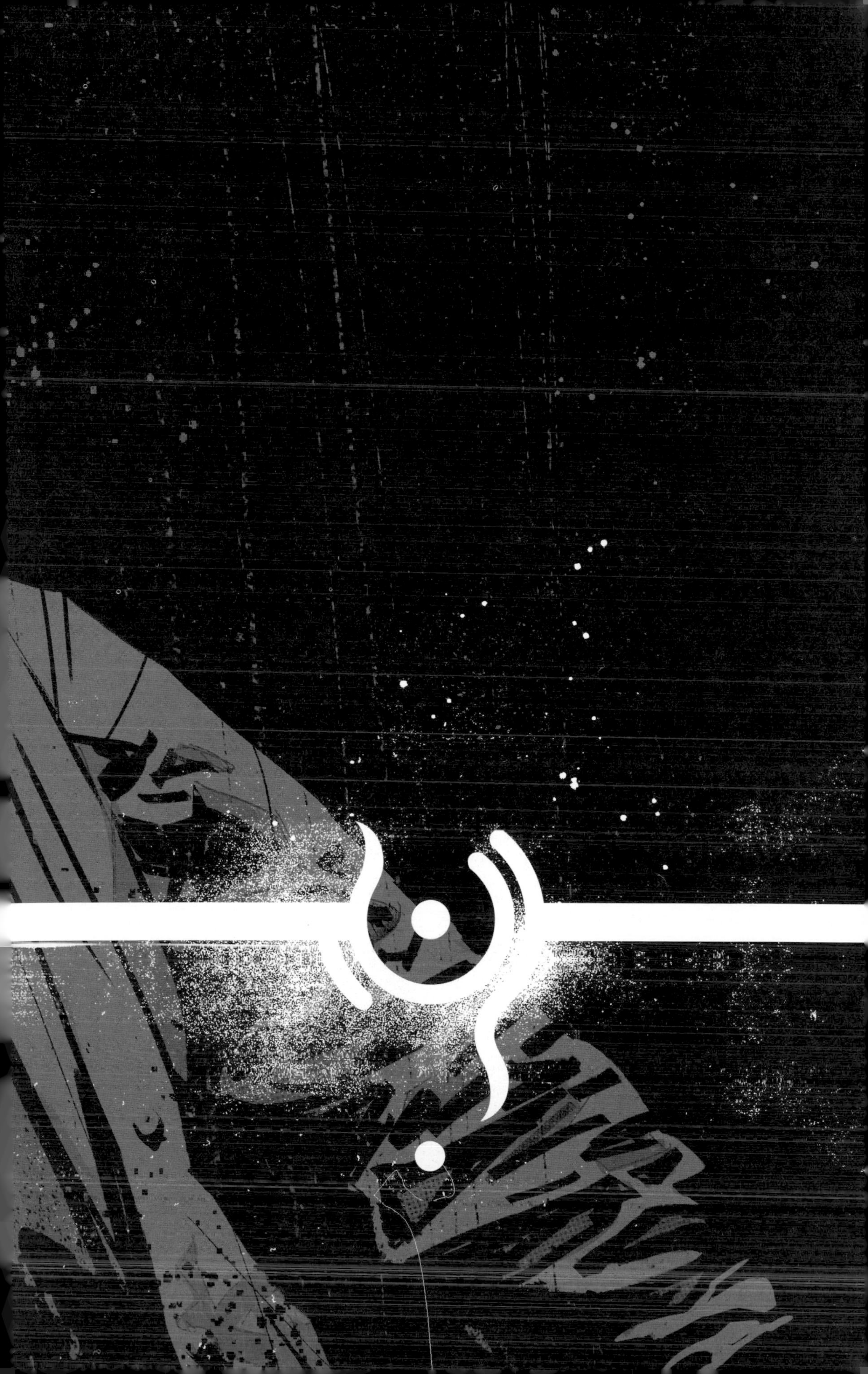

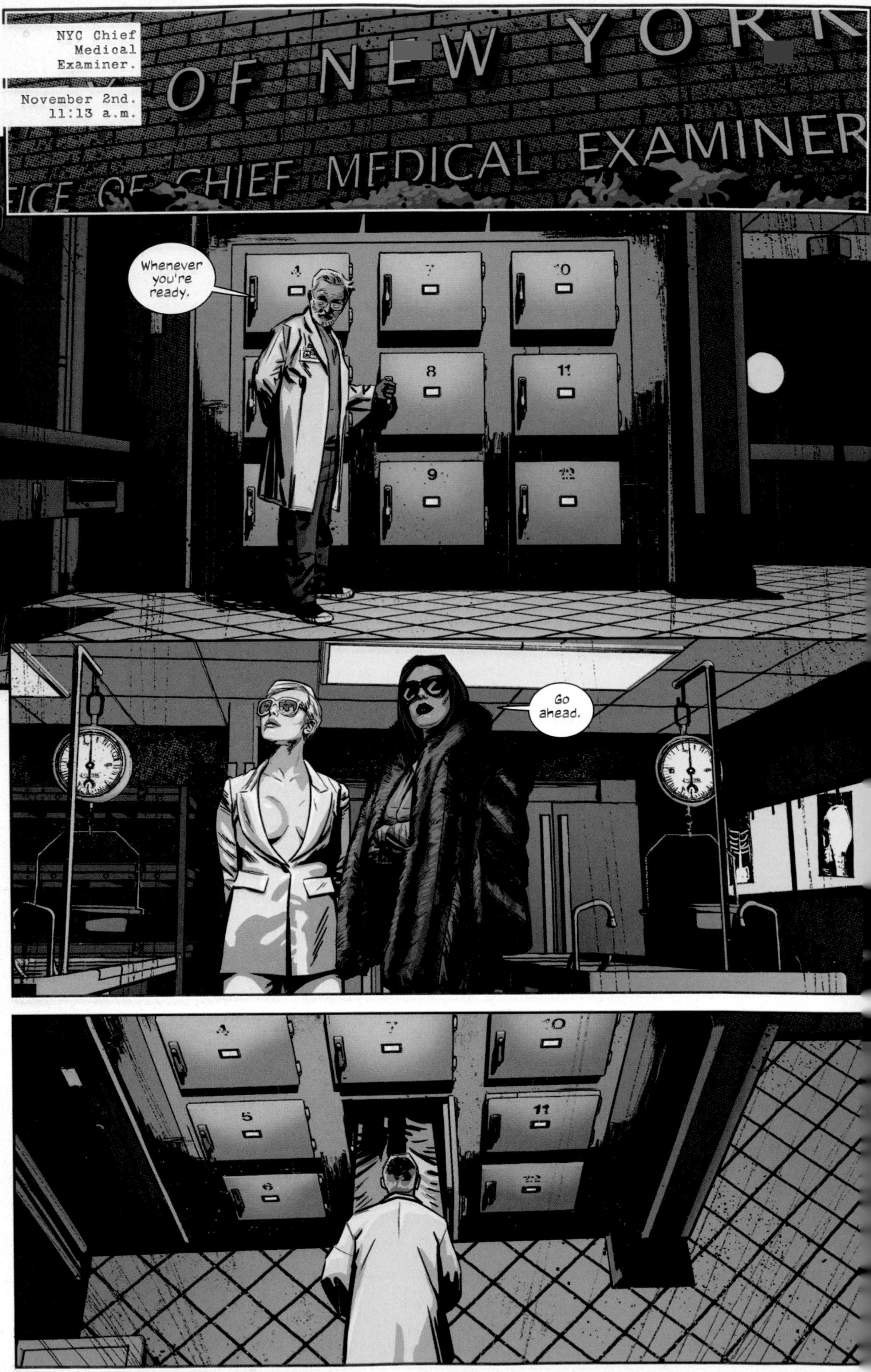
NYC Chief Medical Examiner.
November 2nd. 11:13 a.m.
OF NEW YORK
CHIEF MEDICAL EXAMINER
Whenever you're ready.
Go ahead.

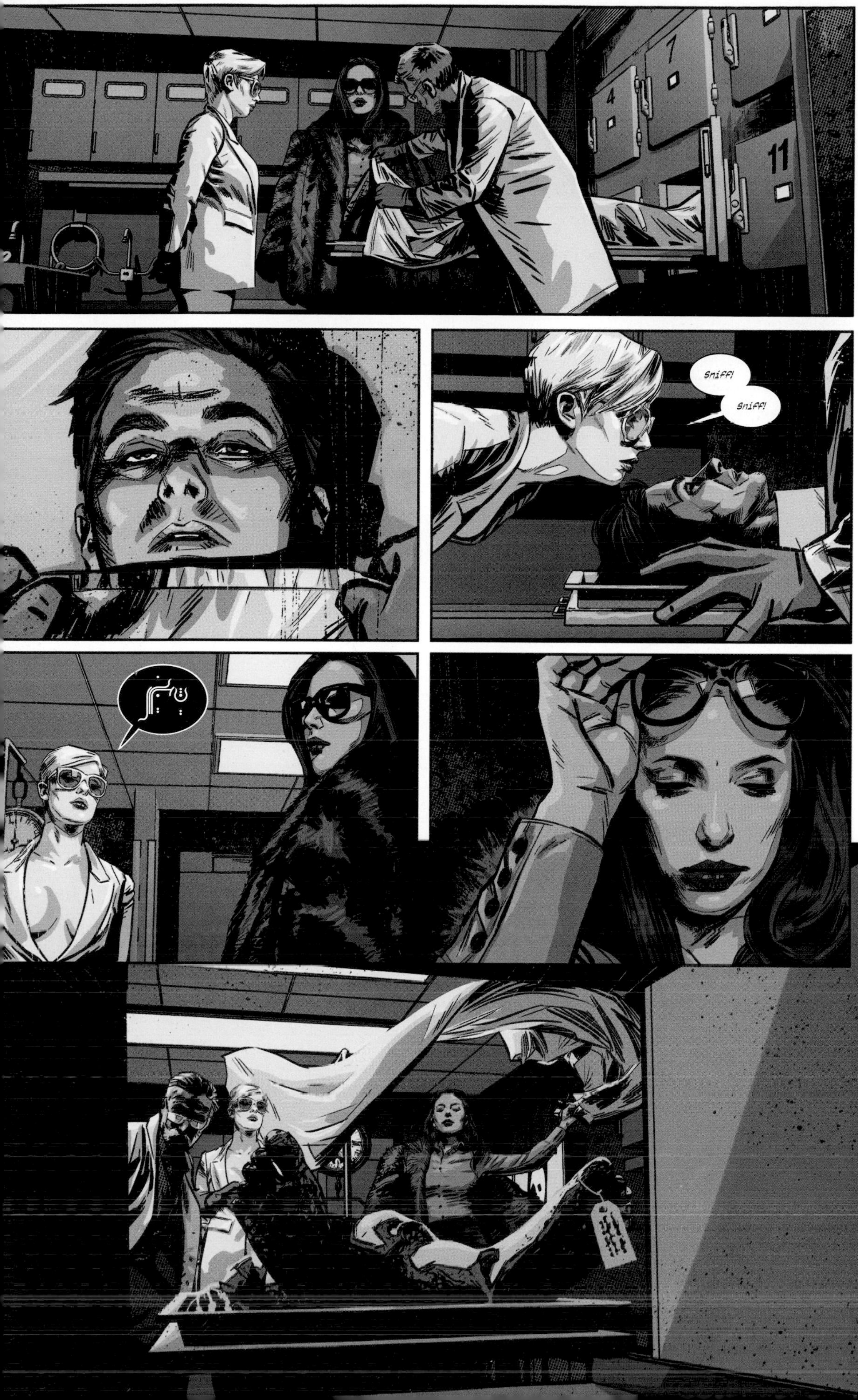
Sniff!
Sniff!

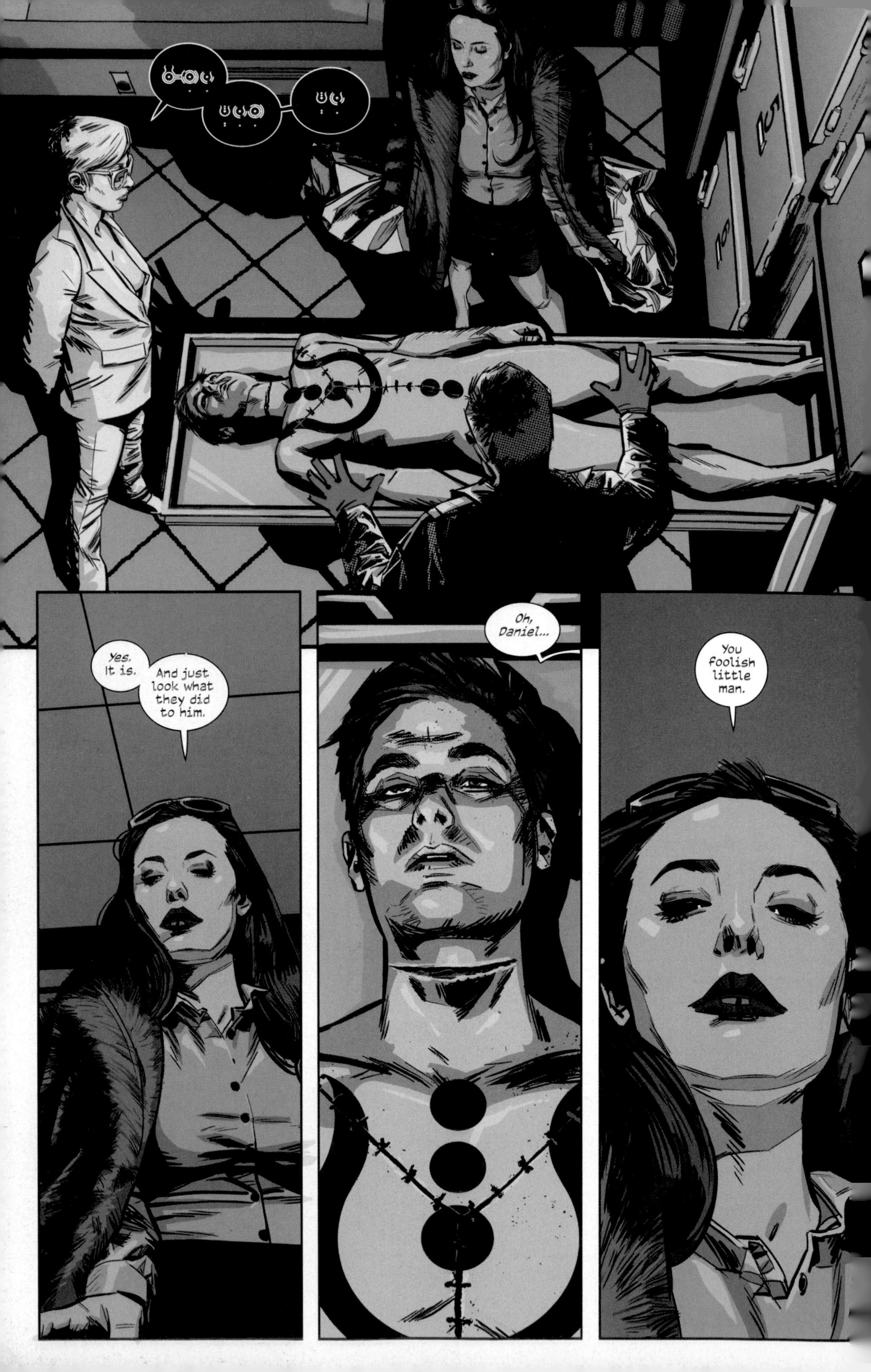
Yes. It is.
And just look what they did to him.
Oh, Daniel...
You foolish little man.

TRANSCRIPT

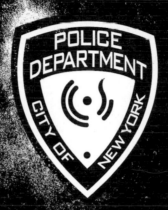

CASE#: 8923-62

CASE #: 8923-62

RECORDING DATE:     November 2nd, 2016

TIME OF RECORDING: 11:44 a.m.

RECORDED PARTIES:   Viktor Eresko.

                    Andrew Wright.

TRANSCRIBED BY:     R. Morgan.

001    (Recording begins)

002

003    ANDREW WRIGHT: Mister Eresko.

004

005    VIKTOR ERESKO: Yes?

006

007    ANDREW WRIGHT: Mister Eresko, I'm chief counsel for--

008

009    VIKTOR ERESKO: I know who you are. Why are you here?

010

011    ANDREW WRIGHT: I'm here for...well, it's obvious, isn't it?

012                   I'm here on your behalf. I'm representing

013                   you.

014

015    VIKTOR ERESKO: You do not represent me.

016

017    ANDREW WRIGHT: I represent your best interests.

018

019    VIKTOR ERESKO: And there we have a problem, don't we? Your

020                   idea of what is in my best interests very

021                   likely runs contrary to mine. Of course,

022                   there's also the issue of you not actually

023                   being my attorney at all.

(b,c,d)
(e,f)

(g)

```
024   ANDREW WRIGHT: Normally, no. No, I'm not. Most certainly

025                 not. But your personal lawyer, Mister Popov,

026                 won't be coming. That's been seen to.

027

028   VIKTOR ERESKO: It has?

029

030   ANDREW WRIGHT: Yes.

031

032   VIKTOR ERESKO: So you are all I have.

033

034   ANDREW WRIGHT: That's correct. Only me, and no one else

035                 coming. That's the reality of your current

036                 situation, Mister Eresko. So let me help you.

037                 Let's help each other.

038

039   VIKTOR ERESKO: If I choose not to?

040

041   ANDREW WRIGHT: That's not an option.

042

043   VIKTOR ERESKO: (Laughs.)

044

045   ANDREW WRIGHT: They're not going to wait. You know how this

046                 works, pieces are already being moved. Plans

047                 set in motion.

048

049   VIKTOR ERESKO: (Laughs.)

050

051   ANDREW WRIGHT: I don't understand...

052

053   VIKTOR ERESKO: People always assume they are the only ones

054                 making plans.

055
```

056   ANDREW WRIGHT: Well, laugh all you want, Mister Eresko, but

057                 I promise you, there is nothing amusing about

058                 your situation.

059

060   VIKTOR ERESKO: Oh, there are many things I find amusing

061                 about my current situation. You thinking that

062                 I need help -- your help -- is one of them.

063

064   ANDREW WRIGHT: You think you can go this alone? Handle it

065                 all by yourself?

066

067   VIKTOR ERESKO: Yes.

068

069   ANDREW WRIGHT: You're sitting in jail.

070

071   VIKTOR ERESKO: I am biding my time. Staring at the pot while

072                 the water gets warm.

073

074   ANDREW WRIGHT: Mister Eresko. Viktor. I have seen the

075                 evidence they have. Your short-term situation

076                 is not...manageable. They have you. They just

077                 do. What you need now is someone who can

078                 navigate your situation. Prolong the process

079                 until more favorable conditions present

080                 themselves. That's what you need. What the

081                 firm needs is someone who understands the

082                 broader, unspoken concerns of the board. I

083                 can do both, so please let me.

084

085   VIKTOR ERESKO: I need to know who sent you.

086

087   ANDREW WRIGHT: Excuse me?

(a)

VIKTOR ERESKO: Who sent you here? Who told you to come?

ANDREW WRIGHT: You know who sent me. I am Caina-Kankrin's chief counsel. I serve at the pleasure of the board, and as I'm sure you've guessed, your situation concerns all of them. So here I am.

VIKTOR ERESKO: So you were summoned before the entire board?

ANDREW WRIGHT: No. That's not what...Mrs. Bischoff requested that I come.

VIKTOR ERESKO: No one else?

ANDREW WRIGHT: I didn't speak to anyone else.

VIKTOR ERESKO: Then she was only acting out of her position. It's a predictable response from the Watcher seat.

ANDREW WRIGHT: [redacted] (a)

VIKTOR ERESKO: [redacted] (b,c)

ANDREW WRIGHT: [redacted] (d)

VIKTOR ERESKO: [redacted]

(b,c,d)
(e,f)

(g)

(a)

ANDREW WRIGHT: [redacted]

VIKTOR ERESKO: [redacted] You should know this.

ANDREW WRIGHT: Well, I...I don't.

VIKTOR ERESKO: Then congratulations, Mister Wright. Today you have learned something about how much you are valued. Don't let it trouble you, it's better that you don't know.

ANDREW WRIGHT: What else do I not know?

VIKTOR ERESKO: I don't think we have that kind of time. You were not chief counsel when I last sat on the board. You were hired in, what, the first quarter of last year?

ANDREW WRIGHT: Yes. March.

VIKTOR ERESKO: Do you know what happened to your predecessor?

ANDREW WRIGHT: He retired.

VIKTOR ERESKO: That's one way to put it.

ANDREW WRIGHT: It's the only way to put it.

VIKTOR ERESKO: If you say it is so, then it must be. But Beatrix Bischoff sent you here to assess the situation and report back to her. It's what

(b,c,d)
(e,f)

(g)

```
152   VIKTOR ERESKO:   the Watcher does. They measure the coming and
153   (cont.)          going of things that have value. Information
154                    being one of them. So, only after you report
155                    -- after you provide them with more
156                    information -- will the board decide on a
157                    course of action. This is how it is done. How
158                    it always has been done. I have confused
159                    them, and so their actions lean toward
160                    conservation. These people, they offer me no
161                    surprises.
162
163   ANDREW WRIGHT:   I'm not sure that's an accurate--
164
165   VIKTOR ERESKO:   Please. Do not represent that you know more
166                    than you do. This has been a long time
167                    coming, and I have left nothing to chance.
168
169   ANDREW WRIGHT:   You need to be very careful with what you
170                    say.
171
172   VIKTOR ERESKO:   So do you, Mister Wright. You are here to
173                    judge me, to determine if the situation can
174                    be controlled. I take it you have formed
175                    something of an opinion at this point?
176
177   ANDREW WRIGHT:   I have the germ of an evolving idea.
178
179   VIKTOR ERESKO:   And?
180
181   ANDREW WRIGHT:   You want my professional opinion?
182
183   VIKTOR ERESKO:   Yes.
```

(b,c,d)
(e,f)

(g)

184   ANDREW WRIGHT: You're arrogant. Even when you find yourself

185               on uneven ground. What I think is that you

186               need both a bit in your mouth and to be

187               brought to heel.

188

189   VIKTOR ERESKO: Search the whole world twice over, and you

190               will never find a man capable of that job.

191

192   ANDREW WRIGHT: (Inaudible.)

193

194   VIKTOR ERESKO: (Laughs.)

195

196   ANDREW WRIGHT: If you want me to leave, just ask.

197

198   VIKTOR ERESKO: No. Stay. I have a point to make, and I've

199               figured out a use for you.

200

201   ANDREW WRIGHT: Well, if you're growing open to counsel--

202

203   VIKTOR ERESKO: No. I've already told you, you are not my

204               attorney. You represent Caina. As it exists

205               now.

206

207   ANDREW WRIGHT: Now? You see it changing soon?

208

209   VIKTOR ERESKO: I see that uneven ground you spoke of opening

210               beneath us, and Mammon getting his due.

211

212   ANDREW WRIGHT: (Inaudible.)

213

214   ANDREW WRIGHT: What do you want me to do?

215

216 VIKTOR ERESKO: This is what is going to happen. I want you
217 to summon another detective in here so that
218 you can offer a statement on my behalf. After
219 that, they will offer me a deal, and after
220 that, I will walk out of here.
221

222 ANDREW WRIGHT: I'm not going to do that until I know what
223 happened. I would be an idiot to let that
224 happen without knowing everything you're
225 going to say.
226

227 VIKTOR ERESKO: And this is what you want to know? What
228 happened?
229

230 ANDREW WRIGHT: You think I should start somewhere else?
231

232 VIKTOR ERESKO: I do not know. Do you really want to know
233 what happened, or would you rather know how
234 I'm going to get away with it?
235

236 ANDREW WRIGHT: I think I need to know the first thing before
237 I can be sure of the second. Okay?
238

239 VIKTOR ERESKO: Okay.
240

241 ANDREW WRIGHT: Well, then. Go ahead. Let's hear it.
242

243 VIKTOR ERESKO: ████████████████████████████
244 ████████████████████████████
245 ████████████████████████████
246 ████████████████████████████
247 ████████████████████████

(a)

VIKTOR ERESKO: (cont.) [redacted] you [redacted] will [redacted] never [redacted] understand [redacted] what I [redacted] really [redacted] am [redacted]

ANDREW WRIGHT: Shit.

VIKTOR ERESKO: Yes.

ANDREW WRIGHT: Shit. Did that really...shit. I can't believe...

VIKTOR ERESKO: There's one thing I do well, Mister Wright -- make believers out of those who do not.

(b,c,d)
(e,f)

(g)

280     ANDREW WRIGHT: You understand what this means, don't you?

281                    You're not leaving them any choice.

282

283     VIKTOR ERESKO: I am putting them to a choice, Mister Wright.

284                    There's a difference.

285

286     ANDREW WRIGHT: Still. I don't see how this helps you with--

287

288     VIKTOR ERESKO: You have to hear the rest before you make

289                    that determination.

290

291     ANDREW WRIGHT: What?

292

293     VIKTOR ERESKO: The rest. I want to tell you what happens

294                    next. How I get away with it.

295

296     ANDREW WRIGHT: I honestly don't know how you're going to do

297                    that.

298

299     VIKTOR ERESKO: It's simple, really. It's the way these

300                    things are always done. You defeat a truth

301                    with a greater truth. A lie, with a greater

302                    lie.

303

304     ANDREW WRIGHT: And which is this?

305

306     VIKTOR ERESKO: Listen. Then I want you to try and tell

307                    me which it is. Can you do that?

308

309     ANDREW WRIGHT: Yes.

310

311     VIKTOR ERESKO: ██████████████████████████████████

(a)

VIKTOR ERESKO: (cont.) [redacted] see [redacted] the [redacted] blood [redacted] pouring [redacted] from my [redacted] mouth [redacted] dripping [redacted] down [redacted] my [redacted] chin [redacted]

ANDREW WRIGHT: (Inaudible.)

VIKTOR ERESKO: Well?

ANDREW WRIGHT: It's...it...that just might work.

VIKTOR ERESKO: I think so.

ANDREW WRIGHT: Where are they now? Wait. Don't tell me. I don't want to know. But, that's...that's perfect.

VIKTOR ERESKO: So, which was it, Mister Wright? A truth or a lie?

(b,c,d)
(e,f)

(g

344  ANDREW WRIGHT: It's perfect. Too perfect, really. So it has

345               to be a lie. But the more I think about it,

346               it's still going to work because it eats all

347               the evidence.

348

349  VIKTOR ERESKO: Yes.

350

351  ANDREW WRIGHT: Okay. I'm going to ask for a detective now. I

352               want you to promise me that you'll let me do

353               the talking. We'll get through this as

354               quickly as we can, and get you out of here.

355               Then we'll move on to the more important

356               matters at hand. Can you do that?

357

358  VIKTOR ERESKO: I will consider it.

359

360  ANDREW WRIGHT: You should. Because this is the easy part,

361               you know? The board, they're going to have

362               questions that will be a bit harder to lie

363               about.

364

365  VIKTOR ERESKO: Oh, for Caina-Kankrin, I will offer only the

366               truth.

367

368  ANDREW WRIGHT: I think that's a bad idea.

369

370  VIKTOR ERESKO: I cared very little for what you thought when

371               you walked in this room, Mister Wright. I

372               care even less now. That bit you were talking

373               about earlier? I want you to bite down on it.

374

375  ANDREW WRIGHT: (Inaudible.) I'll get the detective.

(b,c,d)
(e,f)

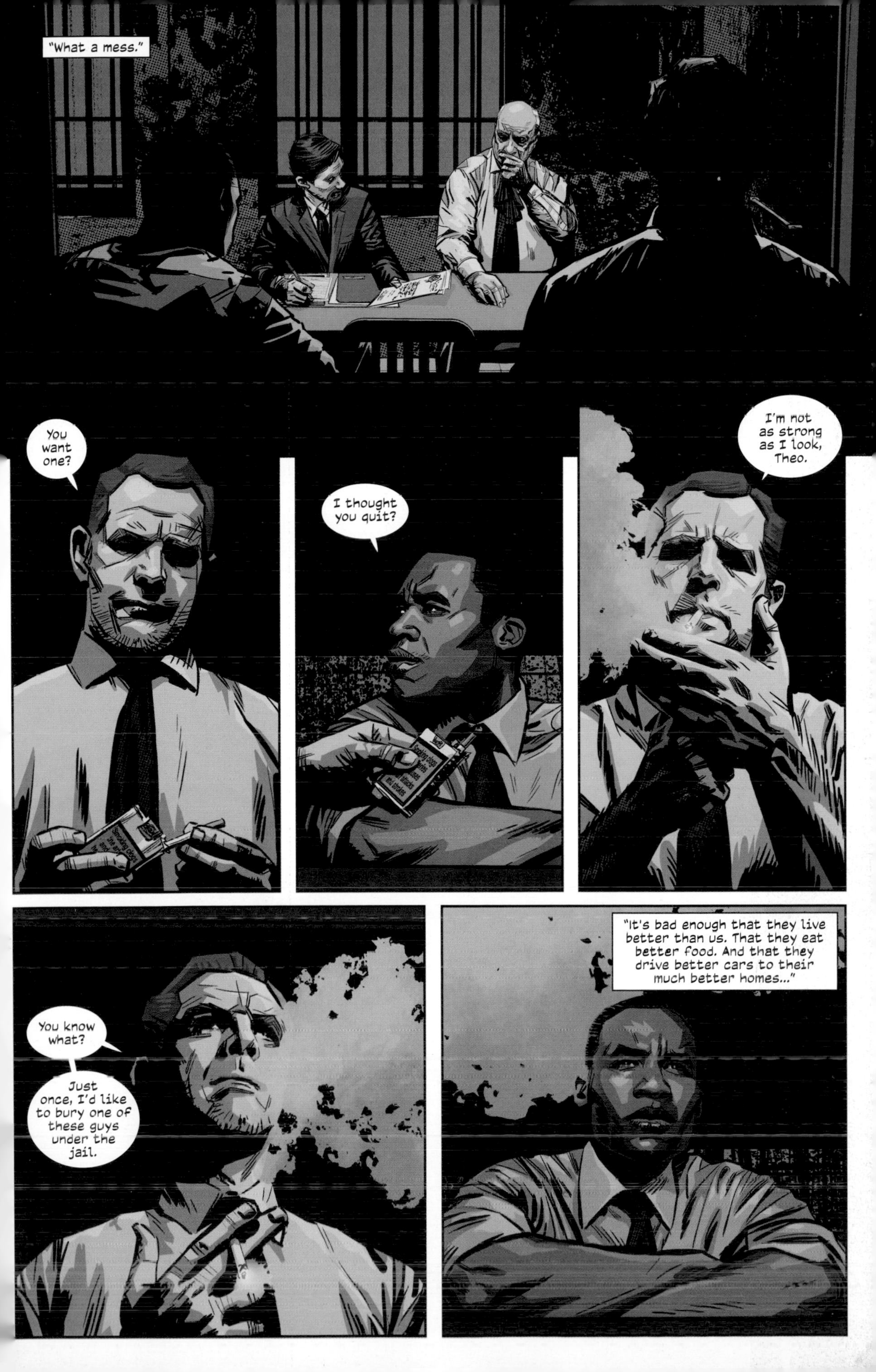
"What a mess."
You want one?
I thought you quit?
I'm not as strong as I look, Theo.
You know what?
Just once, I'd like to bury one of these guys under the jail.
"It's bad enough that they live better than us. That they eat better food. And that they drive better cars to their much better homes..."

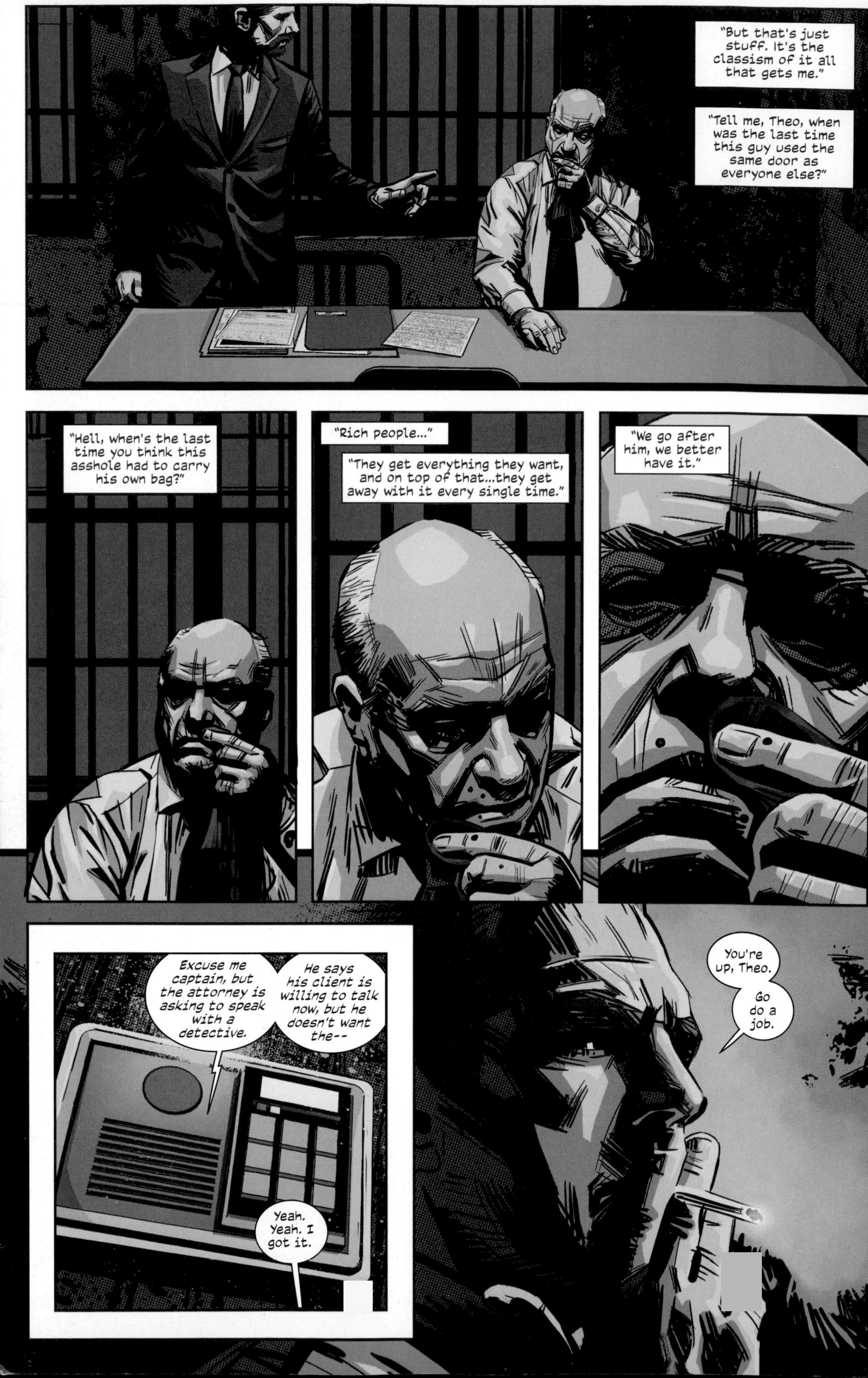
"But that's just stuff. It's the classism of it all that gets me."
"Tell me, Theo, when was the last time this guy used the same door as everyone else?"
"Hell, when's the last time you think this asshole had to carry his own bag?"
"Rich people..."
"They get everything they want, and on top of that...they get away with it every single time."
"We go after him, we better have it."
Excuse me captain, but the attorney is asking to speak with a detective.
He says his client is willing to talk now, but he doesn't want the--
Yeah. Yeah. I got it.
You're up, Theo.
Go do a job.

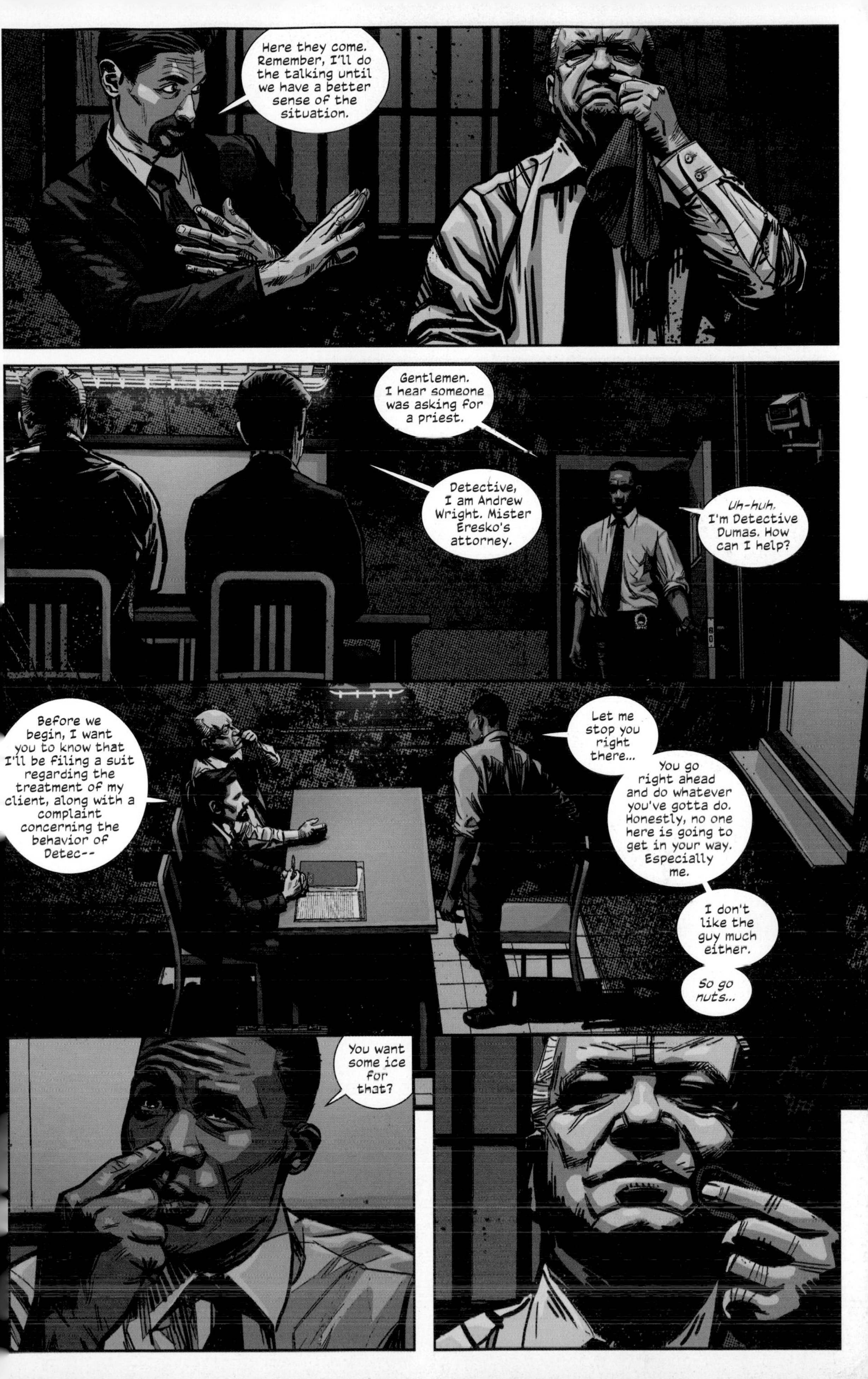
Here they come. Remember, I'll do the talking until we have a better sense of the situation.
Gentlemen. I hear someone was asking for a priest.
Detective, I am Andrew Wright. Mister Eresko's attorney.
Uh-huh. I'm Detective Dumas. How can I help?
Before we begin, I want you to know that I'll be filing a suit regarding the treatment of my client, along with a complaint concerning the behavior of Detec--
Let me stop you right there...
You go right ahead and do whatever you've gotta do. Honestly, no one here is going to get in your way. Especially me.
I don't like the guy much either.
So go nuts...
You want some ice for that?

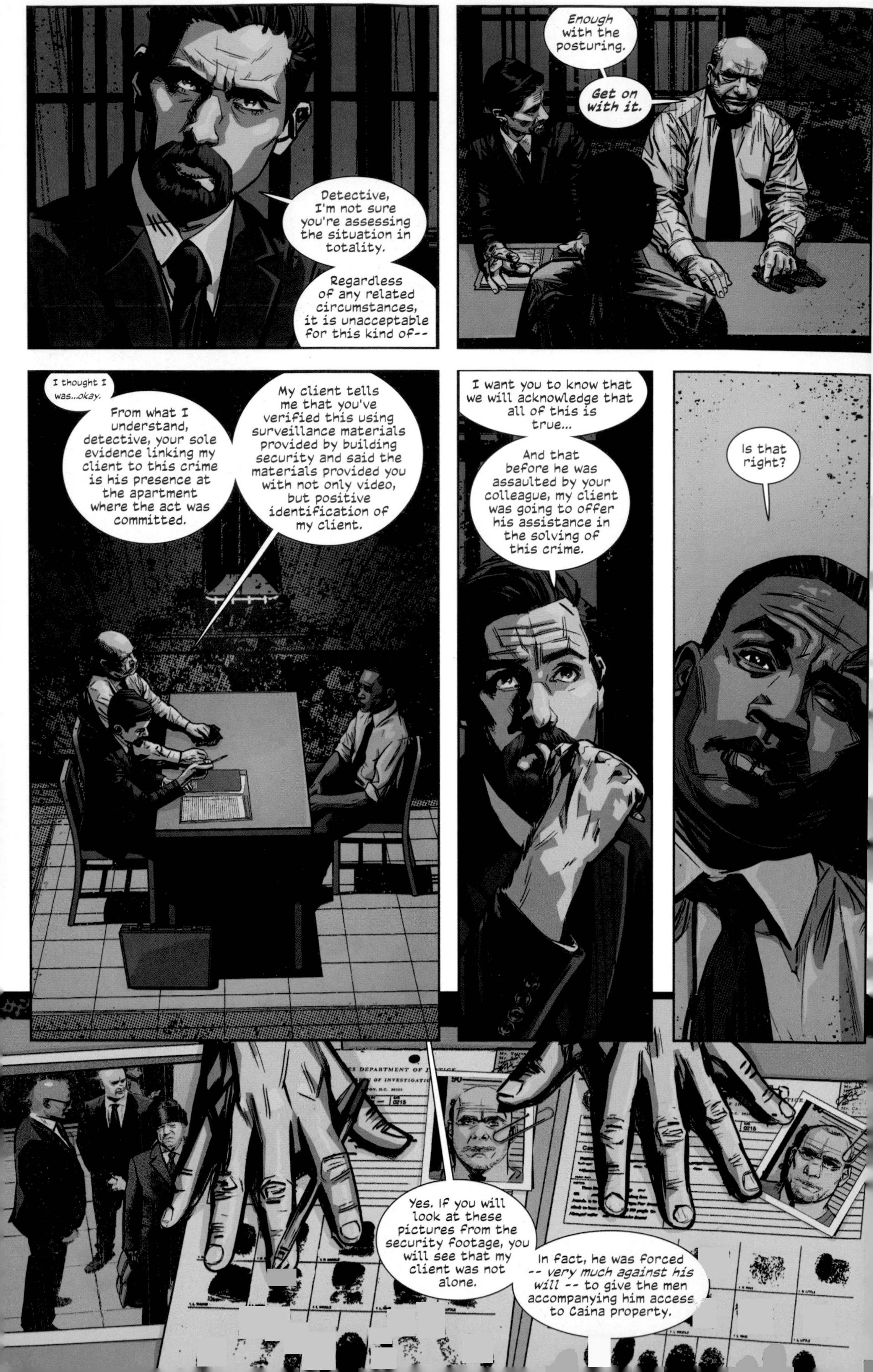
Detective, I'm not sure you're assessing the situation in totality.
Regardless of any related circumstances, it is unacceptable for this kind of--
Enough with the posturing.
Get on with it.
I thought I was...okay.
From what I understand, detective, your sole evidence linking my client to this crime is his presence at the apartment where the act was committed.
My client tells me that you've verified this using surveillance materials provided by building security and said the materials provided you with not only video, but positive identification of my client.
I want you to know that we will acknowledge that all of this is true...
And that before he was assaulted by your colleague, my client was going to offer his assistance in the solving of this crime.
Is that right?
Yes. If you will look at these pictures from the security footage, you will see that my client was not alone.
In fact, he was forced -- *very much against his will* -- to give the men accompanying him access to Caina property.

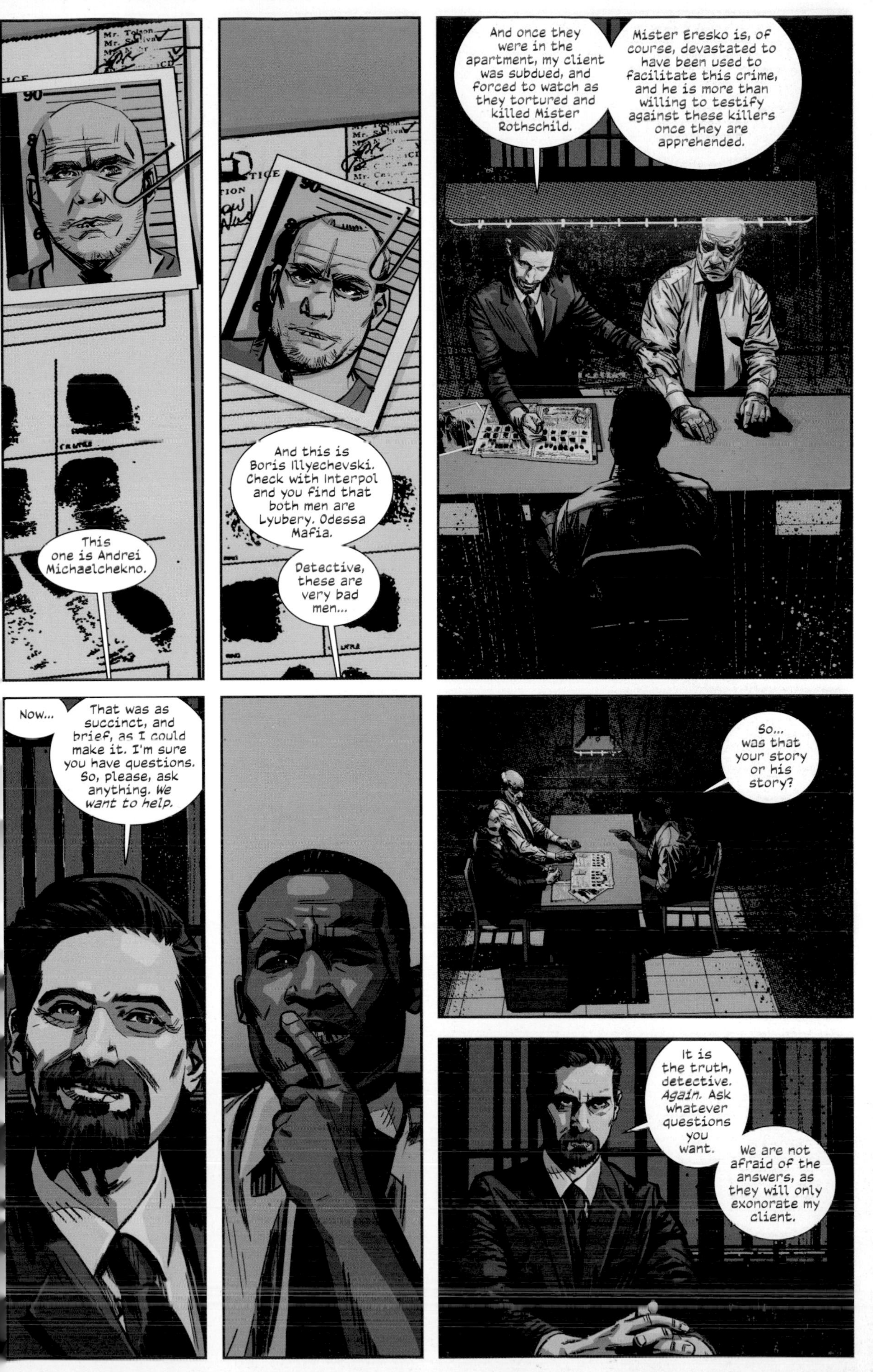
This one is Andrei Michaelchekno.
And this is Boris Illyechevski. Check with Interpol and you find that both men are Lyubery. Odessa Mafia.
Detective, these are very bad men...
And once they were in the apartment, my client was subdued, and forced to watch as they tortured and killed Mister Rothschild.
Mister Eresko is, of course, devastated to have been used to facilitate this crime, and he is more than willing to testify against these killers once they are apprehended.
Now...
That was as succinct, and brief, as I could make it. I'm sure you have questions. So, please, ask anything. *We want to help.*
So... was that your story or his story?
It is the truth, detective. *Again.* Ask whatever questions you want.
We are not afraid of the answers, as they will only exonorate my client.

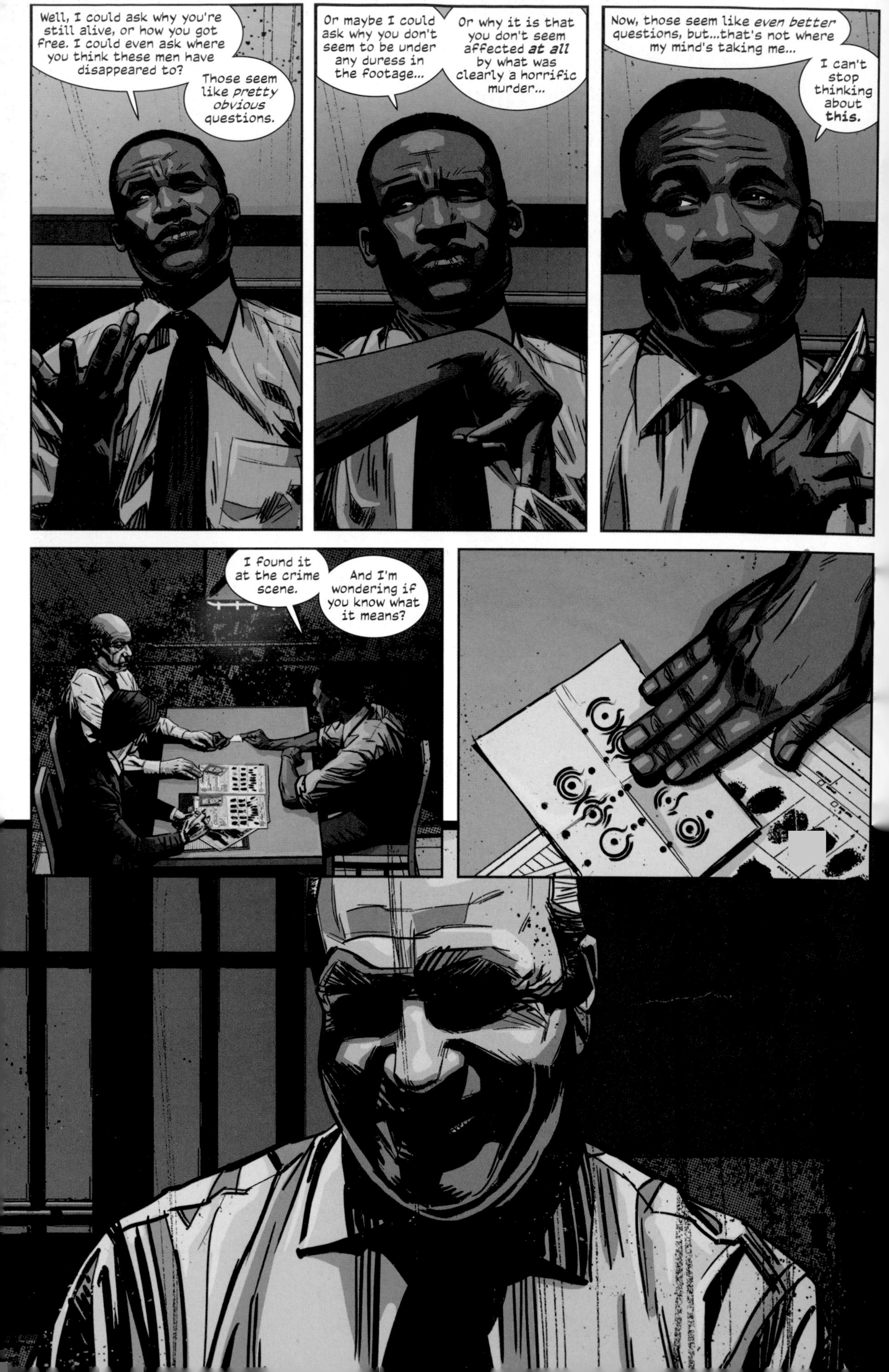
Well, I could ask why you're still alive, or how you got free. I could even ask where you think these men have disappeared to?
Those seem like *pretty obvious* questions.
Or maybe I could ask why you don't seem to be under any duress in the footage...
Or why it is that you don't seem affected ***at all*** by what was clearly a horrific murder...
Now, those seem like *even better* questions, but...that's not where my mind's taking me...
I can't stop thinking about **this.**
I found it at the crime scene.
And I'm wondering if you know what it means?

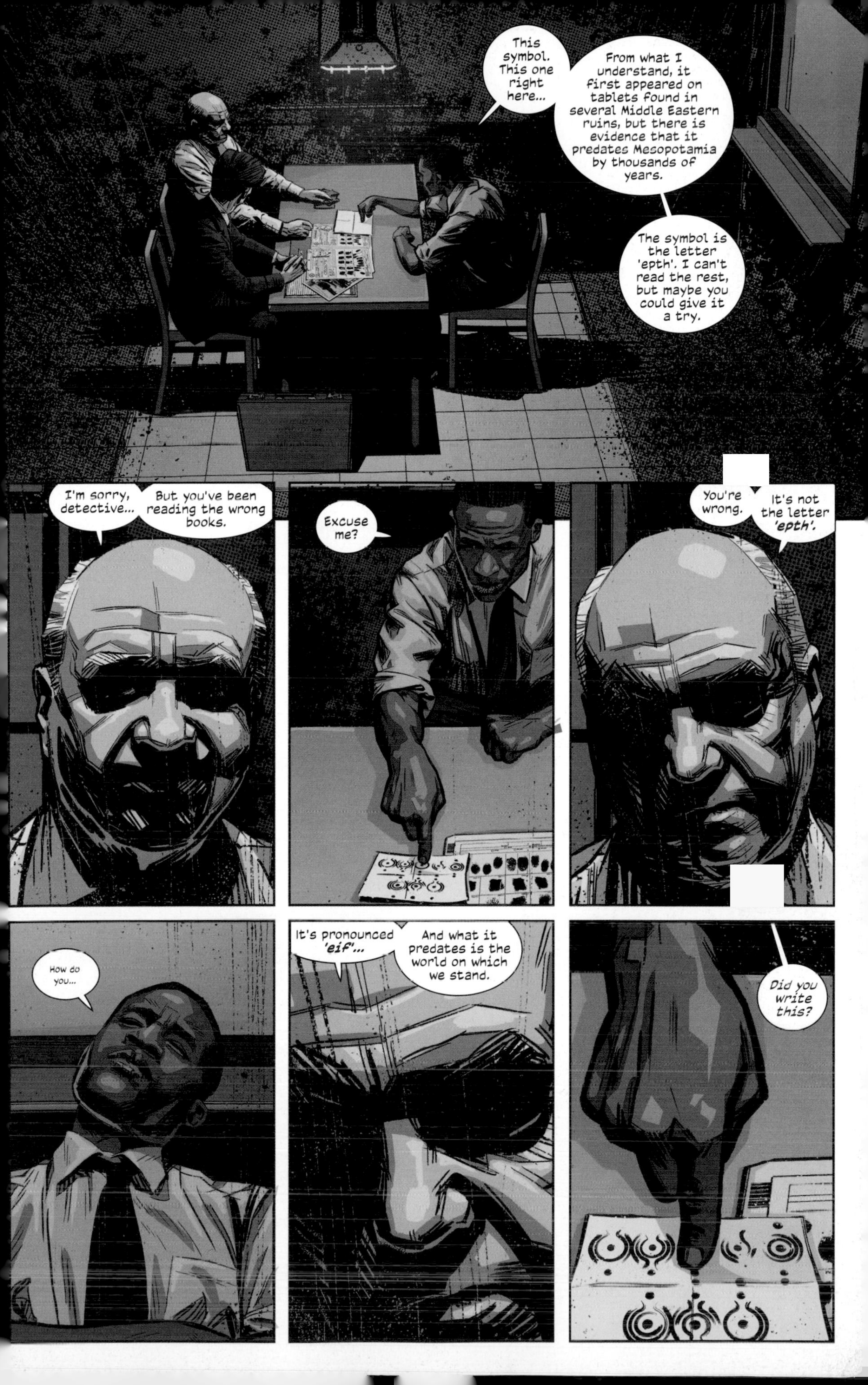
This symbol. This one right here...
From what I understand, it first appeared on tablets found in several Middle Eastern ruins, but there is evidence that it predates Mesopotamia by thousands of years.
The symbol is the letter 'epth'. I can't read the rest, but maybe you could give it a try.
I'm sorry, detective...
But you've been reading the wrong books.
Excuse me?
You're wrong.
It's not the letter *'epth'.*
How do you...
It's pronounced *'eif'...*
And what it predates is the world on which we stand.
*Did you write this?*

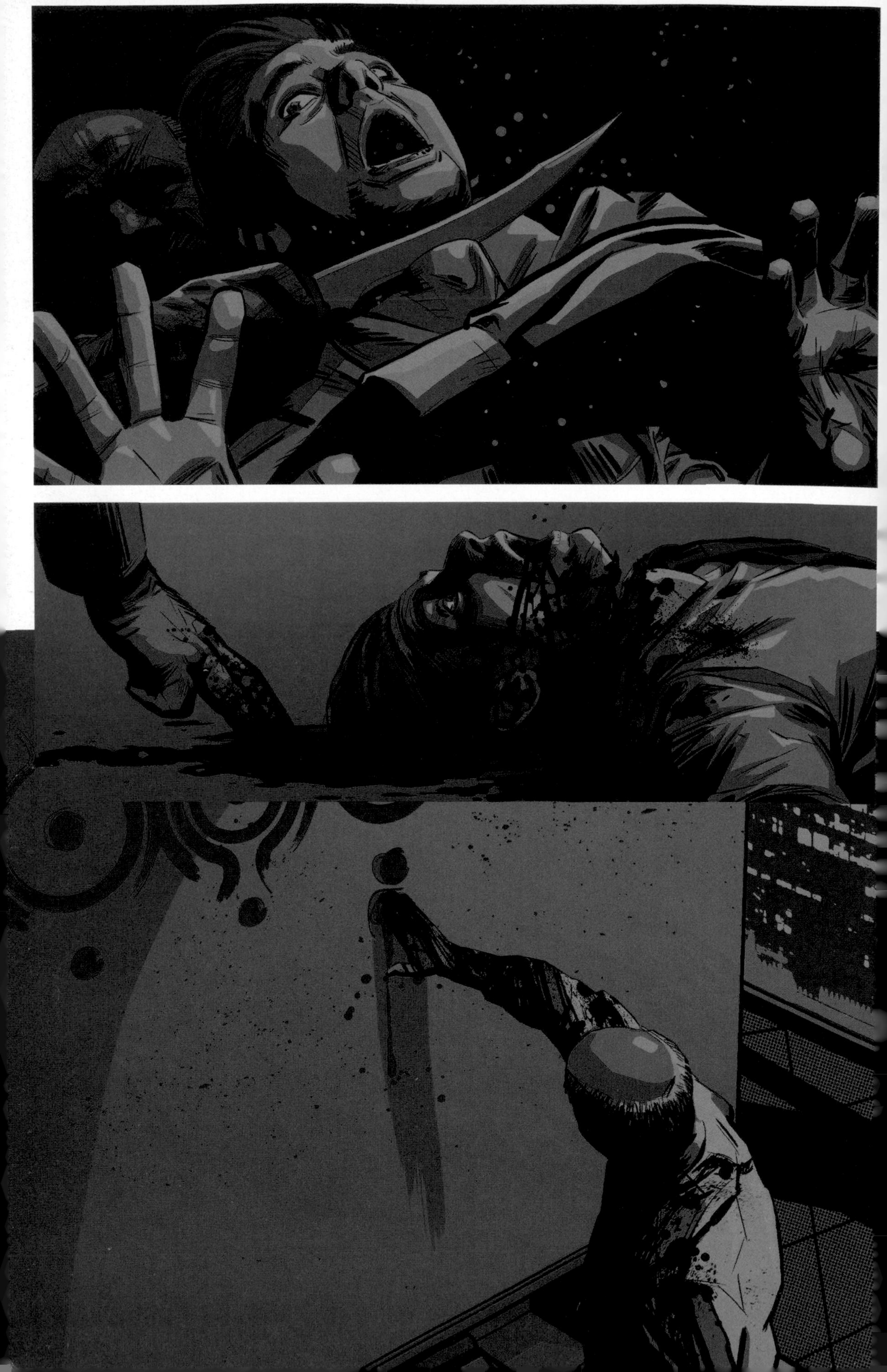

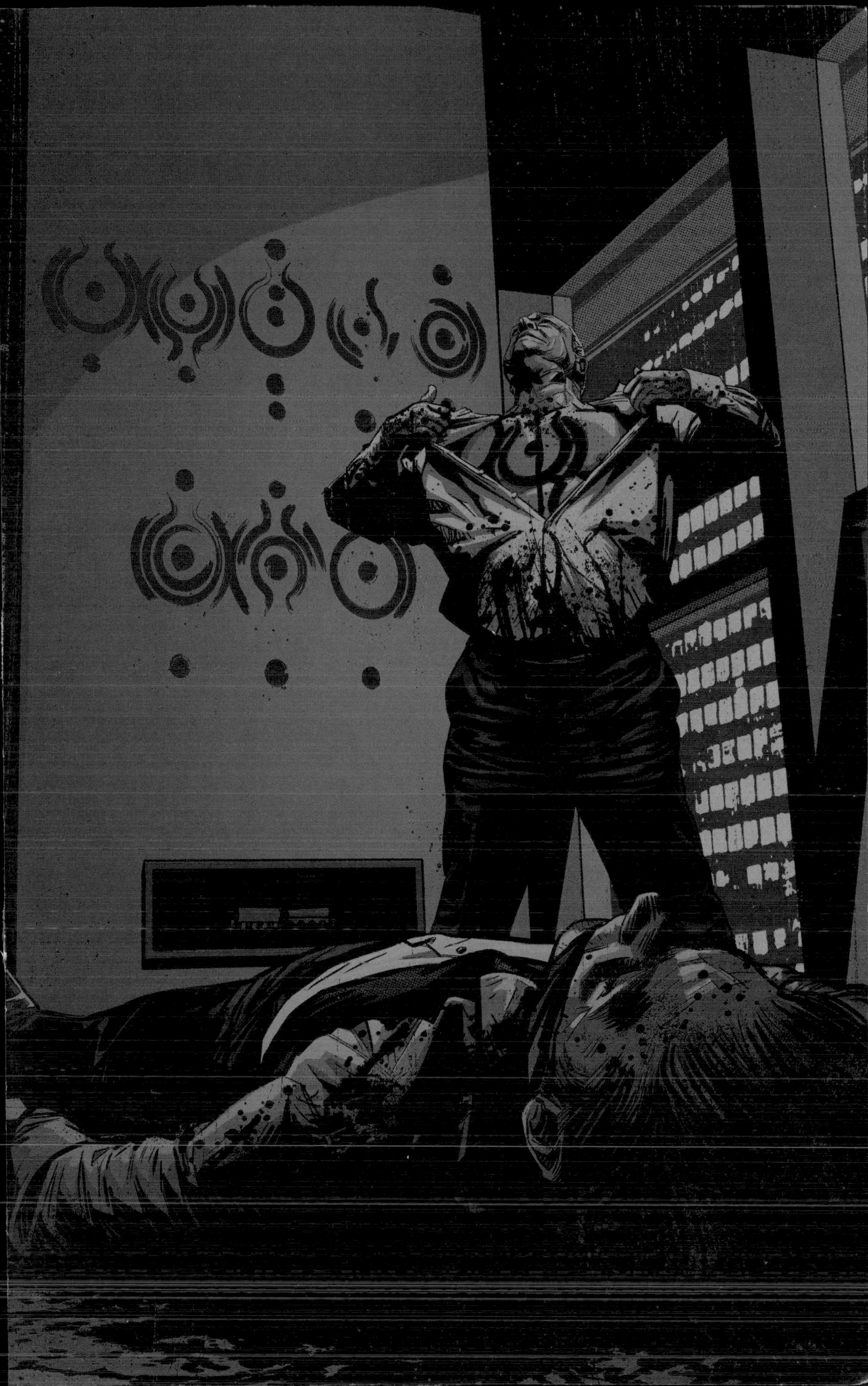

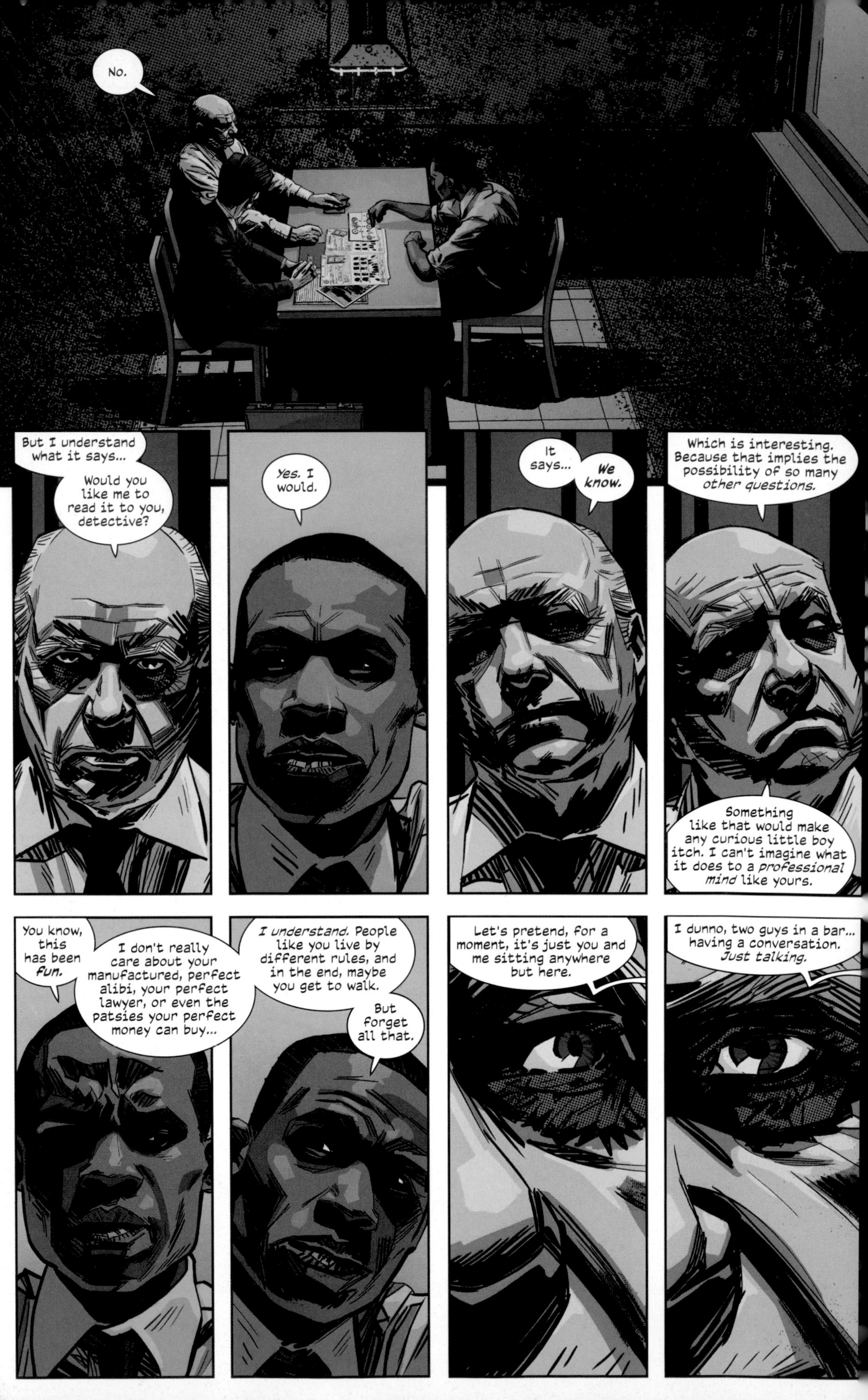
No.
But I understand what it says...
Would you like me to read it to you, detective?
*Yes.* I would.
It says...
*We know.*
Which is interesting. Because that implies the possibility of so many *other questions.*
Something like that would make any curious little boy itch. I can't imagine what it does to a *professional mind* like yours.
You know, this has been *fun.*
I don't really care about your manufactured, perfect alibi, your perfect lawyer, or even the patsies your perfect money can buy...
*I understand.* People like you live by different rules, and in the end, maybe you get to walk.
But forget all that.
Let's pretend, for a moment, it's just you and me sitting anywhere but here.
I dunno, two guys in a bar... having a conversation. *Just talking.*

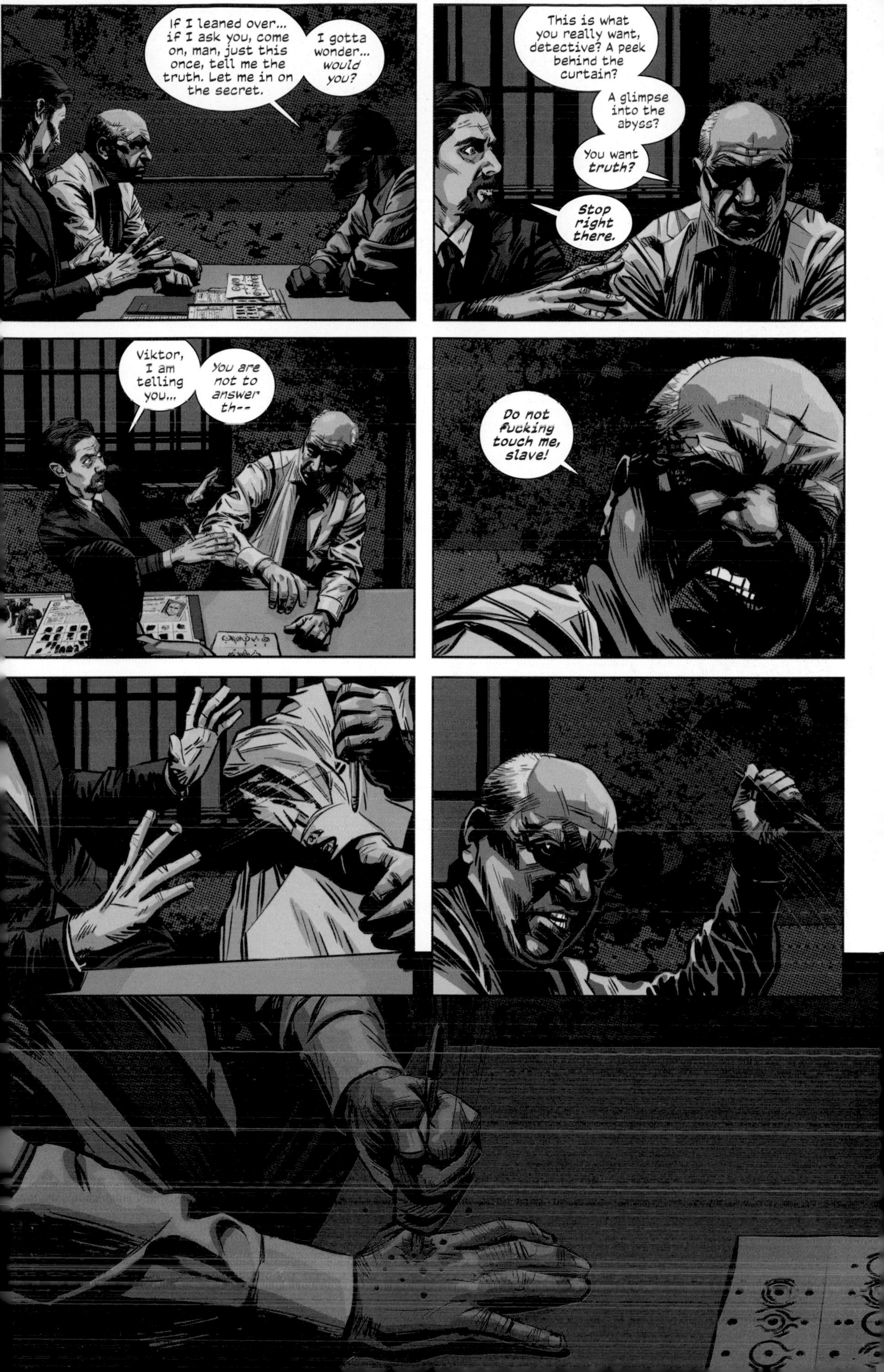
If I leaned over... if I ask you, come on, man, just this once, tell me the truth. Let me in on the secret.
I gotta wonder... *would you?*
This is what you really want, detective? A peek behind the curtain?
A glimpse into the abyss?
You want *truth?*
*Stop right there.*
Viktor, I am telling you...
*You are not to answer th--*
*Do not fucking touch me, slave!*

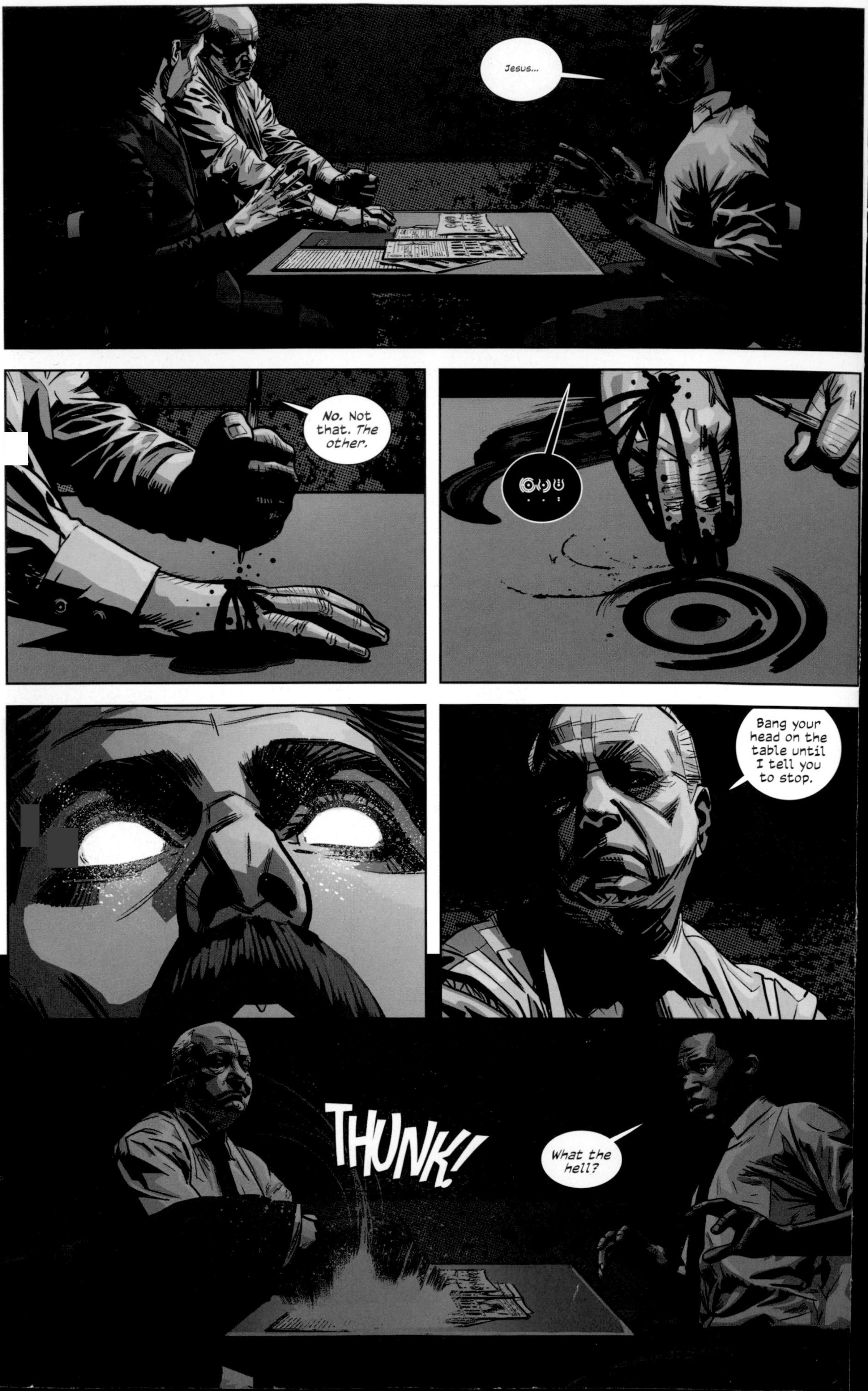
Jesus...
No. Not that. The other.
Bang your head on the table until I tell you to stop.
THUNK!
What the hell?

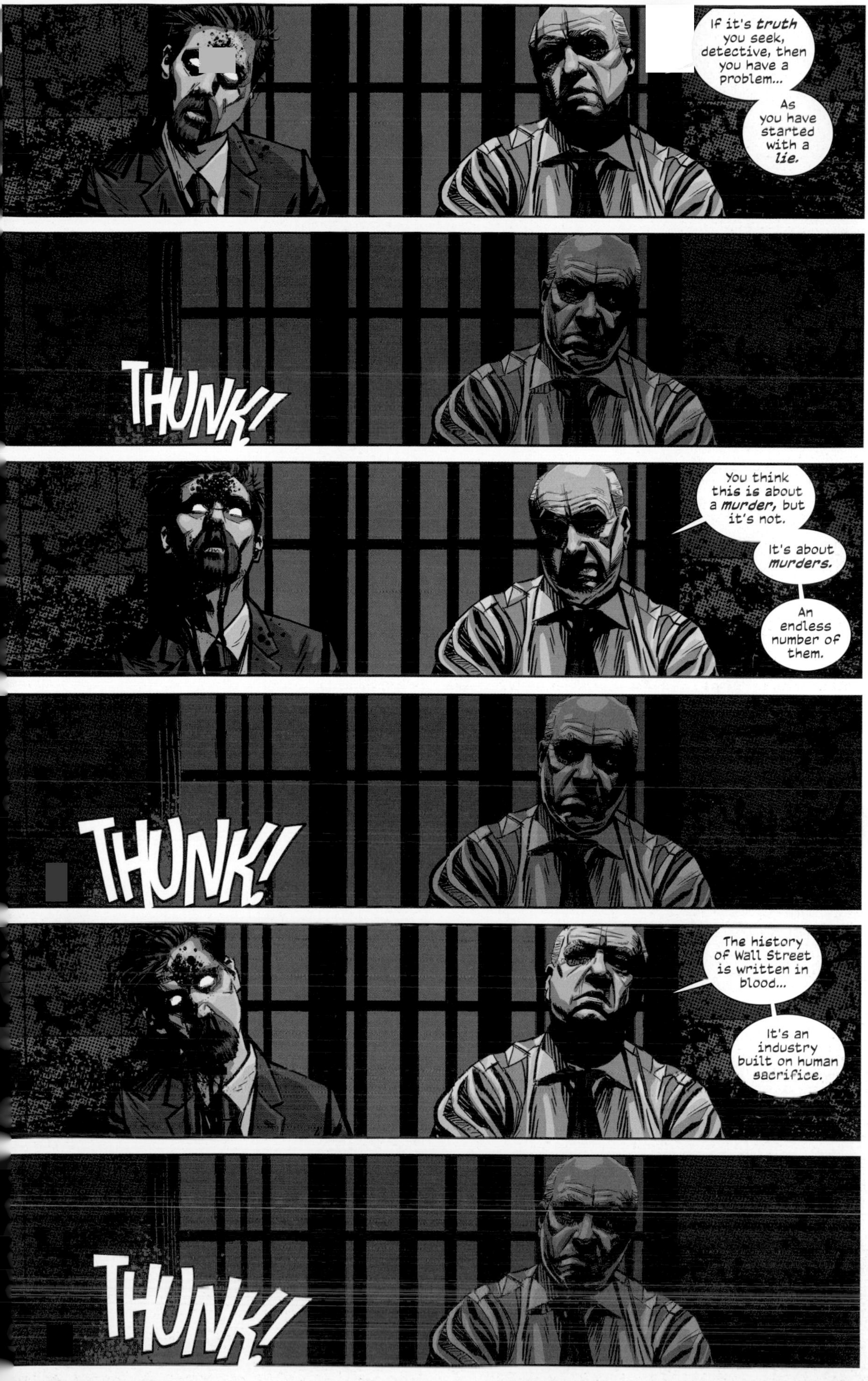
If it's truth you seek, detective, then you have a problem...
As you have started with a lie.
THUNK!
You think this is about a murder, but it's not.
It's about murders.
An endless number of them.
THUNK!
The history of Wall Street is written in blood...
It's an industry built on human sacrifice.
THUNK!

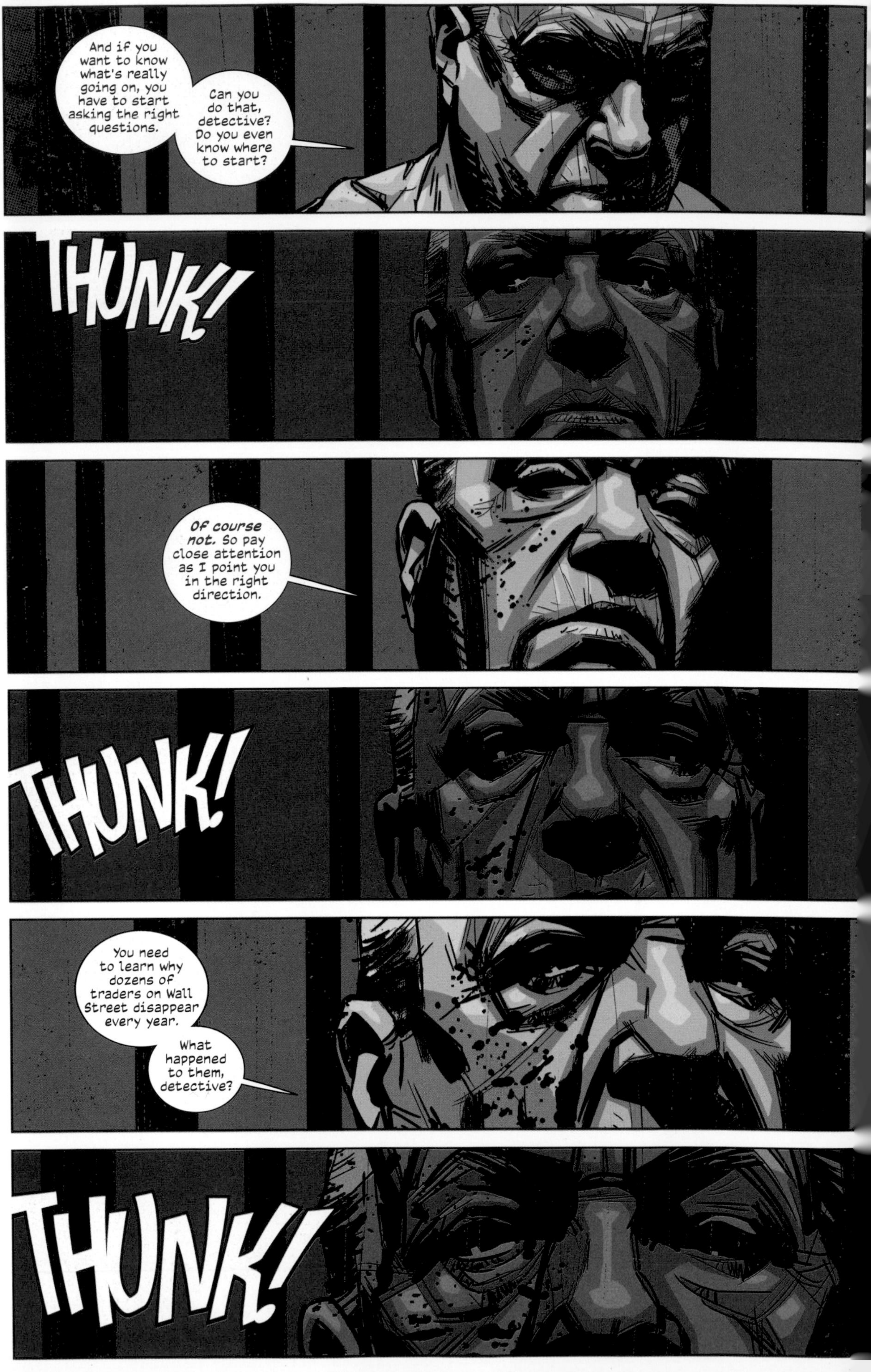
And if you want to know what's really going on, you have to start asking the right questions.
Can you do that, detective? Do you even know where to start?
THUNK!
*Of course not.* So pay close attention as I point you in the right direction.
THUNK!
You need to learn why dozens of traders on Wall Street disappear every year.
What happened to them, detective?
THUNK!

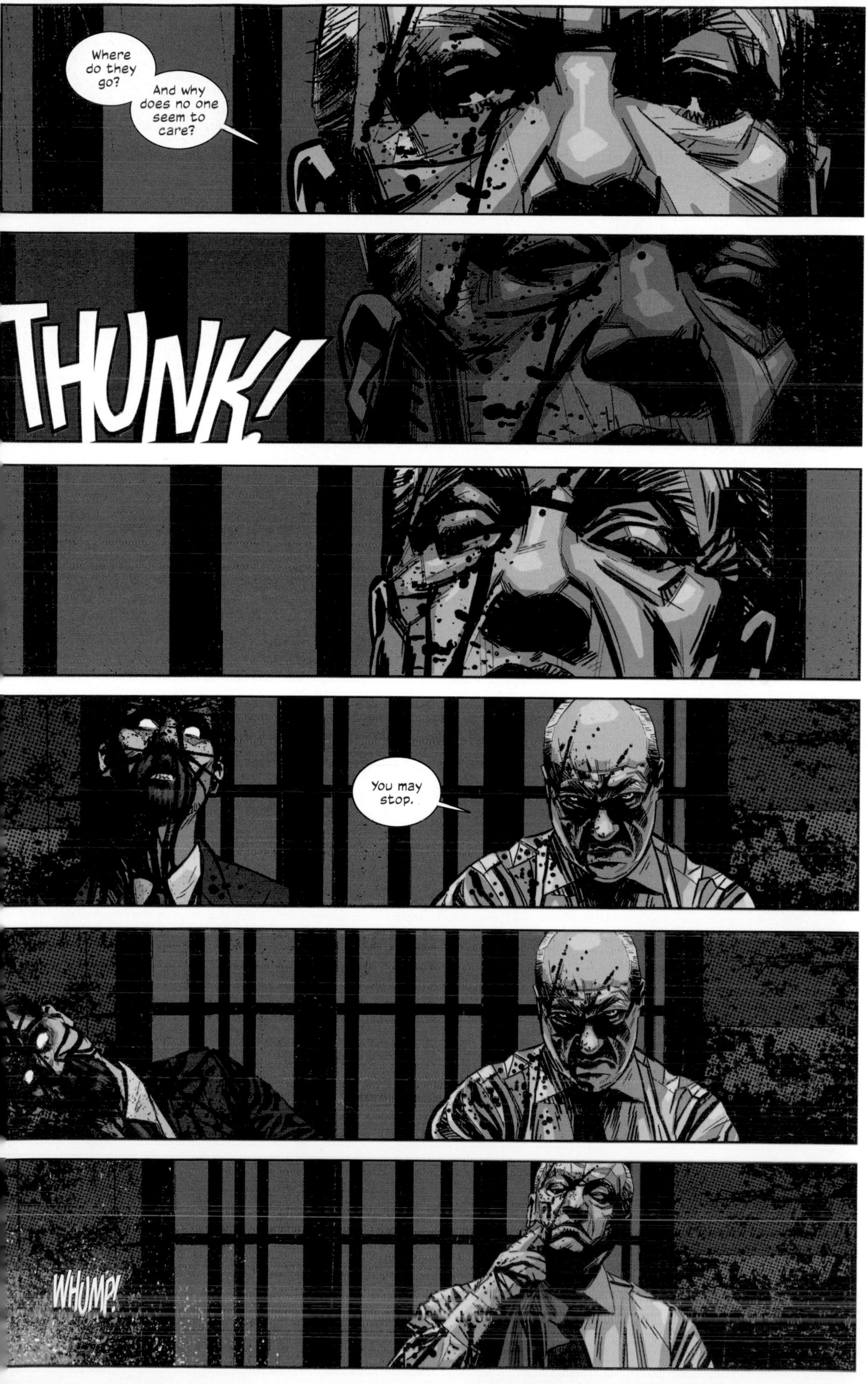
Where do they go?
And why does no one seem to care?
THUNK!
You may stop.
WHUMP!

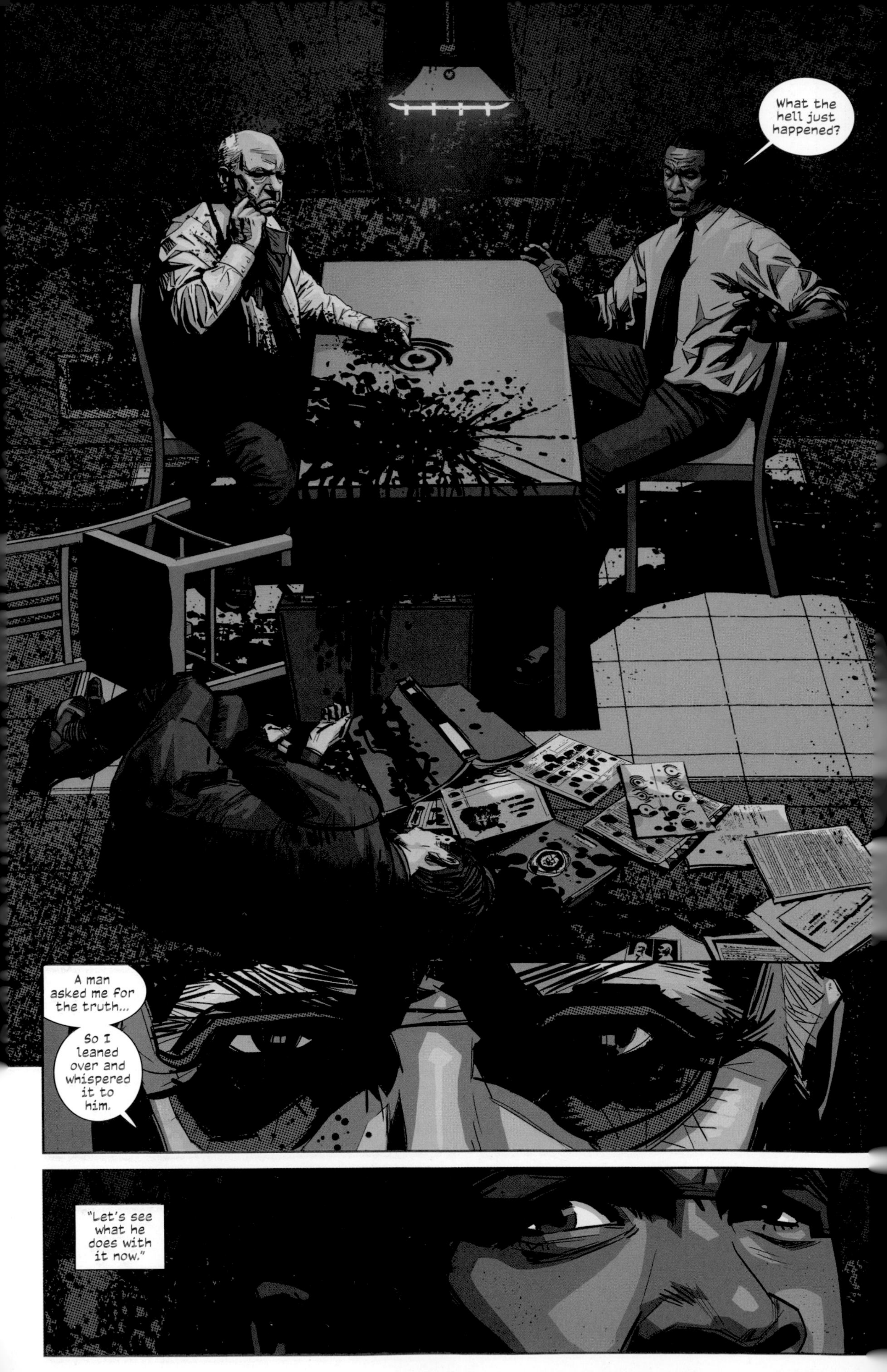
What the hell just happened?
A man asked me for the truth...
So I leaned over and whispered it to him.
"Let's see what he does with it now."

Consume them whole.

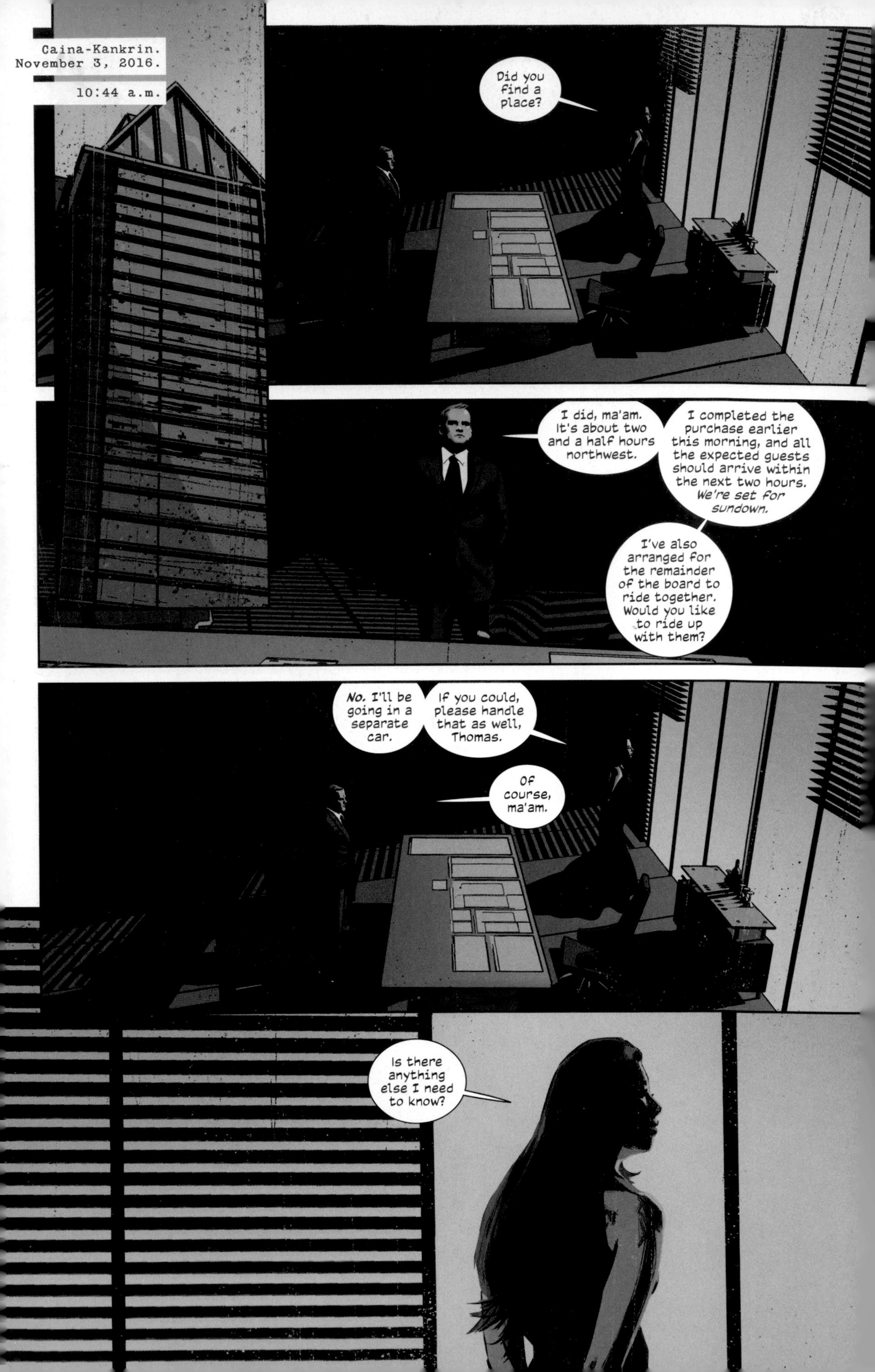
Caina-Kankrin.
November 3, 2016.
10:44 a.m.
Did you find a place?
I did, ma'am. It's about two and a half hours northwest.
I completed the purchase earlier this morning, and all the expected guests should arrive within the next two hours. *We're set for sundown.*
I've also arranged for the remainder of the board to ride together. Would you like to ride up with them?
***No.*** I'll be going in a separate car.
If you could, please handle that as well, Thomas.
Of course, ma'am.
Is there anything else I need to know?

There is... The Black Pope won't be attending. However, a cardinal was sent to preside over the ceremony in the pontiff's place.

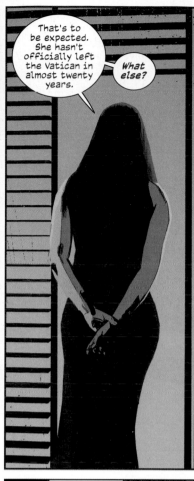

That's to be expected. She hasn't officially left the Vatican in almost twenty years.

What else?

The police...they couldn't hold Viktor Eresko. He made bail this morning.

You should prepare yourself -- he might be in attendance as well.

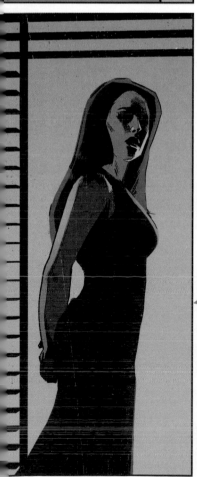

Of course he will be. It's how all wars start. With hollow words and posturing over corpses.

That will be all, Thomas.

Thank you, ma'am.

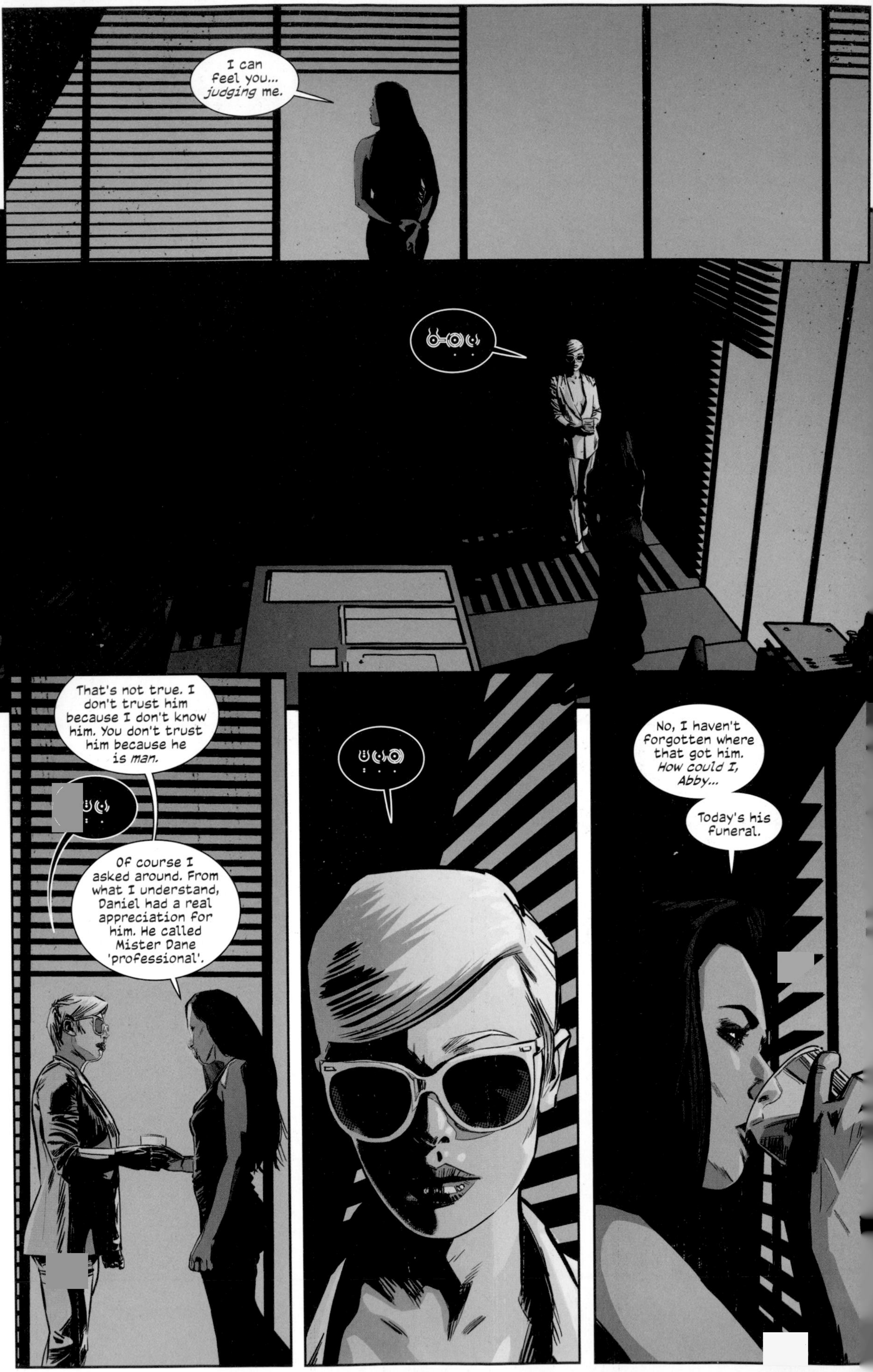
I can feel you... *judging* me.
That's not true. I don't trust him because I don't know him. You don't trust him because he is *man.*
Of course I asked around. From what I understand, Daniel had a real appreciation for him. He called Mister Dane 'professional'.
No, I haven't forgotten where that got him. *How could I, Abby...*
Today's his funeral.

(a)

(b,c,d)

THE DIARY OF WYNN ACKERMANN


Entry 1 - April 5, 1975

Mrs. Raven told me that it would help if I wrote things down. Because
one day if I was still bothered by all this I'd be able to look back at
my diary and remember how I was feeling and what I was thinking about.
She says that it's important to always have a clear mind and that things
like what happened to me tend to mess your head up. But I know that no
matter what, I'll always remember.

The Banes killed my whole family. Now I have to live with Mrs. Raven
because she can protect me. Maybe one day I won't need protecting.

My name is Wynn. I'm five years old. There's still blood under my
fingernails.

(e,f)

(g)

CHAPTER FOUR:

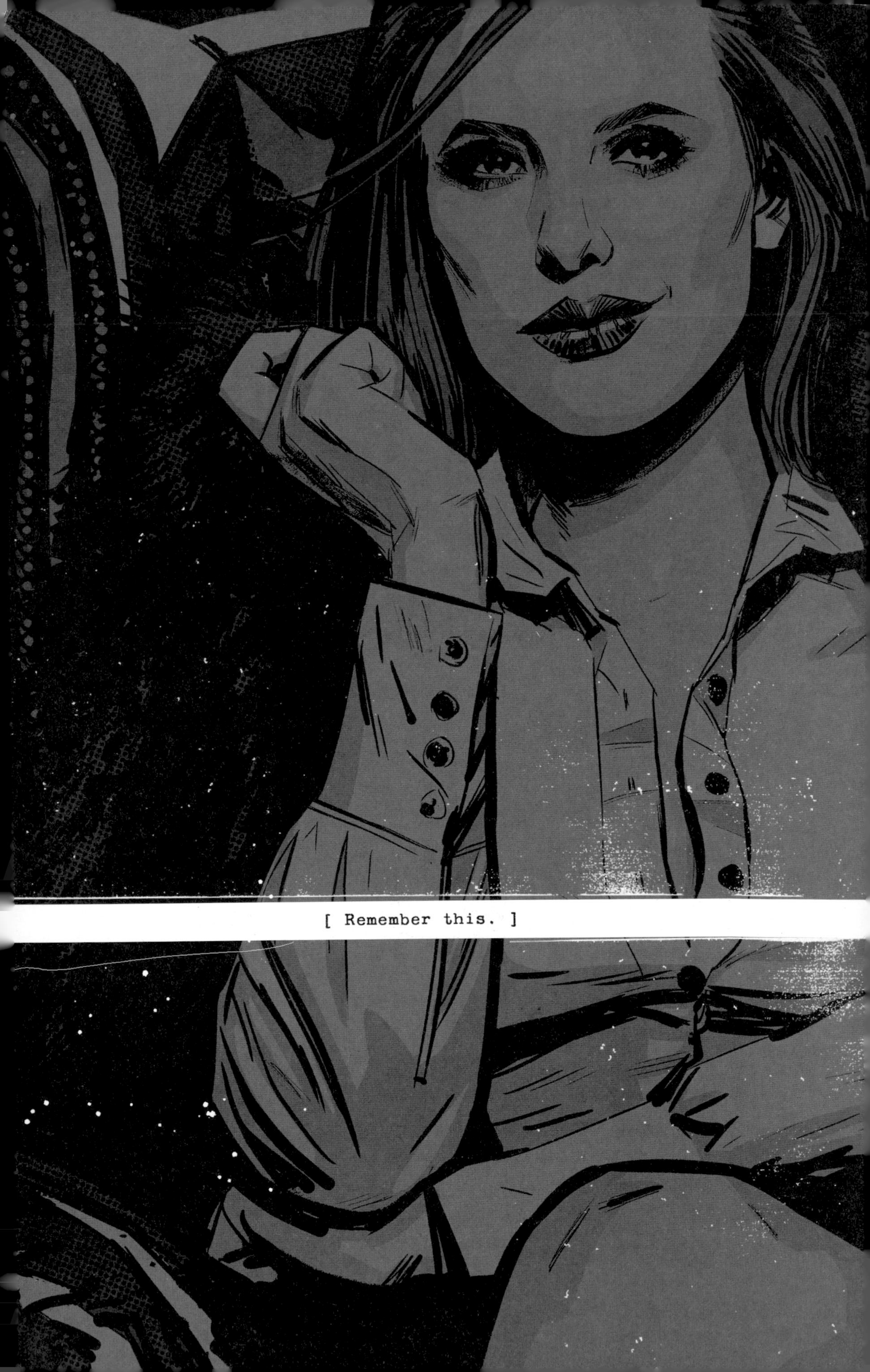
[ Remember this. ]

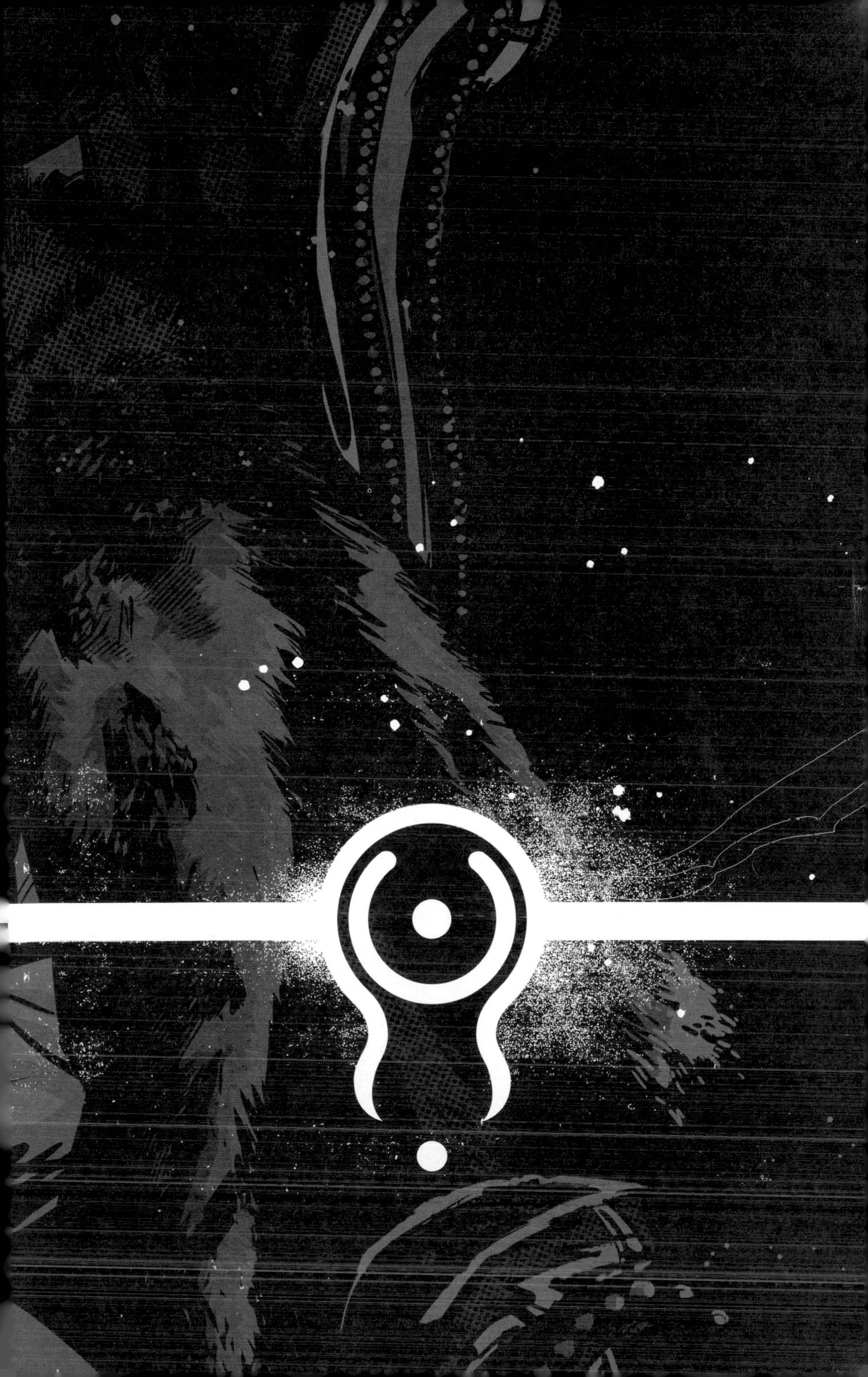

THE DIARY OF WYNN ACKERMANN


Entry 22 - May 19, 1976

Mrs. Raven says it's important that I learn about what our families do
because I have to take my family seat back one day. She says there's a
good chance I might become the youngest board member in the history of
our company. I don't see how that's possible because there are so many
members of the Bane family, but Mrs. Raven says I'm very smart for my
age and I'll figure it out.

The only problem is that Beatrix gets angry at me because Mrs. Raven
makes her leave the room sometimes when she's teaching me stuff, and I
guess I'd be mad too if I was older than her and my mom left me out.

She doesn't stay angry long though. Sometimes when it's bedtime, Beatrix
will read to me. She's not as smart as she thinks she is, and gets some
of the words wrong, but I don't mind. I even tell her some of the things
her mother didn't want her to know because that's what friends do.



Entry 34 - December 9, 1976

The Banes are all dead. Mrs. Raven and the rest of the original families
killed them all. They killed Desmond Bane in front of me and watched as
I ate his heart.

I am Wynn Ackermann. One of the four pillars, returned to my rightful
seat, and am now the Watcher.

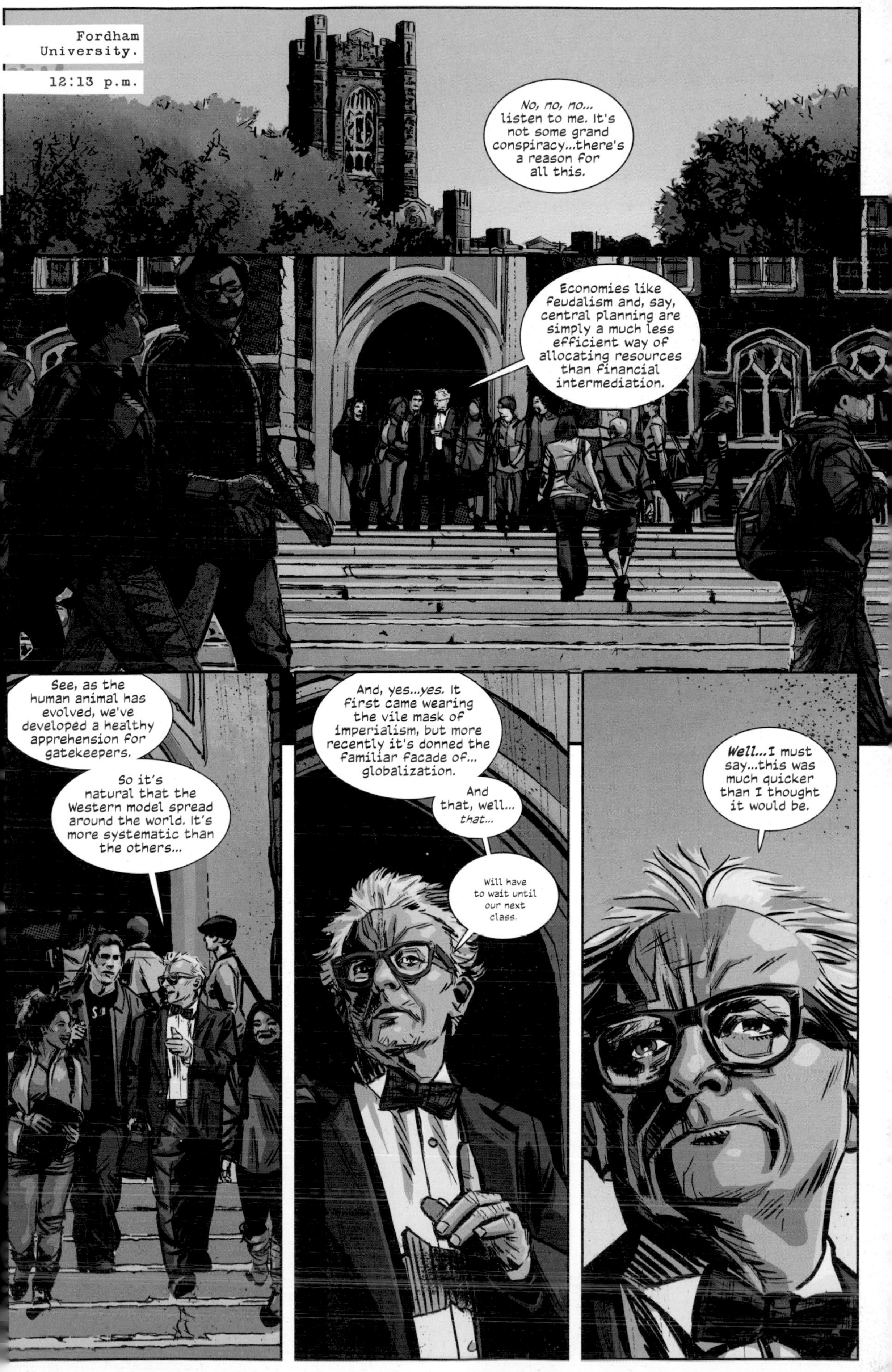
Fordham University.
12:13 p.m.
No, no, no... listen to me. It's not some grand conspiracy...there's a reason for all this.
Economies like feudalism and, say, central planning are simply a much less efficient way of allocating resources than financial intermediation.
See, as the human animal has evolved, we've developed a healthy apprehension for gatekeepers.
So it's natural that the Western model spread around the world. It's more systematic than the others...
And, yes...yes. It first came wearing the vile mask of imperialism, but more recently it's donned the familiar facade of... globalization.
And that, well... that...
Will have to wait until our next class.
Well...I must say...this was much quicker than I thought it would be.

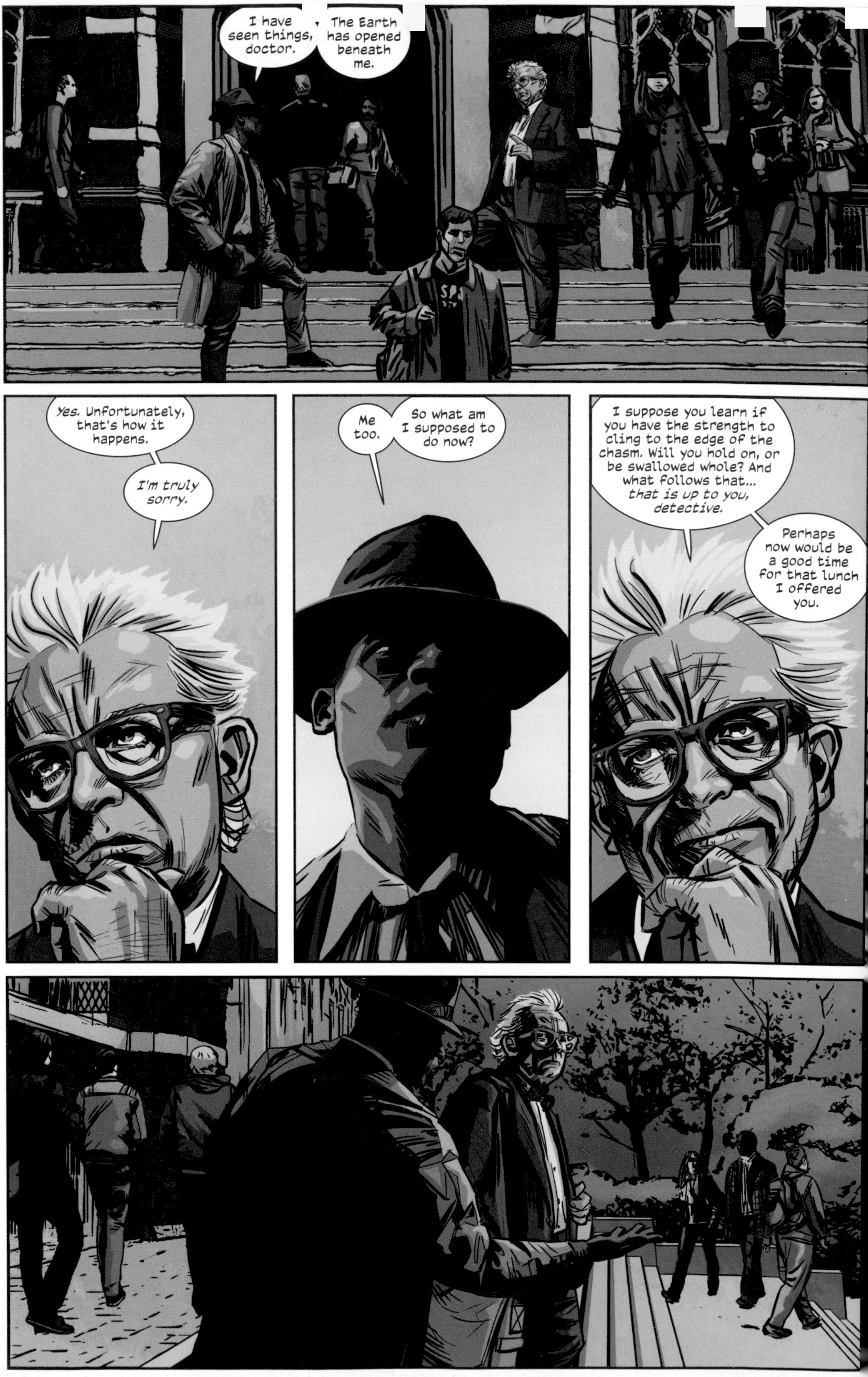
I have seen things, doctor.
The Earth has opened beneath me.
Yes. Unfortunately, that's how it happens.
I'm truly sorry.
Me too.
So what am I supposed to do now?
I suppose you learn if you have the strength to cling to the edge of the chasm. Will you hold on, or be swallowed whole? And what follows that... that is up to you, detective.
Perhaps now would be a good time for that lunch I offered you.

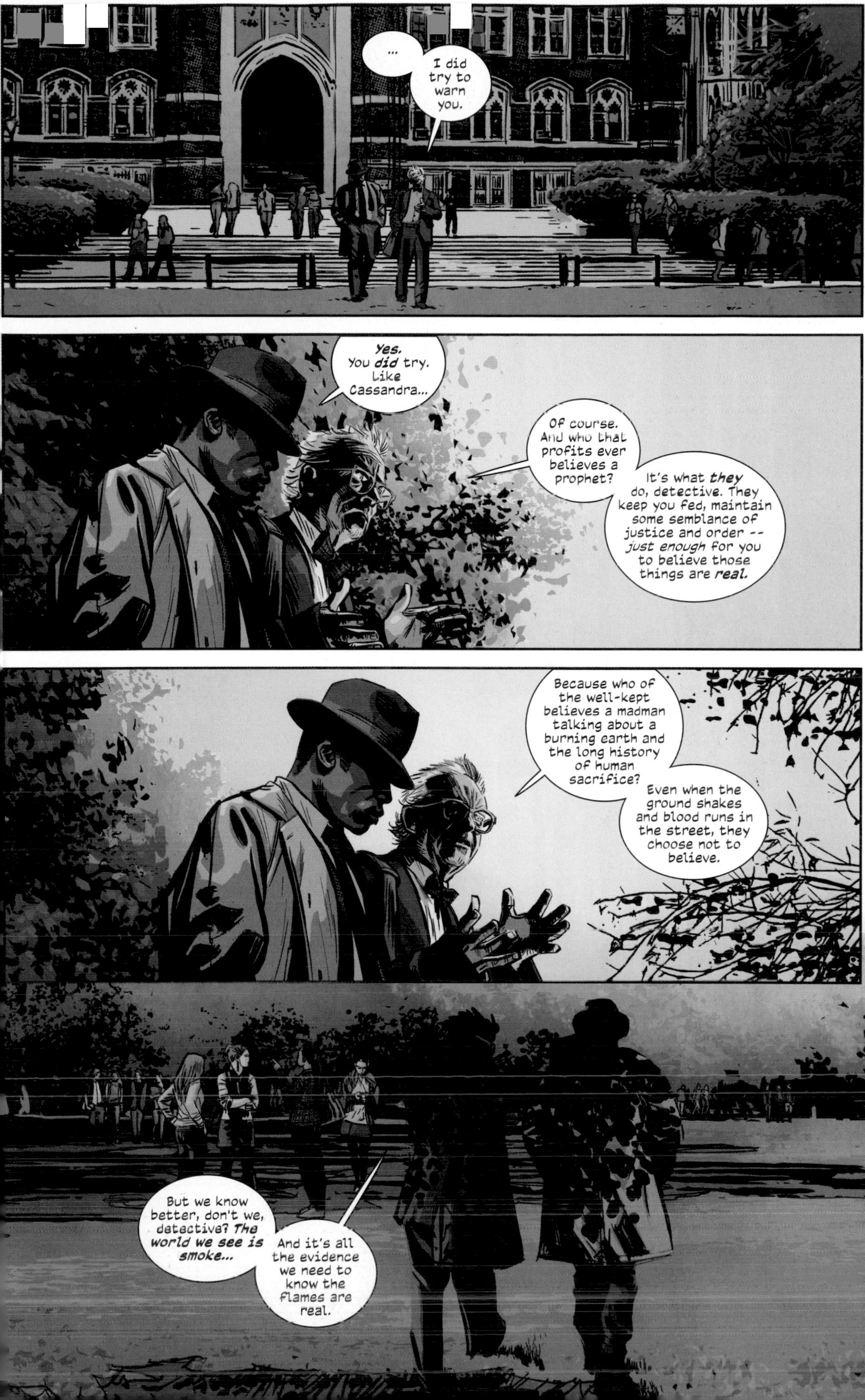
...
I did try to warn you.
Yes. You did try. Like Cassandra...
Of course. And who that profits ever believes a prophet?
It's what they do, detective. They keep you fed, maintain some semblance of justice and order -- just enough for you to believe those things are real.
Because who of the well-kept believes a madman talking about a burning earth and the long history of human sacrifice?
Even when the ground shakes and blood runs in the street, they choose not to believe.
But we know better, don't we, detective? The world we see is smoke...
And it's all the evidence we need to know the flames are real.

THE DIARY OF WYNN ACKERMANN

Entry 157 - February 22, 1979

Sometimes I can hear the market, like it's a sentient thing able to
communicate with those willing to listen. Which, of course, is true, but
traditionally understood to be more of an 'interpreted' thing. Not so
much for me.

To that end, I have arranged a meeting with the Fed tomorrow. Probably
not the wisest thing to do - tempt fate by physically addressing the
embodiment of commerce - but I have a few hunches about market
volatility that I simply have to have either confirmation or denial of.

Regardless of what I learn, I look forward to seeing god face to face.


Entry 158 - February 23, 1979

Hey Wynn, "where'd you get your tan," they'll say. Because I'm a
well-cooked, slightly crispy idiot.

But I'm also right.

Let's never do that again.

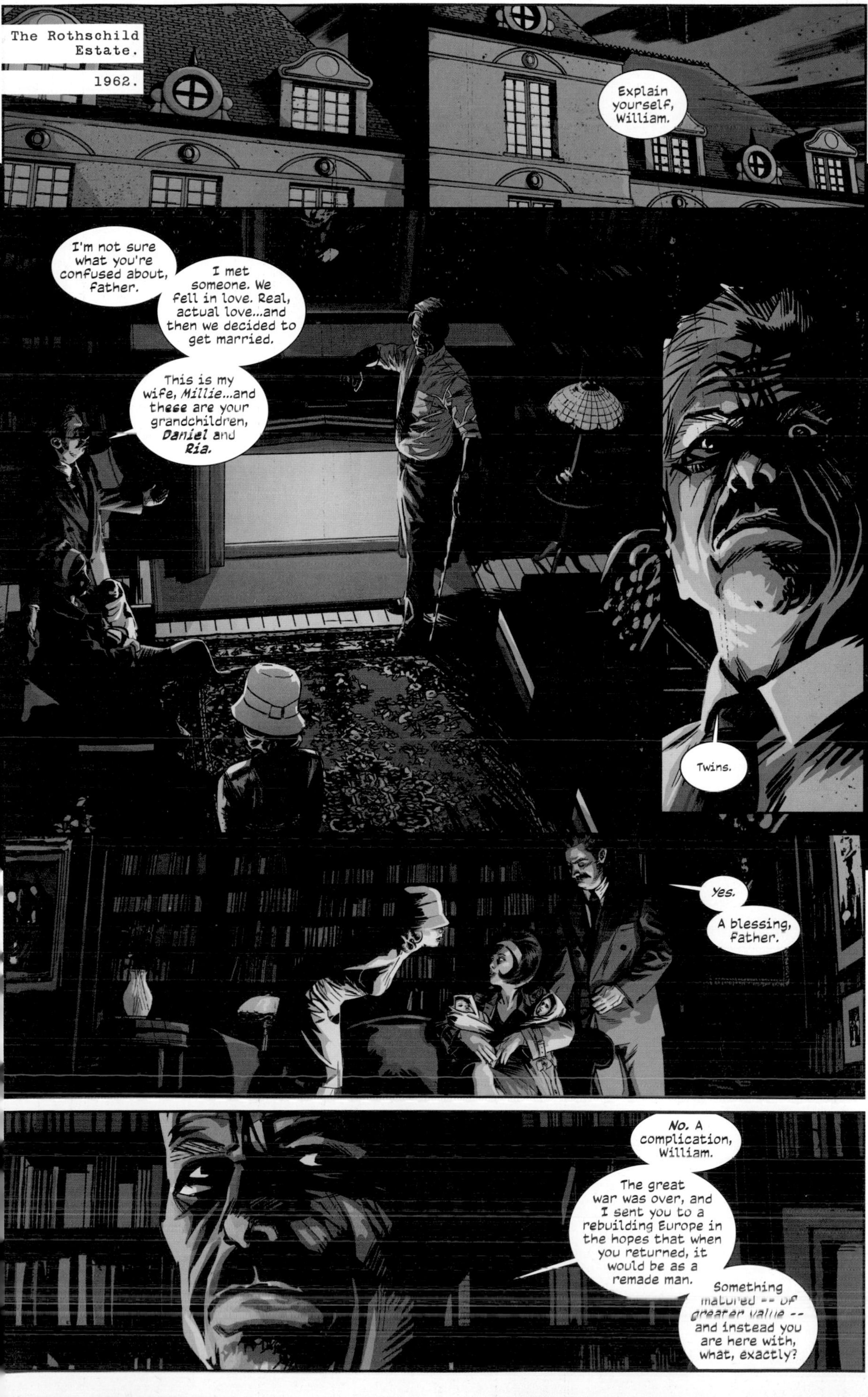
The Rothschild Estate.
1962.
Explain yourself, William.
I'm not sure what you're confused about, father.
I met someone. We fell in love. Real, actual love...and then we decided to get married.
This is my wife, *Millie*...and these are your grandchildren, *Daniel* and *Ria.*
Twins.
*Yes.*
A blessing, father.
*No.* A complication, William.
The great war was over, and I sent you to a rebuilding Europe in the hopes that when you returned, it would be as a remade man.
Something matured -- of *greater value* -- and instead you are here with, what, exactly?

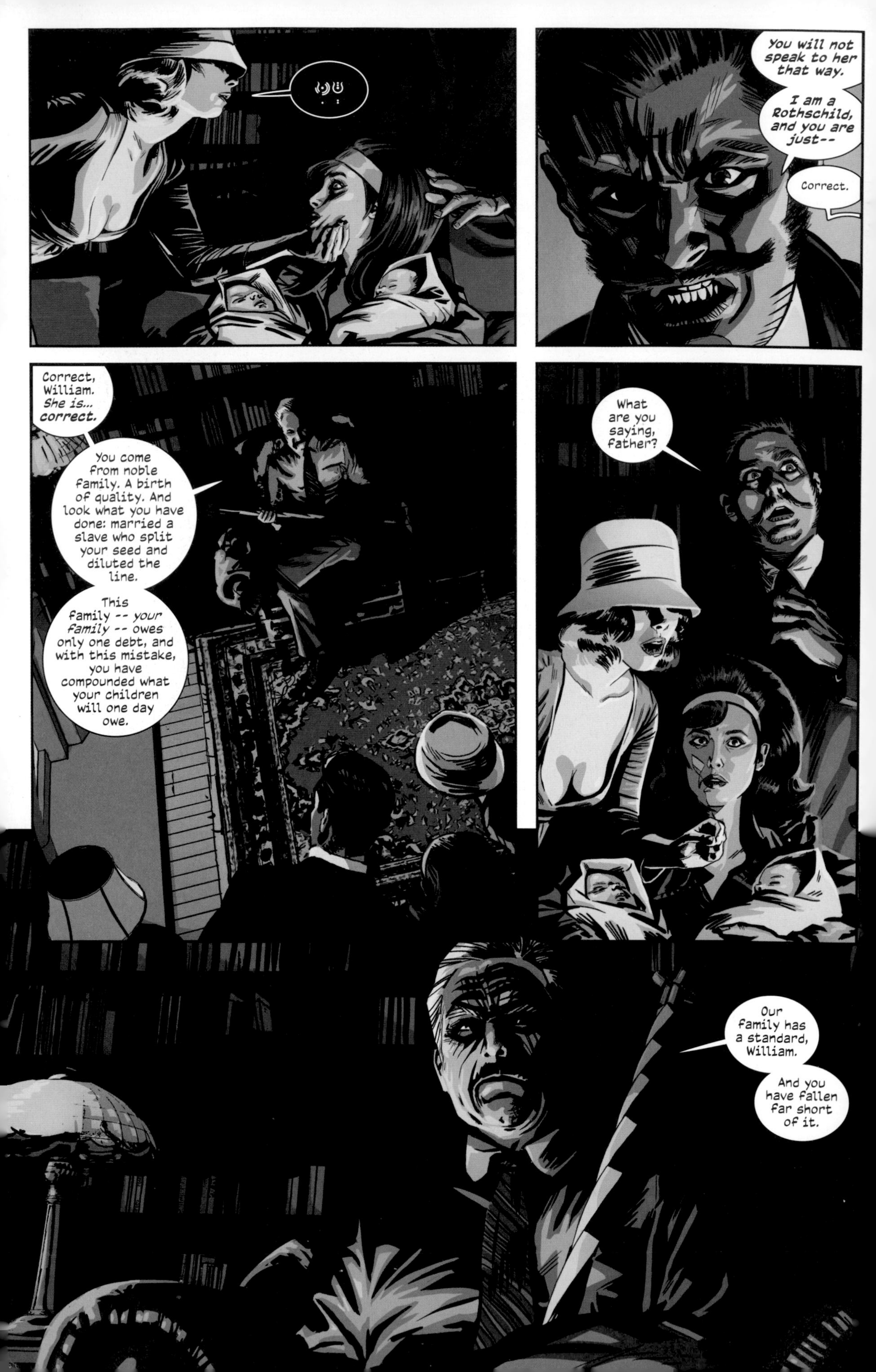
You will not speak to her that way.
I am a Rothschild, and you are just--
Correct.
Correct, William. *She is... correct.*
You come from noble family. A birth of quality. And look what you have done: married a slave who split your seed and diluted the line.
This family -- *your family* -- owes only one debt, and with this mistake, you have compounded what your children will one day owe.
What are you saying, father?
Our family has a standard, William.
And you have fallen far short of it.

In Memory Of

# DANIEL WALTER ROTHSCHILD

February 17, 1962 - October 31, 2016

The Rothschild Family is sad to announce the passing of
Daniel Walter Rothschild on October 31, 2016.

Daniel's honesty, loyalty, and commitment to his fellow man
will be missed by all.

## HIS DEBT IS PAID

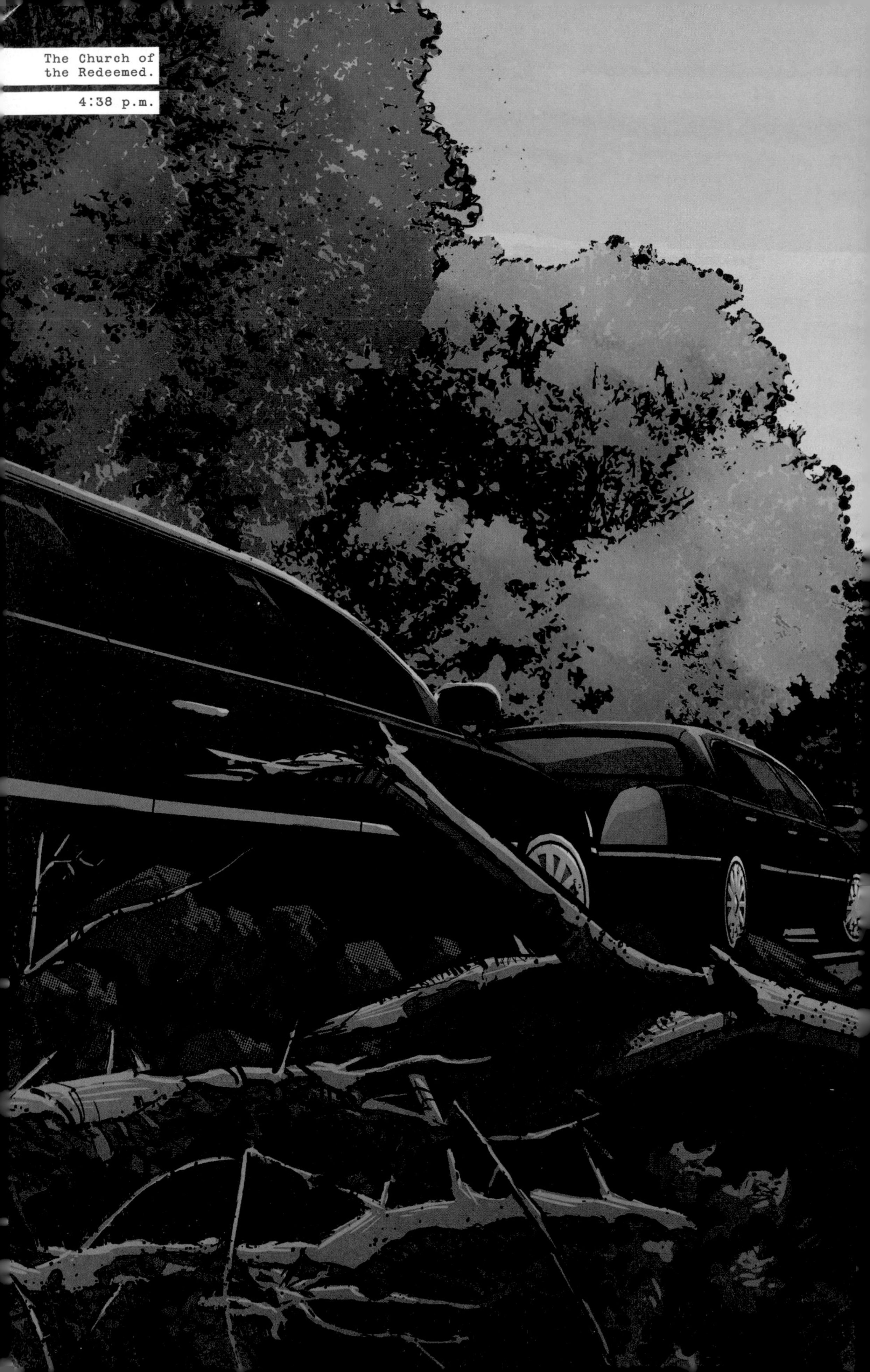
The Church of
the Redeemed.
4:38 p.m.

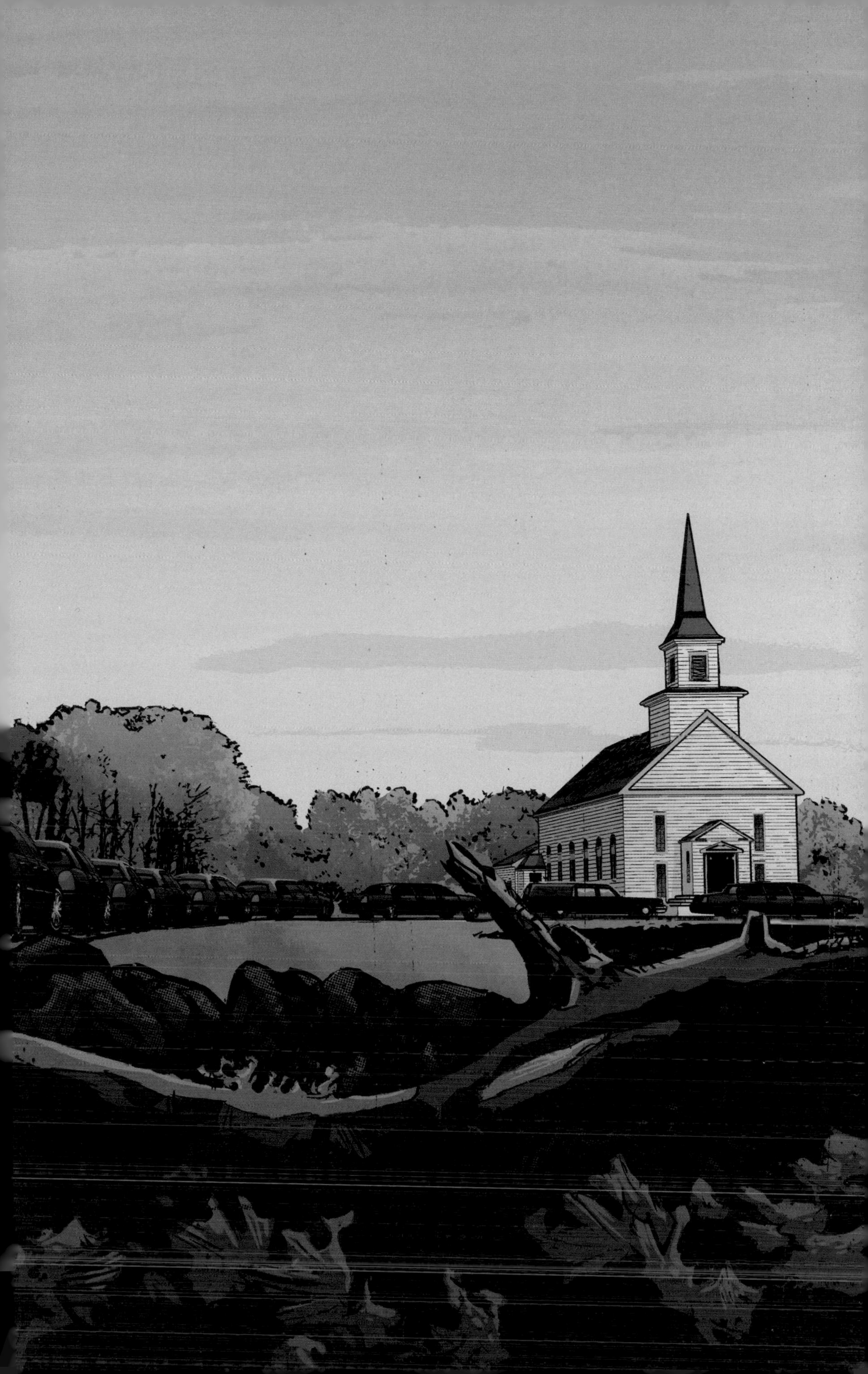

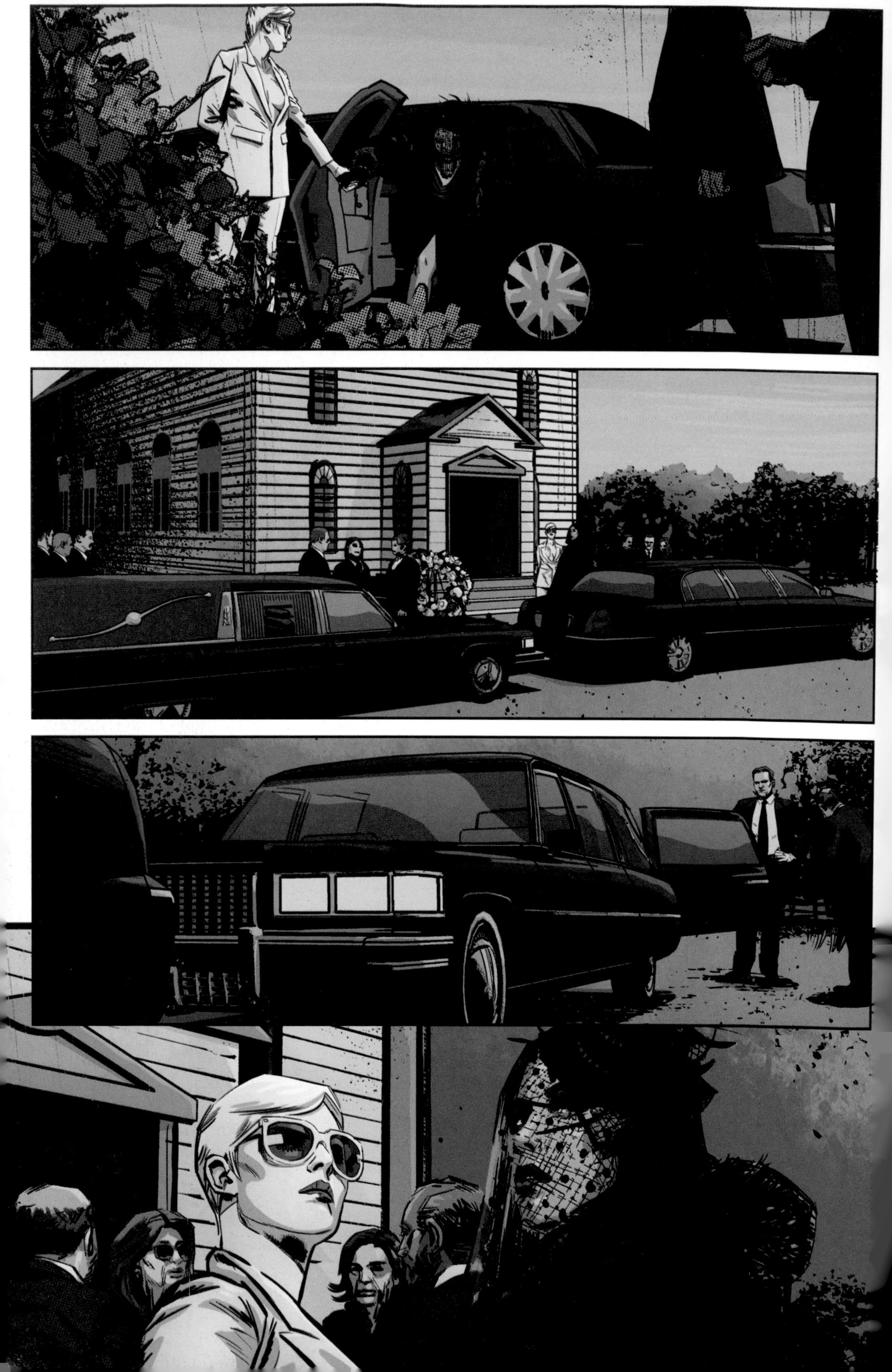

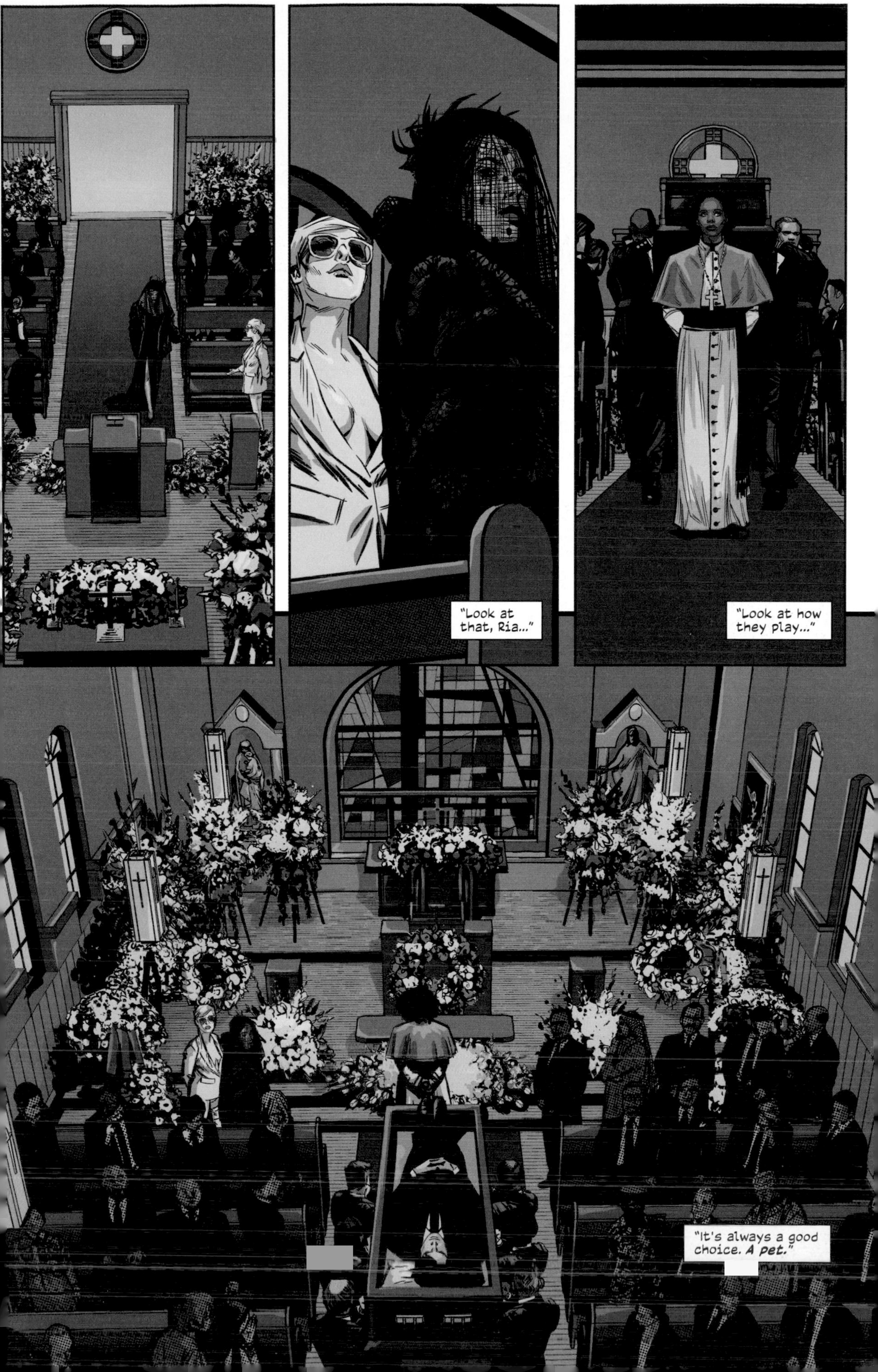
"Look at that, Ria..."
"Look at how they play..."
"It's always a good choice. *A pet.*"

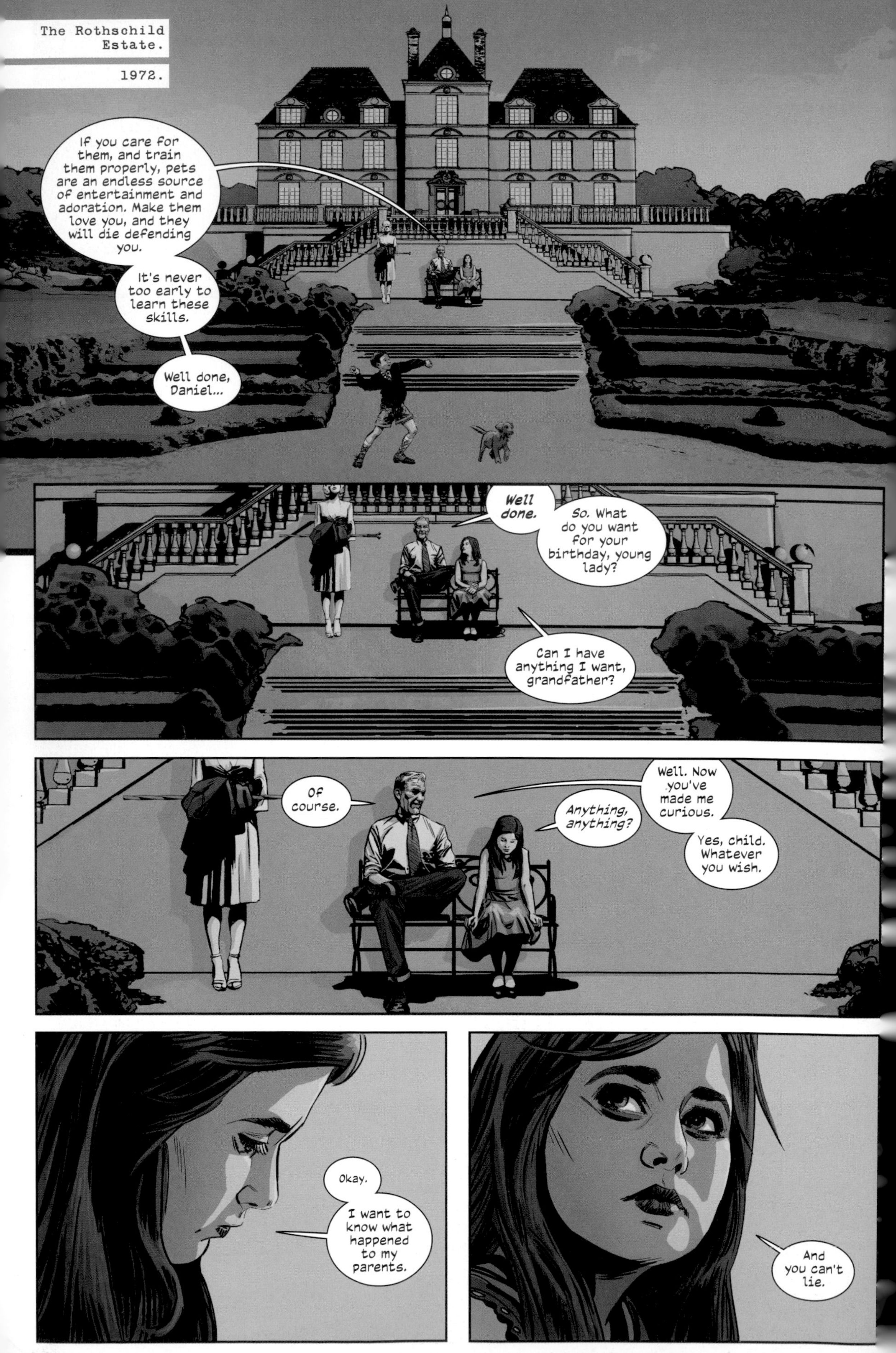

The Rothschild Estate.
1972.
If you care for them, and train them properly, pets are an endless source of entertainment and adoration. Make them love you, and they will die defending you.
It's never too early to learn these skills.
Well done, Daniel...
Well done.
So. What do you want for your birthday, young lady?
Can I have anything I want, grandfather?
Of course.
Anything, anything?
Well. Now you've made me curious.
Yes, child. Whatever you wish.
Okay.
I want to know what happened to my parents.
And you can't lie.

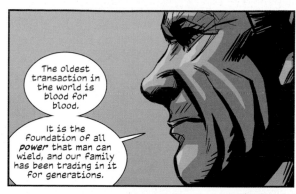

The oldest transaction in the world is blood for blood.

It is the foundation of all *power* that man can wield, and our family has been trading in it for generations.

All that you see -- *all this wealth* -- is simply the physical manifestation of that power.

Now take a good look at me, child.

I was born ninety years ago, but do not look a day over sixty. I am *strong* because I have devoured *many*.

The *purer* the line, the *better*.

One day I will be gone -- my circle closed on a millennial covenant...

When that happens, either you or your brother will become master of this house.

You'll understand better then, but in the future, try and remember these words...

Whenever possible, it's best to eat your own.

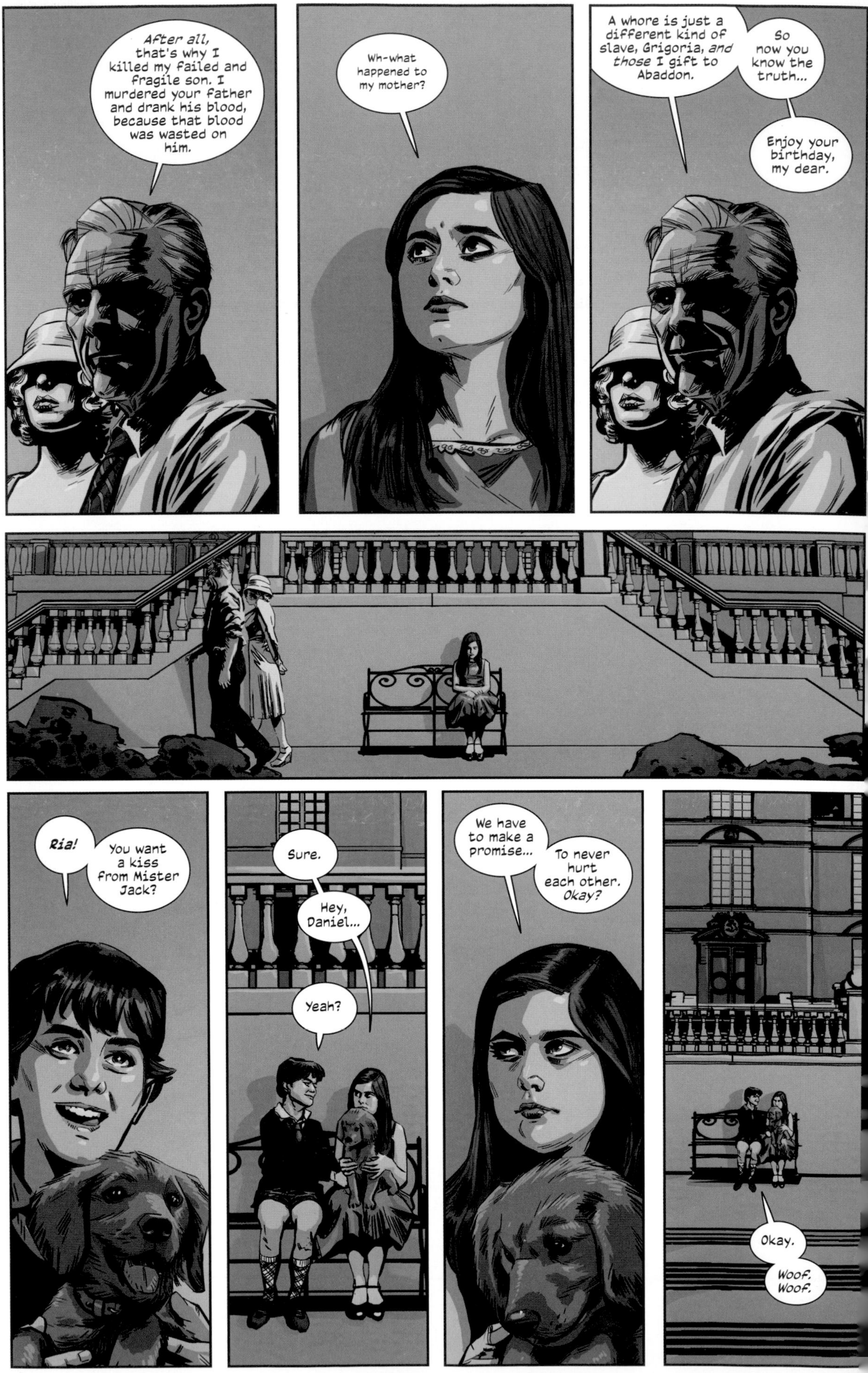

*After all,* that's why I killed my failed and fragile son. I murdered your father and drank his blood, because that blood was wasted on him.
Wh-what happened to my mother?
A whore is just a different kind of slave, Grigoria, *and those* I gift to Abaddon.
So now you know the truth...
Enjoy your birthday, my dear.
*Ria!*
You want a kiss from Mister Jack?
Sure.
Hey, Daniel...
Yeah?
We have to make a promise...
To never hurt each other. *Okay?*
Okay.
*Woof. Woof.*

THE DIARY OF WYNN ACKERMANN

Entry 182 - October 24, 1980

Raven Bischoff is dead. Yet another victim of the Stone Chair. She saved
me when she had no reason, and of all the people I know, she was the
most human.

She was a good, no, great woman, and I'm going to miss her so much.

I wish Beatrix didn't seem so happy about taking her place.

(b,c,d)

(e,f)

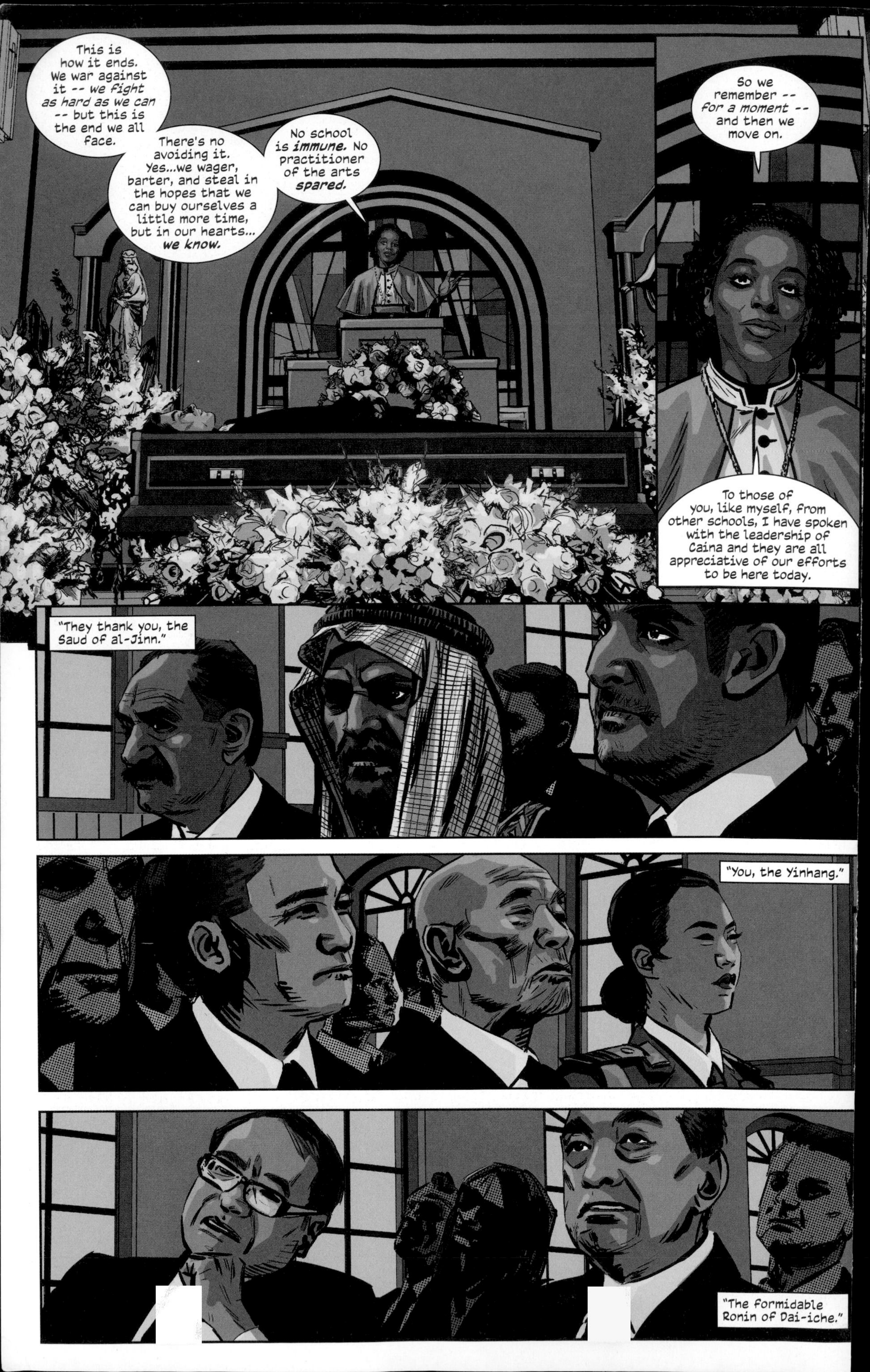
This is how it ends. We war against it -- we fight as hard as we can -- but this is the end we all face.
There's no avoiding it. Yes...we wager, barter, and steal in the hopes that we can buy ourselves a little more time, but in our hearts... we know.
No school is immune. No practitioner of the arts spared.
So we remember -- for a moment -- and then we move on.
To those of you, like myself, from other schools, I have spoken with the leadership of Caina and they are all appreciative of our efforts to be here today.
"They thank you, the Saud of al-Jinn."
"You, the Yinhang."
"The formidable Ronin of Dai-iche."

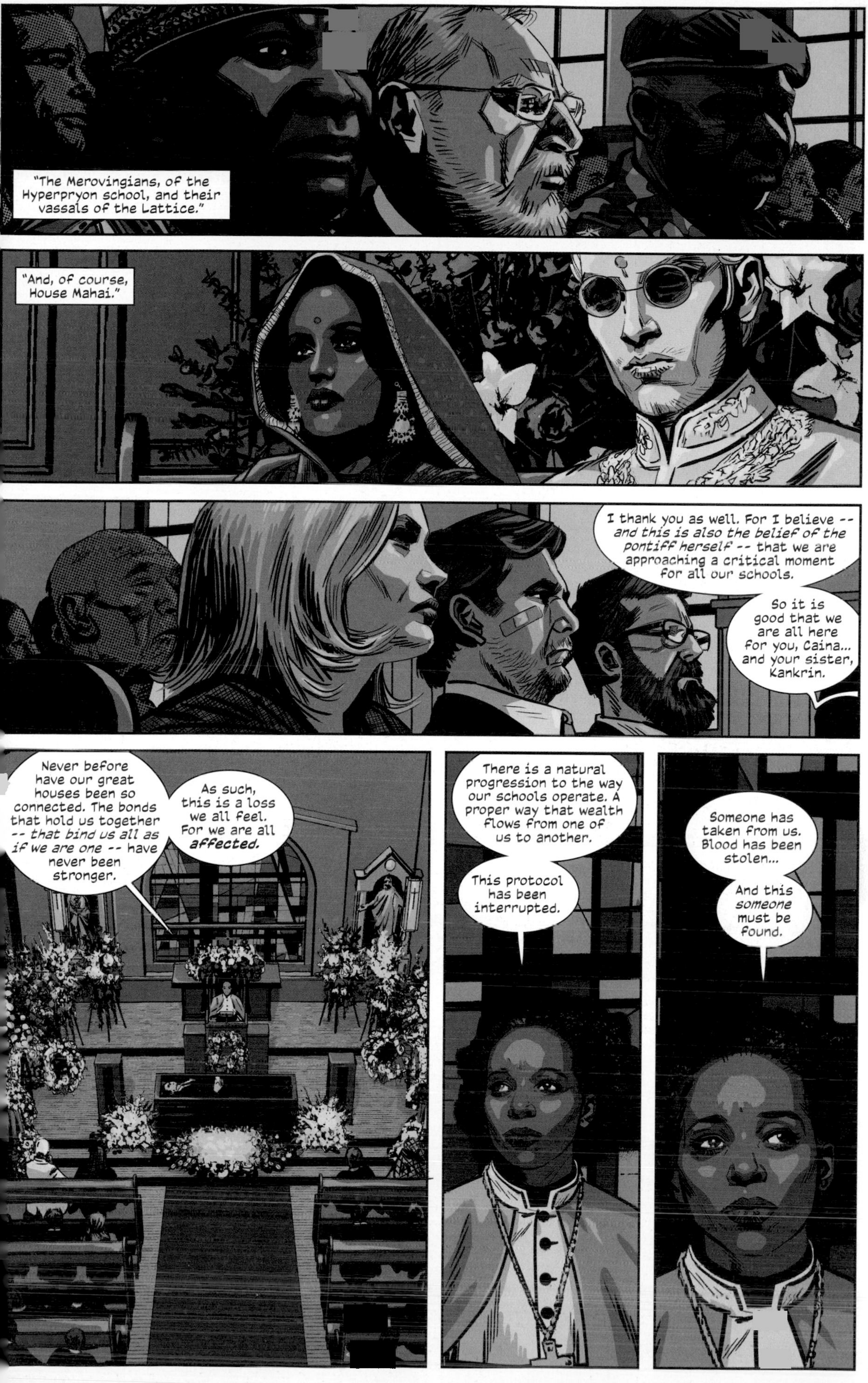
"The Merovingians, of the Hyperpryon school, and their vassals of the Lattice."
"And, of course, House Mahai."
I thank you as well. For I believe -- *and this is also the belief of the pontiff herself* -- that we are approaching a critical moment for all our schools.
So it is good that we are all here for you, Caina... and your sister, Kankrin.
Never before have our great houses been so connected. The bonds that hold us together *-- that bind us all as if we are one --* have never been stronger.
As such, this is a loss we all feel. For we are all ***affected.***
There is a natural progression to the way our schools operate. A proper way that wealth flows from one of us to another.
This protocol has been interrupted.
Someone has taken from us. Blood has been stolen...
And this *someone* must be found.

# *Homicide detectives to interview survivors of missing patriarch*

## Police say the case of well-known financier and philanthropist is still considered a missing person or possible death case.

October 13, 1981 | By Richard Grass, New York Times

After an eighth day of searching failed to produce the body, Hudson homicide detectives said they are now investigating his disappearance and plan to interview his surviving relatives.

Milton Rothschild was reported missing last Wednesday by one of his business partners after he did not return to the city for a previously scheduled board meeting. The partner, Thaddeus Dominic, told authorities he last spoke with Rothschild on the previous Friday. Both are board members of Caina Investment Bank.

After he could not reach him, Dominic travelled to Rothschild's Hudson Valley estate and found both of his grandchildren there accompanied by estate staff. Rothschild, however, could not be located, authorities said. Neither of the grandchildren could recall when their grandfather went missing, but they did confirm that he had been at the estate on Saturday and assumed he had returned to the city.

After searching for seven days on the estate and surrounding area, the case has been shifted from the missing person's detail to a team of homicide investigators. Several law enforcement sources said suspicious circumstances surrounding the case warrant the involvement of veteran homicide detectives.

Reached by telephone this morning, Daniel Rothschild declined to answer questions about his grandfather's disappearance until he talks to detectives later today. His sister, Grigoria Rothschild, could not be reached for comment.

Lt. Andy Simmons said both Rothschilds are cooperating with investigators, and although homicide detectives are investigating, it is still considered a missing person or possible death case.

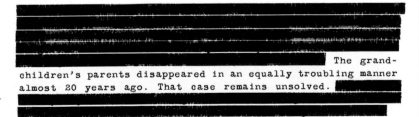

The grandchildren's parents disappeared in an equally troubling manner almost 20 years ago. That case remains unsolved.

Anyone with information should call the department homicide bureau at (845) 666-0000.

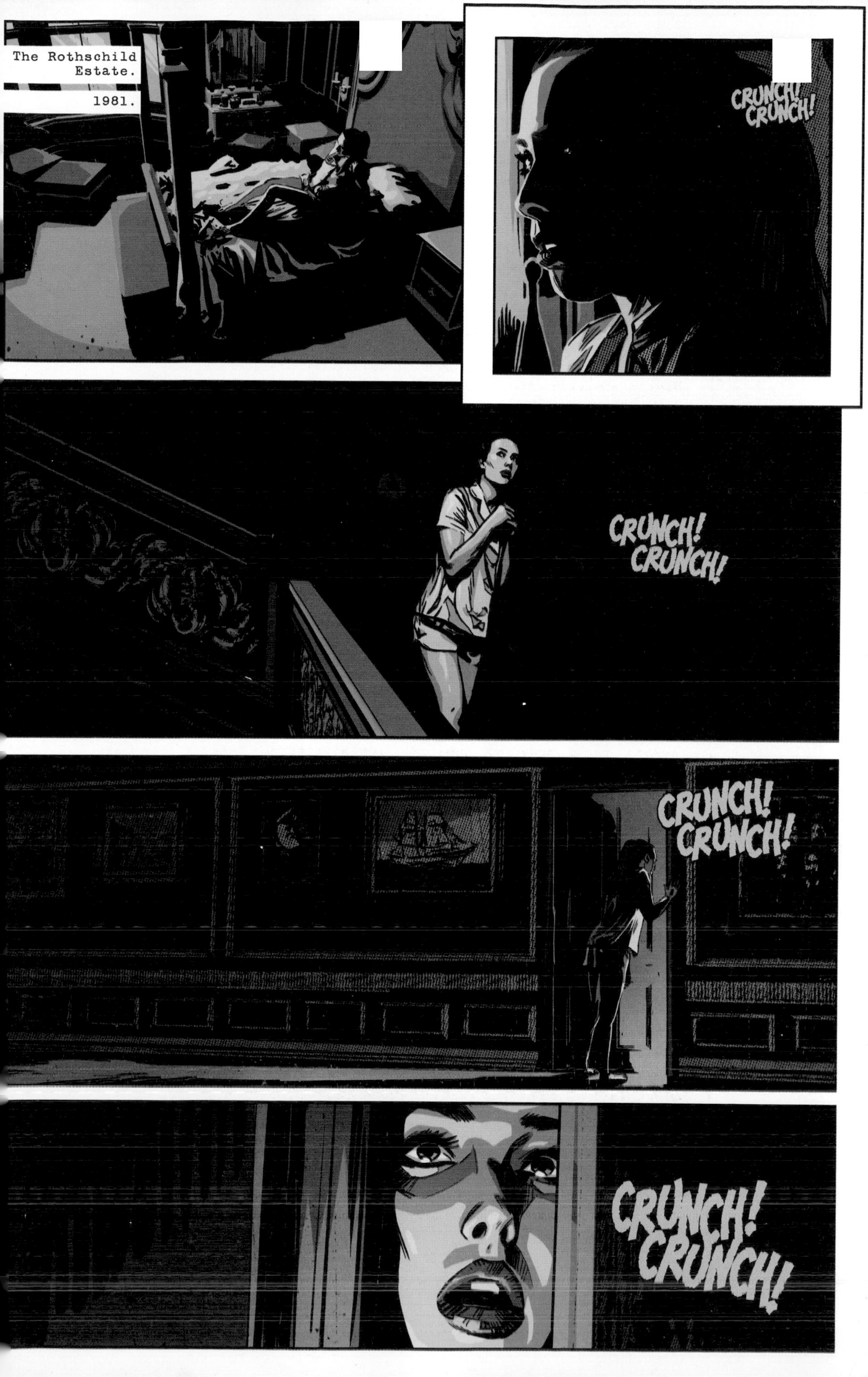
The Rothschild Estate.
1981.
CRUNCH! CRUNCH!
CRUNCH! CRUNCH!
CRUNCH! CRUNCH!
CRUNCH! CRUNCH!

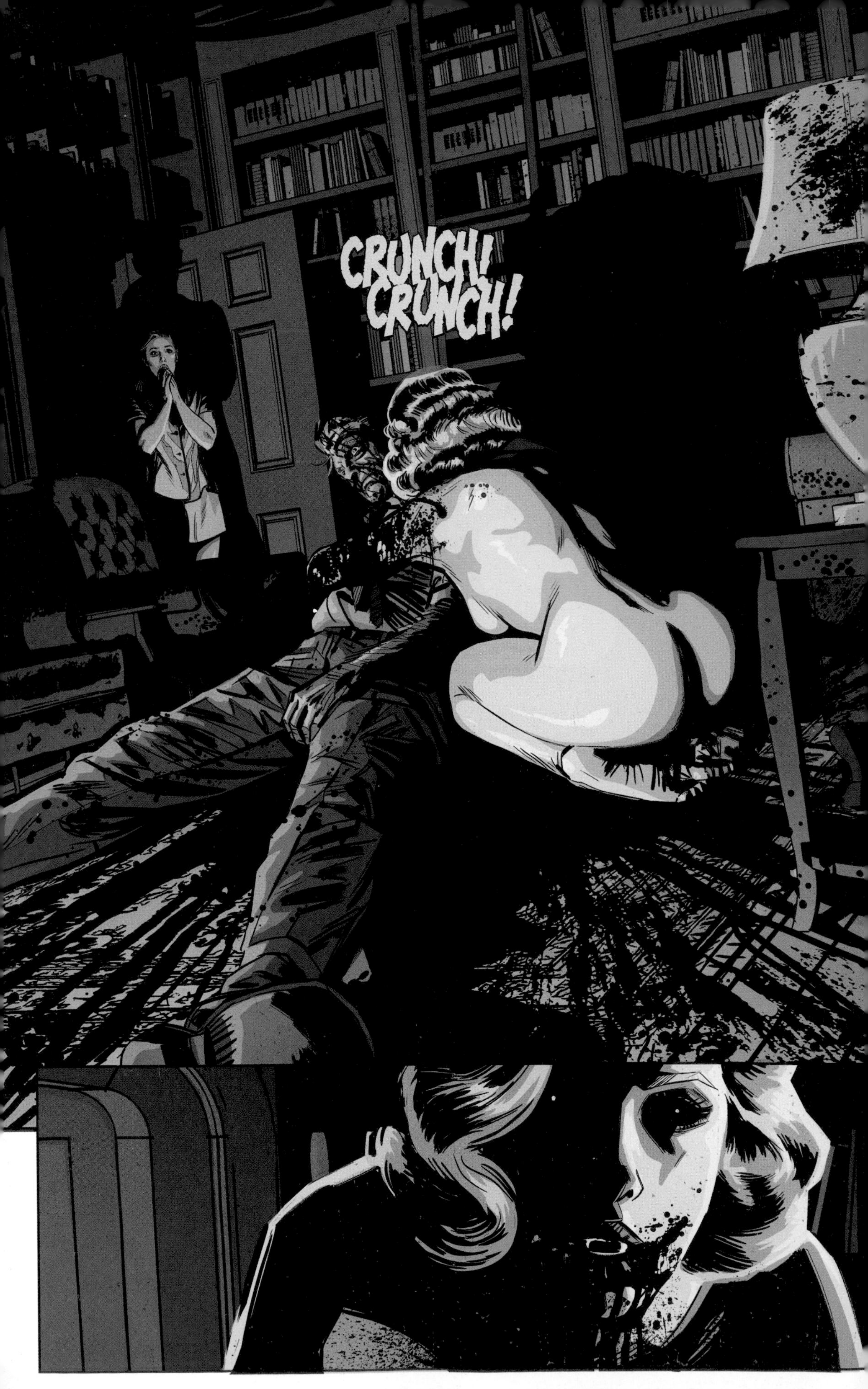
CRUNCH! CRUNCH!

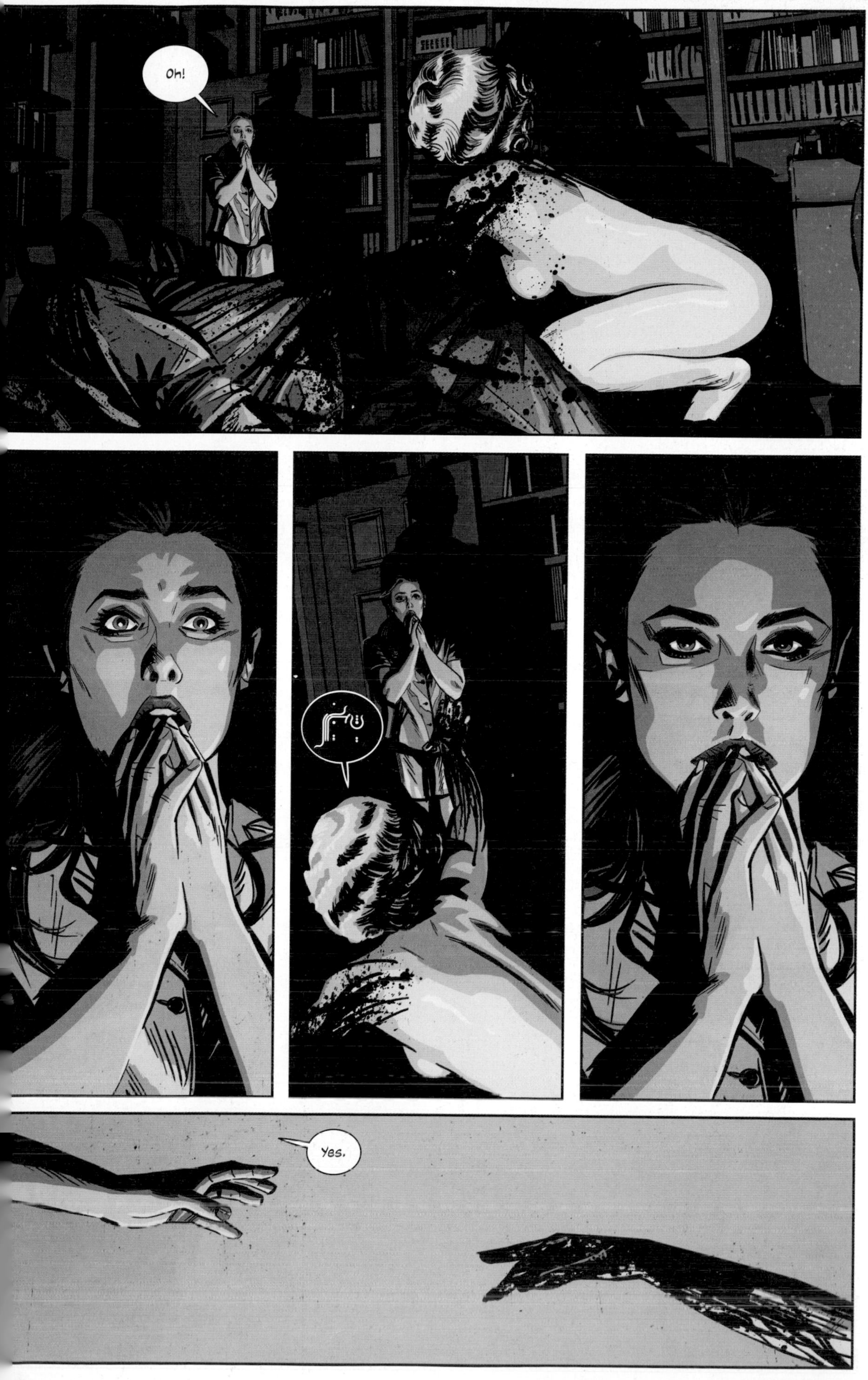
Oh!
Yes.

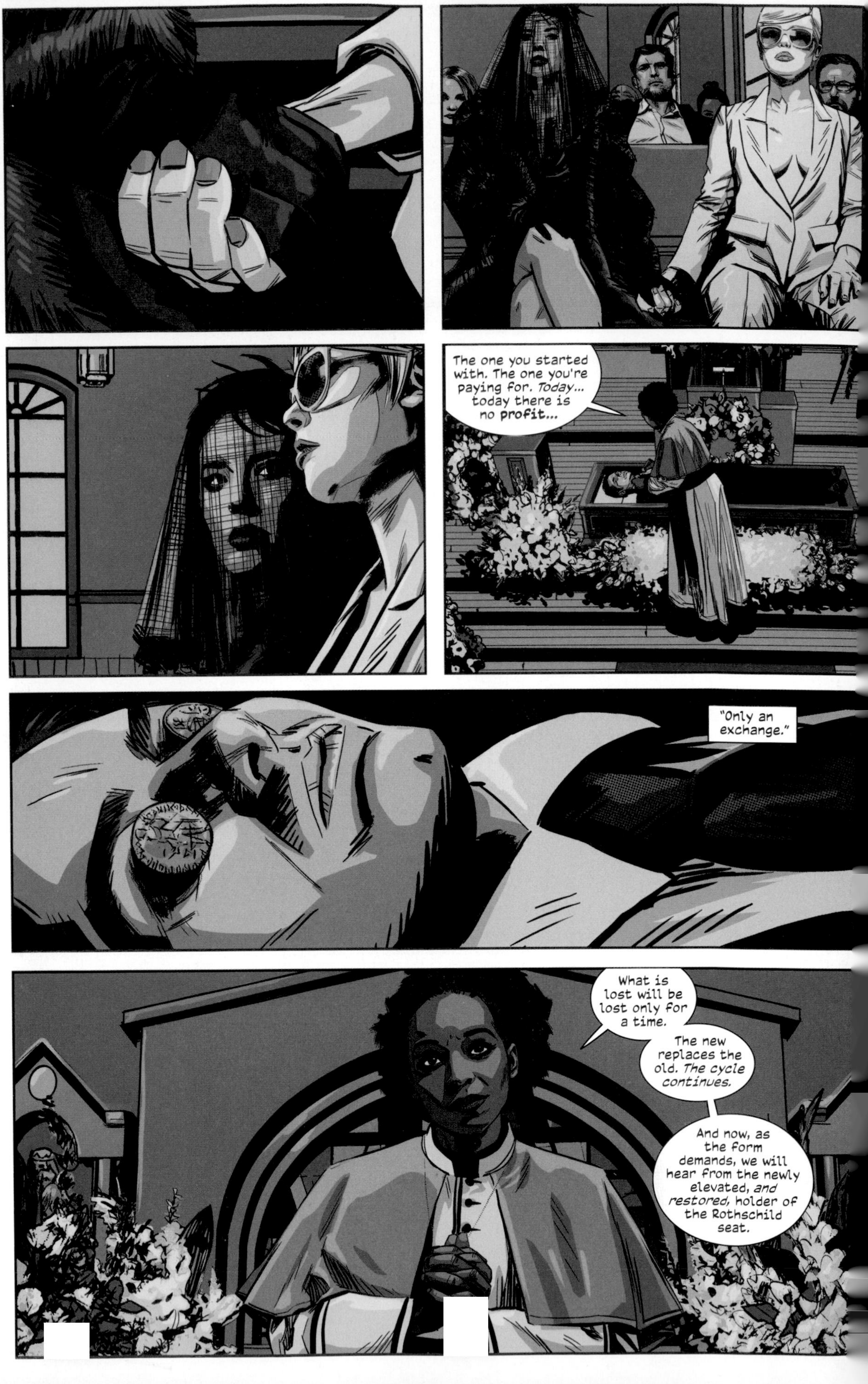
The one you started with. The one you're paying for. *Today*... today there is no **profit**...
"Only an exchange."
What is lost will be lost only for a time.
The new replaces the old. *The cycle continues.*
And now, as the form demands, we will hear from the newly elevated, *and restored,* holder of the Rothschild seat.

THE DIARY OF WYNN ACKERMANN


Entry 193 - November 19, 1980

Spoke with Beatrix regarding ideas to eliminate the Stone Chair. She
seems disinterested, or probably more fairly put, a slave to tradition.

Anyway, I have the germ of an idea. It's risky, and something I most
certainly won't be able to pull off on my own, but I think it's a plan
worth holding on to.

Why we tolerate this noose around our necks is beyond me. After all,
what's the power for if you can't shape the world into something more
accommodating of your desires? Maybe something will change. Maybe an
opportunity will present itself.



Entry 260 - December 30, 1981

I like these new Rothschilds. They are, most certainly, a proper kind of
ambitious.

I may have found what I've been looking for.

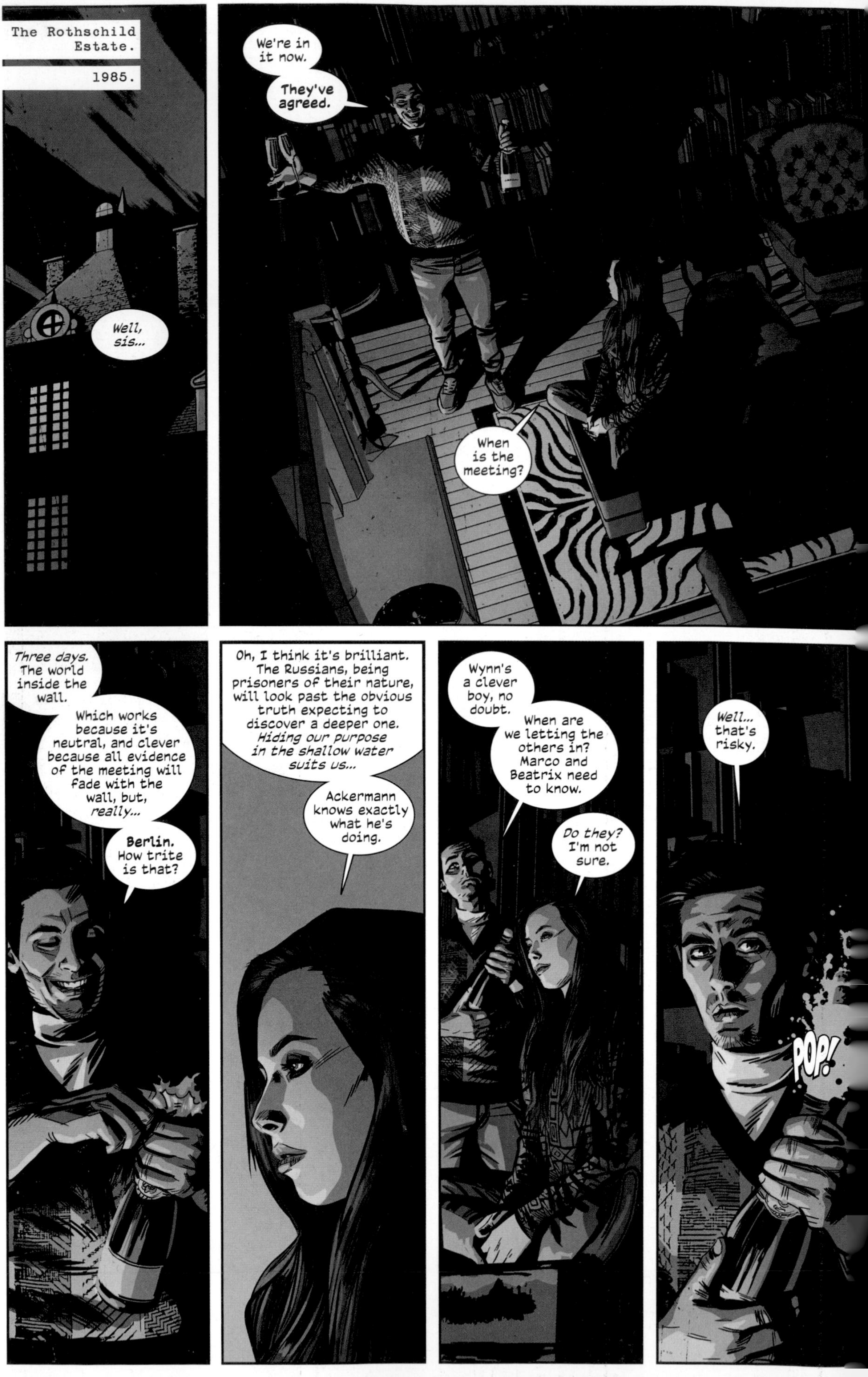
The Rothschild Estate.
1985.
Well, sis...
We're in it now.
They've agreed.
When is the meeting?
Three days. The world inside the wall.
Which works because it's neutral, and clever because all evidence of the meeting will fade with the wall, but, *really...*
**Berlin.** How trite is that?
Oh, I think it's brilliant. The Russians, being prisoners of their nature, will look past the obvious truth expecting to discover a deeper one. *Hiding our purpose in the shallow water suits us...*
Ackermann knows exactly what he's doing.
Wynn's a clever boy, no doubt.
When are we letting the others in? Marco and Beatrix need to know.
*Do they?* I'm not sure.
Well... that's risky.
POP!

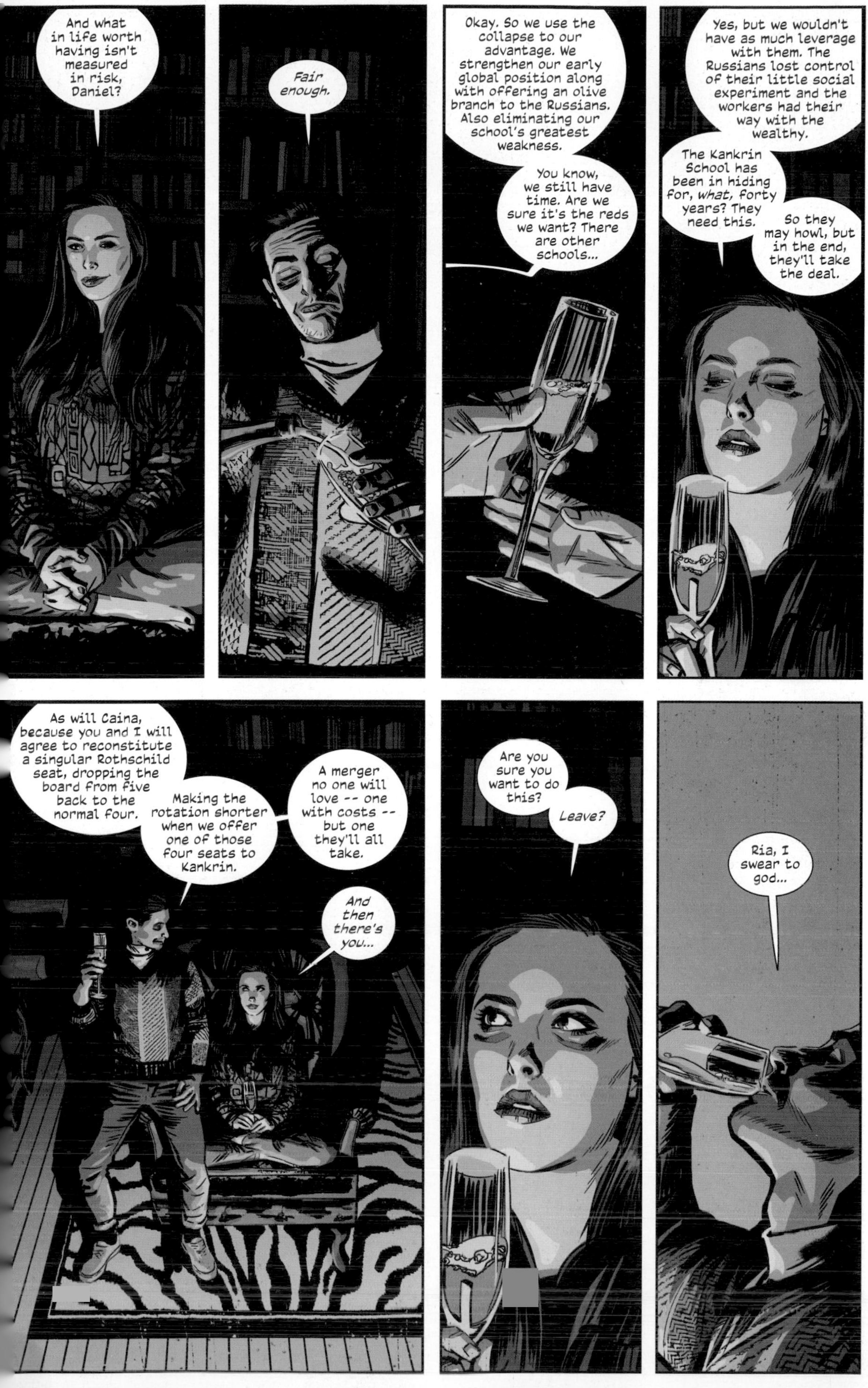
And what in life worth having isn't measured in risk, Daniel?
*Fair enough.*
Okay. So we use the collapse to our advantage. We strengthen our early global position along with offering an olive branch to the Russians. Also eliminating our school's greatest weakness.
You know, we still have time. Are we sure it's the reds we want? There are other schools...
Yes, but we wouldn't have as much leverage with them. The Russians lost control of their little social experiment and the workers had their way with the wealthy.
The Kankrin School has been in hiding for, *what*, forty years? They need this.
So they may howl, but in the end, they'll take the deal.
As will Caina, because you and I will agree to reconstitute a singular Rothschild seat, dropping the board from five back to the normal four.
Making the rotation shorter when we offer one of those four seats to Kankrin.
A merger no one will love -- one with costs -- but one they'll all take.
*And then there's you...*
Are you sure you want to do this?
*Leave?*
Ria, I swear to god...

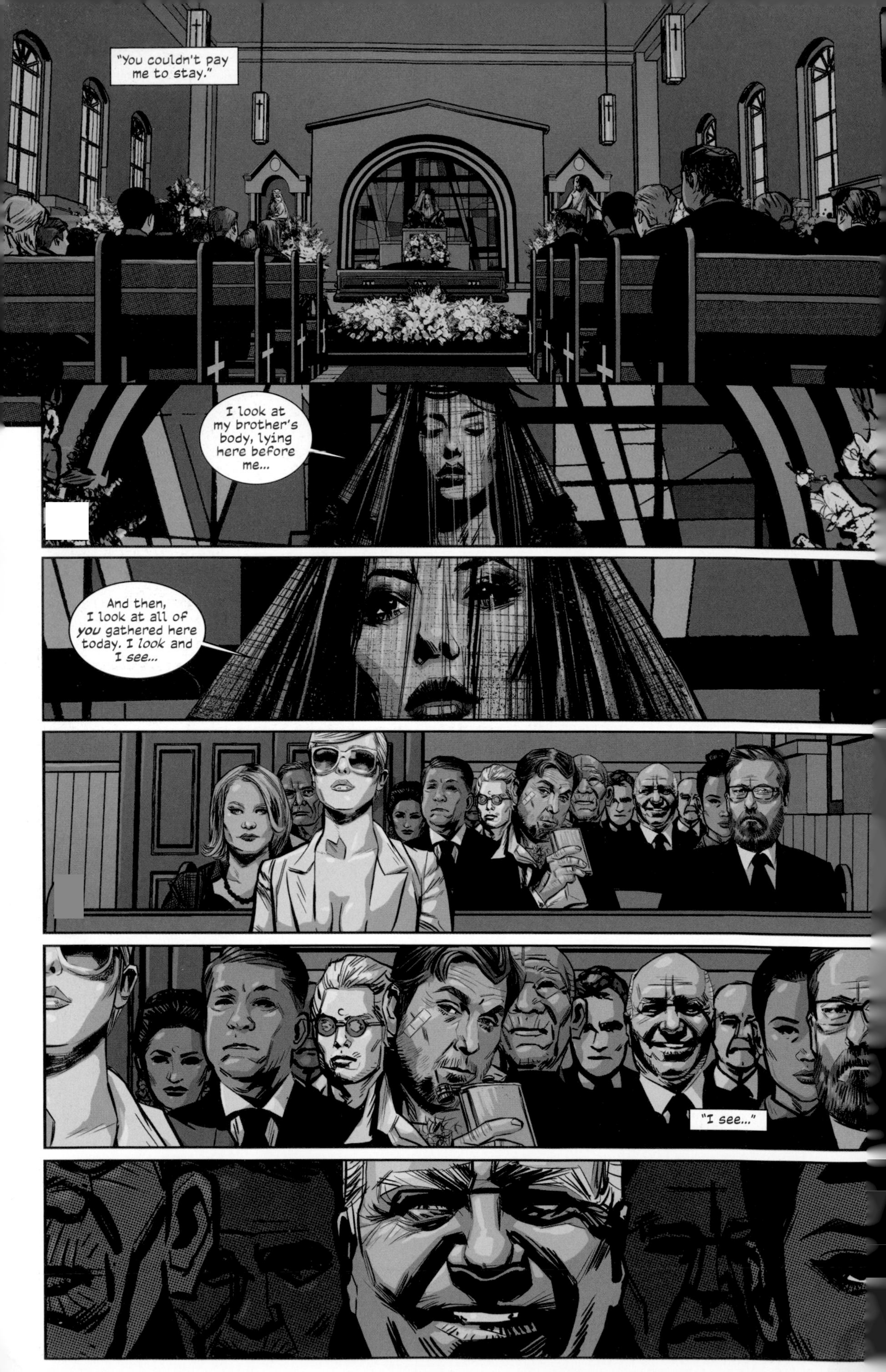
"You couldn't pay me to stay."
I look at my brother's body, lying here before me...
And then, I look at all of *you* gathered here today. I *look* and I see...
"I see..."

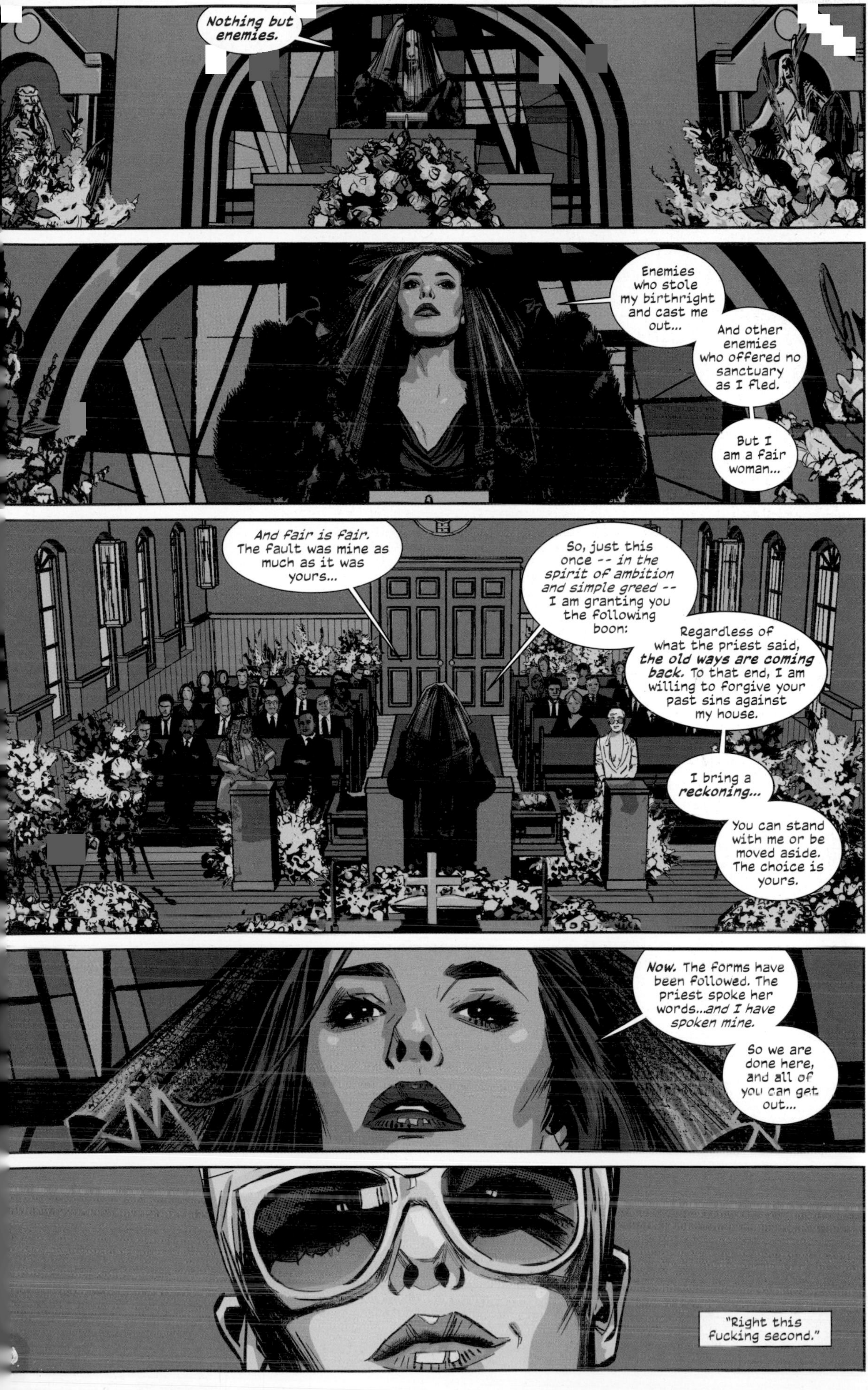
Nothing but enemies.
Enemies who stole my birthright and cast me out...
And other enemies who offered no sanctuary as I fled.
But I am a fair woman...
And fair is fair. The fault was mine as much as it was yours...
So, just this once -- in the spirit of ambition and simple greed -- I am granting you the following boon:
Regardless of what the priest said, the old ways are coming back. To that end, I am willing to forgive your past sins against my house.
I bring a reckoning...
You can stand with me or be moved aside. The choice is yours.
Now. The forms have been followed. The priest spoke her words...and I have spoken mine.
So we are done here, and all of you can get out...
"Right this fucking second."

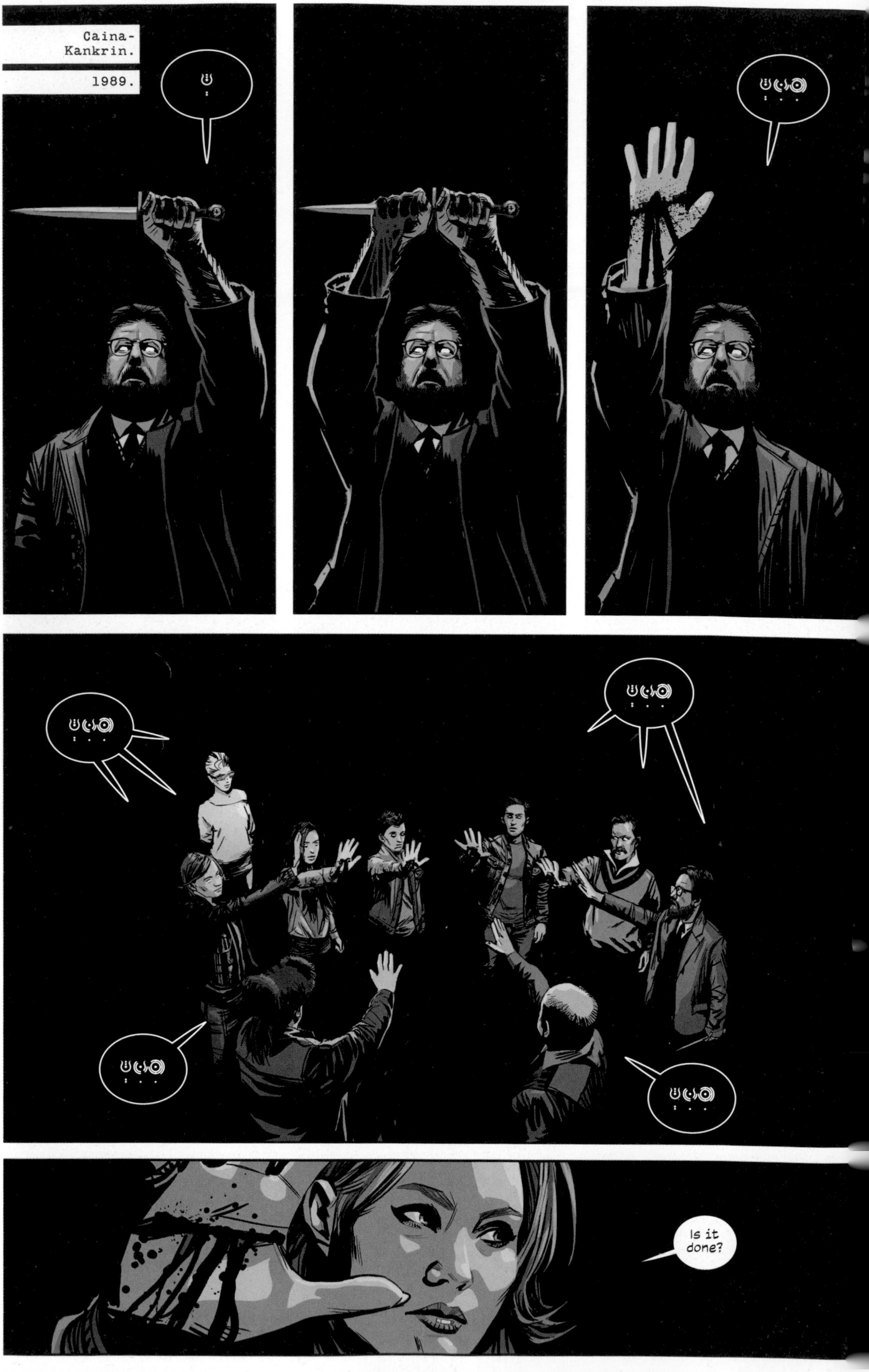
Caina-
Kankrin.
1989.
Is it
done?

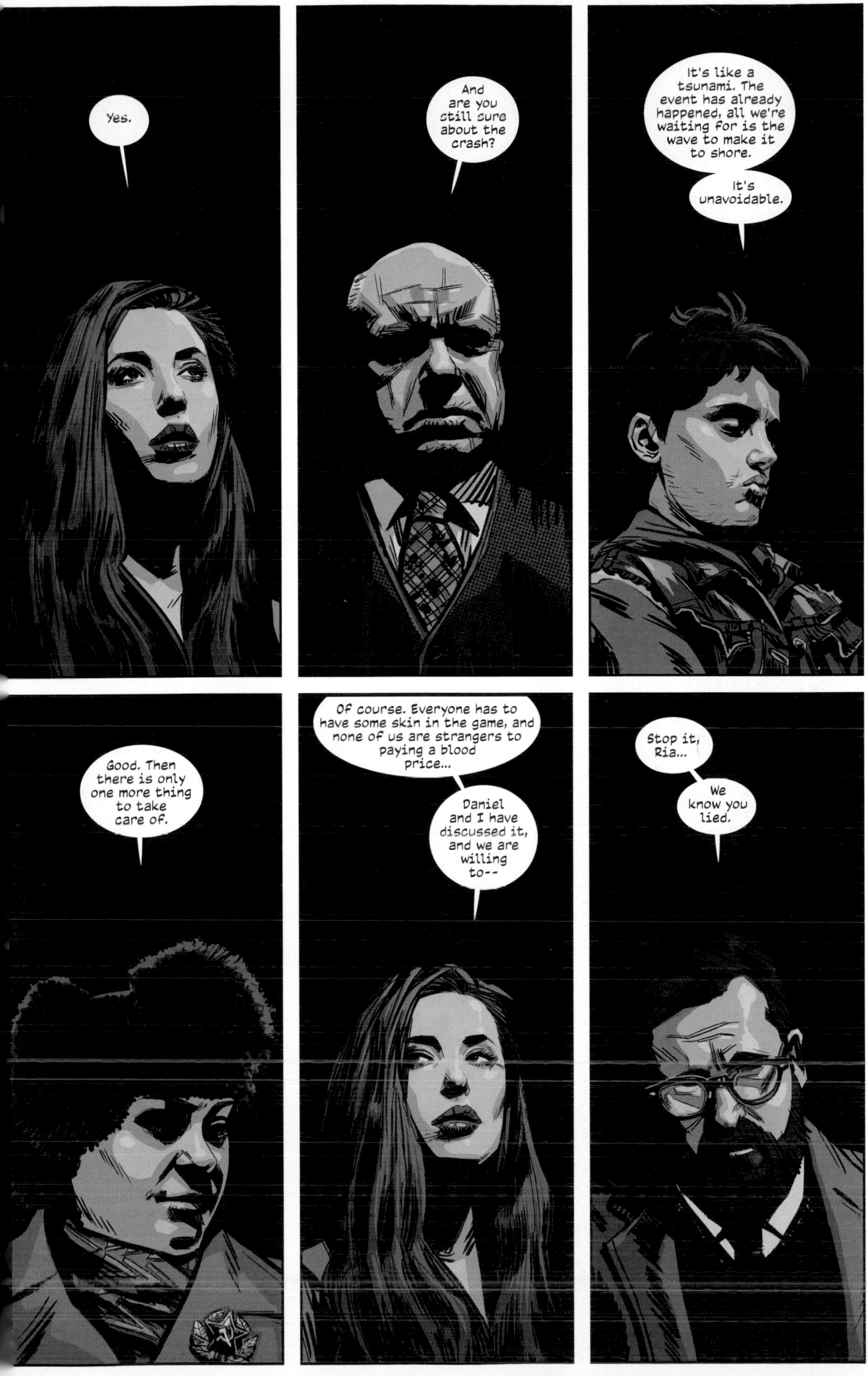
Yes.
And are you still sure about the crash?
It's like a tsunami. The event has already happened, all we're waiting for is the wave to make it to shore.
It's unavoidable.
Good. Then there is only one more thing to take care of.
Of course. Everyone has to have some skin in the game, and none of us are strangers to paying a blood price...
Daniel and I have discussed it, and we are willing to--
Stop it, Ria...
We know you lied.

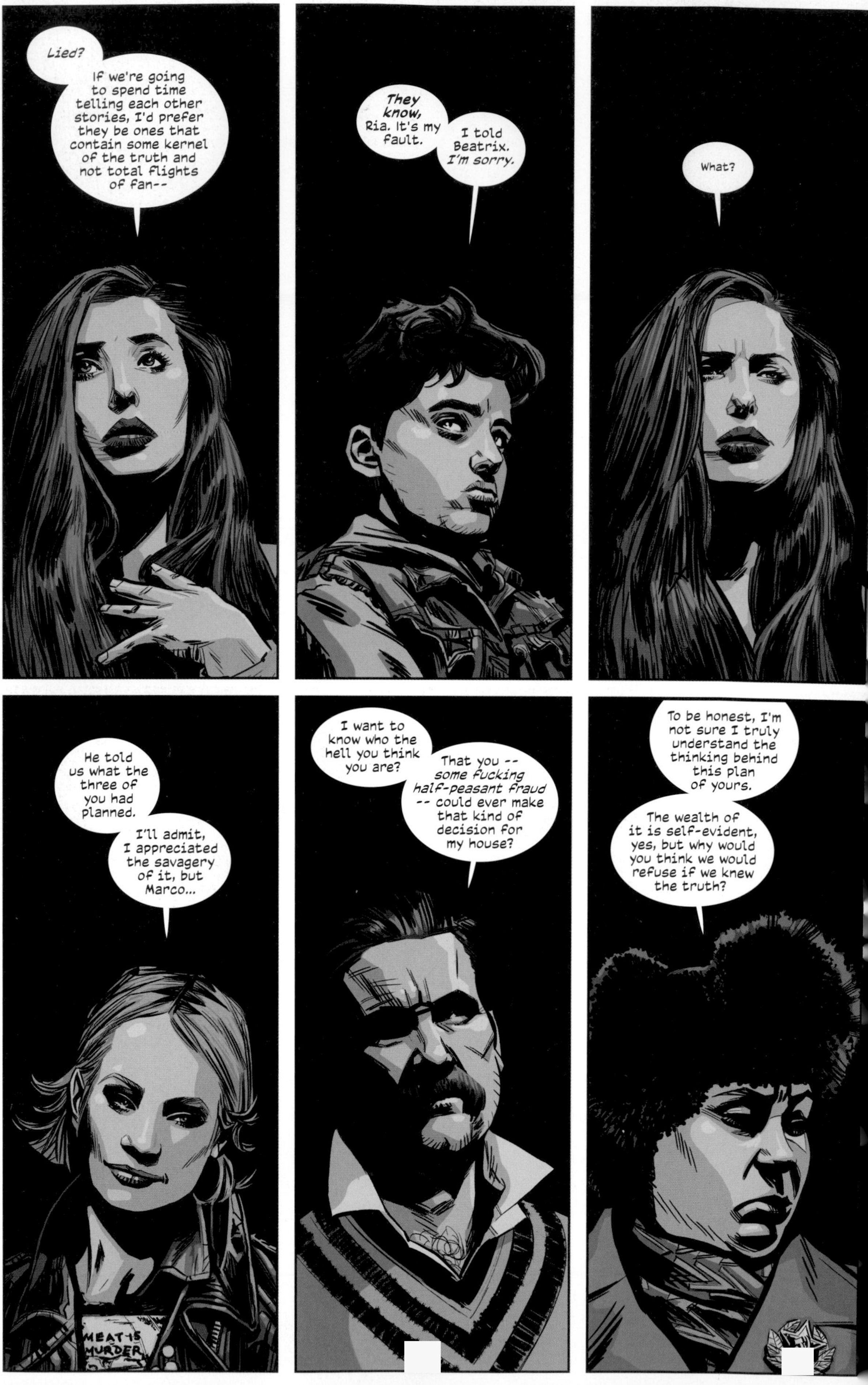
Lied?
If we're going to spend time telling each other stories, I'd prefer they be ones that contain some kernel of the truth and not total flights of fan--
They know, Ria. It's my fault.
I told Beatrix. I'm sorry.
What?
He told us what the three of you had planned.
I'll admit, I appreciated the savagery of it, but Marco...
I want to know who the hell you think you are?
That you -- some fucking half-peasant fraud -- could ever make that kind of decision for my house?
To be honest, I'm not sure I truly understand the thinking behind this plan of yours.
The wealth of it is self-evident, yes, but why would you think we would refuse if we knew the truth?
MEAT IS MURDER

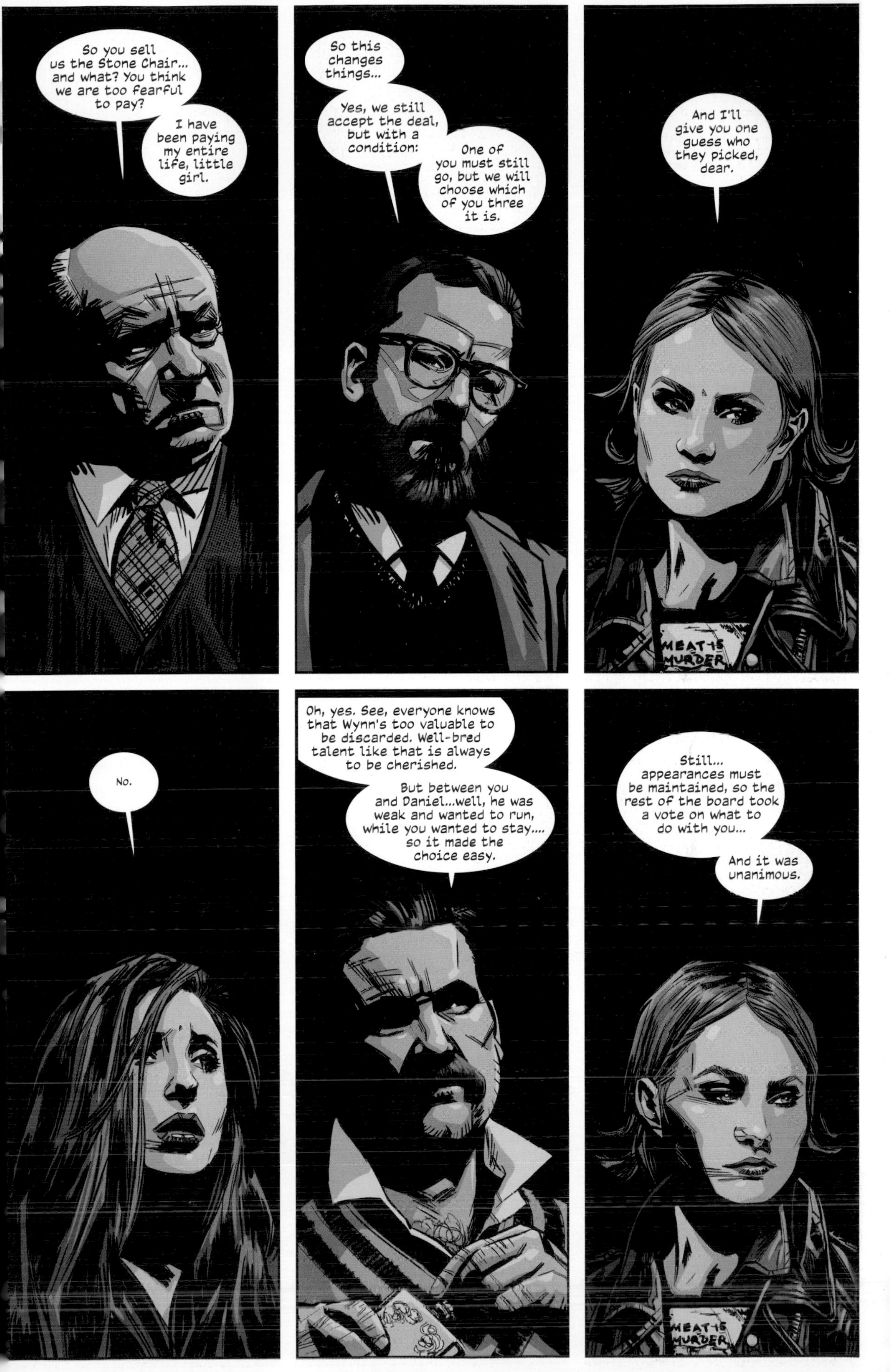

So you sell us the Stone Chair... and what? You think we are too fearful to pay?
I have been paying my entire life, little girl.
So this changes things...
Yes, we still accept the deal, but with a condition:
One of you must still go, but we will choose which of you three it is.
And I'll give you one guess who they picked, dear.
MEAT IS MURDER
No.
Oh, yes. See, everyone knows that Wynn's too valuable to be discarded. Well-bred talent like that is always to be cherished.
But between you and Daniel...well, he was weak and wanted to run, while you wanted to stay.... so it made the choice easy.
Still... appearances must be maintained, so the rest of the board took a vote on what to do with you...
And it was unanimous.
MEAT IS MURDER

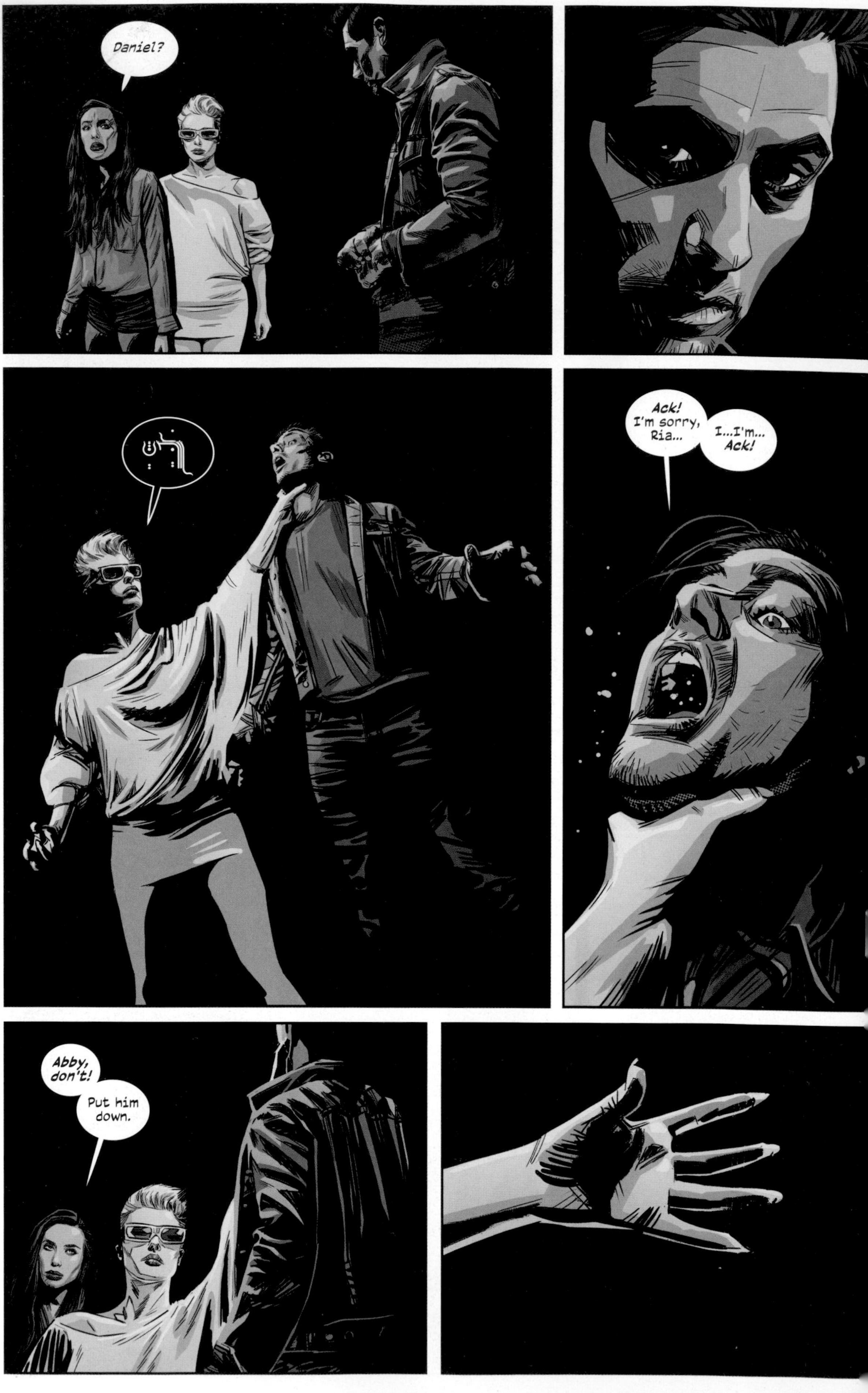
Daniel?
Ack! I'm sorry, Ria...
I...I'm... Ack!
Abby, don't!
Put him down.

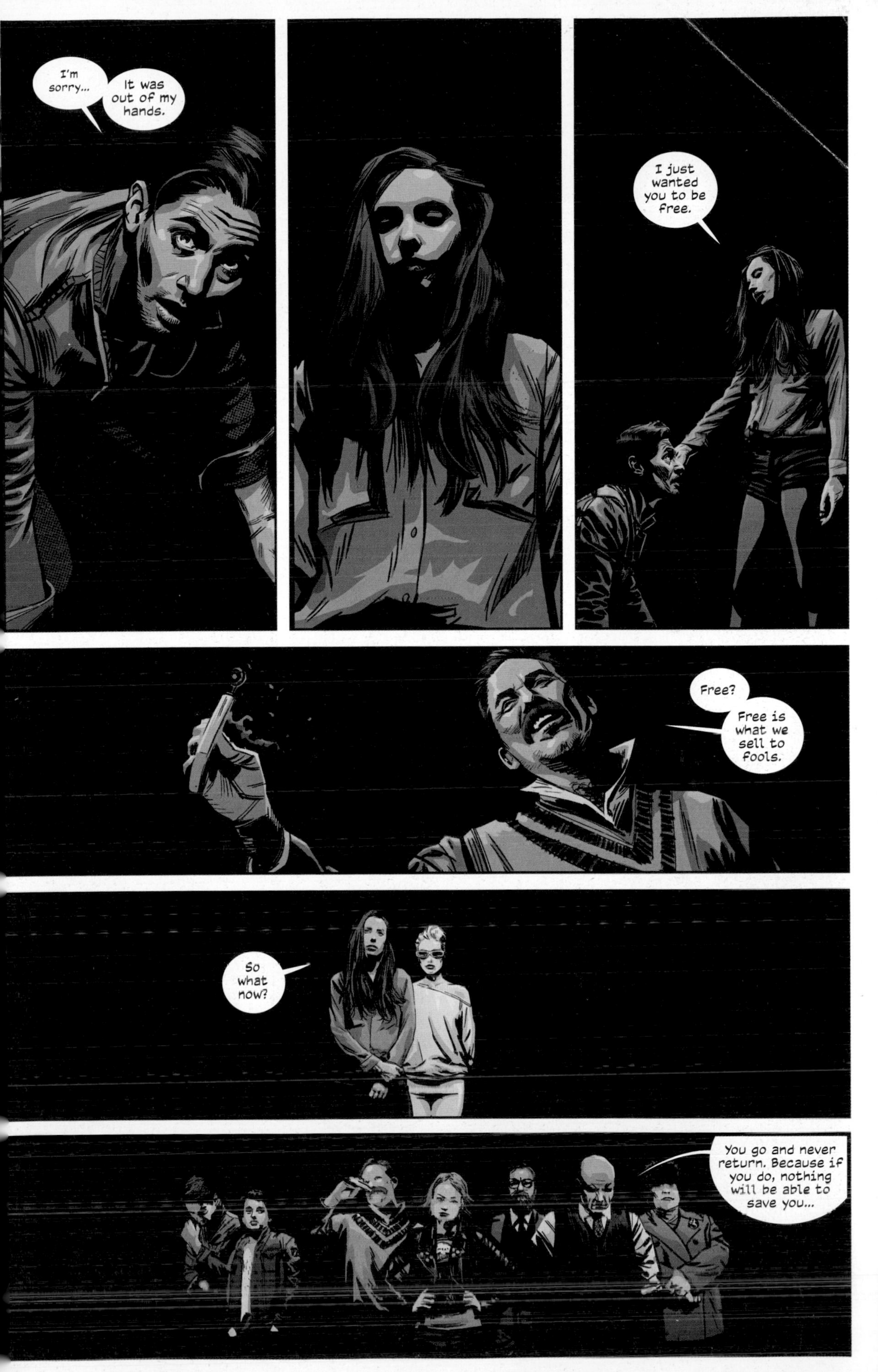
I'm sorry...
It was out of my hands.
I just wanted you to be free.
Free?
Free is what we sell to fools.
So what now?
You go and never return. Because if you do, nothing will be able to save you...

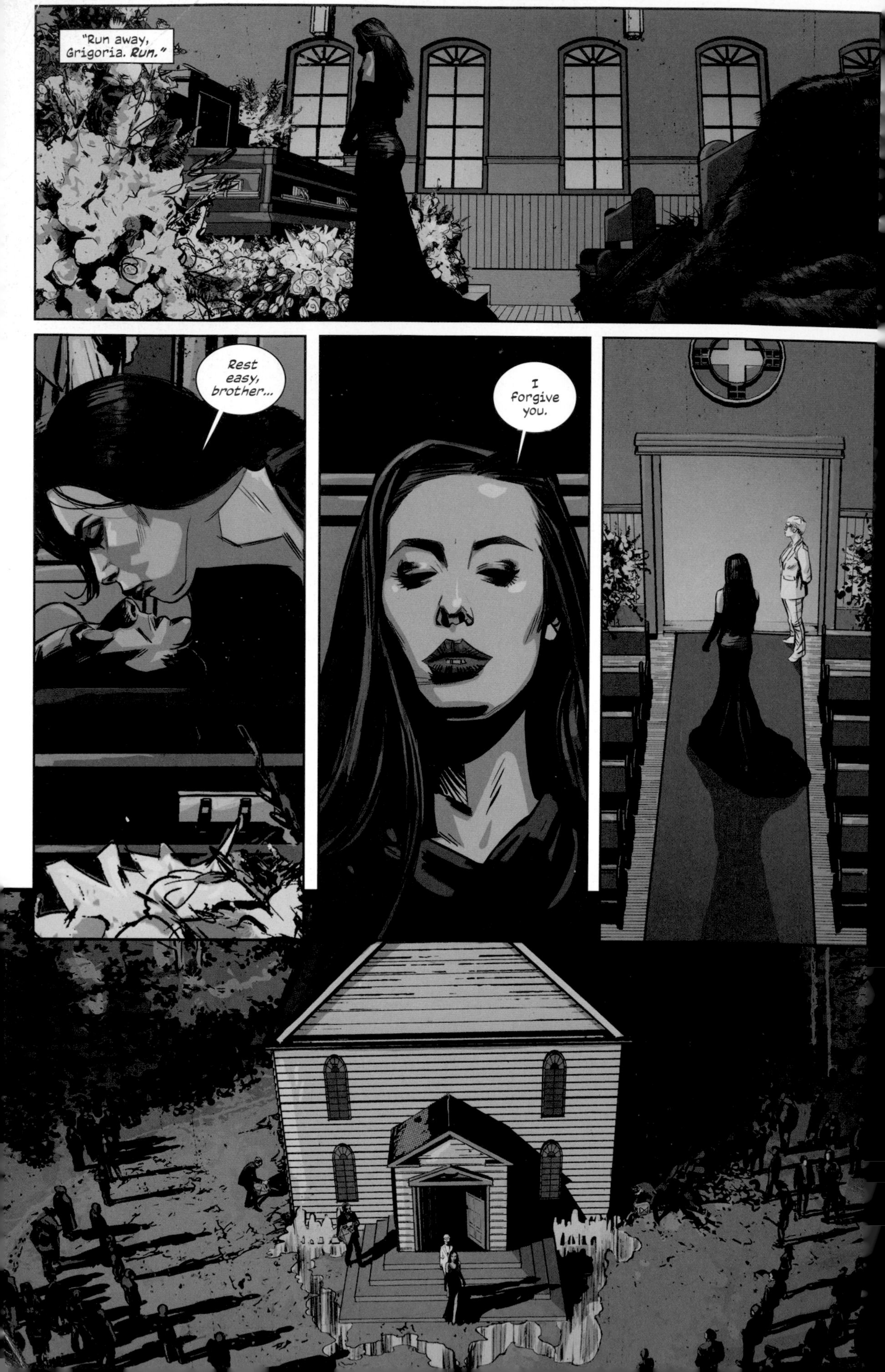
"Run away, Grigoria. *Run.*"
Rest easy, brother...
I forgive you.

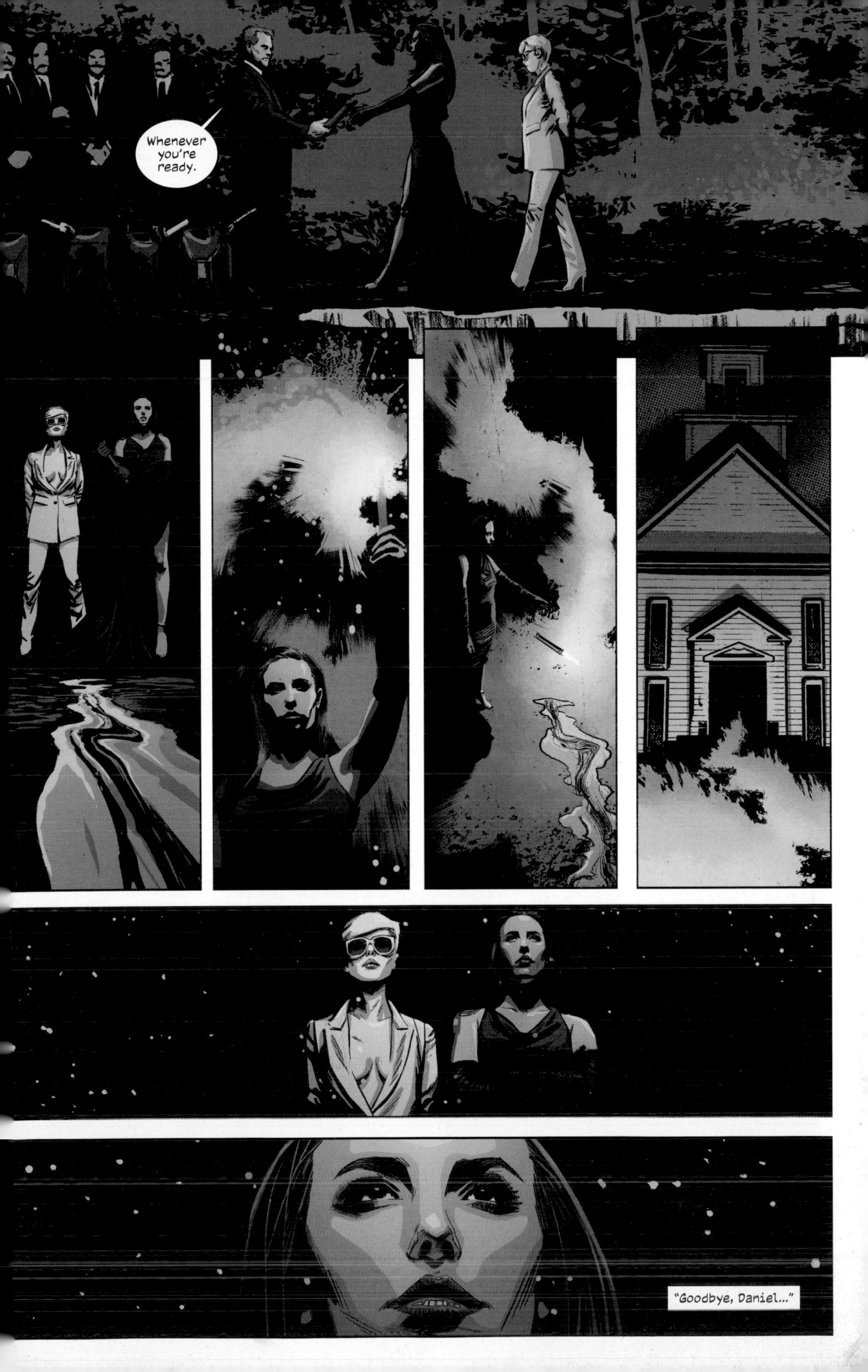
Whenever you're ready.
"Goodbye, Daniel..."

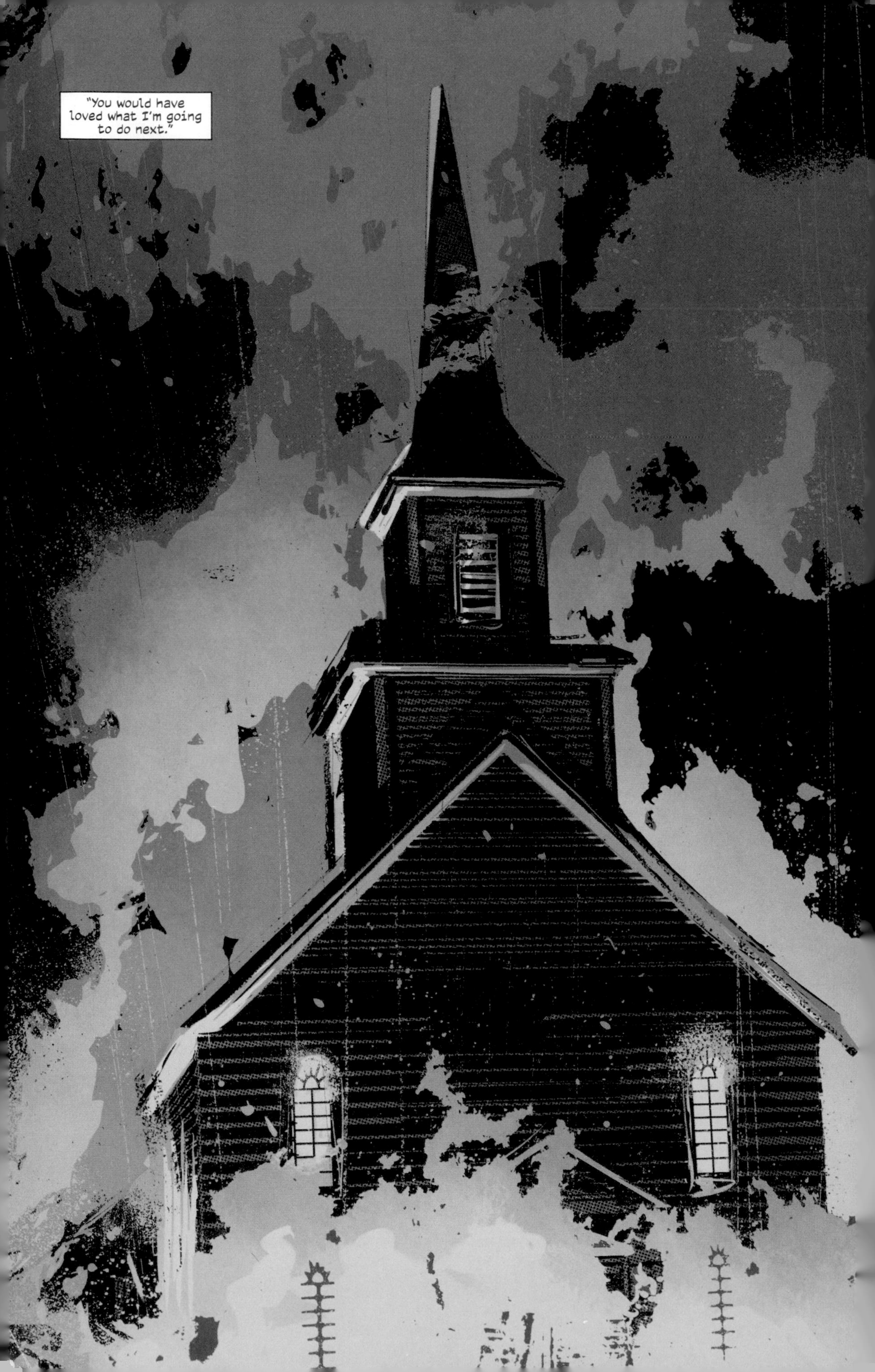
"You would have loved what I'm going to do next."

Burn it all.

SKETCHES

-  COVER DESIGNS  -
- CHARACTER STUDIES -

Artist: Tomm Coker Title: Issue: Page:

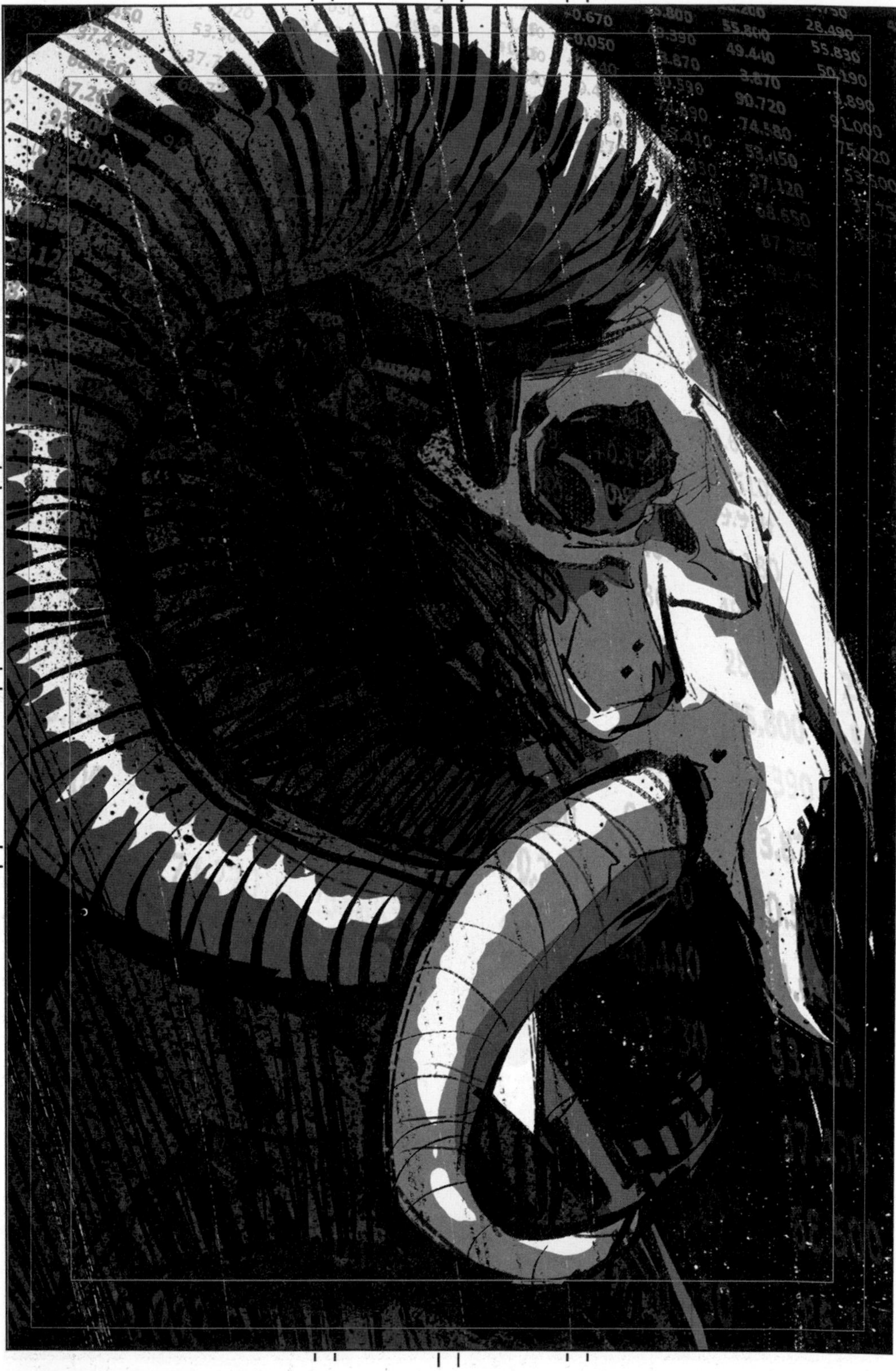

-0.670
55.800
28.490
49.440
55.830
90.720
74.580
53.450
37.120
68.650

Artist: Tomm Coker Title: TBMM Issue: 001 Page:

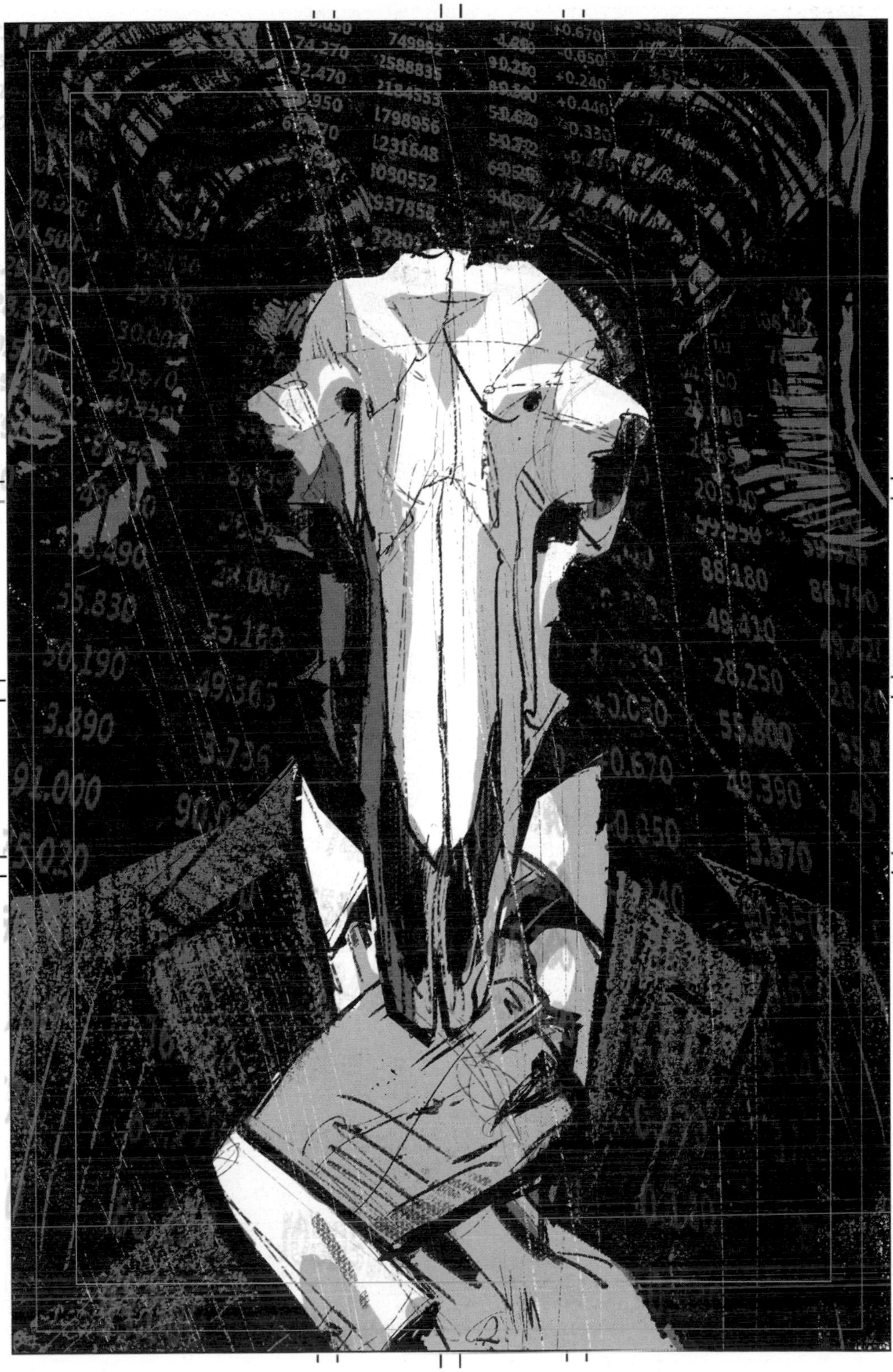

Artist: Tomm Coker Title: tBMM Issue: 002 Page:

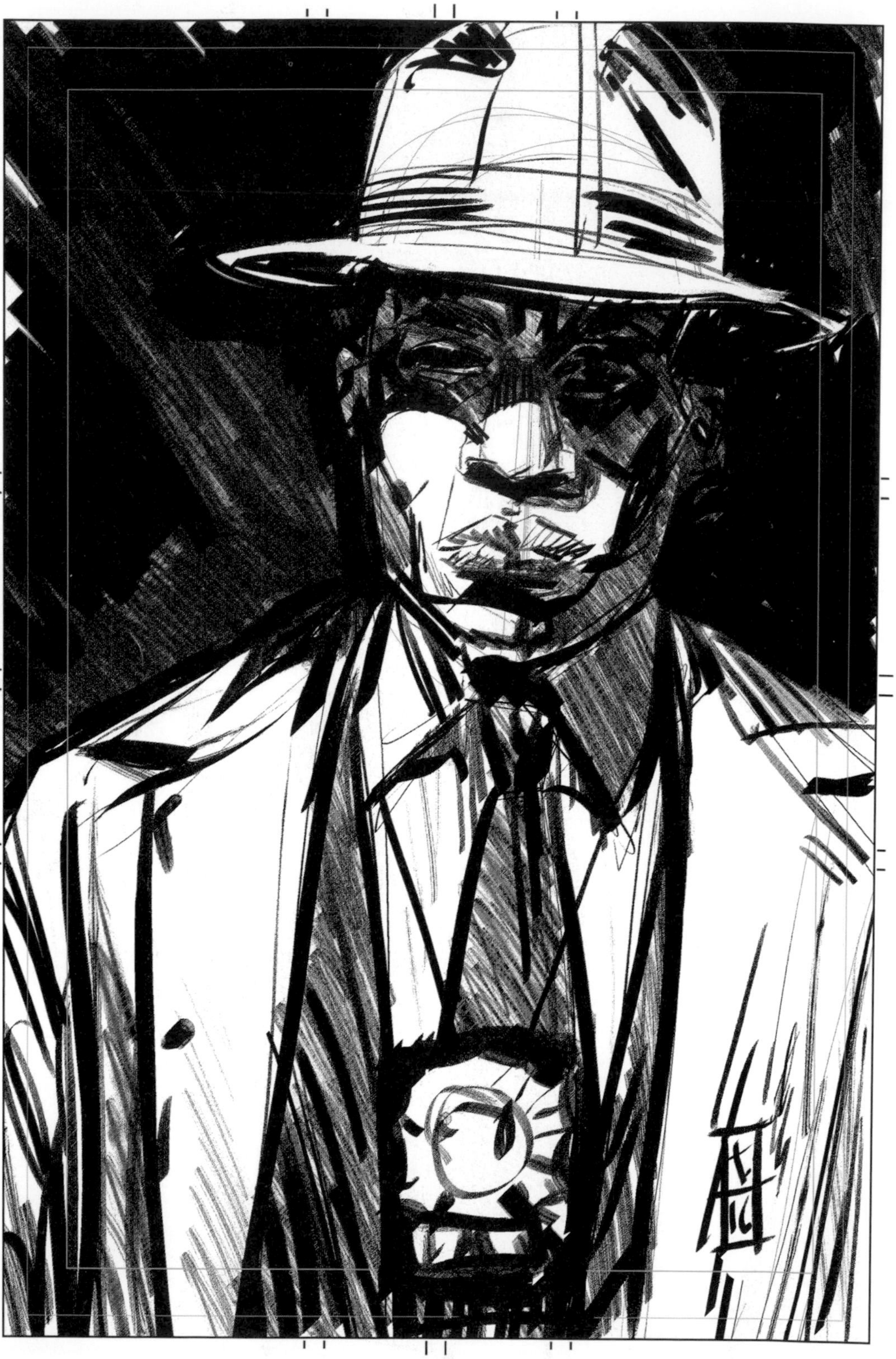

Artist: Tomm Coker Title: TBMM Issue: 002 Page:

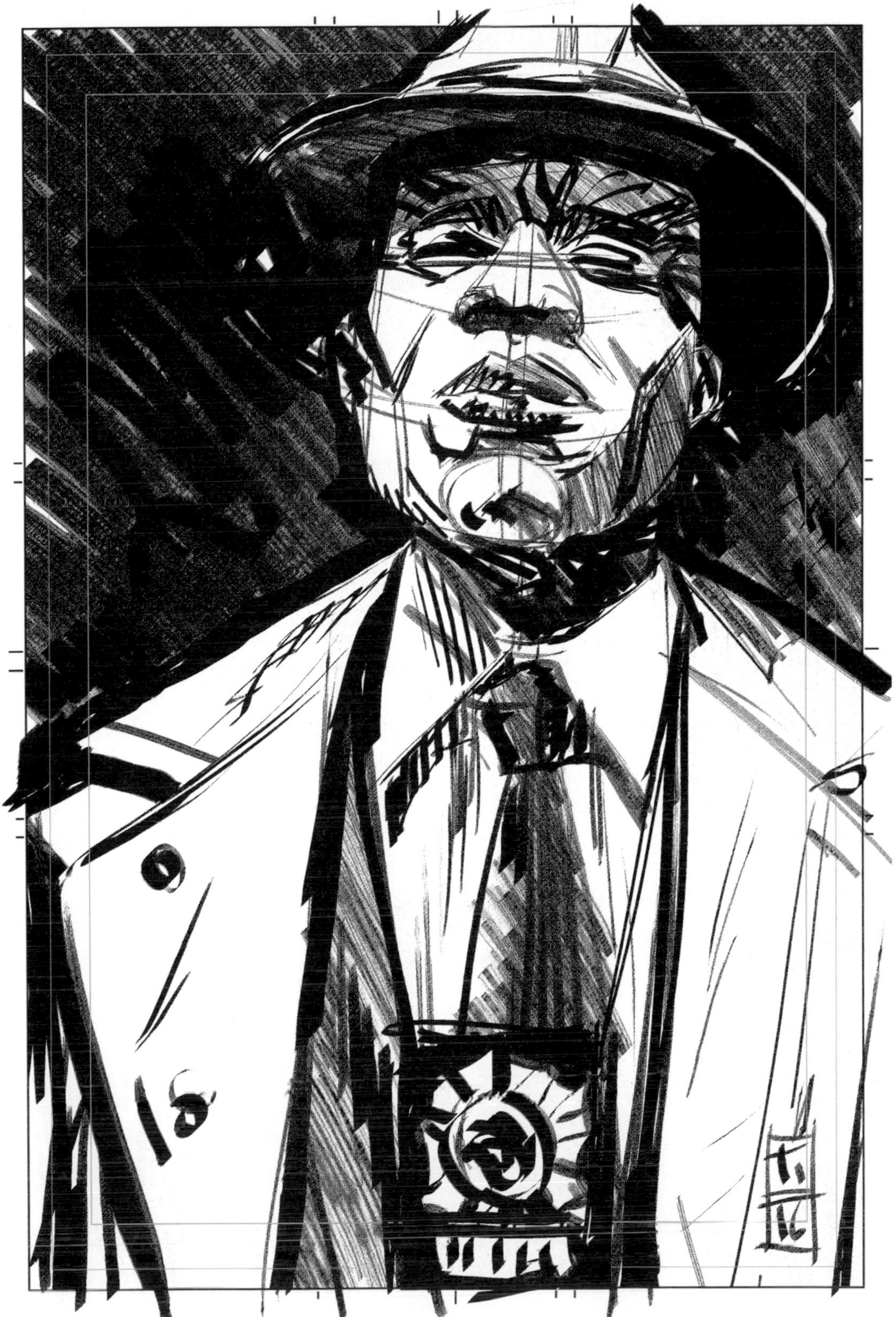

**Artist:** Tomm Coker **Title:** tomm **Issue:** 002 **Page:**

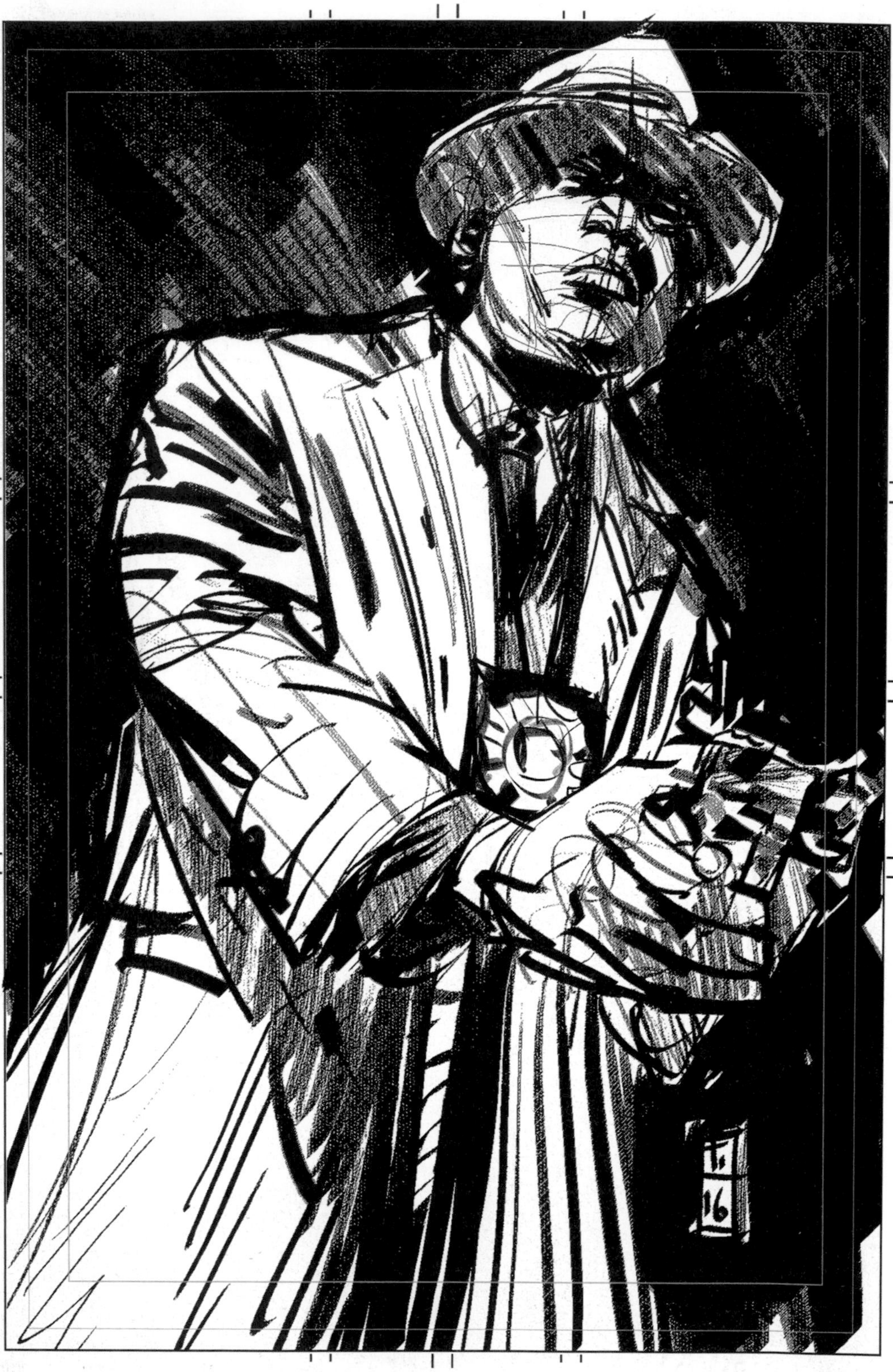

Artist: Tomm Coker Title: TBMM Issue: 003 Page:

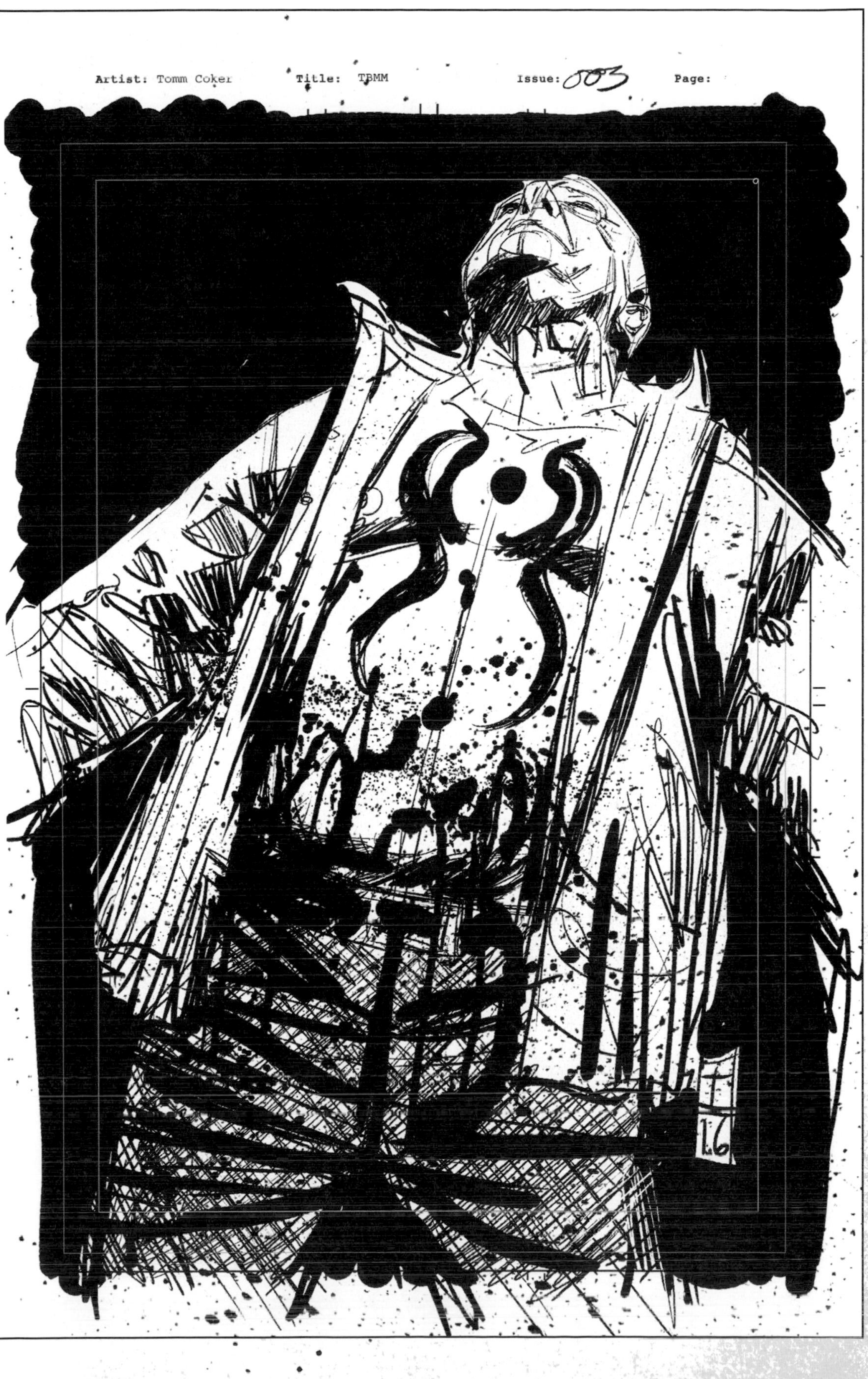

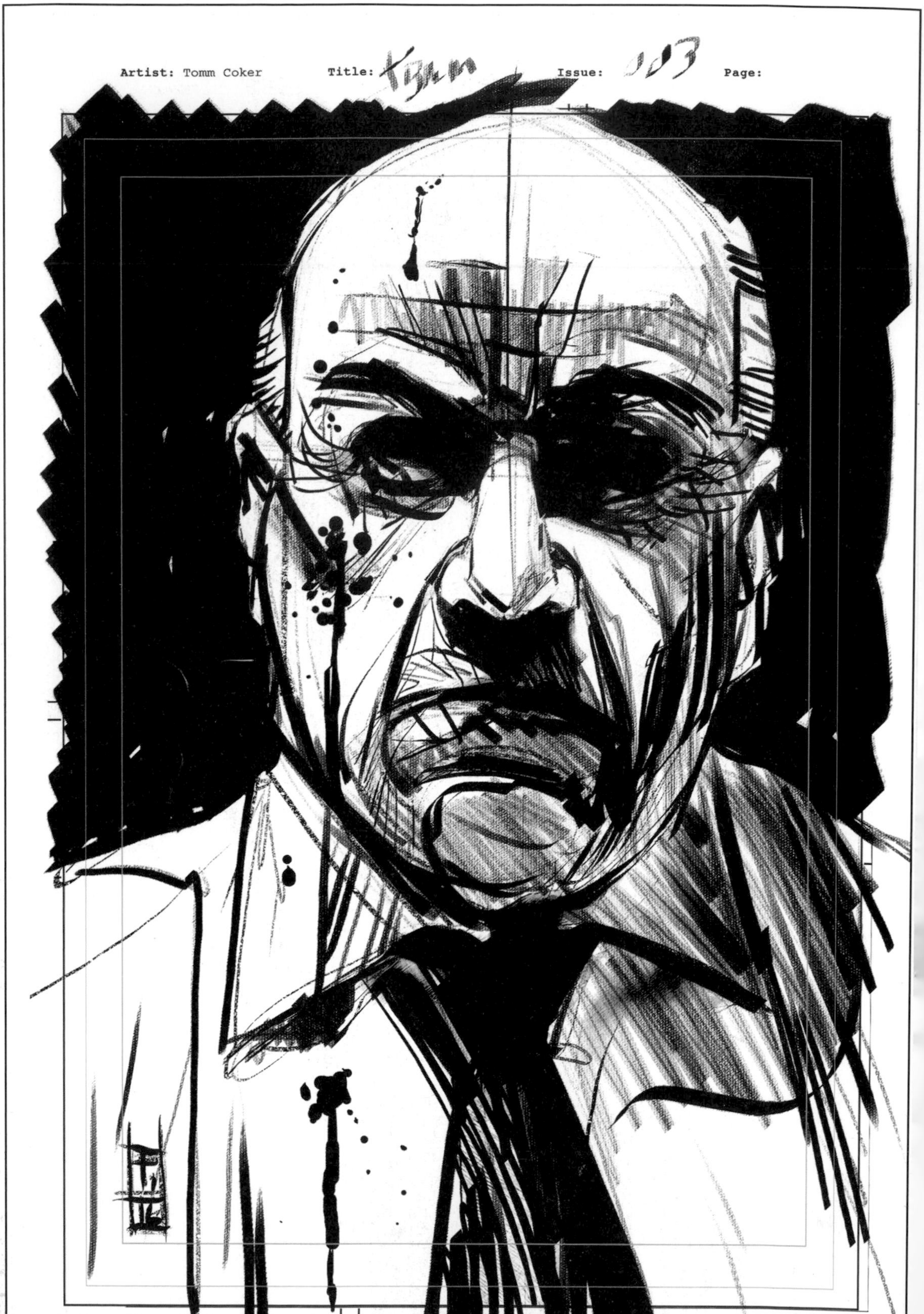
Artist: Tomm Coker
Title:
Issue:
Page:

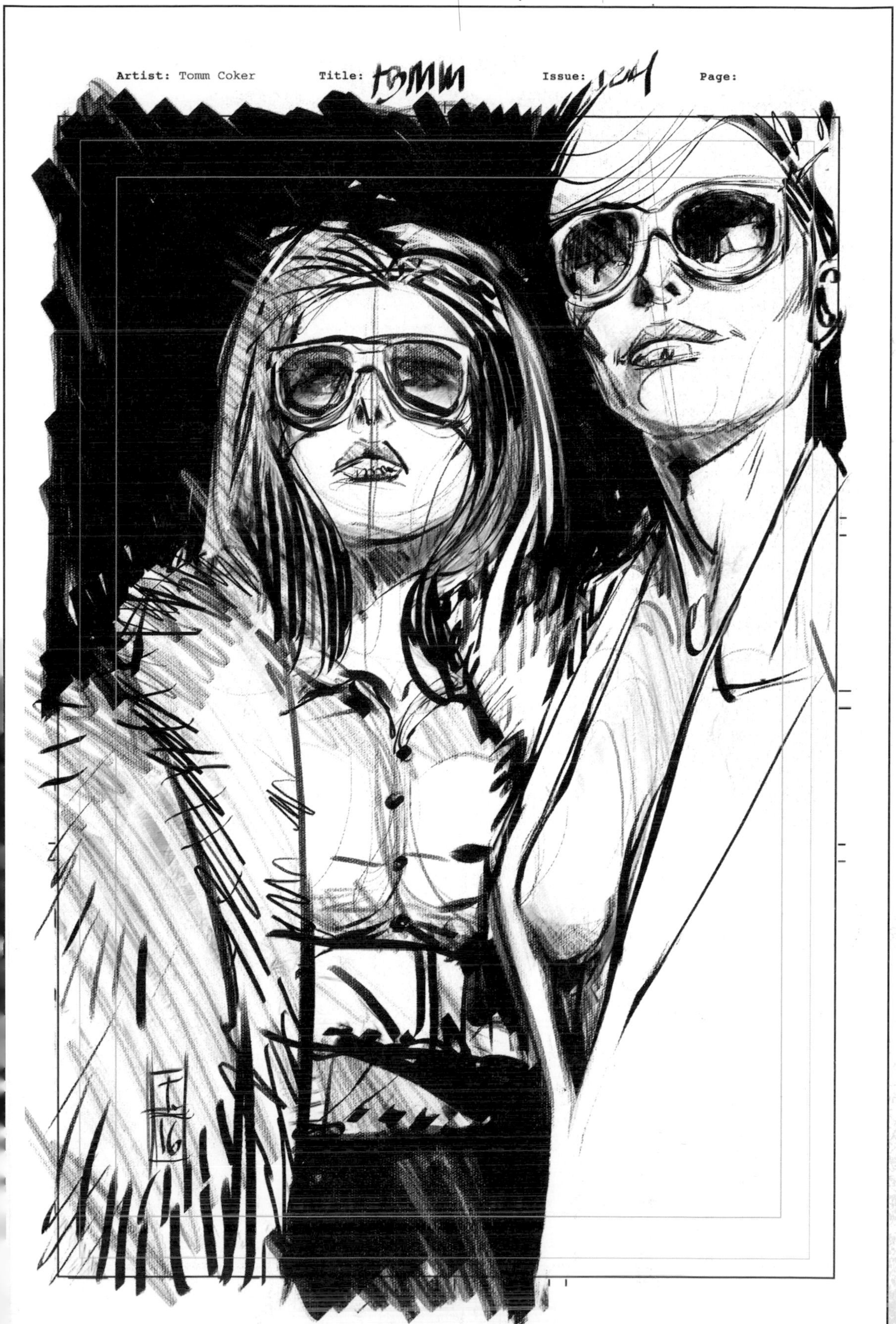
Artist: Tomm Coker
Title:
Issue:
Page:

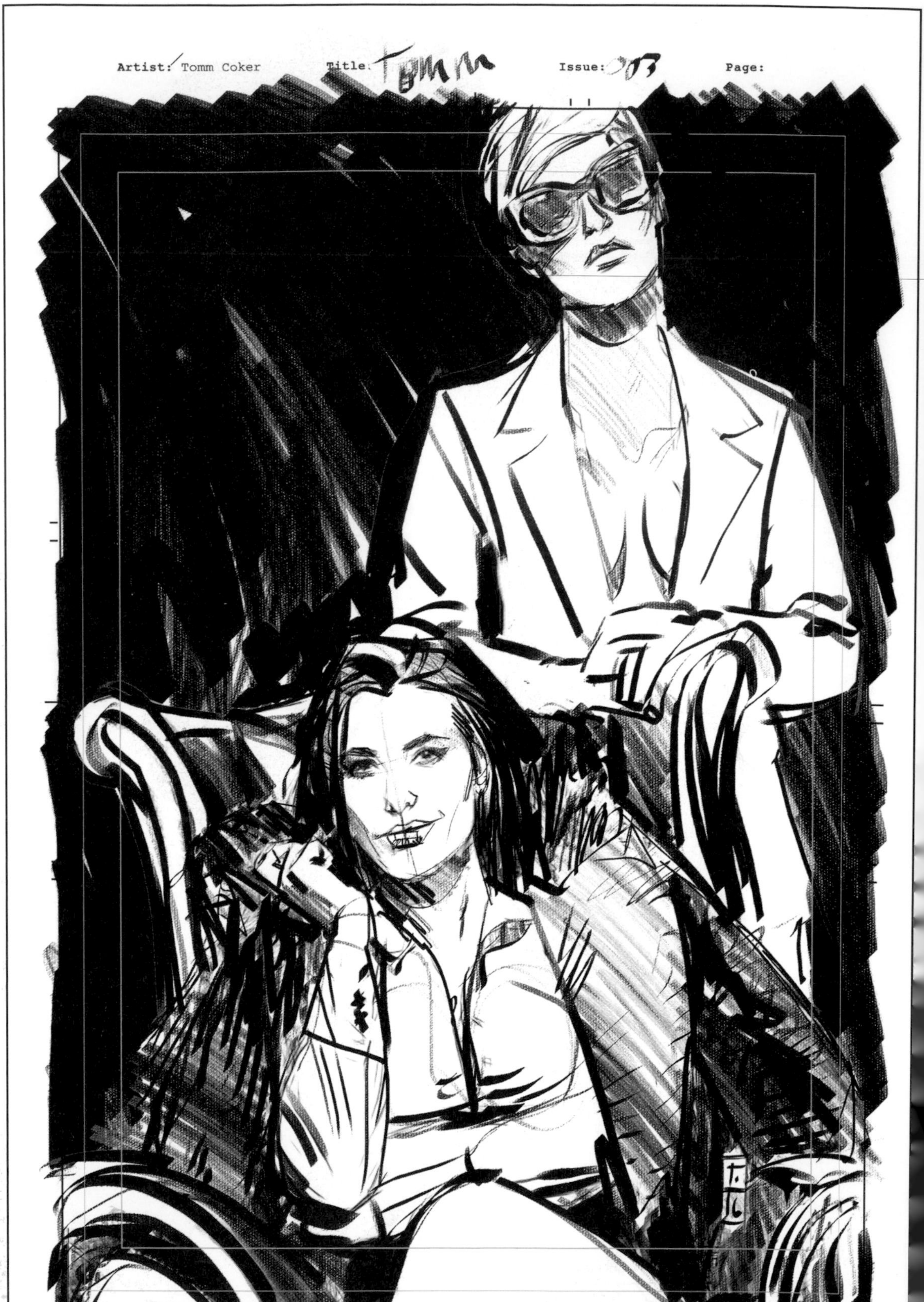
Artist: Tomm Coker
Title:
Issue:
Page:

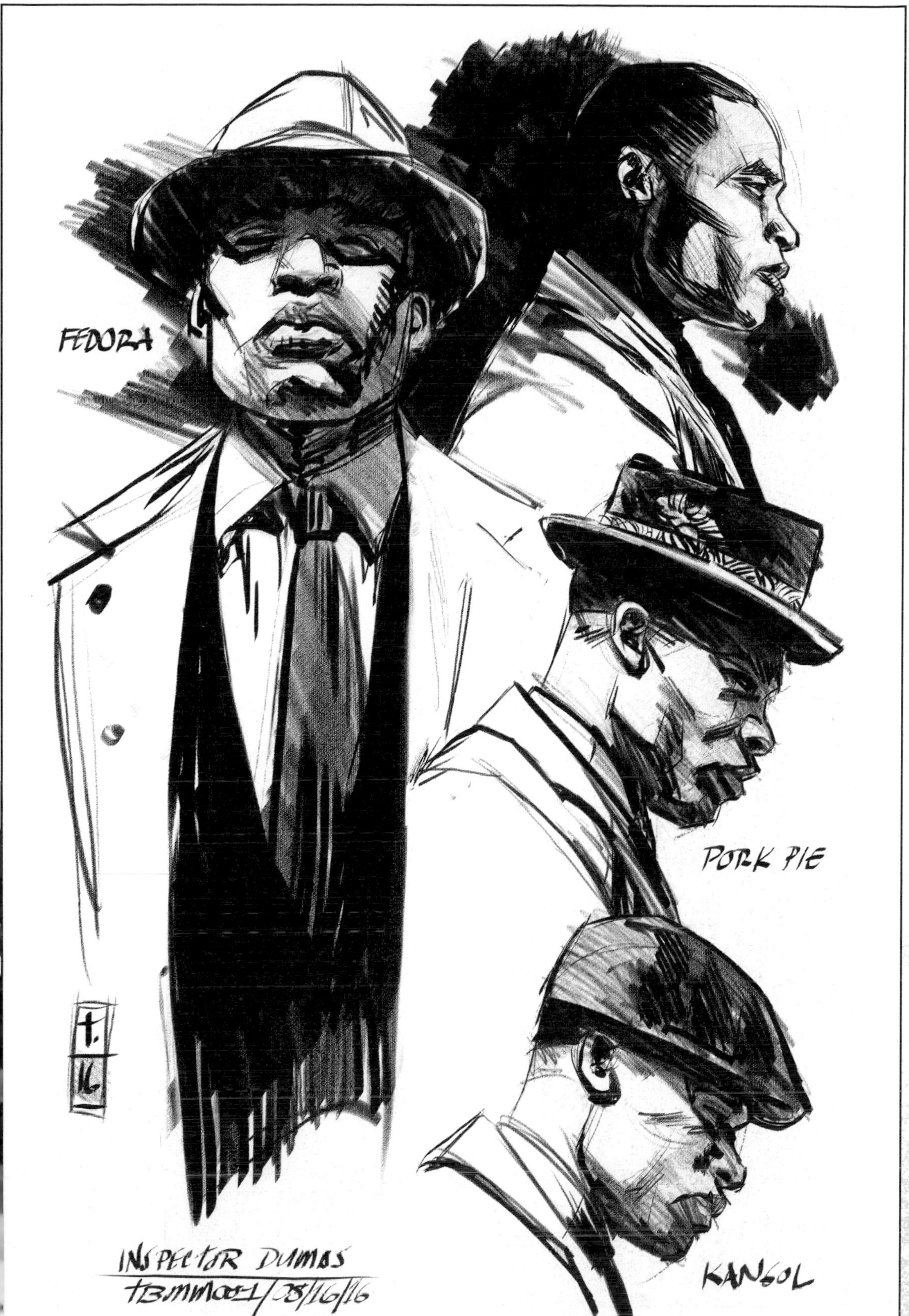
FEDORA
PORK PIE
KANGOL
INSPECTOR DUMAS

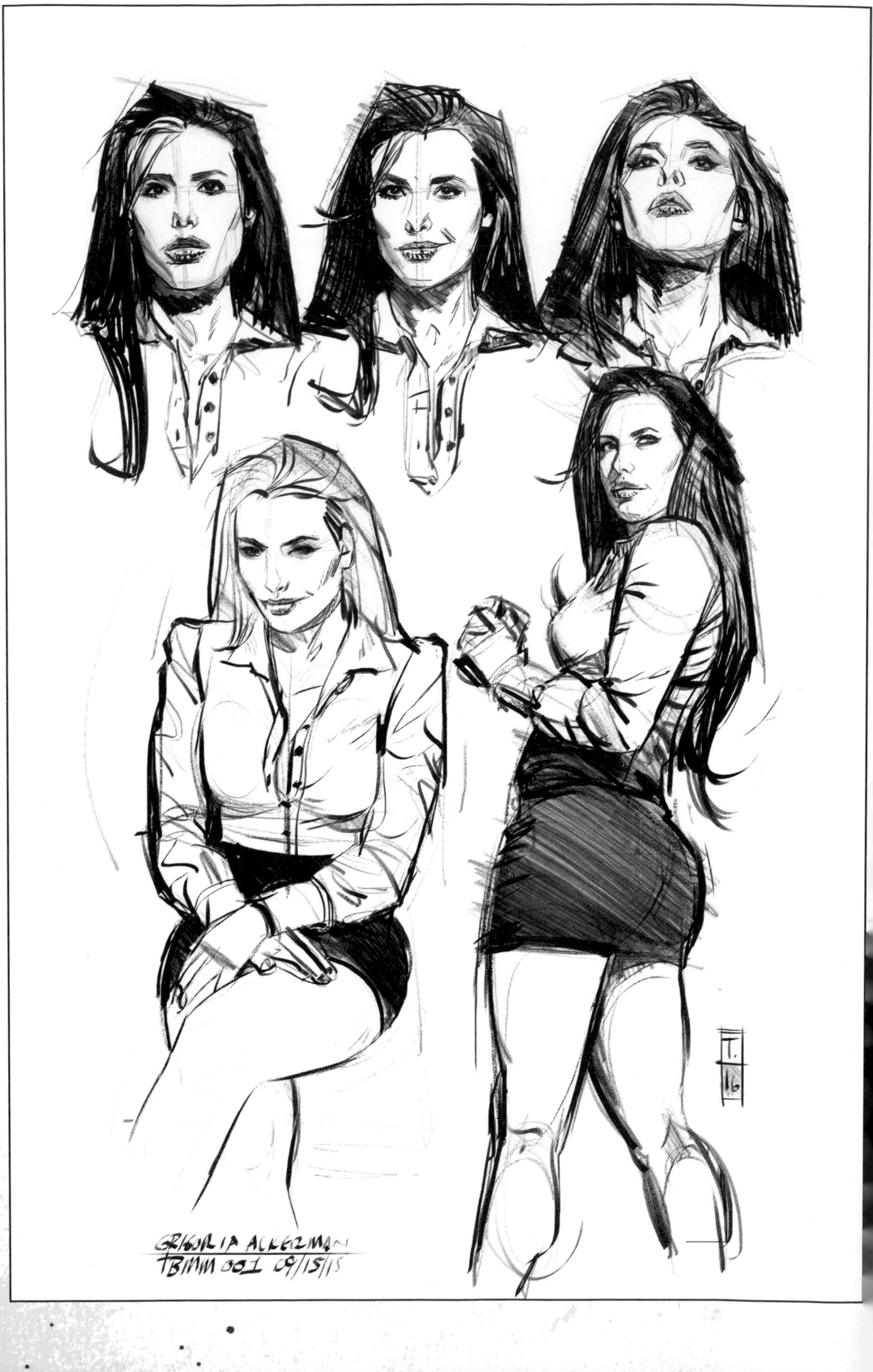
GRIGORIA ACKERMAN
TBMM001 09/15/15
T. 16

Jonathan Hickman [redacted] lies [redacted]

Tomm Coker [redacted] is [redacted] a [redacted] thief [redacted]

Michael Garland [redacted] has [redacted] blood on [redacted] his [redacted] hands [redacted]

Rus Wooton [redacted] cannot [redacted] be [redacted] trusted [redacted]